A Tangled Web

A Tangled Web

eBook ISBN: 978-1-9192261-2-5
Paperback ISBN: 978-1-9192261-3-2

Chapter 1

I tipped my head back and blew a ribbon of blue smoke through the cherry blossom canopy when a low, persistent buzzing sliced into my contentment. At first it was only faint, like the tired rasp of a fly trapped too long behind a net curtain, only occasionally mustering up enough energy for a brief, exhausted quasi-buzz. But then it changed in rhythm, the weak rasp becoming an intermittent thrum that forced me to seek out the distraction.

My ears steered my gaze towards a spider's web which ran from a dandelion cluster to my side fence panel. A bee hung in its threads, twisting helplessly as the spider spun it tighter, wrapping it in silk with patient precision. The strands glistened prettily in the light, a delicate frame for an ugly, one-sided prize-fight. Easy to see how the bee had been drawn in, dazzled by beauty. Now it was sluggish and dazed, drugged by venom, I supposed. The spider's abdomen bulged. Pregnant, I wondered, knowing that it's usually the female spiders that construct webs. Or simply gorged from hunting well.

I toyed with the idea of saving the bee. I recalled reading somewhere that male spiders learn to tap a special code when entering a female spider's web to avoid being mistaken for prey. If only the bee had known the secret, it might have stood a chance. But who was I to interfere? The spider had caught her meal with her own skill and patience. If I released the bee, who's to say the spider might not starve? Or get stung in retaliation, bringing them both to a premature end. Did bee stings even affect spiders? I wasn't sure. Better to let nature run its course, even though I knew the spider had already won.

I took a final, greedy drag of my Marlboro Gold, the acrid smoke burning my throat, and flicked the butt into the bald, earthy patch around my cherry tree's base. Bugger.

1

The ash scattered across my dressing gown. When I tried brushing it away, I only smeared it deeper into the towelling, leaving dirty grey smudges. No matter. Nothing could dampen the euphoria of last night still coursing through my veins.

I surveyed the garden with fresh eyes as warm rays streamed through the cherry blossom branches above. The patch of land the tree sat on betrayed the fact that I wasn't much of a gardener. Its overgrown lawn with more weeds than grass could at best be described as sparse. My solitary pink cherry blossom tree, now twelve years old and pressed against the back wall, was the only sign of life. Still, this scrappy piece of land had become my oasis of calm and still looked a lot better than the concreted-over backyards that seemed to be fashionable in Hackney these days.

The spring air carried a sweetness that felt cleansing, a promise of renewal. Last night had aroused a long-dormant and insatiable spirit in me, a restless certainty that nothing would be the same again. I'd almost forgotten how the thrill of a woman's touch can change your entire world view. But she was gone now, slipped out before I woke, leaving only her jasmine scent in the pillow and an ache in my chest that refused to fade.

I'd escaped the suffocating atmosphere of the firm's end-of-financial-year drinks reception last night. That usual chest-beating, self-serving celebration of profit margins and corporate machismo. The drunken crowd was unbearable, especially for IT geeks like me, either the butt of every joke or completely ignored. I'd taken the stairs up to the roof terrace for a proper smoke, not like those half-hearted vapers puffing strawberry-scented clouds into the air.

That's where I first saw her. Framed against the London skyline, champagne in one hand, cigarette in the other, eyes glinting as if she had been waiting for me. I had no idea who she was, only that I was inexplicably drawn to her. As I edged past the oversized potted plants, we smiled at each other with the easy recognition of people who have just recognised a like-minded soul.

Talking with her felt effortless. She said my suit looked sharp, that its cut on my slim frame set me apart from the stuffed shirts downstairs. She touched my hair, freed from its usual ponytail into a slicked-back wavy bob and smiled. We even smoked the same brand of cigarette.

But then I'd made that stupid mistake. Boasting about being the Chief Executive of some made-up marketing company. Why? She was clearly already keen enough, and I'd never been one to measure myself by poncy job titles before. It was stupid, especially when she admitted she was a receptionist from a small suburban company who'd pinched her boss's invitation for free drinks and canapés. I could have been honest about being a Digital Systems Manager. What a dickhead.

The kiss was electric. I'd whispered, 'I've almost forgotten what it feels like to be kissed...let alone by a woman like you.' She closed her eyes, moistened her lips, and pressed the gentlest of kisses on my cheek. Her jasmine scent filled my senses. Then she kissed me properly, full on the mouth, coaxing my lips apart, and my heart hammered against my ribs. As I slid my fingers into her hair and down her neck, perfectly formed at the nape, I felt long-dormant embers in the pit of my stomach roar back to life.

Now I was alone again, sitting in my scrappy garden, already late for work and not caring. For the first time in years, I felt truly alive.

But she was gone. No note, no number, nothing. I paced from room to room, scanning corners as if she might still be hiding there. Deep down I knew better. Guys like me don't usually get lucky with women like her, let alone have them stick around after sunrise.

I threw myself onto the bed and buried my face in the pillow where she'd slept. Her warmth had left, but her scent still lingered. I twisted onto my back, wincing as my stomach muscles throbbed from last night's exertions. My body wasn't accustomed to such vigorous activity. My hand wandered between my legs and squeezed my exhausted limp genitals with dreamy pride. Damn, it really had been such a long time.

I refused to wallow in self-pity. The fire in my heart was lit, my passion for life re-stoked. I had to find her again, reach her, make her part of my life. Last night wasn't a one-off. I wouldn't let it be.

I'd previously believed that most women, especially attractive ones, were more trouble than they're worth. But she wasn't just another self-absorbed, pouting, selfie-taker. There was something about her that stood out as different. Assured without arrogance, confident without being brash, beautiful without needing to flaunt it. And French to boot. A clichéd male fantasy perhaps but it only sharpened the allure. She was the kind of woman you could change your whole life for overnight. I was hooked.

Carefully, I picked one of her black wavy hairs from the pillow and placed it on the bedside table. A good omen that she'd return.

Estelle.

Chapter 2

The journey from Gore Road, through Victoria Park to Bethnal Green tube was its usual monotonous blur. Passersby shuffled forward, lost in thought. Singles, couples, the scruffy and the polished, all going about their business together but separately. Stressed parents, mostly mums, flustered as they herded their kids along. Commuters narrowly avoiding head-on collisions with each other as they stared at their phones while marching forward. Everyone looked distant and preoccupied with their own set of worries and purpose. None seemed to be enjoying the moment as I was; my private thoughts providing a newfound and superior spring in my step.

People aside, the park's appearance mirrored my mood perfectly. It was coming to life again, taking spring's first breaths under the warm rays of light. Bright green lawns were being tickled by sprinklings of purple and blue crocuses and bright yellow daffodils. Statesmanlike trees stood sentinel around the park's outskirts, their array of varying green backdrops punctuated by the orangey-green leaves of strategically placed Japanese Maples. I'd seen it all before through many annual cycles, but today it all felt new and exciting.

On the tube, I closed my eyes and retreated into my own world of daydreams, my head bobbing from side to side in rhythm with the carriage. Estelle's whispers echoed round my mind, dulling all other sounds. The spell only broke as I found myself being swept along by the crowds across the street from Victoria station into the middle of Columbus House's faux-tropical atrium, the brutal reality of work returning as I waited for the lift to arrive. There was no need to rush. Normally, I could stroll in any time before lunch and, unless anyone had any user access problems, no one would bat an eyelid. Even if there were issues, it only provided others with an excuse to disappear for a coffee in the atrium until I could fix it. I largely operated in a bubble of self-management.

The lift doors pinged open, triggering a jostle for space. I pressed 8 for Effective Solutions, flattened my back against the wall, crossed my arms and held my breath, eyes fixed on my shoes. With each floor, the lift gradually emptied, finally releasing me at the top, free to breathe again.

'Morning Luke,' chirped Lesley from behind a stack of posh biscuits on the reception desk. 'Where'd you disappear to last night? I was looking forward to 'aving a proper catch up.'

I paused before answering to consider whether she might have seen me leaving the party early with Estelle. If so, it might already be all round the office. I gave her the benefit of the doubt.

'Oh...I...er...wasn't feeling great,' I lied. 'And you know what I think of these dos.'

'Well, you might 'ave found it a bit more fun than usual if you didn't run out on me like that,' she said with a playful scold. 'Anyway, you'd better shift yourself. The chairman's address starts in just over 15 minutes.' I stared back blankly. 'You'd forgotten, hadn't you?' I had, and this wasn't the first time I'd switched off to the extent I'd risked losing my job.

'Thanks,' I replied, trying to look unfazed, while inwardly screaming *you bollocking idiot* at myself. How could I have forgotten the chairman's address at 10:30? They didn't take place often but when they did they were usually for the purpose of making major announcements, new office openings, a lucrative contract, an industry award won or the like. Attendance was compulsory. Sometimes I suspected he liked the sound of his own voice so much he simply relished having a captive audience. And the chance to pop into the office, and leer over the latest intake of young female marketeers and PR staff. Whatever his motive, his presence on the floor always brought out the ugliest competitive element amongst staff. Even Change Implementation Director John Salter seemed to ooze an extra layer of smarmy cockiness on these occasions, his bald head shining as much as his pointy shoes, exposing his narcissistic traits.

I cursed myself again for forgetting. I hadn't washed, my clothes were stale, and now I was going to be trapped inside a stuffy conference room marinading in a heap of corporate bullshit for an hour instead of getting online and tracking Estelle down. Not good.

There was a noticeable buzz in the room. More than half the staff were on their feet, posturing and parading, gesticulating for attention. Ralph and Jacqueline, the firm's Consultant Analysts, had donned their smartest outfits and most serious expressions. I stifled a cynical chuckle at Ralph's glasses, a prop I knew he only wore to give his nice-but-dim persona an air of intellect. It didn't work, of course. He still looked as if he was singlehandedly responsible for putting the 'anal' in analyst.

Elaine and Theo, the CHange Implementation Managers – or CHIMps as they were known behind their backs – fussed over Gannt charts like a couple of modern-day war colonels planning a campaign. Elaine's ample bottom, still wobbling long after she stopped moving, reminded me of the unkind online nickname - *Greggs on Legs* – her colleagues used for her.

Salter strutted back and forth like a preening rooster, firing questions for the sake of asserting his authority and making himself feel good. Tosser. Salter was all gloss and no substance, a living embodiment of the Peter Principle. Years in management had made him fluent in corporate jargon – 'helicopter views', 'low-hanging fruit', 'idea showers' - you name it, he could always find a phrase to use as a smoke grenade to hide his lack of any real insight or intelligence. He reminded me of those toys with a string at the back you pull to repeat a familiar phrase.

Nor was he averse to dumping blame on others, using their efforts as stepping stones while neatly sidestepping his own mistakes or inactivity. In a just world, he'd have been rumbled and booted out years ago, but he'd made a superpower out of his superficiality.

Neil's fate served as a cautionary tale to the rest of us. One of our most diligent digital architects. he'd spent months pouring his soul into a report, only for Salter to swoop in at the eleventh hour of his presentation to claim the credit and associated bonus. I caught Neil's eye across the room. He sat slumped, drained and resigned to a life of exploitation in exchange for his meagre salary. I could understand it, mind. Neil knew, as we all did, that ambition and capability were dangerous traits in Salter's orbit. Those who dared snap at his heels were quickly cast aside. What pissed me off most about him was how his phoney charm continued to fool the Chairman and Board Members who were blind to his useless Teflon-coated persona, seeing only what they wanted to see. But that's corporate life for you. Better to stay safe under the radar than to compete and risk losing all.

I retreated to my corner desk unnoticed, switched on my computer and left it to boot up while I went to the kitchenette to make coffee. By the time I returned, a calendar reminder told me the Chairman's meeting was due to start in five minutes. The search for Estelle would have to wait. So would the 26 unread emails that had accumulated during the morning. I locked my screen and took my coffee through into the conference room to get an early back seat. I was first to arrive.

Within minutes, the buzz of others from the open-plan area migrated to join me. A wave of chatter and nervous energy filled the room, speculating on the meeting's purpose. I slid down in my seat, using my coffee cup as a shield against unwanted interaction. The hot liquid burned my tongue. I might as well have been invisible for all the attention anyone paid me.

With the room almost full, the corporate hierarchy - Peter Richardson (Finance), Salter (Marketing) and Mitch Fletcher (Sales) - took their places at the top table alongside Stephen Waring, the Chief Executive. Their carefully cultivated air of relaxed authority couldn't quite mask the undercurrent of tension I sensed beneath. All four of them were doing that thing where they deliberately ignored each other while fixing their gaze on random points at the back of the room. 'Visionary posing', I called it. Stephen staring intently towards the top corner of the room, as if in private communication with some celestial corporate presence, Peter squinting with characteristic intensity, probably fantasising over a sexy spreadsheet, and Salter, true to form, looking down his nose at the assembled mass before him, while Mitch passed the time trying to catch the eyes of his team with cries of 'like me, like me'.

But there was something else behind this well-rehearsed performance. Something different. A tremor in Stephen's hand as he scrolled his phone. A tightness in Salter's eyes. A falseness to Mitch's smile. Something was afoot. I found myself leaning forward in anticipation.

Then, in an instant, the room fell silent, and heads turned towards the entrance as Gordon Freeman strode in, the shiny buttons of his blazer heaving under the strain of his puffed out, barrel-shaped torso. He looked serious. Self-satisfied and jovial, but serious.

I froze and kept my head down as he stomped past. A cloud of cheap aftershave hit the back of my throat in his wake.

A second set of footsteps followed behind him. Instinctively, and without looking up, I knew it was her. I could feel her presence. It was almost as if she was radiating a sphere of magical warmth a couple of metres either side of her. I kept my head down, staring at my shoes while a surge of adrenaline coursed through my veins. My thumping heart against my ribcage told me it was her. My breathlessness told me it was her. The dry lump of cement that had formed at the back of my throat told me it was her.

I fought the urge to look up as she glided past, two paces in sync behind the Chairman. She walked tall, sleek leather folder under her arm, radiating a potent blend of business-like purpose and unapologetic sensuality. This was a woman who knew precisely what she wanted and how to get it. I could only catch her profile but that was enough to set my stomach fluttering as I took in her black eyelashes and the contours of her porcelain cheekbones and nose. Her lips were painted a defiant shade of red and fixed in a half-smile that could have meant something – or nothing at all. The collars of her blouse were turned up, brushing against her bobbed black hair which bounced with an array of stray waves fighting to break free as she quickened her pace to keep up. She looked like a force of nature, and that both thrilled and terrified me.

As Estelle moved, her tight-fitting two-piece suit accentuated every curve of her hourglass figure, sending a rush of warmth back to my previously frozen limbs. I straightened my back to take her in more fully. It wasn't just me. The collective gaze of the room had shifted their sights from the Chairman to Estelle. Next to me, Jacqueline, having spotted me craning my neck, let out an audible snort. Ha! If only she knew.

As the Chairman and Estelle took their seats, I sank into mine. I could see Estelle through the gaps between people's heads in front of me but felt safely concealed enough that she wouldn't be able to spot me in my far corner. She looked fantastic considering how little sleep she got last night. But what was she doing here? Why did she leave without a word this morning? A rush of questions flooded my mind, turning my joy into a bittersweet state of neurosis. And then, I wondered selfishly, what does this all mean for me?

The elation of a few moments ago twisted into a knot of anxiety. My angst turned to panic and, in a botched attempt to sneak out, I managed to spill my coffee on my lap, prompting Jacqueline to sneer at me as she inched her chair away from mine. I put the cup on the floor and sat as still as possible, while coffee seeped through my trousers onto my thigh.

The Chairman's voice boomed around the room as he delivered a self-congratulatory monologue, referencing the success of last night's drinks reception, the renewal of client contracts – all due to his personal charm, of course - and the need for everyone to keep their 'foot on the gas' to ensure future success. Only fleetingly would he throw morsels of praise out to his select inner circle in the same way that owners give their dogs treats for not shitting on the kitchen floor. Estelle's gaze was focussed solely on him, her expression unreadable. The Chairman was lapping it up, his chest puffing out a little more with each sentence. I felt a twinge of…jealousy? Fear? I couldn't quite place it.

To listen to him on such occasions, you'd think that Gordon Freeman single-handedly dragged the company to success through sheer force of will. The truth was, he was both aloof and elusive and did nothing to justify his inflated salary. Gordon had stumbled into the Chairman's role at Effective Solutions like a drunk falling up stairs after blagging about his past successes with Winibrand plc. In reality, he'd been nothing more than a figurehead there who'd hoovered up the successes of the team and passed them off as his own.

These days, he only popped into the office a couple of days a month when it suited him. The rest of his time was spent in the emerging markets of the Far East, particularly Thailand, where he disappeared for weeks at a time at the firm's expense. 'Networking', he called it, from which he emerged only occasionally to attend a lavish function or deliver a paid keynote speech. Even then, he was too lazy to write his own speeches and would pay some bloke from Bespoke Speechwriting Agency to write them for him. On company expenses, of course. Bloody good speeches though, it had to be said. Always articulate, impeccably structured and with good visionary metaphors that sent shivers down my spine. But today, it was painfully evident that he'd penned his own monologue.

My eyes kept drifting to Estelle. What was she doing here, perched alongside him? What business did she have sitting at the top table with the senior leadership team? Gordon's voice droned on like the adults in the Charlie Brown cartoons. My mind drifted until a single word snapped me back to attention – 'Estelle'. My heart rate doubled in an instant, blood rushing in my ears.

'Meet our new Chief Operating Officer, Estelle Merisier.' The words shot through me like a succession of thunderbolts. My vision swam as he continued, explaining that the role of Chief Executive would become redundant, and Directors would report directly to her with immediate effect. She, in turn, would report directly to him. With each revelation, I felt the world I thought I knew crumble away.

Her role, Gordon elaborated, was to audit the firm's practices within HQ and its overseas franchise offices. His voice dropped to a conspiratorial whisper as he added 'where it appears there's a discrepancy between the amount of business referred to them and the profits returned'. Gasps and whispers rippled up and down the rows of seats.

The resulting stench of panic in response to this unforeseen development was overwhelming. Stephen Waring, the exiting Chief Executive effectively sacked? He didn't look too disappointed about it; presumably a payoff was his sweetener. So who was Estelle Merisier? Apparently, a freelance consultant with an impressive track record from within the French office. But why had I never heard of her? How had she leapfrogged over the three existing Directors? How had I missed this? I had access to every file in the organisation - HR files, emails, memos - but had seen nothing of this. What else could I have missed? And why didn't she let me – or anyone else for that matter - know who she was at last night's party? What game was she playing?

It didn't make sense. None of it did. The pieces refused to fit together. An incomplete puzzle.

Gordon, clearly relishing the chaos he'd unleashed, encouraged a perfunctory round of applause for Stephen Waring. For 'his sterling efforts over the years', he said flatly, 'and good luck for the future'. He then invited Estelle to say a few words.

As she rose, I sank further into my seat, keen to remain unseen. I was struck by how much shorter she seemed than my memory of her. Five-foot-four at most, and she looked especially petite alongside the seated bulk of the Directors. Yet, as she surveyed the silenced room, she seemed to fill it with her presence. I hid my face behind a hand and felt my blood run cold with fear.

'Good morning,' she projected in that same seductive accent that had mesmerised me last night but now carried an additional layer of business-edged authority. She paused and surveyed the silent room once more.

'It is a pleasure to be here in London,' she continued, perfectly measured. 'And more so to have been given the opportunity by your Chairman, Gordon Freeman, to enter your firm as Chief Operating Officer.' Gordon was staring at her, drooling at her every movement. 'As Gordon said, I have been involved in some of your overseas projects...' Her words were cut short by a derisive snort from Salter behind her, prompting Estelle to pause to direct a raised eyebrow in his direction which said *silly little boy*. '...and I have learnt much about your operations,' she continued softly, '...and have been impressed by your achievements.' An unspoken *so far* hung in the air.

Her voice weakened me, and my confusion over the whole situation made my stomach bubble with nausea. The work part of me felt frail and fearful, vulnerable even, as if her arrival signalled the beginning of the end of my eighteen years with the firm. Yet, the other part of me felt besotted, desperately wondering if last night's liaison could blossom into something more. I was discombobulated.

'Some of you may have noticed me wandering around your drinks reception last night...' Estelle continued.

'Spy, more like,' someone up front whispered.

'I was fortunate to meet some of you and look forward to spending time with each of you in the days and weeks ahead.' Did her eyes linger on me for a fraction of a second, or did I imagine it?

She was careful and purposeful in the way she spoke. To me, it sounded as if she was trying to pronounce each word with perfect English diction, but slipping into a breathy French accent whenever she relaxed slightly which I imagined was melting the men in the room. The women, I could see, were sitting tall to admire the fact that she'd managed to land such a senior role in this male-dominated company. They weren't just listening to her; they were hanging on to her every word for clues as to what might have helped her on her path. Estelle exuded strength and comfort in her new position and, if she felt any first day's nerves or vulnerability, she kept them well masked.

'I have been impressed with what I have heard so far about your energy, talents and passion,' she continued. 'I am sure I have much more to learn from each of you. I can also see that my arrival here may seem like a surprise but don't worry. I am not here to shake things up or change anything overnight.' Again, her eyes seemed to stop at me as she scanned the crowd. 'In the first instance, I want to spend time with each of you to understand your priorities, processes and strategies. For starters, I have asked Lesley to set up 15-minute one-to-ones with each of you.' She paused, allowing her words to sink in. 'I think that's all for now. Thank you for your time and I look forward to getting to know you.'

With a polite bow of her head, she sat down. A ripple of applause, more courteous than enthusiastic, spread across the room. I found myself clapping too while my mind raced.

Gordon stood up abruptly. 'Right, that's all. Back to work everybody,'

And that was that. No questions. No invitation for the Directors to contribute. Meeting over. I kept my head low and filed out with the rest of the staff.

Stunned, I couldn't work out why, how or what was happening. Or what might follow. Everything was out of control. It seemed inevitable that, one way or another, my cosy job was under threat. And despite the fact she'd specifically said she wouldn't be seeking to change anything within the firm, I knew – instinctively and definitely – that a big shake up was just around the corner.

The one thing I was certain of was that nothing would be the same again.

Chapter 3

I sniggered as I watched the Directors regroup inside Gordon's glass-fronted office, their frantic discussion a sharp contrast to the calm façade they'd maintained during the all-staff meeting. The blinds were pulled down just enough to give them a false sense of privacy, while leaving a sufficient gap for me to see what was going on. They sat facing each other on the comfy chairs. Stephen had already packed up and left. Peter, true to form, sat in stoic silence, nodding along to what was being said with furrowed brow. Mitch and John, in contrast, bristled with agitation, their arms gesticulating wildly. A crimson-faced Gordon paced up and down amongst them like a caged tiger. His hand movements switched back and forth from assertive dictatorship to patronising 'calm down dear' signals which, it was plain to see, had the effect of pouring petrol on Salter's flames of frustration.

Estelle sat just outside their circle, her back perfectly straight. In contrast to the others, she looked very much at ease. Occasionally she would sweep a loose lock of hair back behind her ear, only for it to break free again. When she took a turn to speak, always with slow controlled posture and careful movements of her lips, she provoked more patronising hand gestures from Mitch and John, which Gordon would shoot away with a single point. It was easy to follow the gist of what was going on, but I did wish I could hear them.

Estelle sat as serene as a cat amidst the chaos of voices surrounding her (bar passive Peter's). When she did speak, the slow accompanying movements of her hands created an impression of someone at ease and in control. She was divine, her style evident with each movement. It was impossible to take my eyes off her. Or the unfolding drama. My inbox could wait.

Each time she turned her head to follow the exchange of discussion, I couldn't help likening her elegance and grace to that of a classic film star like Audrey Hepburn. Or a modern-day model. The delicate sinews in her slender neck twisting with each turn sent bolts of heat to the pit of my stomach. Her movements couldn't have been better choreographed for greater effect and beauty.

My heart raced with a paradoxical mix of hope and dread that her gaze might find mine. I craved even the smallest acknowledgement. But nothing. Her eyes swept past me as she looked out onto the office, leaving me hollow.

When the Directors eventually left the room, it was amusing to watch the scowls on the faces of Mitch and Salter transform into masks of in-control-authority as they stepped over the threshold into the general office area to face their teams. Peter looked unfazed and not at all worried. But it was clear to me that Mitch and Salter felt under threat and, I well imagined in their insecure minds, not at all happy about being overlooked for promotion by a woman. I relished the thought of Estelle's understated professionalism metaphorically knocking the stuffing out of those self-serving corporate psychopaths.

The day dragged on, each hour marked by Estelle's closed-door meetings with various team members. I watched the office slowly empty as five o'clock approached, but I lingered well past my usual departure time, hoping to catch a word with her. As the sun set outside, it cast long shadows across the office, transforming the few remaining souls into quiet silhouettes. When she did finally emerge from Gordon's office, with him laughing heartily by her side, a sharp pang of jealously stabbed at my chest. In a brave effort to be noticed, I stood up as they passed my desk. She looked straight at me, nodded, and said 'have a good evening' without displaying the slightest glimmer of recognition. As if I was a stranger. I was gutted.

A cocktail of emotions welled up inside me, bringing a bitter taste of bile to the back of my throat.

At home, I found myself pacing from one end of the flat to the other, restless and uneasy. It somehow felt smaller. Part of me hoped Estelle might return. But deep down I knew I was harbouring false hope. She wouldn't. I poured myself a large brandy and sat in the wicker chair in the bay window, angled perfectly to observe the entire length of the street outside. The sight and sound of others going about their business dampened my loneliness and provided a sense of company.

A silhouette of a shadowy figure approaching - a woman in a business suit carrying a small briefcase with a purposeful stride was aimed at my flat. I jolted to my feet, spilling brandy on my lap. What was it with me spilling drinks on myself lately? She had purpose in her stride and was five foot something. Could it be her? I must have been staring too hard, too intently, in the same way as one checks and re-checks a losing lotto ticket hoping the losing numbers might magically change into winning ones, as she quickened her pace to a fast trot past my flat. Closer inspection showed very clearly it was not her. Her movements were far clunkier and lacked grace.

I refilled my glass and felt a cold wind of loneliness howl through my insides, rattling with sadness and loss. My passion had been stoked only to be dashed again. My heart awoken only to be put back to sleep. Restlessness took over as I found another excuse to walk to the rear of the flat, check the back window and return to the front. I wondered what tomorrow would bring. And the day after that. I knew I was being melancholic and losing my sense of proportion, but fear of the unknown had wormed its way to the forefront of my mind and was beating like a drum. I was unsettled and unhappy. My rational mind kept interrupting to tell me that nothing had changed, but I also knew that everything had. My encounter with Estelle was not one which could simply be left to sail on by. It happened for a reason.

I held my generously filled glass up to the window and swirled it round, releasing its fumes and allowing the streetlight outside to shimmer through its caramel colours. I held the glass up to my right eye and squinted through the soothing oily residues sloping down the inside of the glass towards the street outside.

Another woman was approaching. I flattened myself against the side bay window and held the net curtains to one side to get a clearer look without being seen. It was only when I started to feel dizzy I realised I'd been holding my breath. It wasn't Estelle - too tall and no twists and turns to her step. I placed my palm on my chest to calm my thumping heartbeat, but it did nothing to lift the dreamlike fog engulfing me. The hazy approaching figure appeared to be looking straight at me, despite my disguised position. There was something familiar about her I couldn't quite put my finger on. Until she slowed down and stepped beneath the stream of light shining down from the streetlight on the other side of the road.

*Then it clicked, like a loaded gun pressed against the back of my head. But it couldn't be. Impossible. A buried spectre from the past, one I thought was safely buried, yet there she was. Standing. Staring. I hadn't thought of **her** for years, and now, of all days, she appears. Without taking my eyes off her, I gulped my brandy down in one go, followed quickly by gulps of air to soothe my burning throat. I couldn't see straight. My vision twisted itself into a long dark tunnel as I struggled to gain focus on her shadowy face. Her gaze remained firmly fixed in my direction, her pace fast and confident, and a look of determination in her eyes. Or was it vengeance?*

*Memories of **her** flooded back, shooting an instantaneous weakness through my veins. The thunderbolt*

19

*effect of seeing her exposed a deep weakness within me, intensifying my frustration. Another deep breath, a blink of my burning eyes, and she was gone. I didn't see **her** turn off or enter any of the houses, or the park on the other side of the road which was in any case fenced off. **She'd** somehow disappeared into thin air, and I'd missed it. Or was it a cruel hallucination? I couldn't be sure. Click.*

The street outside returned to late night emptiness. Hope and brandy had kept me up for long enough. I took myself through to the bedroom, threw my clothes off and lay on one side of the bed. The ceiling swirled like a giant replica of the brandy in my glass, leaving long oily legs dripping down the sides of the walls. Chance of sleep seemed unlikely. I let the day's events replay themselves out in no particular order. Characters from work held bit parts of the plot while Estelle held centre stage.

'Estelle, Estelle....,' I whispered, as if the sound of her name would make her appear. 'Come back.'

Then the impossibly mysterious figure in the street interrupted the scene, upsetting my dreamy dynamic by standing in the corner of the conference room and staring straight at me. 'No, no...stay away,' I mumbled as pain and confusion returned. Jumbled thoughts made me feel like I was somersaulting forward at uncontrollable speeds as I struggled to push painful memories back to where they belonged.

It was no good. Sleep was impossible. I got up and knocked back a fourth large brandy to numb the pain and returned to bed.

Better to be drunk and forget than to remember and regret, I told myself as I drifted into a fitful sleep.

Chapter 4

The clock in the corridor displayed 08:34 as I arrived at the eighth floor, my head surprisingly clear given last night's restlessness. My uncharacteristically early start didn't go unnoticed.

'Oh. My. Gawd,' Lesley called out from behind reception as I approached. 'Did you put your clocks forward an hour by mistake?' I forgave her sarcasm in exchange for a much-appreciated coffee from the cafetière behind her, its scent providing as much relief as its invigorating hot, bitter taste.

First job of the day was to reorganise my desk so that I had a clear line of sight between my monitors into Estelle's newly adopted glass-fronted office. Although early, Estelle already had Sophie and Judith from the Campaigns Team in with her for what looked like a friendly chat. As with yesterday, Estelle carried herself with a cool, calm and relaxed manner whilst maintaining an air of supreme authority and professionalism. She wore minimal, if any, make up - maybe some eyeliner, a hint of blusher and a touch of lipstick at most. Her understated effort, compared to the other two's Sharpie-pen-esque eyebrows, filler-filled lips and foundation shades to rival the Tango Orange man only accentuated her natural beauty. And, if body language was anything to go by, Sophie and Judith thought so too.

My coffee grew cold before I'd managed to finish it, so I logged on and turned my attention to the day ahead. Busy days were not something I was accustomed to, and Fridays were no different. In fact, Fridays were generally reserved for snooping on others' plans for the weekend.

A calendar invite popped up in the middle of my screen, telling me I had a 1-2-1 with Estelle at 10:00am. Only half an hour away.

'Thanks for that!' I called out sarcastically to Lesley, who responded with a *'what-can-I-do?'* shrug. My stomach churned and my hands felt clammy with anticipation. The meeting, billed as an 'Introductory Chat', was scheduled for 15 minutes. This would at least give me a chance to pick up from where we'd left off the other night and find out what was next. But I also had a rumbling fear that she might choose to keep it professional and stick to work issues, in which case I needed to be prepared for the fact that my cosy position within the firm might be about to be derailed. I had to focus.

09:58. I paused outside Estelle's office before entering, mentally rehearsing the approach I'd devised in the toilets beforehand. Be self-assured. Confident, but not cocky. Calm, polite and charming is good. Hesitant, needy or adoring is bad. Be modest but hint at my indispensability to the firm and to her. And do not, repeat not, mention the other night. Unless she does. I smoothed my shirt down, took a deep breath, and entered.

'Good morning,' I said, with such perfect pitch that I impressed myself. 'How are you settling in so far?'

'Sit down please,' she said, doctor-like, gesturing towards the large cream sofa that ran along the side of her office. She was leaning against her newly delivered, presidential-style desk, studying me with narrowed eyes. I maintained my cheery disposition, wondering whether she'd devised her own strategy and goals for our meeting.

'Thank you,' I replied, as confidently as I could manage. In truth, I was relieved to sit down for the chance to steady my legs and fold my shaking hands on my lap. She continued to study me with a sideways glance as she pushed away from her desk and moved towards the window overlooking the Thames. Every step was taken with mesmerising grace.

Before I could think of anything to say to break the silence, she spun round, strode back towards her desk, sat

22

down and picked up a folder, all the while avoiding eye contact. The silence was unnerving. I occupied my mind by admiring the way in which the contours of her cheekbones sloped down towards her fine lips.

'So...' she purred, emotionless, while thumbing through the folder. 'Tell me what the point of you is.'

'The point of me?' I echoed.

'Yes,' she snapped, maintaining her terse expression.

'Well,' I said, straightening my posture. 'I basically manage the firm's whole IT storage and service delivery network. I'm solely responsible for managing the tricky relationship with our IT provider – Inter Solutions.' I tried to establish friendly eye contact, but her face remained frozen with no sign of thawing.

I sat forward, determined to continue my self-pitch. 'I safeguard IT security, manage IT audit procedures, maintain an information repository of intellectual property, ensure data protection, and report directly to the Chief Executive – which I guess should be you now? – on client confidentiality issues.'

I waited a few silent moments. She clearly had no intention of answering my question. Remain polite, charming and respectful, I told myself as I leant in closer, trying my best to recapture some of the twinkling I knew our eyes were capable of exchanging. She maintained an icy gaze.

'And, on a more routine level I also take responsibility for archiving, managing shared drives, storing backups, and resolving any hardware or software issues amongst staff.' I was running out of things to say and was aware that the tone of my voice was rising with panic.

'And finally,' I added, 'I am, of course, keen to further the success of the business with whatever expertise and skills I can offer.' As soon as I heard the words out loud, I knew it made me sound like a complete corporate wanker. But wily habit had taught me to always appear willing, especially when there was no chance of my offer being taken up. Overall, I was pleased with my opening performance but disappointed to have only managed to encourage a stifled yawn from Estelle.

'If you have *any* questions – about *anything* – at all, I would be more than happy to elaborate.' There. That was it. The ball was in her court now.

Patience, I told myself, watching her as she flicked her deep brown eyes from the folder to me and back again. Her silence was killing me, and she knew it. The situation's only consolation was being able to take in every detail of her at close range. The stray wisps of hair seeking escape from her bob to the delicate beauty spot on the top left of her lips; her tiny, perfectly formed ears with short lobes and the most intricate of studs in them.

'Bull. Shit!' Her words sliced through the silence. I flinched, my hands gripping the sides of the sofa, ready to rise.

'Stay seated,' she spat. I folded my hands on my lap, keen to avoid confrontation. 'Everything. Everything you have just told me is complete bullshit and almost word for word what I have already read from your fictitious performance management objectives. You are *such* a disappointment.' There was an undertone of a sigh in her voice.

'I'm sorry, but that's what I do here.'

'So, you are admitting you are a total bullshitter?' Her cheeks flushed below her stern look.

'Estelle, please.'

'Don't.' The word cracked like a whip. She turned her back to me, framing herself against London's panoramic skyline. 'Let's be clear about our relationship. I'm your Chief Operating Officer, not your friend. Any... familiarity between us ended the moment I walked into this building.'

'I'm sorry. I don't know what else to say. What can I do to make this right?' I must admit, I was slightly taken aback by her obvious reference to status.

'Make what work?' she scoffed.

'If you feel I've let you down in some way, we'll need to find a way to work together.' As soon as I heard the words leave my lips, I knew I'd overplayed my hand.

'Let me remind you,' she said, facing me. 'My position here as Chief Operating Officer gives me a free hand to hire and fire as I see fit. *I* decide if we still need to work together, OK?' There was no doubt between us that the balance of power here lay firmly in her favour.

'Nobody likes you,' she added. There was no comeback to that.

'You have no network. No friends. No allies here, nor any respect from what I can make out,' she continued, looking as if she was enjoying twisting the knife.

'What makes you think that?' I challenged.

'You are an overpaid waste of space, and the Leadership Team think we can make an immediate saving by letting you go. To be honest, Luke, I am finding it very difficult to find a single reason to disagree with them.'

'I'm sorry?'

'You are a bullshitter, Luke. A complete fraud.' She uttered the words so matter of fact that she might as well be commenting on the weather. This was not playing out to plan. My confidence was draining away and her will and determination – attractive as they were – were gaining strength with each syllable. I was going to have to change tack.

'I'm sorry,' I said apologetically with a downward look at the carpet. 'I never set out to cause you any problems. What are you going to do?'

'In this economic climate, and the direction the firm is heading, there is absolutely no justification for keeping your role or you on. I'm sorry.' The finality of her words echoed round my head.

'I thought you said you weren't going to change anything?' was the best I could come back with. Inwardly, I cringed at the weakness in my voice, aware the cracks in my confidence were starting to show.

'You don't believe that corporate bullshit any more than I do.'

'And I thought I was supposed to be the bullshitter here?'

'I beg your pardon?' she asked, pronouncing each word slowly.

'A receptionist from the suburbs, huh?' It was time to gamble.

She visibly stiffened and stepped towards me, chin forward. I did well to avoid any direct eye contact that could be perceived as threatening.

'I do hope you are not looking to make any trouble out of this,' she spat through a tightened facial expression.

'Estelle, please. I'm the one who should be sorry.' She prickled at the mention of her first name. 'I apologise - Ms Merisier. But I think we both have more to gain from each other than we have to lose from this situation.' I was careful to pronounce her surname correctly.

She glanced first at her watch and then through the glass partition wall behind me towards the general office. Our meeting must be close to overrunning.

'I lied about who I was,' I continued, 'simply because I liked you and didn't want to spoil the fun we were having. I'm sorry.' She stared back silently. 'You can't deny we had great chemistry?' I ignored her deliberate scoff in response.

'You were wonderful the other night. Great company, refreshing, fun...' Stop. I was starting to fawn. 'Why did you leave without saying goodbye?'

She sat back down behind her desk, picked up the phone and asked Lesley to postpone her next meeting. I'd won some extra time.

'Luke. The other night was a very big mistake,' she said, exhaling deeply. 'Yes, it was fun, but when I saw your Effective Solutions security pass on your chest of drawers I had to leave. I'm sure you can understand how complicated my position here makes this. If I had known you were attached to the firm, I never would have let things go as far as they did, but we are where we are. I will make sure you receive the appropriate severance payment and a good reference.'

'Estelle, please. You can trust me. I promise. I won't say a word. Promise.' A wave of self-loathing washed over me as I heard myself, but it needed to be done. 'Plus, I can help you here.'

'Luke. Regardless of what happened between us, I'm afraid your position here has been decided already. Your performance is unanimously described as unremarkable. Your lack of business planning and open contract management has been noted, nobody can work out what you do all day, and you appear to add no value to the firm whatsoever. On top of that...' She paused to glance at her folder. '...your salary is disproportionately high, your teamwork and corporate contribution is non-existent, and you don't appear to have a scrap of positive feedback from any of your colleagues here.'

'Support from colleagues?' It was my turn to scoff. 'I'll tell you something. Whether I stay or go, you'll do well not to expect any support from your colleagues here.'

'What do you mean?' A flicker of interest crossed her face. I'd hooked her. Now, to reel her in.

'Gordon, Mitch, John. Complete self-serving psychopaths. Untrustworthy, predatory cannibals who lie and undermine others to destroy any competition in their path. And you're right in their line of fire.'

She raised her eyebrows; out of interest or shock, I couldn't tell. I continued. 'And Stephen Waring? An alright bloke but totally ineffectual in managing anyone in this firm and too ignorant, powerless or both to stop the corruption and kickbacks going on behind the scenes. Completely impotent, metaphorically speaking. He just wasn't smart enough to get to grips with all the money sloshing around under the counter or the personalities in this place. Salter and Mitch have been syphoning the firm's profits off for themselves for years under the radar and never been close to being caught. He couldn't even book the team's overnight awayday without receiving a kickback from the hosting hotel. He's as self-serving as they come.'

'Those are serious allegations you are making. What evidence do you have to support this and does Gordon know?' Ha! She was interested now.

'I'm sure Gordon knows there's corruption. The firm's profits are healthy, but they don't reflect the size or scale of the business being won. Unfortunately for him, he's not close enough to the detail to figure out who, how much and how. Besides, he's having too much fun travelling the world. You'll find out soon enough if you last, but when it comes to bullshit, the real masters are in marketing and sales.'

'OK. Tell me more.' As she leaned in, I caught a glimmer of intrigue in her eyes - the first crack in her professional facade. Finally!

'I'll tell you how it really works here. This whole firm operates on false promises,' I explained. 'They promise small to medium sized firms an objective, independent assessment of their business. Send in sales, under the guise of a *'free strategic audit'*. Every audit results in a list of recommendations. Then all we do is convince the struggling firm their problems can be solved if they reorganise themselves to either – depending on their current structure – a) create a centralised.in-house service model, or b)

28

decentralise services by contracting services out to our network of trusted suppliers. At which point, we get paid by the client and commission from any sub-contracting arranged.' I paused while she stared at me in stunned silence. 'Our website might look impressive with all its talk of Business Design Architects and Change Implementation Managers, but Effective Solutions basically sells overpriced cut-and-paste reorganisation plans to firms in need. That's the real bullshit here!'

Her eyes flickered around my face, perhaps an indication that she was having second thoughts about me. I continued.

'In a nutshell – sorry – basically, they work on the principle of the three 'r's – restructure, relaunch, resign. The firm puts effort into the supposed analysis of businesses and then launch whatever change is recommended. Whether the ship can sail after its launch is immaterial to Effective Solutions' margins. If it leads to success, we take the credit and bask in the glory – see website testimonials. If it leads to failure, and the firm sinks quietly, we still get paid. And we replicate that model in twelve countries across the world. It's a nice earner.'

'That's a very cynical view of the company. Is there anything else you'd like to add?'

'Er...yeah,' I thought I may as well mix things up a little. 'How did you find Sophie and Judith this morning?'

'Not that it's any of your business, but good. They were both extremely enthusiastic and helpful,' she added.

'Watch Sophie. She's sleeping with Mitch and will do anything to keep him happy.'

'Really?' Again, she failed to hide her interest. 'And how do you know all of this?'

'Like I said at the start, I manage the firm's intellectual property and ensure all communications are stored securely. That includes *all* communications', I emphasised. 'Including those on our online chat systems. And I'm the only one with unrestricted access.' I paused to let that sink in. 'There's little I don't know about how this firm operates or what its people are up to. If anyone has the real power in this firm, it's me. Forget those corporate cowboys out there. It's not what you show, it's what you conceal that counts. And I've just chosen not to show it, that's all. For now.'

I may have over-egged it, but my outburst triggered the change in dynamics I was looking for. Estelle was starting to look like the woman I snuck away with on Wednesday. The warmth and sparkle returned to her face, and I was sure she was suppressing a smile.

A minute's silence passed. 'Hmm. I may have underestimated your value.' The corners of her mouth curled upwards. 'I knew there was something different about you. Despite the steer I've been given here, I may keep you on for longer than others would like.' Her tone was firmer than the warmth in her eyes.

'Thank you,' I said as humbly as I could manage.

'Do not think it will be easy though,' she added, keen to maintain an air of authority. 'You will have to change. The current estimate is that your job could be absorbed within 10% of one of Peter's team. I will have to think about that further.'

'As you see fit,' I said, smiling broadly.

'And this is no guarantee that you have a long-term future here', she added unnecessarily.

I got up to leave and was almost at the door when I heard her say, 'We can continue this discussion over dinner tonight. There is a small Italian restaurant in Pimlico called Il Fagioli. Meet me there at eight.'

'It would be my pleasure,' I said, beaming.

'And lose the ponytail,' she added without looking up. 'Your hair looked better loose.'

'As you wish,' I replied.

I left the room elated. It had not been an easy ride, but everything was back on track with some doors left ajar for future possibilities. And a dinner date to boot. I'd survived.

It was only after returning to my desk that I remembered my security pass had stayed in my jacket pocket - where it always is – that night, not on my chest of drawers as Estelle had claimed.

Chapter 5

I replayed my conversation with Estelle on a loop, as other members of the team were called into her office one by one. The rest of the office filled with the hum of gossip, like a swarm of bees keen to sting with their poison. Frequently, people looked in my direction before putting their heads together and muttering inaudibly. I could guess what they were saying. They were so predictable. They think it's over for me. Little did they know that Estelle had just thrown me a lifejacket, albeit temporarily. Time to emerge from the shadows and show this lot what I'm made of. Long overdue, in fact. I'd show them.

I stood tall and started clearing through the piles of paper that had accumulated in my desk trays, systematically working through what needed to be kept and what could be binned. Old reports, invoices, receipts and circulars had piled up over years of neglect, a stark contrast to my meticulous electronic storage systems. Within ten tedious minutes, I'd decided to simply feed the lot of them through the shredding machine. A fresh start.

Reorganising my workspace took less time than anticipated and, before long, I'd created a minimalist setup consisting of my laptop connected to two screens with a slim gap between them for peering into the rest of the office. For show, I cleaned the whiteboard behind me and stuck up a fresh organogram and a couple of colourful line graphs showing recent sales and customer ratings figures. Though I thought so myself, my mini makeover left me looking pretty damn professional.

It even caught the attention of Salter, who swaggered over and broke the silence we'd maintained between us for years by asking how my meeting with Estelle had gone. The gloating sneer on his face revealed his true sentiments which were confirmed when he started speculating loudly that I was clearing my desk in preparation to leave, much to the amusement of his sniggering team in the background. I leaned in close enough for only him to hear. 'Fuck off back to your side of the office, you cockwomble,' I whispered through gritted teeth. Warning shot delivered, he returned to his team, leaving me to wonder whether it might not be him whose days were numbered. I could but hope. Shits like him only made me more determined to succeed.

I never participated directly in office gossip, but I couldn't resist the urge to see what others were saying about Estelle's arrival. Taking care to ensure my screen was angled away from prying eyes, I fired up my ingeniously named office Communicator Remote Access Portal (the acronym never failing to amuse me). It gave me the ability to simultaneously display all Office Communicator conversations taking place across the organisation at any one time. And it was a hive of activity this morning. Call me a voyeuristic geek, but I could lose hours – days even - reading all the individual and group chats taking place on my widescreen monitor.

Today, office gossip was rampant and full of the usual indiscretion they'd never dare communicate face-to-face. The whole firm was united in achieving a single goal - trying to suss out what Estelle's arrival meant for them. They were obsessed. Ironically, for a firm that makes a living out of change management, they seemed resolutely resistant to change.

Salter and Mitch had been exchanging messages with each other all morning. Ordinarily, they rarely had any form of direct communication, preferring instead to avoid any potential conflict by allowing each other to strut around their own domains unchallenged. But here they were, exchanging one-liners and put-downs of their new boss and making a pact to watch each other's backs and swap notes daily. Did Estelle really pose such a threat to them?

Sophie was displaying her insecurities through a chat she had opened with Mitch, saying things like, *'she's much older up close than she first appears,'* and *'I don't know how Gordon thinks he can appoint someone above you with less experience.'* Mitch, in response, was encouraging the anti-Estelle sentiment with superficial generic comments such as *'she's fresh', 'she'll learn'* and *'we'll teach her how things work round here'.* He emphasised the need for *'everyone in the team to make sure they clear everything destined for Estelle through him, so he can watch their backs.* That old trick - create the threat and present the solution. Sly bastard. He must be worried.

Even Peter's team had turned to online gossip (although Peter himself was being his usual wooden self and refraining from getting involved). All three accounting officers – Brian, Carl and Natalie – were commenting on her starting salary - £95,000 + a transitional living allowance + £15,000 travel budget per year. It sounded generous, even by the firm's standards, but as Brian rightly pointed out, it was only for a six-month renewable contract with targets designed to save much more than she was going to cost, and with break clauses if these weren't met. What I found even more interesting was the fact that none of them could find any trace of her receiving any work she'd done for Effective Solutions before, either as an employee or a consultant.

Windows full of bitching and corporate bravado were popping up on my screen faster than I could keep up with them. Neil and Theo from Salter's team, with encouragement from Salter himself, had already created a male group chat which seemed to have the sole purpose of dissecting Estelle into component pieces of meat, graphically describing what they'd like to do to her in *'a just world'.* Their chat was pure Andrew Tate bollocks. My fists clenched as a surge of protective anger rose in my chest.

Sandra, Anna, Cecilia and Michael from the Sales Team were focussing most of their attention on her sense of style and dress. *'I like her suit; you can tell it's not High Street'*; *'you can tell she's French from her figure'* – I couldn't work out the logic behind that thinking! – *'I like her eyebrows'*, *'I wonder if she'll last; she talks tough, but she seems too nice to change anything'*, *'I hope she does'*. Idle, but not exactly welcoming chat.

Apart from aloof Peter, and Lesley, who was stuck out on the front desk on her own, everyone else in the office morphed into mindless amateur pundits, trying to predict what sort of trouble their new COO might cause them, all while taking every opportunity to put down her ability, experience and appearance. It was like a cross between *Lord of the Flies* and *The Office*.

Thank fuck Estelle's keeping me on, and not just for my sake – she'll need someone to watch her back in this snake pit. Sure, she was strong and self-sufficient, but she'd need some inside help if she was going to survive. I was going to make it my job to fulfil that role and provide her with whatever help and support she needed. We'd make a formidable team together. And more.

As if perfectly timed to interrupt my thoughts, a message from Salter to Mitch popped up, *'If that useless wobblehead Luke's managed to talk himself out of being fired, I doubt you or I have anything to worry about'*. Bastard. Why can't he just leave it?

The constant drivel of messages was becoming tiresome, so I turned my attention to the more constructive task of trying to piece together Estelle's past. After all, she had a neat folder compiled on me, and I barely knew anything about her. A bit of background briefing wouldn't go amiss before our meal later. Knowledge is power and all that.

However, as Peter's team had already discovered, this was not as easy or as simple a task as it first seemed. There was no 'Estelle Merisier' on our systems, within HQ or abroad. No mention of her name came up in a search of our TeamSite, even when removing the privacy filter from individuals' folders. It was strange. No mention of her name on any consultant invoices, nor – even more strange for someone in marketing – any social media presence to speak of either. No LinkedIn, Facebook, Instagram or anything else – absolutely nothing. She might as well have been beamed down from another planet.

I peered between my screens into her office. She was on her own, leaning back in her cream leather chair, eyes fixed on a point in the distance, lips moving at high speed as she held her phone to her ear. In addition to the overwhelming physical desire I felt for her, I was consumed with a compulsion to find out everything I could about her. The Estelle I met at the party – flirty, passionate, playful – seemed miles away from this sharp, professional businesswoman. But beneath that tough exterior, I caught glimpses of something... softer. Vulnerable, even. I was itching to know her better. To discover the real woman.

My own online attempts at finding any insight into Estelle's past, I turned to AI to initiate some deep research. Who needs flesh-and-blood IT nerds when you've got an army of AI Agents at your fingertips?

Up until as recently as a year ago, I'd have sought help from the members-only online forum I'd created when Effective Solutions dropped its IT staff count from eight to one. It was a short-sighted decision at the time to save on headcount and overheads in favour of outsourcing and had left me as the firm's one remaining member of the IT crowd while others moved on to bigger and better things. I'd created the anonymous forum to allow ex-colleagues and associates to stay in touch and share IT systems, software and solutions with each other under the radar. Collectively, we must have saved each other thousands of pounds' worth of contracts and months of manhours. Our welcome message when entering the chat was *'Never knowingly overworked'*, a nod to John Lewis's famous slogan. Who says IT guys don't have a sense of humour?

And it was pretty much above board. Ish. If you ignore breaching intellectual, software and property rights of course. The risk of getting caught was low, especially given its obscure and private web location. But the fact remained there were humans behind the pseudonyms. And with humans came risks.

So, frustrated with the inefficient mindless banter and risks of human interactions, I replaced them all with a new army of digital allies. My very own, very efficient, very subservient online team of AI Agents. Each designed to excel in a specific task. Need an IT solution? Ask TechWhizTony. Need advice writing an email? Ask EloquentEric. Need help balancing the books? Ask HeathLedger. I'd even created JesterJoe, an Agent ready with ballsy banter and sassy lines to feed into the online conversations I uploaded if I so chose. Not that I ever did – but it was still fun to read them in isolation.

However, this was a job for HRHarry, my friendly background checker on new personnel. I typed, *'Hey Harry, what can you tell me about Estelle Merisier, Effective Solutions' new COO from France?'* I sat back and smiled in anticipation, wondering why I hadn't thought of employing my agents sooner.

Within seconds the response came back.

'Running a background check on someone typically involves accessing various types of public records and databases…try social media…try public records…try professional networks,,,try court records..blah blah, fucking blah!'

I tried again. *'But what can YOU tell me about Estelle Merisier?'*

'Without specific details or access to private databases, I can only provide general guidance on how to search for

information about someone named Estelle Merisier. I don't
have the ability to access private data directly…'

'Oh, fuck off,' I said out loud, slamming my laptop shut.

That's me done. It was time to go home and get ready for my dinner date.

Chapter 6

There are only so many times you can check a menu outside a restaurant before quizzical glares from the staff inside make you feel uncomfortable and unjustly guilty. I'd arrived at Il Fagioli far too early and had already walked round the block five times to calm my nerves, alternating cigarettes with extra strong mints to stay mildly fresh. It was 20:13 when I recognised her outline approaching from the bottom of the street.

She wore a simple A-line plain skirt, a flower-patterned blouse and a small, crocheted cardigan over her shoulders. She carried herself with relaxed confidence while I stood gawping with a sheepish grin on my face. My stomach churned with nerves as it dawned on me I wasn't sure if I was on a dinner date or an extended business meeting. Obviously, I hoped for the former.

As she approached, I stepped forward and extended my hand. I felt like such a fool when she shook it and said, with mock formality, 'Good evening, Mr Shenstone'. But how was I to have greeted her? It would have been cold and standoffish to not offer her my hand and a peck on the cheek would surely have been considered presumptuous. The lack of ground rules did nothing to dampen my social awkwardness. 'Aaaargh', I screamed inwardly, realising that the awkward angst of my teenage years still lingered.

'You look fantastic,' I said, resisting the urge to stare.

'Thank you,' she acknowledged. 'Have you got any cigarettes? I finished all of mine and couldn't find anywhere to buy some on the way here.'

I took two Marlboro Golds out and cupped my hands around my plastic lighter for her to lean in and take a light. She waited patiently as I repeatedly struck the flint unsuccessfully before she pulled out her own silver Dupont lighter and, with a snap of her thumb, created a clean flame for us, leaving me wishing I had the foresight to practice looking so cool before coming out. We stood outside the restaurant, silently exhaling streams of smoke into the evening air, my mind frustratingly devoid of inspiration for small talk. The harder I tried to think of something to break the silence, the more my mind hollowed. I was relieved when Estelle stubbed her cigarette out halfway through, providing the cue for us to enter.

The clientele inside consisted mostly of couples, with a single group of eight in the central tables area with a spread of ages that suggested they could be one family. Steamy scents of creamy vegetables, herby meats and garlicky seafood filled the air. Wine flowed freely, laughter exploded at regular intervals from different corners, and unobtrusive Italian café music played in the background. Perfect ambience.

A heavily accented waiter greeted us and led us to a small table in the far corner, leaving us with a bowl of olives, some warm bread, a small plate of olive oil and a couple of menus. He showed no subtlety when pointing out *'what a lucky man I was to be out with such a lovely lady,'* while pulling Estelle's chair out for her. She remained standing and stared at him until his smile faded and he scurried off. It was impressive to watch and, although he deserved it, I hoped I wasn't in for similar stern treatment.

My attempts at small talk over the menu's contents failed to elicit any sort of response from Estelle, who stared silently at the menu and around the restaurant as if absorbing its every detail, heightening my stress levels. So much so, I was relieved when the waiter returned to offer drinks.

'Wine, sir?' he sang with effortless charisma. I looked at Estelle and mouthed 'White?' She shrugged in agreement, so I opted for a bottle of house white.

'May I recommend the Orvieto, sir?' the waiter suggested in return. His Italian accent gave him an air of authority which made his suggestion sound like an invitation to an exclusive club. I couldn't help thinking that he didn't look particularly Italian and wondered whether he might drop it and revert to a London accent when he kicks back with a cup of tea in an evening. 'It's a little bit fruity, but very refreshing,' he added, winking at Estelle. Before I had a chance to say, 'yes please', Estelle took charge.

'No. We will have a bottle of Sancerre instead. I prefer something with finer maturity and more subtle qualities than the common Orvieto,' she said, handing the wine menu back while staring unblinkingly at me. I stifled a grin as the waiter's smile faded.

'Certainly Madam,' he said in a clipped tone, withdrawing as quickly as he could. I chuckled and complimented her majestic way with words.

'I have had to deal with lecherous bastards like him all fucking week. I do not want to be objectified and treated like I'm just someone's accessory tonight too,' she spat with passion. I was reassured by the fact she was talking to me as a fellow member within her circle of trust.

'You can't blame him,' I said. 'It's just light-hearted banter. Part of the 'ambience' of this place.'

'No, Luke. You may not have noticed, but he has been looking me up and down since we arrived. And I saw him give you that envious look when we walked across the restaurant. Men like that are not light-hearted. They are one-dimensional bastards who treat all women like meat.'

'I'm sorry. I didn't notice that,' I said honestly, keen to steer the conversation into calmer waters.

'I mean, he has no idea...' she continued, 'who either of us is. He just assumed we are a couple, assumed that you are in charge and the one to ask about the wine and has no idea that I am in fact the more senior colleague here, out for an innocent dinner with a member of staff. He should show more respect rather than make foolish assumptions.'

Being reminded of my place stung, but at least I wasn't in the firing line. In any case, she had a point, so I nodded along politely as she continued to deconstruct every minutia of the waiter's behaviour until he was starting to sound like a dedicated predatory rapist masquerading as a waiter. Instead of returning to our table, he sent a young waitress over with our wine.

'Oh, I'm sorry, I didn't mean to interrupt your conversation,' the waitresses said with cheery innocence, showing us the bottle's label.

'That's perfectly fine,' Estelle replied. The waitress poured a small sample of Sancerre into my glass. I kept my hands folded on my lap and stared fearfully at the glass, afraid to sample the wine that Estelle had chosen. After an uncomfortably long pause, I asked Estelle, 'Perhaps you'd like to try it?' This triggered much laughter from her and the waitress as she gestured for both our glasses to be filled up. She said she was sure it would be fine.

I breathed a sigh of relief when the waitress left our table and, while Estelle was still chuckling to herself, held my glass up and offered a toast to 'a respectful and successful working relationship'. Estelle paused before returning the toast with a small but genuine smile, following which I rewarded myself with a couple of successive sips to steady my nerves.

A few swigs later and the conversation was flowing at a much more relaxed pace. Estelle did most of the talking – a good sign - telling me about her first week at Effective Solutions, her initial impressions of the business and her thoughts on some of the characters she had met so far. I sat in awe, flattered and honoured that she felt she could trust me enough to confide on that level. And yet, I still felt quite alone and detached. Happy enough to be sipping my wine and listening to her melodic tones while staring into her enthused eyes, the faint creases around their corners telling me that she was smiling from within. But I was still very much the obedient recipient of her stories rather than an equal.

As our original waiter returned, Estelle stiffened and turned away in stony silence. I cringed, caught between her obvious disdain and his patient anticipation. I ran my finger down the menu and ordered a pancetta and balsamic vinegar starter, followed by pan-fried calves' liver and vegetables (or Fegato Burro e Salivia as written on the menu). Without turning her head to face the waiter, Estelle nodded and said, 'the same' through pursed lips. As soon as the waiter turned his back to leave, she pulled a face behind him and said, 'pig'. He paused mid-step as he headed back towards the kitchen.

Estelle continued to outline, with passion, her ideas for reshaping the firm, increasing her involvement in the overseas offices and building a team which shared her vision. I admired her enthusiasm but couldn't help but think she was being slightly over-ambitious in thinking it would be that easy to cut through the controlling personalities of the Directors. Despite her obvious strength of character, I still sensed an air of vulnerability – perhaps even naivety about her - that I wanted to protect. For now, I was happy to listen intently and let her take the conversation wherever she wanted.

More than once, I did try to ask what she did before coming to Effective Solutions but was met with a wall of polite evasion. She skilfully sidestepped my question with a vague mention of *'French office projects'* before pivoting to her recent master's in business administration. Her evasiveness was as intriguing as it was frustrating.

'Anyway. Enough about me,' she declared. 'Tell me more about you and how you are going to help me achieve what I need at work.' She placed her elbows on the table and rested her chin in her hands, giving me a look that was both playful and authoritative - like our first night together. I got the impression that perhaps the wine was taking effect.

'Er…I'm still a bit confused over what relationship we have here,' I blurted out with a lack of filter.

'Luke,' she replied, moving closer, intensifying eye contact. 'We are just two work colleagues catching up with each other after work.' The playful tone in her voice did not match the literal meaning of her words. But they combined to tell me that was the best I was going to get. 'Two very attractive colleagues from work,' she added suggestively with a raised eyebrow.

Our exchange was interrupted by the arrival of our pancetta starter and further silence as the waiter introduced what we could see was in front of us. She visibly ignored him and busied herself by topping up her empty glass.

'Is that all we are?' I asked feebly once the waiter was out of earshot. 'Couldn't we pick up where we left off?'

'Luke. You are *so* funny,' she dismissed, cementing my sense of inadequacy. 'Anyway, my attractive work colleague. You were about to tell me all about how you are going to help me.'

I ignored the question and started on my pancetta. 'Mmm. This is good,' I said. 'Just the right balance of flavour between the salted meat and sweetness of the balsamic vinegar.' The pepper and shavings of Parmigiano Reggiano added an extra subtle delight without dominating the dish. We nodded together in appreciation while chewing, allowing me to avoid responding to her question and divert the conversation towards our shared passion for food. We discovered that we shared a preference for Italian cuisine with an emphasis on freshly cooked ingredients, although Estelle did make me laugh when she described having an equal passion for staying out of kitchens.

'While we could talk about food all night, I do believe you were about to tell me more about how you can help me at work,' she reminded me.

Estelle's rapid shifts between flirtation and authority made my head spin, but I decided to go with the flow and let her into the more secretive side of my work. I held back from revealing too much in one go. Partly to make sure she maintained interest in me, but also because I wanted some fun. Before revealing anything, I invited her to guess, from her half-hour introductory meetings with staff, which of them might have secret lives they don't want anyone else to know about.

She didn't look comfortable with my question, but reluctantly offered a couple of incorrect suggestions. I teased her gently, pointing out that she clearly wasn't getting to know her staff as well as she thought. However, her impatient stare told me I was pushing my luck by playing with her, so I blurted out:

'Well, I won't mention any names for now, but I could tell you about two members of the finance team who've been having a secret affair and cheating on their partners for over a year now. Or another guy who likes to present himself as a real ladies' man – there are a few of them in the firm – whose highlight of the week is visiting a gothic gay bar south of the river before returning home to his family. Or, how about one senior manager who's regularly online into the early hours keeping the most depressive online diary you've ever read and who regularly contemplates whether he and his family would be better off without him. Or…perhaps you could guess which member of staff brings in supplies of coke and Viagra to sell on to others.'

'Seriously?' Estelle asked, her back stiffening and both eyebrows raised. She looked both shocked and disgusted. 'A lot of that is really very sad and none of anyone else's business. I don't see how any of that gossip is relevant to their ability to get the job done. And, to be honest, I am disappointed in you and more concerned about the invasion of privacy taking place here than anything else.'

Some empathy was needed. 'I agree, it is sad, but I meant it when I said I could help you. Understanding what

45

motivates and helps your teams and people - or where the threats lie - could be very useful to you.' I said earnestly.

'And should I ask how you come to know all of this?' she asked from behind her refilled wine glass.

'I'm responsible for monitoring use of computer systems, remember?' I replied, sounding smugger than I'd intended.

'But do they really reveal that level of personal detail through our computer systems? And, if they do, are they not protected by some sort of privacy law?'

Her genuine shock at the discovery that every key tapped on a keyboard might be read by someone else was indeed naïve. I wondered if her concern stemmed from her position as COO, or whether she might be concerned about what might be visible of her own online activities. I tried to reassure on the point of propriety by pointing out that the company's computer privacy policy very clearly stated that its systems were *'provided for the purpose of work business only'*. It was so clear, in fact, that a reminder statement popped up on everyone's monitor every time they logged in, together with a warning that *'all computer activity may be monitored by the Administrator'* and *'inappropriate use of the computer systems may result in dismissal'*. Monitoring others' activity was therefore perfectly above board and her knowledge of this fact did not come with any risk.

Estelle seemed to accept this point but remained stony-faced with discomfort.

I went on to explain that no matter how strongly worded the warning was, like foolish attention-seeking lambs to the slaughter in a Big Brother house, it was never long before individuals forgot about the risk of being monitored and relaxed into revealing their innermost secrets in online conversations. The fact that they were a bunch of ambitious, risk-taking, go-getters – often working long hours against tight deadlines – meant that using the Office Communicator system to share their idle, but very personal, thoughts with each other was an inevitable consequence. As inevitable as leaving a pubescent teenage boy on a desk in the middle of an unsupervised library full of porn magazines and expect him not to go for a wander and a peep through the shelves.

I may have been more surprised than Estelle at the sheer fact she was surprised by this.

'I'm still not convinced that it's right,' she said, biting her lip and shaking her head.

I shrugged and repeated the spiel about the firm (or, rather, I) having the right to restrict and monitor their systems as it saw fit, but her crinkled brow leaked her ongoing concern.

A silence crept over us while we returned to our wine. The flow of the conversation had been lost. I racked my brains for something to say but the returning nerves in my stomach robbed me of my voice. Occasionally, I'd catch her eye and smile shyly, although I was sure that my discomfort was patently visible. 'Say something, say something, you fool,' I urged myself. The more I squirmed, the more relaxed and amused Estelle appeared to become as my line of vision flicked to and from her.

Eventually, and thankfully, she broke what had become a painful silence. 'I'm glad we came out together tonight,' she declared conclusively, much to my surprise. 'To be honest, I asked you here tonight so that, one way or another, we could reach an agreement – in a civilised fashion - over you leaving the firm.' Despite the fact she was speaking in hushed tones, her words rang through my head like claxons. I felt winded. 'However, I may have been a little too quick to dismiss your value. But…,' she paused for effect, 'you must understand this situation still leaves me in a very difficult position. Your dismissal from the firm has already been discussed and is expected imminently. Your role - and, if I'm honest, you - are simply not valued enough.'

The finality of her words was punctuated with the return of our waiter. We reverted to silence, maintaining eye contact with each other while our plates were gathered.

'Was everything OK, Madam?' he asked.

'Fine, thank you,' Estelle responded tersely, maintaining her sight on me.

He turned to me. 'Sir?'

'Yes, very good thanks.' I smiled in return.

As soon as he was gone, Estelle leaned forward to complain that he had again been leering at her and sneering at me. I didn't disagree but honestly hadn't noticed and wondered if we'd witnessed the same situation. However, she was adamant that he was an arrogant and disrespectful creep who was not fit to serve in a restaurant. This was awkward. I didn't want to disagree with her, nor did I want the scene to escalate, which it looked as if it might.

'We were talking about work,' I reminded her. 'Let me be honest with you. I really don't want to lose my job and if you could work it so that I could stay I'd do everything I can to help you. I've got a feeling I could be useful to you, especially if you want to get a grip on the overseas offices' funding and operations. If I put my mind to it, I'm fairly sure I could help you find ways to increase the overseas revenue by 20 percent in your first year. What can I do to make that happen?'

Her cheeks flushed, she stopped ranting about the waiter, looked thoughtful for a moment and then, much to my relief, relaxed into a smile.

'Luke. You have already convinced me you have a lot to offer in more ways than one.' Not for the first time, I was unsure whether we were talking business or pleasure. 'But if you are to survive at Effective Solutions, then your job will have to be visibly redesigned and made more challenging.'

The cold, factual nature of her words was not important. Her tone had warmed, as had her body language and facial gestures. I was ready to agree to anything.

'Naturally,' I said out loud. 'What did you have in mind?'

'Well, if only for presentational purposes, we need to expand your role and responsibilities.'

'No problem,' I replied. There was so much slack in my day, I was confident this concession was more than manageable.

'I suggest you build on your Digital, Data and financial management skills by taking on some Programme and Project Management responsibilities.'

'PPM?' I asked, less than keen. 'Such as? Do you have any projects in mind?' I tried to hide the lack of enthusiasm in my voice.

'Not specifically. But you need some realistic targets and results for what you do. Apply the same overarching PPM principles to them as other teams do. Just write some objectives around co-ordination, advising others and creating some project templates to track the firm's strategic performance for now. Oh, and include some training objectives to show you're serious about development. It will help.'

'Ok.' I knew there were online courses I could click through easily enough.

'And get them signed off by Peter.'

'Why Peter?' I asked, slow on the uptake.

'Because someone needs to manage you directly and that's not going to be me. You're going to have to move out of your corner and become part of his team. I'm giving him greater strategic oversight of the firm and you can help him pull that together with your digital knowledge,' she said grinning. It was almost if she had a plan all along.

Integration and subordination did not appeal. 'I'm not sure that'd work from a security point of view. There's a need to keep IT management separate from other teams for a reason. Plus, there's the security and practical issues...'

'Luke.' Her non-negotiable tone was back. 'If this is going to work, you're going to have to start working more closely with others, OK? There's no reason why you can't manage IT security while reporting to Peter. Plus, working with him will involve you in the strategic side of things which will help secure your position.'

I hated the woolly term 'strategic oversight' and the thought of increased interaction with other teams, but there was no point resisting. 'Of course,' I said, smiling compliantly. Her shoulders visibly dropped as our working arrangements were officially concluded.

'Good. That's settled then,' she replied with an air of self-satisfied victory.

An air we both felt, but one that I was more than happy to concede to her.

Chapter 7

With perfect timing, our waiter reappeared with our Fegato Burro e Salivia.

'For Madam,' he crooned, carefully aligning a steaming plate of calves' liver in front of Estelle. 'And for Sir,' he said, dropping his accent and parking my plate in front of me. I caught a twinkle in Estelle's eye from across the table. I was hungry, the food looked great, and my mouth was watering with anticipation.

'See?' she said as soon as the waiter left. 'He is a creep. I'm going to complain.'

'Let's leave it,' I suggested softly. 'He's gone now. Let's enjoy our food.' At which point he reappeared with an oversized pepper grinder.

'Black pepper, Madam?' he asked.

'No,' she spat, turning her head away from him.

'Sir?'

'Yes please,' I replied. A few twists of his wrist, and he was gone again.

'I don't care what you say, he deserves not to get away with treating people like that,' Estelle continued, riled. 'Waving his big substitute penis over people's dinner like that. It's pathetic and obscene.'

I wasn't sure if she was being completely serious or just venting. I struggled to find anything non-inflammatory to say in response, so it was a huge relief when we both broke into spontaneous giggles and started to eat.

Noticing our bottle of Sancerre had managed to empty itself rather quickly, I caught a passing waitress's attention to order another bottle to see us through our main courses while our demon waiter was busy at another table. Overall, despite Estelle prickling each time the waiter passed our table, the evening was going well. The food really was excellent, and the conversation had reverted to the more relaxed topic of our favourite Italian dishes (mine being lasagne, hers being tagliatelle al fungi), and good places to eat near the office. As our meal came to an end and the conversation took over, Estelle took a deep sigh and stretched her arms out behind herself.

'Oh, I am pleased my first week is over with,' she exhaled. 'It is not easy moving to the city, especially a new one, and a new job.'

'You seem to be handling it all in your stride though,' I said encouragingly, carefully resisting the temptation to let my gaze delve below her neckline, although I did start to wonder – or hope - if her stretching was for her benefit or mine.

'Yes, très bien. I'm pleased with how everything's gone so far,' she said, taking a deep breath and surveying the restaurant. 'New city, new job, new life,' she mused, more to herself than me. 'And now it is time to start the weekend.' She took two large swigs of wine and placed her empty glass down, declaring herself full.

'A top-up?' I offered. 'Or some coffee, perhaps?' I added while mopping up the remaining sauce from my plate with a corner of bread.

'No, thank you,' she said abruptly. 'I am ready to leave when you are. I am just going to freshen up.' She paused before leaving the table to remove a small make-up bag from her handbag and give me a subtle half smile while biting the bottom corner of her lip. My stomach flipped with excitement.

She disappeared in the direction of the ladies', behind the kitchens. I sat back, took stock of where we were and what was happening. A good meal, excellent company, I still had a job, and we'd agreed a plan for work. However, I was still niggled by the fact I was none the wiser as to where that left us. If there was indeed an 'us' beyond the work relationship. There had been some positive signs. She had relaxed throughout the course of the evening, and her body language and facial expressions had become increasingly warm. And yet I did not feel confident enough to presume I might be able to tempt her back to my place for coffee. I'd have to play it by ear.

I couldn't help reflecting that it's always the one who is least interested in a relationship who dictates the pace of it. My overthinking of the situation annoyed me, and I resolved to loosen up before Estelle returned.

In the absence of any waiters in sight to get the bill from, I started to sweep piles of crumbs into small mounds on the tablecloth with my hands and stack our plates together when I heard men shouting and the sound of banging from the direction of the kitchens. As necks craned towards the commotion, and the clattering and shouting increased, so did my concern for Estelle's absence. Suddenly, a big metallic crash, a man swearing loudly, followed by more shouting, followed by a stream of waiters and kitchen staff filing out of the back, accompanied by a thick stream of black smoke and the unmistakable smell of burning.

Instinctively, I rushed towards the toilets to find Estelle but was pushed back by a rush of waiting staff shouting instructions for everyone to evacuate the restaurant, one of them gripping my wrist to move me towards the front entrance. A thick fog of smoke continued to chug out from the back of the restaurant and started collecting at ceiling level. Two male kitchen staff with chequered trousers and fire extinguishers rushed past me towards the kitchen. I shook my wrist free and called out Estelle's name repeatedly as loudly as I could manage.

'There's no-one in there,' one of the waiters shouted back, before kicking the doors to the kitchen open. It was a foolish mistake. The intake of fresh air to the kitchen caused a bright flash and a burst of flame which sent both staff onto their hands and knees, abandoning their extinguishers and spluttering their way to the front entrance – the only accessible exit - gesturing at me to follow. All other customers had already left. The kitchen doors were now concealed behind a thick curtain of dark grey smoke. The only visible light was the brightly glowing portholes in the doors, through which the savagery of flames was visible as they flared up and down in waves, ramping up their notches of heat. I was panting with panic and desperate for sight or sound of Estelle, but the heat was too intense and any movement towards the kitchen caused my skin to scream with pain.

'Get out of there, you idiot,' a deep Italian-accented voice barked from behind me.

There was no option. The heat was overwhelming. Smoke spilled out everywhere, sending sharp spikes into my throat and eyes. I grabbed Estelle's handbag from our table and rushed outside, joining the crowd that had gathered across the street, staring back at Il Fagioli, now brightly lit against the evening sky, sending polluting plumes upwards.

I looked around the crowd. Distressed staff, confused diners and voyeuristic passers-by. But no sign of Estelle. I willed her to appear, hoping I'd turn and find her sneaking a cigarette somewhere nearby, safe from the flames now engulfing the front of the restaurant.

In the middle of the road outside the restaurant, furiously pacing back and forth was the waiter who'd served us earlier, waving his free hand in the air while pressing his mobile to his ear with the other. I guessed he was actually Il Fagioli's manager from the urgency with which he was reacting to the situation. Tears of rage or upset poured down his cheeks towards his spit-encrusted mouth. Over the chatter of the crowd, I tuned into his rant as he spat out obscenity after obscenity: *'...fucking fire engine...my fucking business...thirty-five fucking years up in fucking smoke...mad fucking bitch...fucking hurry up...'*. He was definitely more London than Italian. The crowd of spectators lowered their chatter to get their phones out and record the manager's rage while his restaurant burnt in the background. I wondered if any of them had thought to call the emergency services before doing so. I almost felt a pang of sympathy for him. Almost, were it not for the fact that my main concern remained for Estelle's safety.

I weaved in and out of the crowd looking for her, my heart thumping with adrenaline. I held her handbag close to my chest, convinced that the tighter I held onto it, the more likely she was to be safe. I traced the leather pattern with my fingers before opening it, hoping to find an address or way to contact her or some other insight into her personality that might help me understand her. I didn't even have her number. Nothing aside from a purse, mobile phone (switched off) some lip balm, a hairbrush and some keys. I closed it and tucked it under my arm for fear someone would recognise it and realise that it was me who was with that 'mad fucking bitch' in the restaurant.

I needn't have worried. The crowd's attention shifted to the arrival of two fire engines. Firemen sprang into action, guiding the crowd to a safe distance from the restaurant while they unravelled hoses and unpacked equipment. Their flashing blue lights turned the area into an unreal disaster scene film set. There were around a hundred people gathered to watch now. I moved to the crowd's edge to get a clear view of what was happening and who was about. Leaning on a parked car to steady my shaky legs, I pulled out a cigarette to calm my nerves.

'Boo!' Estelle's voice startled me as she grabbed my arm from behind, giggling like a girl.

'Need a light?' she offered, flicking her Dupont flame under my nose.

'What the fuck happened? Are you crazy?' I hissed through gritted teeth, simultaneously wishing I asked how she was first.

'I needed to pee,' she replied, still giggling. Her big brown eyes were fixed on me, warm, open, full of affection with small reflections of blue flashing lights dancing in their corners. The way she was clinging onto my arm took me back to the night we first met. There was a playfulness in her eyes that far outweighed the amount of wine we had drunk.

'I was worried you were trapped in there. What the hell happened?' I handed her handbag back and, without thinking, put my arms around her and gave her a big reassuring hug. She snuggled into my chest and squeezed my waist. I felt a surge of relief in the same way I imagine an addict must feel when he gets his first hit of the day. She ignored my question and, rightly or wrongly, I wasn't going to ask again. Maybe because I was worried what the answer would be, or maybe because I already knew.

'Come on. We ought to get out of here sharpish,' I said against the backdrop of firemen shouting instructions at each other and directing their hoses towards the restaurant. 'You can come back to mine if you want?'

'Yes please,' she replied with a subdued sense of calm, her doe eyes fixed affectionately on me. 'I'm hungry,' she added.

'We could always find something else to eat if you prefer,' I suggested.

She stopped and gave me an earnest look while biting her bottom lip. 'Not that sort of hungry, silly'.

We had only made our way halfway down the street when she stopped dead and looked me in the eye. 'Luke?' she asked. 'I feel like I have got to you know a bit better tonight. But you have told me everyone's secrets apart from your own. What is your secret?'

'I don't have any,' I replied. 'What you see is what you get.'

'I don't believe you,' she pressed. 'Everyone has secrets. What's yours?' I shook my head and gave her a smile.

'I'm as straightforward as they come,' I lied. Some things are best left unsaid.

I slipped my arm through hers and gave it a squeeze to signal our need to quicken our pace. I felt euphoric. Still shaky, but ultimately euphoric. The evening air was fresh and sweet even if our clothes were tinged with stale smoke. The sky, a crisp and clear deep blue, speckled with stars and framed by a clear crescent moon. The most perfect woman in the world was holding my arm and we were heading back to my flat. What more could I ask for? The whole fire incident already seemed distant, crazy and surreal. All that mattered was me and her. Here and now.

As we made our way towards Victoria station in silence, I couldn't help likening my situation to that of a man who had just mounted a wild horse he knew was too dangerous to ride but was too swept away with passion to get off.

Chapter 8

Clattering sounds from the kitchen woke me. Not for the first time in a week, my head was cloudy, eyesight blurred, tongue as rough and foul tasting as (I imagine) the bottom of a budgie cage. I squinted out from under my duvet to verify my surroundings. Aside from a small stream of morning sunlight breaking through a crack in the curtains, the room was still dark. The window was open, letting the fresh scent of spring enter the room along with the sound of chirping birds.

The clatter-clatter of teaspoon against cup rang through the flat accompanied by the soft tones of Estelle melodically humming to herself. I sat bolt upright, surprised but pleased that she was still here. As my ears attuned to the sounds coming from the kitchen, memories of last night flooded back to my waking mind - lips to lips, flesh to flesh, squeeze to grip, kisses to bites, passive to passion. I felt sore but kinglike.

Estelle took complete charge last night, reducing me to a compliant ingredient in her recipe of desire. As soon as we'd entered the flat, she denied me permission to speak, holding her finger to her lips and shushing me every time I tried. She'd led me to the bedroom by my hand and stood me up beside the bed. She told me not to move or speak without her permission while she circled me, tracing her finger round my face and throat, before unbuttoning and undressing me. When I responded by putting my hands on her waist, she'd slapped them hard and told me to keep my hands to myself. I'd complied, of course, part out of desire to fulfil her wishes, part out of curiosity to see what would happen next. Piece by piece of clothing, she'd stripped me bare, leaving me standing before her, completely exposed while she slowly paced around me, looking me up and down. There was nothing embarrassing or demeaning about it. Her touch was tender and her eyes, full of desire, rarely left me. Even when she had to remind me to keep my hands by their side by placing my wrists hard against my hips, it had been done with an element of not wanting to spoil a game rather than out of maliciousness. It was more affection than control. Being denied an active role in the scenario had only increased my desire and hunger for her.

I sat up in bed recalling every small detail to relive the night before. When I was completely naked, she'd stepped back and admired me, whispering compliments on my sinewy contours that I was not allowed to respond to. She'd started undressing herself while maintaining eye contact, leaving herself with only an open blouse and bra on, while her underwear had been pushed down to the floor. I was aroused again just thinking about the scene. When she stepped towards me again, she surprised me by placing her palm on my chest and pushing me backwards onto the bed, my arms spreading out to break my fall as she pinned my shoulders down and straddled my waist as she positioned her exposed self over me. 'Now you can have me,' she'd more demanded than offered.

The rest of the night was a blizzard of twisted passion full of scents, sensations and surprises. It was not just my stomach muscles aching this morning. Parts of me were very sore.

I pulled a pair of shorts on, tiptoed down the corridor and paused by the open kitchen door to watch Estelle. She had her back to me and was preparing a cafetière of coffee. She was rocking from side to side while humming and looked a picture of adorable innocence. Gone was any trace of the hard-nosed businesswoman about her. Nor was there any hint of the uncompromising seductress of the night before (even if she did ultimately choose to submit). She'd found and was wearing an oversized t-shirt of mine. Her hair was untamed and had increased in waves. The left side had been gathered and pinned back behind her ear, the right side was sticking out at ninety degrees, presumably where she had been lying. A faint red mark was visible on the back of her neck.

'Good morning,' I said brightly, slipping my arms around her waist from behind and softly kissing the back of her neck. 'It should be me making coffee for you.'

'Oh, good morning, Luke.' She turned within my hands to face me, smiling. 'You were sleeping so soundly I was hoping to surprise you. Wouldn't you like to stay in bed longer?'

Her eyes – soft, hypnotic, smouldering - drew me in closer so that our bodies were touching from head to toe. Her body twisted against mine as we kissed deeply. I wished I'd stopped off at the bathroom to make my mouth as minty fresh as hers. She broke away and stretched up on her toes to peck my forehead. 'Come on. Let's take these back to bed.'

After a quick freshen up - face, hands, eyes, ears, mouthwash, bits and pieces - I returned to the bedroom to find Estelle stretched out on the bed, legs folded strategically to avoid revealing too much, blowing clouds of smoke up towards the ceiling. It was a sight I knew I'd remember for life, her face radiating warmth and her unblemished body looking magnificent. As I stood savouring the scene, she took another draw from her cigarette which triggered what sounded like a huge snap at the back of my brain.

*Click. 'NO SMOKING IN THE FLAT!' came a screaming voice out from the distant recesses of my memory. I hadn't heard **that** voice for years. 'It stinks, put it out!' came the shrill instruction, causing me to freeze on the spot. Oh, how **she** would have a heart attack if **she** could see the scene now, I thought to myself. The shock at hearing this distant voice from the past quickly turned into annoyance at myself for allowing **her** to enter the room - if* *only in spiritual memory - and interrupt what should have been a blissful morning with my newfound lover. Keep it boxed up and focus on what's in front of you, I told myself. My heart sank at the realisation that, despite the elapsed time, history still had the power to haunt, even when the present promised so much.*

'Luke, what's wrong?' Estelle asked, sitting up. 'You are staring at me like you've seen a ghost.'

I shook myself back into the moment and sat on the bed next to her and lit a cigarette. 'I'm sorry,' I said. 'I guess I just can't believe how lucky I am to have you all to myself.'

She pulled me back onto the bed and lay my head on her stomach. She looked down at me. Her big brown eyes were so warm and relaxing as they searched every detail on my face. 'You haven't fallen for me already have you, Luke?' She was stating the obvious, of course. She knew it and I knew it.

'I can't remember the last time I felt like this,' I admitted, not directly answering her rhetorical question.

She ran her fingers through my hair, sweeping it off my forehead. 'Well, maybe you had better get used to it,' she whispered, bending forward, and pecking light kisses across my forehead. Cigarettes extinguished, coffee untouched and going cold, we kissed, stroked, and caressed without words. Our dreamy eyes with dilated pupils stared yearningly at each other with every shift of position. She cupped my face and wrapped her limbs around me. Her cheeks flushed and the rhythm of her breathing changed to deep pleasure-moans, punctuated by occasional intakes of breath. Our bodies formed the perfect jigsaw against each other. I could envelope her completely in my arms. Our legs could grip and lock each other into position with tailor-made precision. My firmness against her softness. My twists against her turns. My stubble against her smooth skin. Endless spiralling, kissing, exchanging of pleasures. Mutual worship of each other's spirits and bodies. We were completely intoxicated with each other. Two lost souls who had finally discovered their other halves. Absolute trust. And love. I hoped.

I wrestled with our positioning so that I was hovering over her, while she lay on her back. There was no denying my state of arousal, causing Estelle to give a half-smile and raise a single eyebrow in mock shock and anticipation.

'Good morning,' she said, the corners of her mouth turning upwards and her dimples becoming more prominent. 'Looks like someone woke up with a healthy appetite today'.

She gripped me between her legs and, in contrast to last night, applied no rules or restrictions on me as she relaxed her hold on me. I felt as if the roles had reversed, or switched, as she raised her knees and wrapped her legs around me and whispered 'I'm yours' while maintaining full undivided eye contact. I whispered 'mine' in response, and slowly pushed myself inside her, causing her to release a deep moan of satisfaction.

A sense of relief washed over me as our bodies and souls rocked back and forth together in gentle unison, the present firmly slamming the door on the past.

Chapter 9

Late afternoon. Estelle had left the warmth of bed to stretch in front of the window, her raised arms inadvertently lifting the t-shirt she'd stolen from me to expose the lower curves of her bottom. I propped myself up on my elbow, admiring her as she shifted her weight from foot to foot. She turned to face me as my stomach let out a loud rumble, betraying a hunger I was previously unaware of. We'd survived on coffee and cigarettes alone since our meal at Il Fagioli. And those calories had long since been burnt off.

'I wondered how long it would be before you got hungry for something other than me,' she said laughing, sitting herself down on the side of the bed.

'I'm sorry,' I said, blushing unnecessarily. 'You must think I'm terribly selfish. I haven't even offered you anything to eat yet.'

'That's OK. You've been looking after me in other ways.' She reached over and squeezed my hand. 'Anyway, I need to think about heading back to my own accommodation soon.'

'How about a homemade dinner for two?' I offered with a fresh wind of energy. 'I could make some pasta. Or something lighter if you prefer?'

'Hmmm…' she mulled, pursing her lips and twisting her nose to one side. 'I really ought to head back. I need to freshen up and my clothes smell of smoke from last night.'

'There's no need to rush,' I said, lifting myself onto my knees. 'I'll get you a fresh towel for a shower if you like and you can wear some of my jogging bottoms. They're clean and comfortable, promise.' Before Estelle could reply, I was up and pulling out a fresh towel and a choice of clothes from the chest of drawers. 'I'll make us an early dinner while you freshen up.'

Estelle flicked her eyes from the clothes to me, sighed, and agreed she could stay a little longer. She made it sound like a concession, but her face told me otherwise. She told me not to go to any trouble and asked for something quick and light on the basis she didn't think she could manage a portion of pasta.

'No problem!' I replied cheerfully. 'A light dinner of some sort will be ready in about half an hour in that case.'

Solo living does not create much of a need for cooking fancy meals, but I always made sure I was stocked up on fresh and tasty ingredients. I'd never acquired a taste for the over-processed ready meals that so many modern-day singletons survive on. My fridge didn't contain a huge amount of choice, but there was some goat's cheese, a jar of beetroot, cherry tomatoes and some salad which would do for now. I also found a small bottle of truffle-infused olive oil that I'd hidden away at the back of a cupboard for special occasions. That would add a dash of sophistication.

From down the hallway, the sound of the shower started up, accompanied by the humming of a happy Estelle lost in a world of her own. I tiptoed down the hallway and listened outside the door, trying to imagine her every movement in response to the sound of the fall of the shower. After a couple of minutes' indulgence, I returned to the kitchen to wash, chop and throw the ingredients into a large salad bowl before rushing round the flat picking up the remains of the night before, smoothing the bedcovers down, opening windows, and laying a table for two in the living room.

While rushing back and forth from the kitchen to the front room to set the dinner table to look as romantic but spontaneous as possible, I realised I'd picked up Estelle's habit of humming to myself. I threw a light cotton tablecloth over the small, rounded table by the window, set the glistening bowl of salad in the centre with my homemade vinaigrette on the side, placemats, coasters, the only set of knives and forks I could find in the flat that actually matched, and a pair of tall-stemmed wine glasses. Or would water be better? Or both, so we have a choice? I hurried back to the kitchen to pull out a bottle of sparkling water and a bottle of Muscadet from the top of the fridge, so we had options.

Was a candle too much for a casual evening salad, I asked myself? Not sure, so I lit one, thought it screamed of trying too hard, blew it out, stood back, and then lit it again before a final trip to the kitchen to freshen myself up with a quick wash in the sink and return to pour two full glasses of water and two half glasses of wine.

Estelle joined me within minutes wearing one of my t-shirts and a pair of pyjama bottoms I couldn't remember last wearing. Her hair was still damp and wavy. Her skin glowed red and rosy in the way that only a hot shower can produce.

'Wow, this looks lovely!' she fluttered, admiring the table and choosing to pick up the wine over the water and raise her glass. 'Santé! I promise to do my best not to stain your t-shirt with any beetroot. I hope you don't mind...'. Of course I didn't mind. She was staying for longer and that was all that mattered.

'Not a problem,' I replied, encouraging her to sit down while I served a couple of medium-sized salad portions, being extra careful not to spill any beetroot.

'Mmm, this is perfect,' she said, drizzling vinaigrette over her portion. 'Not bad for an Englishman,' she teased with a wink. 'This is exactly the sort of meal I would make for myself. Thank you.'

'Good!' I replied, consciously trying not to wolf my food down to satisfy my growling stomach and wishing I'd brought more bread to the table. While we ate in silence, I could see that Estelle's line of vision kept returning to my left hand, making me aware that I had inadvertently failed to keep the tip of my left ring finger concealed as I usually do by keeping my hand closed.

'I know, I know…', I said, holding my hand up and spreading my fingers and waving my hand from side to side. 'Slightly short of a full house. Not quite the full kit-kat. High four-point-five!' I joked, fully revealing and displaying my reduced ring finger, extending it to its smooth rounded stub at the second knuckle with no tip or nail. Even after all this time, the missing tip still took me by surprise some mornings.

Estelle frowned and stuck her bottom lip out in exaggerated sympathy and asked how it happened. I never like talking about it but have learnt to accept others' curiosity so have a standard abbreviated script for such occasions. I'd been working late, was tired, hungry and had rushed into preparing dinner as soon as I'd got home. After managing to slice and dice onions, garlic and ginger for my stir fry, and having swept them to one side of the chopping board to bring out a couple of peppers from the fridge, I'd been careless in chopping them. In my carelessness and haste, and with the tip of the blade fixed on the chopping board to allow me to deploy a rocking downward chop and tug to the side to slice the peppers, I had somehow managed to position my hand in such way as to leave my third finger in the line of fire of the approaching guillotine.

'I'm sorry, it's not very nice to talk about while we're eating,' I concluded, but she was more interested than squeamish and encouraged me to tell her more about what happened while she placed another forkful of salad into her mouth.

'Well, the fragility of a human finger does not fare well against a razor-sharp knife in the hands of a hungry cook,' I continued. 'Silly as it sounds, it's much easier to chop off a finger than you might think. To be honest, the movement – the accident - happened so fast that most of the pain was caused by the wrench of the tip being pulled away from its final attachment to the rest of the hand, rather than the initial slice through skin and flesh. From what I remember, even the bone didn't feel much tougher than dissecting a thigh off a roast chicken.'

'My God, Luke, that's awful,' she said, continuing to chew. 'The pain must have been intense. Was it?'

Her eyes showed intent interest, so I continued. 'Well, surprisingly, the pain wasn't as bad as you might think. The cut was so clean and firm it went through in almost one go. There was more blood than pain at first. That said, once I'd dialled 999 and sat down to wait for them to arrive it did start to throb like hell and I felt like I was going to fall asleep as shock set in. But once I'd been taken to hospital, they did a great job of cleaning up what was left and it hasn't given me any trouble ever since,' I held out my hand for her to inspect the stump's thin and silky scar tissue. I omitted to mention the fact I was not alone at the time. No point opening up another unwanted strand of conversation.

'You poor thing. That must be really difficult to adapt to.'

'Not really,' I answered honestly. 'I could never fully touch type before, so I don't think I'm missing much. It's more of an issue when people stare, and I have to explain my clumsiness.'

'You must have an unusual chopping technique to have managed to cut though that particular finger without damaging any of your other fingers,' she said, making her statement sound more like a question.

'What can I say? I was careless and learnt the hard way.' Estelle continued staring at me as I returned my attention to my plate.

'Well, you must take better care of yourself in future,' she eventually said with an air of finality.

'I will,' I promised. 'I have good reason to now.' I smiled, relieved to have concluded this particular conversation and took the opportunity to ask Estelle what growing up in France was like.

She did not disappoint and opened up immediately, treating me to vivid descriptions of what sounded like a fairy-tale upbringing. She spoke with enthusiasm, passion and a romanticism for the French countryside and a way of life that I could only imagine but was in love with already. As she spoke, her eyes grew bigger and livelier and had a childlike excitement to them. I listened attentively as she spoke of the stone farmhouse she was brought up in with freedom to roam the whole village. Of the way she could step out of the back of the house into a garden that rolled endlessly down acres of hillside with an array of fruit trees to distract her on the way down – apples, cherries, plums, peaches, apricots. How all the scented plants and flowers were kept close to the house – mint, thyme, lavender, rosemary, jasmine. And how the trail of fruit trees led to an open meadow full of wildflowers. Her face lit up as she told me how she used to spend days on end exploring different corners of her picturesque surroundings, wandering through wildflowers, lying in the sun and making dens to hide in. She laughed as she told me how she loved to climb a large crooked walnut tree at the bottom of the garden where she could sit on a branch and watch everything and everyone within distance without being seen. She giggled naughtily as she told me how she would deliberately panic her father into thinking she'd gone missing while silently watching him pace around the garden calling for her.

I listened with amusement as she went on to tell me of the get-togethers that used to take place with other villagers. How they used to gather around a bonfire at the edge of the village for seasonal celebrations, singing and dancing to the sound of violins and clapping. She sipped on the Muscadet in between sentences to keep her mouth moist. Her speech got quicker the more excited she became. She told me how they'd sit around long tables, brought by neighbouring villagers, pushed together and laden with contributions of freshly picked or caught food. Homemade breads, stews, soups, varieties of soft and hard cheeses, punnets of tomatoes, nuts, grapes and freshly picked salads. She told me how she would sometimes take lettuce leaves from the table and sneak away to the edge of the gatherings to tempt wild rabbits out of hiding to join in. It all sounded idyllic. It all sounded like a complete contrast to life in my small Bethnal Green flat.

However, although I was enjoying the descriptive journey through Estelle's village, the earlier storytelling of my stunted finger kept fighting its way to the forefront of my mind. I was struggling to stay in the moment. Behind the mask of my smile and attentive nods I could feel the pressure of the past once again creeping up on me, dragging me away from present reality. The past should stay put, the present was more perfect than I could wish for, and the future held more hope and promise than ever, I kept telling myself. Perhaps it was the combination of the wine and lack of sleep, but my mind was slipping into a downward spiral, and I could feel myself losing control.

Chapter 10

*Click. A rush of jumbled up pixelated thoughts and memories finally settled into vignette focus as I saw my younger self, back in the kitchen chopping vegetables. **She** was there, just as she was all those years ago, taunting me, belittling me. We were engaged to be married although even to this day I'm not sure why **she** ever suggested it. Status? Boredom? A wish to show others the power and control she had over me? I'll never know now, but it surely wasn't love or attraction on her part. What was for sure was how hurt I was when **she** told, no screamed at, me in no uncertain terms how **she** wished I could be more of a man; someone like Salter who was her boss at the time. I kept my head down and held my breath and tears inside while **she** ranted at me, for lack of status, ambition and success within the company we both worked for.*

*I kept up my rhythmic chopping of the dinner's vegetables while **she** continued her tirade, me wondering why **she** stayed with me if **he** was the sort of man she really wanted. 'Look at you – you even chop vegetables in an OCD way,' **she'd** said laughing and pointing at my neat rows of evenly chopped up garlic and onions. 'Can you imagine John chopping vegetables like that?' **she** taunted.*

For a change, I snapped back. 'Why don't you go and find out then?'

*I can remember **her** stepping towards me so that she was a couple of inches away from my face and slowly saying 'I have, and I can tell you that his talents go much further than making dinner…'.*

*Why **she** ever felt the need to tell me that if not for the sole reason of causing me pain, I will never know. How anyone can get a kick from causing others misery remains a mystery to me. That's probably why I've chosen to spend more than the past decade alone.*

She snorted as *she* caught sight of a tear escaping my eye, spraying my face with her saliva. I can remember wiping my face down with kitchen towel before turning back to the chopping board to continue preparing dinner in silence. But *she* couldn't just leave it 'See? Spineless! Even now you can't display any passion. Go back to chopping your vegetables.'

The lump in my throat was choking me, my heart was thumping, and blood was racing round my brain faster than I could cope with. Even with the benefit of hindsight, I don't know what made me do it, but it seemed a sensible and rational reaction to the situation at the time. Keeping my hands steady, I fanned my fingers out on the chopping board and slowly lifted the knife above the top knuckle of my ring finger, tucking my forefinger and second finger into my palm and out of the way. I paused for a moment to turn and look her straight in the eye, repeated the word "spineless" back to her, and rocked the knife down in one hard, decisive movement. The force almost detached the tip in one clean effort. Almost. It took a second weighty press and twist to completely remove it from my hand.

There was no pain. At least initially. I can clearly remember my initial emotion being one of elation and enjoyment at being in absolute control of the situation. Accompanied by some satisfaction at seeing *her* screaming and retching over the sink with her arms flapping about. Physically, I could feel only numbness in my hand and up my arm as I stared at the bloody mess seeping out onto the chopping board. I remember thinking that I would have to start chopping some fresh vegetables from scratch. And then the most intense pain and feeling of sickness kicked in as I went into shock and my recollection from that point onwards becomes hazy.

She didn't challenge my version of events at the hospital, nor say anything to the emergency paramedic at the flat, when I explained how the accident had happened. Nor did *she wait around for me while I spent the following hours with my hand anaesthetised waiting for a qualified surgeon to clip back the remaining exposed bone from my finger and stitch the surrounding folds of skin from each side together. That was a night I won't forget.*

'I am sorry, am I boring you?' Estelle's hand on mine brought me back to the present.

'No, no, not at all,' I replied quickly. 'Sorry, I was miles away enjoying how different and perfect your village life sounds.'

I sat forward and took a deep breath, mentally blowing away past ghosts on the exhale.

Estelle continued to talk of rolling hillsides, fields of wildflowers, stone houses, shuttered windows, farmers markets, local foods, and lazy afternoons sleeping in the sun. However, despite the detailed descriptions, I soon began to notice that none of her stories or descriptions were accompanied with any mention of any significant friends or family. Nor were there any clues as to how such an upbringing and background could lead to her becoming the COO of Effective Solutions.

Despite my curiosity, I was in no mind to disrupt her flow and, besides, no one wants that awkward conversation about their past too early on in a relationship - if at all. Earlier in the conversation, she had paused to ask me briefly about my past love or loves, but I had skilfully evaded the question and so it would seem wholly unfair of me to quiz her on that point.

As we finished our food and the view through the front bay window of the sun's shadows across the park got longer, we moved across to the sofa with our glasses to settle into each other's arms. Low-level light streamed in across the room. I lay across the sofa, and she cuddled up beside me with her head resting on my chest, making it impossible for me to raise my glass to my mouth.

Her hair was still damp from the shower and soaking through my t-shirt. My back was starting to hurt from the twisted position I'd adopted to accommodate Estelle, but I didn't want to adjust my position for fear of spoiling the moment. So I remained still and uncomfortable. The move to the sofa had fast-forwarded her tales of growing up in France to the need for her to make a completely fresh start away from home.

She described joining a local English group to brush up and perfect her secondary education English before going on to complete her online MA in Business Administration and work towards her long-held ambition to escape the monotony of the French countryside and come to London. She spoke with clear pride of her achievement in landing her new role so quickly, and her excitement at taking the firm to higher levels of efficiency and profit. She spoke with hope and optimism for what she described as a fresh start.

I found her journey to date from small village to big city incredible, and felt an element of pride, not only for her but also for myself and the fact that here she was, opening up her inner thoughts, curled up beside me in my flat. It was one of those moments I wished I could freeze forever, where I didn't think I could be happier.

As she continued to open up about at having attained independence for the first time in her life in the city she loves and having severed any obvious connections to her past life, her tone became softer and slower until eventually her head relaxed and went limp on my chest.

The expression on her face was one of peace and contentment. The warmth of her relaxed body against mine was pure heaven.

My mind, however, was far from being ready to sleep. Although I had learned more about Estelle in the past couple of hours than I had hoped for, I was struggling to reconcile the different facets of her character as one whole person. Everyone has different sides to their character, but there was something unique and unusual about the fact that the woman sleeping peacefully on my chest was the same senior leader who had threatened my security in the workplace, the same seductive dominatrix who had stripped me of any remaining inhibitions, and the same chatty woman who had described her childhood to me. The same reckless arsonist in the restaurant yesterday? And what did she mean by a fresh start? From what? Her life in France sounded ideal.

The fire at the restaurant had been periodically nagging at the back of my mind and there were moments when I had thought of asking her again whether it was more than a coincidence that it started while she had disappeared from the restaurant floor. Yet at the same time, I knew such a question would have changed the mood again, so I had kept my focus on enjoying the moment instead. Besides, no one wants their past mistakes dragged back into the present.

I swept a strand of hair that had fallen across her face behind her ear and pecked her lightly on the forehead. She was now fast asleep and showing no trace of the hard-nosed businesswoman I'd seen at work. For some reason, at that precise moment, it dawned on me that we hadn't even paid for our meal. Not that detail like that would be at the forefront of the manager's mind. Probably best, anyway - no card payment could be traced back to either of us.

Curious, intriguing, intelligent and mysterious were the words rattling round my head to describe her. On one hand, incredibly open and chatty and yet at the same time a complete enigma. I was frustrated that although it had appeared that she was sharing all with me earlier, her story only seemed to have a beginning and end to the present day. There was no middle to it, nor any accompanying characters. She had spoken a lot without really telling me very much. A technique I was familiar with.

I was in no doubt that there was a whole lot more to her that she hadn't yet revealed. What I had seen so far was akin to a puzzle whose picture had yet to fully emerge, but one which I had to stick with to find out. Granted, I was not in control and had no idea where we were heading, but I felt alive and was looking forward to the future for the first time in ages.

A feeling of total contentment swelled up inside me until I felt I was floating above the pair of us, looking down onto our interlocked bodies on the sofa and admiring what was arguably the greatest feeling in the world – when two people find their ultimate match.

Chapter 11

As the lift doors pinged open, the digital clock in the corridor switched from 07:56 to 07:57. I hadn't heard from Estelle since she snuck out while I was sleeping on Saturday night and had spent all day yesterday hoping she'd return or at least call. I'd sent a couple of messages to her work mobile – the only number I had for her - and none of them appeared to have gone through.

'Morning Luke,' Lesley beamed from behind reception. 'What's up? Couldn't you sleep?' I forgave her sarcasm for the fresh cafetière coffee she poured me.

'New week, new start,' I replied, straightening up and tightening my tie. 'I'm moving into Peter's team today so thought I'd make the effort.'

'You're looking good,' she said, peering over her desk to take in the detail of my three-piece suit and freshly polished shoes. 'It's taken you long enough.' After barely sleeping last night, wondering what sort of reception I was going to receive from Estelle today, her words gave me the boost I needed. 'Are you sure that's the only reason for the makeover?' she probed with a cheeky smile.

'I don't know what you mean, but thanks for the compliment' I replied innocently, picking up my coffee cup. She dipped her head and looked up at me with a single raised eyebrow in that way that can only mean *'Really?'*.

As I made my way to my desk, I could see Estelle securely positioned in her glass-fronted office, mouthing into her phone. She looked totally at home. Comfortable in her environment, at ease and confident. I slowed as I passed to give her ample opportunity to catch sight of me and acknowledge my presence, but she was engrossed in her call.

I headed to my desk, switched on my laptop and stared into Estelle's office through the gap between my screens for some, any, form of acknowledgment. None came. She was clearly busy and keen to maintain the air of professionalism she'd created as she remained focussed on the various calls and meetings she had arranged while I was left to watch from afar.

As the rest of the office filled up, I logged straight on to the C.R.A.P. system to see what the gossip of the day was. I'd set the system up to display a conference room environment with each of the firm's 24 employees represented by an avatar with their name displayed below while the text of their messages appeared in speech bubbles above them. It was an ingenious design, though I say so myself. I wouldn't like to count how many hours I'd spent reading the never-ending stream of mindless gossip pinging back and forth within the firm. Some days left me wondering how anyone managed to do any actual work on top of their online chat.

Today's chat was more interesting than usual and contained an almost live stream of people reporting the content of their conversations with Estelle as she carried out short and private get-to-know-you chats with everyone. Nothing revelatory was being said and the gist of discussions seemed to be focussed on what skills people had, what they thought worked well in the firm, and what improvements they thought could be made. No hint of a hidden agenda but that wasn't stopping Salter or Mitch from whipping people up into a state of fear with speculation that Estelle was mapping everyone's skillsets to help inform the next reorganisation or clear out of staff. Of course, their solution to this perceived threat was to instruct everyone to keep them informed of everything being said so that they *'could look after everyone's best interests and protect them'*. The old *'create the fear, present the solution'* strategy. They really were so lame. Two-faced as well, because while they were whipping everyone up into a state of fear and mistrust, they were also creating confusion by tacitly showing support for Estelle by saying things like *'she's got some interesting ideas'*, *'we need to think about whether that fits with Estelle's vision'*, *'I'll need to run that past Estelle in my next 1-2-1 with her'*. Thus, leaving everyone totally confused as to who they should be trying to please, but totally dependent on Salter and Mitch for validation. Passive bullying, if you like.

Peter on the other hand was as straight as they come, as were Carl, Brian and Natalie in his team. They were the unrecognised and undervalued backbone of the firm and provided all the governance, finance and audit functions needed to satisfy the firm's legal requirements and keep it in favour with its Board and investors. Despite their solid reputation for being quietly efficient, reliable and straightforward they lacked the charisma, aggressive attention-seeking and risk-taking personas of the sales and marketing teams and were therefore often dismissed as being geeky and boring.

Peter had been in the firm for just over 10 years. He'd started as an apprentice and worked his way up slowly, taking his accountancy exams along the way. He was quiet, shy and very private, both in person and in his online communications which never seemed to stray from the utmost professional, and certainly never into divulging any personal information. But everyone accepted him as a nice guy. Always polite and respectful; never devious or duplicitous. Even when others were staying late and going for after-work drinks or food, he would be the one who would leave first to return home to his family.

Come to think of it, being pushed into his team to report to him rather than Mitch's or Salter's was a blessing (or, at best, the least worst option) that I hadn't appreciated up until now. The gossip on the C.R.A.P. had fast become monotonous and boring, so I decided to switch from observer to proactive team member by messaging Peter to suggest an introductory meeting. To my surprise, he messaged me straight back to say he'd been thinking the same, and before I could respond, he was standing in front of my screens suggesting we pop out to the Costa across the road for a coffee to *'escape the toxic atmosphere in the office for a while'*. I hadn't been particularly looking forward to talking to Peter. Or joining his team. Or having to do the whole corporate objective setting and discussion about development that was being forced upon me by Estelle. But, as much as I hate to admit it, my conversation with Peter left me feeling a lot more positive about myself and the workplace than I had for a very long time.

He'd insisted on paying for my coffee, which is always appreciated. He'd then diffused my social awkwardness by leading the conversation and explaining exactly what Estelle had asked of him – namely to absorb my contract management functions within his team and to more formally incorporate my activities and milestones into the firm's overall work programme.

He talked about arrangements for managing me, which wasn't nearly as awkward as it could have been. In fact, he'd been extremely complimentary and told me he thought I'd been under-valued and under-utilised for years now – *'ever since that business between John Salter and **her**'*, he'd said. He went on to say how brave I was to conduct myself throughout that whole episode with such dignity when being treated so appallingly by others and that he respected me for that. If only he knew the full story. For a moment, I was taken back in time to a memory of **her** sitting within his team, tossing her head back and twisting her hair into curls with her fingers while Salter was sitting on the edge of her desk, the pair of them leaning into each other to whisper and snigger at my expense. Still, although I don't like reliving the past, it was nice to know that someone else had recognised what I had been put through at that time.

I agreed to attend his team meetings (on Tuesdays and Thursdays), a regular 1-2-1 over coffee with him every

Monday morning, and I promised to consider some training courses and qualifications to work towards. It was all the sort of stuff I'd normally be dismissive of, but somehow Peter's warmth had made agreeing a natural outcome. It felt like a chance to break away from the ever-decreasing circles of my past and an opportunity to create a totally new routine and persona for myself.

All in all, a good morning's work!

Whether Estelle's day was going as well I had yet to find out and was fighting the urge to send her any more messages via the Communicator system. I'd sent her three messages already since 16:30 – *'what time are you finishing?'*, *'I'm going to head off shortly if you'd like to join me?'* and *'see you later?'*, all of which I could see had been read, but none of which had tempted a response.

It was gone 18:00 now and I could see she was locked in a fast-paced discussion with Salter and Mitch about something and I was only drawing attention to myself by staying so late.

I said goodnight to Peter, hit send on one final message to Estelle - *'going home x'* – and left the office with a heart full of hope.

Chapter 12

Fuck! The sound of a cockerel crowing at 01:17 is enough to jolt anyone from their sleep, if not give them a full-blown bloody heart attack. Stubbing my little toe on the corner of the bed as I rushed to the front door, I cursed myself for ever having bought that stupid novelty doorbell. Sitting on the steps outside was Estelle, smoking a cigarette, wearing an overcoat too heavy for March, and wedged between a large old-fashioned leather suitcase and a smaller, more modern, plastic one.

'My god, I'm so tired. What took you so long?' she said, exhaling a stream of smoke into the night air. 'Can you take my bags in please? I'm afraid they're rather heavy.'

'Of course. Sorry, I was sleeping...I wasn't sure if you were coming back tonight or not.'

'Neither was I,' she said, lifting herself up from the steps and walking past me into the flat. 'But here I am.' She paused to sigh. 'It will save me time and effort if I stay here rather than travel back and forth between the office and my temporary accommodation. I cancelled my booking. That's not a problem, I assume?'

'Of course not,' I said, still not fully awake. She left me to heave her cases indoors corner by corner without betraying how heavy I found them. 'I wasn't sure if you were coming or not. I did message you a couple of times...' My voice trailed off as I realised she'd disappeared towards the back of the flat. 'Estelle?' I called.

'In here,' she called from the kitchen. I could hear the distinct plip-plop sound of wine being poured from a bottle. 'Pinot Grigio, huh?' she called out rhetorically, followed by another sigh. 'It will have to do, I suppose.'

I squinted into the bright light of the kitchen. She looked surprisingly fresh considering how late (or early) it was and how much more intense her day had been than mine. I smiled weakly and, still in a sleepy haze, made a clumsy attempt to welcome her with a kiss on her cheek. A misjudgement on my part, clearly, as she held out one arm towards my chest to stop me getting close to her while raising her glass to her lips with the other to take another sip.

'Some ground rules, mon chéri …' she started, continuing to sip her wine and circling me slowly. 'Private life is called private life for a reason. It is totally separate from work life and the two should not be mixed.' Her circling me like a sergeant inspecting his parade was making me dizzy. 'While I am at work, do not forget that I am your Chief Operating Officer, and that you are an employee on trial…' The reminder was unnecessary as was the need for me to say anything in response. 'What happens between us outside of work stays between us only and is not to enter the workplace.' She stopped pacing. 'Do you understand?' She remained frozen until I nodded. 'That means no staring into my office like a sad puppy, and no messaging me expecting us to hold hands on the way home together. Yes?' I nodded compliantly again.

'However, mon chéri,..' she continued. I was curious where this performance was leading and wondering whether her use of the term "mon chéri" was genuine or not. Had I really been upgraded to being her "chéri"? I hoped so. It was more than a little arousing to be spoken to in this way, but part of me was struggling with whether it was real.

'When we are together in private…' she continued, circling me again and trailing her finger across my chest as she moved. '…I do hope you will continue to show me the level of attention I'm starting to appreciate?' The corners of her mouth curled upwards.

'Of course,' I replied, turning to rest my hand on her neck and kiss her.

'Ah, ah, ahh!' she scolded, grabbing my wrist with one hand and placing a finger on my lips with the other. 'Not yet, Luke. You are too fast and presumptuous. You need to slow down.'

Reading her signals was hard! 'Sorry, I thought…'

'Sometimes you think too much, Luke. Besides, you look sleepy and it's late.' I couldn't help but return a look of chastised disappointment in response to her playful glint. 'Poor Luke,' she continued. 'I tell you what. Why don't you take a few minutes to freshen up and brush your teeth and I'll see you in the bedroom?' Her eyes seemed to soften, and her tone was soothing. To be honest, she could have asked me to do anything and I'd have complied.

I must have been lying alone in bed in the dark, fighting the urge to sleep, for almost an hour before the sounds of Estelle pottering around in the kitchen and bathroom finally stopped and the bedroom door opened. As a thin sliver of hallway light shone in my direction, I sat up and pulled a corner of the duvet over to allow her to climb into bed more easily. She remained with her back against the door, hands behind her and legs crossed underneath her thigh-length cotton dressing gown. She shook her head slowly, her predatory eyes still fixed on me while biting her protruding bottom lip slightly.

'You're going to have to come and get me if you want me,' she breathed slowly.

I got up and walked towards her. In keeping with the mood she'd created, I leant in and kissed her gently on the cheek. She 'mmm'd' and closed her eyes in response. I moved closer so our bodies touched lightly while trailing small kisses down her neck towards her chest. She turned her head upwards and closed her eyes. I put my hands on her waist and slipped them towards her back and rested my head on her breasts.

Until she grabbed my wrists harshly and pushed my hands and myself a body-width away from her. 'Luke, you seem tired tonight,' she said in an accusing tone. 'Perhaps we should sleep after all…'

'No,' I replied stepping forward into her warmth to resume the mood. Again, she pushed me back. Not for the first time, I was having trouble reading her mood and getting frustrated by the hot and cold signals.

'No, Luke,' she spoke slowly. 'I think you must have misunderstood when I reminded you who is boss at work.' Her dark brown eyes seemed almost black. 'Sometimes, just sometimes, I would like you to be the boss, and now is one of those times.' The corner of her mouth turned upwards into a playful half smile that I couldn't help replying to with a seductive grin. Well, I like to think it was seductive, although I wouldn't be at all surprised if it looked sheepish from where she was standing.

Again, I stepped towards her with more confidence and put my hands back on her waist firmly. And again, she grabbed my wrists and pushed me back.

'I'm still not sure you want me enough yet,' she scolded with a challenging stare.

There was no doubt I did. Both visually and from my quickened heartbeat and a fire burning in my lower stomach. There was no way I could simply go straight to bed and sleep now.

I flicked my hands around hers, freeing myself from her grip and grasping hers instead. She gave a surprised but approving look. My confidence boosted, I fixed my gaze on her, so my hands were out of vision and, as quick as I could, let go of her wrists, grabbed the cord to her dressing gown and tugged it as hard as I could. She gasped, as her gown fell open, exposing definite proof that she was completely naked underneath, but made no attempt to stop me.

Without saying a word, nor breaking eye contact, I removed the cord from her dressing gown and wrapped both of her wrists in a figure of eight knot. Not too tight, but firmly enough to ensure she couldn't easily wrestle free. She bit the corner of her lower lip while maintaining a half-smile of approval. I then took the other end of the cord and threw it over the top of the ajar door. Stepping closer to Estelle, and without resistance this time, I reached behind the door and pulled the cord down bit by bit until it lifted her wrists above head height. I kissed her cheek and neck. Again, no resistance. I looked into her eyes and nodded slowly…questioning. She nodded back…approvingly.

With that, I pulled the cord down sharply wound the end around the door handle, and slammed the door shut so the cord was trapped at the top of the frame, her hands unable to chastise again. The room was dark but contained enough light for me to see what I was doing. I took a step back, looked Estelle confidently face-on, took hold of her dressing gown and flung it wide open, causing her to gasp again and close her eyes. If taking charge was what she wanted, that is what she was going to get. I felt a switch of hunger flick inside me as I stepped towards her, hands on her waist, knee between hers, and started kissing her from her shoulder down until I found myself kneeling before her.

The feeling of total control was exhilarating, even though in my heart of hearts, I think we both knew who was really in charge of the situation. It was going to be a long night.

Chapter 13

The morning passed in a complete blur. I'd heard Estelle's alarm go off at 06:00 followed by the sound of her getting washed, dressed and calling 'à bientôt' before the door slammed shut. I was sore and exhausted and stayed curled up in bed for as long as I could manage to recuperate. I'd eventually managed to get myself out of bed and kick start my system with a ritual coffee and cigarette before heading to work in a daze.

'Morning Lesley, morning Peter…Brian…Carl…Natalie.' It felt weird exchanging salutations with others after so many years of hiding away in my own corner. It wasn't as bad as I thought, and I must confess to letting a genuine smile creep across my face when they reciprocated the greeting.

I didn't need to log onto the C.R.A.P. to hear the morning's gossip as I could watch it unfold in 3D before me, more vividly than any App could provide. Estelle was in the general office area, sitting on the edge of the bank of desks in John's team, chatting away to Elaine, Sandra and Vicky about their favourite films and the best nearby places for lunch. It all looked very relaxed aside from Salter scowling silently in the background.

Peter's bank of desks had a different air about it. They too were chatting idly with each other, but their eyes remained focussed on their screens while they simultaneously kept bashing away at their keyboards. Efficiently civilised.

Mitch, despite having the largest team, covering both advertising and sales, was the least chatty. Sophie and Judith, his loyal executives, were craning their necks towards Estelle, eager to be brought into her conversation. Like Salter, Mitch eyed them with silent suspicion.

Yes, things were changing. For me, my run of 12 years in virtual self-isolation was coming to an end and I found myself looking forward to coming out of hibernation for a new season.

Estelle flitted from desk to desk, taking the time to chat effortlessly with everyone. leaving them with a smile on their face before moving on. It was quite the contrast to the impression she'd created the previous week when she'd spent almost all her time holed up in her office in private 1-2-1s and appearing completely aloof to the outside office. This week felt as if the whole organisation was breathing a sigh of relief.

That was until Gordon Freeman bounded in, booming a big 'good morning, everyone' with his trademark false smile, gold-buttoned blazer and shiny bald head. Salter and Mitch snapped out of their sulky solitudes and were up on their feet, returning false smiles like a pair of eager-to-please puppies.

'Shall we?' said Gordon to Estelle who, judging from her unfazed demeanour, had been expecting him. 'You may as well bring the Directors along with you,' he suggested unnecessarily, as they were already tailgating their way into Estelle's office behind her, leaving me once again relegated to having to watch the goings-on from outside.

They sat in the comfy seating area and faced Gordon, who appeared to be doing most of the talking, nodding along intently as he spoke. The outside office maintained its cheery high. I still ached from the night before and hoped the day would give me enough downtime to recover. No such chance - Peter stuck his head out from around Estele's office, beckoning me to join him. My immediate thought was that I was about to face redundancy again.

'Come and join us,' he whispered as I approached him. 'We're talking about a new project, and I thought it might be helpful to involve you at the outset.' He pointed towards an upright chair outside the inner circle of comfy armchairs.

'Luke's going to link up the project management side of things with accounts, so I thought it'd be useful to include him in this,' he explained. Gordon grunted. Estelle gave a welcoming smile. The others ignored my presence.

'As I was saying,' Gordon continued. 'You're all doing a fantastic job, and I've got no complaints. But I'm under severe pressure from the Board to explain why the firm's profits aren't higher than they are. Or, more to the point, why their dividends aren't paying out as much as they'd like.' Over Peter's shoulder, I could see him taking studious bullet point notes on the A4 pad he carried everywhere. Mitch and John exchanged shifty glances before returning their gaze to the floor with concerned expressions.

'We've had some clear successes over the past year,' Gordon continued as if delivering well-rehearsed lines. 'Some new big-ticket clients at home, more domestic implementation programmes than we can handle, and the number of overseas referrals has more than doubled. All great achievements, and that's recognised. But the bottom line is they want to see more bangs for their bucks and higher returns. They're starting to ask a lot of questions along the lines of whether we're running ourselves as efficiently as we should be.' Gordon's tone suggested he was seeking ideas, rather than reveal a predetermined plan.

Estelle ventured first. 'Could it be that we're frontloading our investment in winning new clients abroad too much? From the short time I've been here, I have noticed that our spend on travel and entertainment is considerable while the return has been minimal or slow at best.' The suggestion was met with such firm rebuttals from Mitch, Salter and then Gordon himself that curtailing their travel budget wasn't a path they wanted to venture down.

'No, no, no…impossible,' he bumbled. 'It's precisely because of our face-to-face interaction, customer focus and hospitality that we're able to land so much business and success in the first place. It's how we've always run things and is part of the firm's success. I've already made the point to the Board that our strength is in our people and their ability to be able to work with clients face-to-face to see projects through from start to finish. These things can't just happen through video meetings you know. That's not an option. We're not going back to that.'

He was wrong of course; thousands of pounds were spent every week on flights, hotels, meals, visits, etc with clients who simply wanted to get down to business quicker, but there was no way he was about to change his jet-set lifestyle (or that of his all-male Directors' club) for the sake of the Board's dividends. Mitch and John visibly breathed a sigh of relief. Peter wrote *'Expenses and benefits?'* down as a fresh bullet point.

'But what about the number of...?' Estelle didn't get to finish her sentence as Gordon cut back in, palm raised to indicate he hadn't yet finished.

'Estelle and I have already discussed this, and she's had some great ideas. What we've agreed for now is to carry out a set of efficiency and effectiveness reviews across our international network over the summer to demonstrate we're operating at optimal levels already with no missed opportunities or slack. No cut-and-paste jobs, here mind. These will need to be done properly to give them the reassurance they need, and us the licence to operate in the way that we want.'

Estelle's expression suggested that Gordon's suggestion wasn't entirely familiar to her although she chose not to object to it. 'We can do that,' she said compliantly. 'Mitch. John. Peter. What are your thoughts?'

The three men took turns to look at each other while raising and lowering their eyebrows in the same way a mechanic does when thinking up a price for repairs.

'Why not? We've got nothing to hide.' Salter's agreement was unconvincing.

'Yeah, same. If we can be left to get on with our jobs, I don't see why not,' added Mitch, with all the enthusiasm of a bored teenager.

Peter, by contrast, wild-eyed with excitement, held up the page he'd been manically scribbling on to display tiny flowcharts and bullet points with arrows pointing in all directions that no one could make out the detail of. He spoke at a hundred miles an hour about efficiency and effectiveness reviews, governance, progress reporting, milestones, timelines and all sorts. It all made sense, but I'm not sure that anyone other than me and Estelle were really listening to him.

While Estelle and Peter continued bouncing ideas off each other enthusiastically (Estelle now on her feet, mapping out a project timeline onto a whiteboard), Salter and Mitch fidgeted, making no effort to hide their lack of interest. I too was fidgeting in my seat, but out of discomfort rather than boredom. I remained the silent observer while admiring Estelle's innocent passion for wanting to get things done. Her passion for the task was infectious and I was aware that I'd have to help and protect her from the undoubted resistance she'd be up against from so-called colleagues within the firm, both at home and overseas.

Gordon sat back in his seat, hands folded across his bulging shirt, clearly satisfied with what he saw as his brilliant suggestion having lit the fuse that sent the firework of ideas rocketing in all directions. Of course, he was happy; he'd constructed the perfect win-win scenario for himself. Increased company profit if the review produced results, and a convenient fall guy (or female equivalent?) if it didn't.

Estelle paused from the excitement of mapping out a timeline to read the room and realised it was time to dismiss the passengers.

'Ok,' she said, commanding attention. 'With Gordon's clear direction and the buy-in of all of you, I think we have the start of a plan that's going to lead to future-proofing the firm's profits for the next decade.' Gordon leaned forward, lapping up the reference to his direction. Salter and Mitch, without needing to utter a word, couldn't have looked more condescending if they tried.

'Peter will lead the work under the umbrella of a programme of work that will conduct a series of audits with each HQ and overseas team. Luke will ensure the process is managed within a project management framework. Together they'll form the Review Team. We'll devise a timetable of interviews and aim to complete the review by early September, before the next Board meeting…'. Her enthusiasm was unstoppable.

'Er, I manage the overseas offices so I can handle that side of things,' Salter piped up predictably.

'No, I shall personally conduct those interviews.' There was no doubt from her tone that this was non-negotiable. 'We need to demonstrate to the Board that these reviews are conducted objectively, not by someone marking their own homework.' I almost snorted at Salter's chastisement. 'You'll be kept informed of the findings of course and any changes that need to be made.' Estelle was firm and matter of fact.

'But the overseas offices aren't even legally part of Effective Solutions,' Slater continued. 'They're separate entities, exclusively contracted to provide consultancy services, so they're not subject to the same controls as the rest of us. I can't see them giving up their time to take part in this.' He spoke with the air of an eight-year-old pleading *'but why?'*.

Estelle remained cool. 'I would say that the fact that their sole source of income comes from our referrals is precisely why they would want to cooperate with us.'

Gordon was beaming at the sight of his management team at odds with each other. The old divide and conquer strategy suited him.

'But their contracts only require…' John continued to bleat.

'If they don't want to cooperate,' I interjected, 'I'm sure we could amend their contracts to require it. I'm pretty sure I've seen a clause that requires them to act *"in the spirit of mutual trust and cooperation"*.' I'd done my homework. 'I would immediately suggest that they provide us with an open set of accounts every quarter, rather than the current end-of-year spreadsheets which are impossible to verify and read.' I offered, causing heads to turn in my direction. Both Salter's and Mitch's faces were red, but they said nothing to challenge me.

'I can't imagine that will be necessary, but that's a good point to bear in mind,' replied Estelle with what looked like a small smile of approval. 'Anyway,' she continued, 'if we're going to work towards a September deadline, I'll need you, Peter, to work with Luke to prepare a short Project Initiation Document by the end of the week, so we've got something in writing to work towards?' Peter was nodding and scribbling into his pad vigorously.

'What about objectives?' I asked.

'What do you mean, Luke?'

'I mean personal objectives. Should we make sure that everyone incorporates a commitment into their own objectives to make this review a success?'

'Excellent suggestion - I like it!' said Gordon, lifting himself up from his seat and clapping his hands together to signal we were done. 'I'm going to leave this in your capable hands, Estelle,' he said, putting his hands on her shoulders and, I think, attempting to peck her on the top of her head. Wholly inappropriate! Estelle sprung up and sidestepped his reach.

'Leave it with me, Gordon. I will let you have sight of the Project Plans by the end of the week.'

'Excellent, excellent! I'll give the Board an informal heads-up that their concerns are being addressed. We'll need a name for this project, of course. Any suggestions? Something transformative. Something to catch their imagination.'

This guessing game captured everyone's attention, and a few names were called out and quickly dismissed. Something positive, nothing too clever, something easily relatable, was Gordon's only steer. And with that, Gordon leapt on Salter's immediate suggestion to name it 'Project Butterfly', ignoring Estelle's view that it was too fragile and not strong enough to represent what we were trying to achieve. However, Gordon's short attention span did not allow him time to consider the pros and cons of it, so he excused himself and left the room repeating it to himself on the way out.

And with that, Estelle, as the project's Senior Responsible Officer, was unofficially nicknamed Madame Butterfly. Following that train of thought, I liked to think that that made Gordon a fat, hungry caterpillar. Putting the office name-calling aside, I gave myself the objective of making sure that Estelle's Project Butterfly didn't turn into Project Titanic.

Chapter 14

Back at my desk, I reflected on how, ordinarily, that conversation with the Directors would have sent me to the height of boredom with all their corporate jargon. But things were different now. Estelle was passionate about her job and had something to prove. The thought of her being undermined or set up to fail gave me a level of passion and motivation to match hers. I was desperate to protect her against the sort of underhanded shenanigans I knew Salter and Mitch were capable of.

Peter was the only other person in the firm who I considered to be safe and loyal. I questioned everyone else's motives. Neither Salter nor Mitch had any real desire for change. Their efforts were purely focussed on self-validation, protecting their fragile egos, and getting rid of Estelle so they could return to their cosy little routine of international travel, backhanders and sucking up to Gordon's ineffectual buffoonery.

My unwritten objective was simply to make sure that Estelle didn't fail. Not only did I need to support and ensure her success, but if I could bring down Mitch and get revenge on Salter in the process, that would be a bonus. It would not be easy though. Reading their online communications for over a decade might have provided plenty of suspicion, but it had failed to provide any conclusive evidence of wrongdoing. They were slick operators and skilled at providing a steady trickle of successes and good news stories for themselves to stay on the right side of the Board. But the profits generated for their small successes were disproportionately small compared to the noise they made about them.

Even with my inside technical know-how, I'd been unable to figure out or challenge the financial statements they submitted for each client. Breakdowns of costs and receipts were never transparent and email exchanges between them and clients would often go silent after the *'let's pick this up on WhatsApp later'* line was played. I had a good idea what was going on, and their obvious increasing wealth and lifestyles far exceeded their salaries, but I hadn't yet figured out a way of being able to infiltrate or prove precisely what they were up to.

Nor was I sure whether Gordon was really behind Estelle with the project. Sure, he'd highlighted the need for action and made supportive noises, but I wasn't convinced he actually wanted her to succeed. My sense was that he probably just wanted to keep the Board happy so he could maintain his lifestyle of travelling round the world until he decided to retire. I was also in no doubt that he had appointed Estelle purely to have an attractive subservient to hand.

The more I thought about it, the more my admiration for Estelle's drive and dedication grew, and the stronger my dislike – no, hatred - of Salter and Mitch became. And if Gordon had appointed her in the hope that she was going to be his obedient puppet, he'd made a big mistake. I knew from first-hand experience she was not cut out to be anyone's subservient. Not really.

Chapter 15

'So, let us keep this quick. I am sure you're all keen to get home.' Two weeks into the project and Estelle had been convening 08:30 and 17:00 checkpoint meetings with Directors and me, as project scribe. 'No more than two minutes each to check off actions and next steps. Mitch?'

'Continuing to analyse advertising spend through different channels over the past three years' campaigns with a view to recommending where future spend should be focussed. Sophie and Judith are working on it, and we should have some ideas to share by the end of the month,' I zoned out halfway through his update but nodded along.

'Luke?' Estelle snapped me back into life.

'Two weeks, Mitch,' I said, checking the actions log. 'We agreed you'd share initial recommendations by next Friday.'

'Yep. Can do,' he clipped, knowing full well that that was his deadline.

'Good. Let's try and stay on track guys. We don't have time for slippage if we're going to deliver this project in twelve weeks.'

Personally, I had no doubt the project would be delivered on time. The past couple of weeks had been a whirl of activity with the whole end-to-end review process being mapped out, individuals tasked with small research projects, past project implementation reviews, interview appointments booked, questionnaires designed, and these compulsory twice-daily meetings put in place to make sure that any delays to delivery were nipped in the bud before they became problems.

I was exhausted. Not only was I having to work most evenings, but I was also keeping an eye on online office gossip and feeding Estelle tips on which individuals needed help or reassurance. As a result, the tide was turning in her favour, and it wasn't uncommon to read messages being exchanged praising her ability to understand the company and its people. I'd noted that Vicky from Salter's team had even started to emulate Estelle's favoured style of two-piece business attire and had had her hair cut into a similar style. I know that must have grated with Salter. Good!

'John, how are you progressing?' Estelle was keen to keep the meeting moving.

'All on track. Seven of the twelve country and overseas office background briefs are complete and the rest will be done by the end of the week.' He paused to wink at me, before adding, 'Ahead of target.' Smarmy git. 'I've also developed a series of review questions for each overseas Director and made some notes for how they could report their financial highlights as well.'

It annoyed me how his head rocked from side to side with self-satisfied smugness as he spoke. The way he leant into Estelle while he spoke, maintaining direct eye contact with her and invading her personal space also wound me up. I couldn't help but wonder if his approach wasn't a deliberate but futile attempt on his part to seduce her. However, I did realise that may be a case of over-sensitivity on my part

*Click. The memory of **her** perched on the edge of a younger Salter's desk, throwing her head back while laughing, crossing and uncrossing her legs without any thought for modesty, touching his arm unnecessarily as he spoke, appeared in the back of the room, like misty black and white holograms. **She** kept glancing over at me and smiling – no, sneering, while Salter continued to entertain her with stories of his endeavours abroad, his head rocking annoyingly from side to side as he spoke and his hand emphasising points by resting it on her thigh. Although I could not be sure, the angle at which she was perched probably gave John a clear line of vision to her underwear.*

*Salter too would glance in my direction occasionally, but with a smug look of triumph at my expense, causing my innards and eyes to burn with suppressed rage. The pain and humiliation of the situation being played out for all to see. And she was supposed to be **my** girlfriend!*

The misty figures evaporated before me, snapping me back to the present with my cheeks burning red. 'Luke?' said Estelle abruptly; I got the impression she had maybe had to repeat herself.

'Yes?'

'Come on. The questionnaire. Keep up.'

I'd let myself be caught off-guard. It was not just the long working days that were getting to me but the late-night chats with Estelle and being woken in the middle of the night with one need or another. Her drive, both mental and physical, was manic, and although I was trying to give her everything she needed, it was hard to keep up with her.

'Yep. Thanks John,' I said in a deliberately dismissive tone. 'I've already devised the overseas office questionnaires. Send your suggestions through and I'll take a look at them.'

'It might be easier if you just send through what you've managed, and I'll finish them off,' he replied.

'No need. They're good to go already and we're deliberately not sharing them with the overseas Directors in advance of their reviews.' I ran my hand through my newly trimmed hair and looked over his shoulder.

'But *I* manage their contracts and performance,' he asserted, sitting forward and clearly not happy. 'Fair enough not sharing them with the overseas Directors before their reviews, but *I'm* the Change Implementation Director and it's not right that I don't get to clear them or check if they're asking the right sort of questions.' His mouth tightened and his teeth clenched as he spoke.

The truth of the situation was that neither I, nor Estelle (on my advice) trusted him not to water down the questions or leak them to overseas directors in advance of us meeting them, and doing so ran the risk of turning the whole review into a back-slapping exercise of self-validation. I looked at my watch, returned his hard stare with a soft gaze and replied, 'Well, that might be so, but we already agreed to keep the review questions deliberately independent and objective.' I paused and held his stare long enough to make him uncomfortable before adding, 'You'll just have to trust the process.' I do love a good cliché.

In the corner of my eye, I could see Estelle suppressing a smile. Salter was continuing to protest, but I wasn't listening to him.

'OK, let's leave that there for now,' Estelle interrupted. 'We will stick with keeping the questionnaires entirely independent and you can always add your thoughts when the results are written up. Let's move on. Peter? Luke?' John was left red-faced and seething.

'Well, Luke's done most of the work and I don't want to steal his thunder, so I'll hand straight over to him,' said Peter, always the gentleman. In truth, Peter was being modest as it was he who'd been guiding me through everything and imparting knowledge that I was happy to soak up. I was enjoying working with him. His whole team, in fact. They'd all been extremely welcoming and friendly towards me since I joined them.

I sat up and provided a thorough yet concise run-through of progress. All the supporting project management documents had been drawn up, commented on, and signed off. A forward plan, the questionnaire and a template for the final report had been drawn up, and key milestones entered into calendars. Hotels and flights for visiting the overseas offices had been booked, and briefing packs for each visit were in preparation, complete with local travel directions to make things as easy as possible for Estelle. It was still early days, but delivery of a final review report to the Board was on track for mid-September. Overall project rating was green.

Salter and Mitch shuffled in their seats as I spoke, but I didn't care. Estelle was nodding along approvingly to my update; Peter was smiling quietly with what looked like pride and I felt good. I was achieving. As I was talking, I had a weird sensation of stepping out of my body for a few seconds and watching myself speak. I looked and sounded good. The new suit, the slightly shorter hair being held firm with wax and the crisp new shirt, the two top buttons left undone, made me look as professional as I was sounding. I'd come a long way in the short time Estelle had entered my life.

'Thank you, Luke. It's good to see you've settled into Peter's team so well and are on top of everything.' My grin betrayed the pride I was trying to contain. Salter and Mitch were already heading for the door, keen to show they had something better to do or somewhere better to be. I thought I heard Salter mumble *'Madame fucking Butterfly'* on the way past but couldn't be sure.

'Forward look at 08:30 tomorrow,' she called as they disappeared out of earshot.

'Before you both leave,' she addressed to Peter and me. 'I wanted to let you know that I really appreciate just how much effort you're putting into this project. I know not everyone is as enthusiastic about it as us, but you are both doing a great job, and I couldn't do it without you. Thank you.'

Peter smiled politely and, incapable of accepting any individual praise, felt duty-bound to add, 'No problem. It's a team effort. Anyway, I'd better head home to the family now. See you in the morning'. And off he scurried, keen not to miss his usual 18:14 train.

I was following Peter out the door when I heard Estelle behind me.

'Luke. Can you stay behind for a few more minutes please?'

Chapter 16

'That seemed to go well,' I said, hoping to maintain the positivity I thought the meeting had left. Her face was emotionless while she reassumed her position of power behind her desk.

'Yes,' she chirped, causing me to breathe a sigh of relief. Whether we were at home or work, I still found it hard to read Estelle's moods. There was always an element of unpredictability with her that always kept me on my toes and, when she was happy and excitable, made me feel a real sense of achievement. 'I just wanted to give you some quick feedback,' she continued, the raising of her left eyebrow suggested she might be in play mode.

'Firstly, I have to say you look *good* today.' My smile was instant. Like a pupil from the back of the class who'd just been called up to receive a gold star. 'Your new look is working for me.' I looked round to check the door was closed for fear of us being overheard.

'Why, thank you,' I replied gratefully.

'You should stick with that look. It suits you.'

'I will,' I replied, my recent efforts in sprucing myself up feeling validated. It was not usual for Estelle to deliver compliments in my direction, not least in with workplace.

'Take your jacket off. Let me see your shirt better.' I put my jacket on the back of a chair, put my hands in my pockets and moved side to side, adopting my best impression of a catalogue man.

'Very nice,' she smiled. 'It is good to see you're taking your second chance here seriously. Really good, Luke. Her praise made me glow from within. 'And you are working well with Peter's team too, it seems?'

'Yeah, I'm actually enjoying it. He's a good guy and his team have really welcomed me into their fold.'

'That's great. I'm pleased it seems to all be working out so well. But what about John?' she asked, lowering both brows to resume a more serious demeanour.

'Salter?' I said, more aggressively than intended. 'I don't really have much to do with him other than by email.'

'I picked something up between you just now. You really don't like him at all, do you?'

'No, I don't like him at all, but you know why. He's a self-serving, smarmy git who'll try to undermine you at every opportunity. Plus, I'm sure he's on the take at the firm's expense and that's what's draining profits. I just can't prove it yet. I'm watching your back that's all.' All true.

'Hmm.' She raised her left eyebrow. 'I got the impression there might have been more to it than that.' Her statement felt more like a question that I left hanging. 'A little rivalry, perhaps?' My warm glow turned to a chill. Had someone been talking?

'No. What makes you think that?' Again, I was sloppy with my tone and sounded more defensive than intended.

'It's OK, Luke,' she said, walking around her desk towards me. 'Someone did mention to me that you and John were once love rivals, that's all.' She rested her hands on my shoulders as if she was talking to a child. 'I just wanted to check that your behaviour towards John isn't being driven by anything that happened between you in the past?' She slid her hands down my arms to my wrists and held them gently by my side with a look that provided more reassurance than accusation. 'Maybe I'm watching your back too?'

I felt sick. I didn't like the fact that *she* was being alluded to in our conversation. Past and present *had* to be kept separate at all costs. My eyes burnt from dryness, causing me to blink rapidly. I held my third finger tightly within my fist to stay calm and present. 'It was a long time ago,' I said, steadying my voice. 'It's all forgotten about now,' I lied.

Estelle let go of my wrists and stroked my cleanshaven cheek. I turned to look out into the general office, fearful that someone might be able to see us. Her strict rule of keeping our work and private lives separate was screaming in my head. But it was the playful, not the strict, Estelle standing before me. The outside office was mostly dark, with only the far corner where Brian and Natalie were sitting, quietly working, still lit up.

'Shhh. Don't stress,' she said, turning the knob attached to the double-glazed surround that shut the integrated blinds, ensuring our total privacy from the outside world. Aside from the fact anyone could walk in through the door. The thought of someone walking in on us panicked and thrilled me in equal measure.

'Well, I just wanted to let you know that you should have nothing to worry about.' She smiled, her left eyebrow dancing playfully on her forehead. 'You are much more handsome than him.' She stroked my shoulders. 'You are also much smarter than he is.' She started to unbutton my shirt, that now familiar playful glint in her eye having returned.

'Estelle, no. Work and home separation remember?'

'Shhh, mon chéri. Who is the boss here?' She was giggling and I knew there was no way of changing her course of action. 'Mmm, you smell good too,' she added, taking in the scent of my newly purchased Dior Sauvage. The tension I had felt minutes ago over mention of *her* had evaporated, replaced with the warmth of lust flowing through my veins.

My attempt to kiss her was met with a scolding finger on my lips.

'Not yet, Luke. Remember where we are...' she tutted hypocritically whilst pulling my shirt open and running her hand slowly down my sinewy chest. 'Mmm, and have I told how sexy you look today?' she giggled as she started fumbling with my belt.

'You haven't,' I replied, worried that anyone could stick their head round the door to say goodnight at any moment and catch us. She positioned herself in front of me so that I was backed up against her desk, looking round nervously, my breath fast and shallow.

'Don't stress, Luke. The shutters are down, remember?' she said as she managed – finally - to undo my belt. The light in her office was low, the situation high-risk, but she was impossible to resist.

The glimmer in her eyes turned to a slow-burn smoulder, while she lowered and slowed her voice and whispered, 'I just want you to know that you have absolutely nothing to worry about with me, OK? No one here comes close to matching what you give me.' I don't think she'd ever said anything so reassuring to me before.

I leant forward in another attempt to kiss her, unashamed at how aroused and exposed she'd left me. My lips met her cheek as she stiffened and stepped back to look me up and down. The contrast between her pristine business presence and my dishevelled state of arousal immediately apparent.

'I'm sorry, mon chéri. You are right.' Her voice had switched back to work mode. 'We should keep work and home separate. I just wanted to let you know that I think you're great.' The speed by which she'd transformed from determined seductress to practical-minded professional left me feeling both disappointed and relieved. As well as confused and dizzy.

I tucked my shirt in and did the buttons up in silence. Estelle watched me with what looked like a sense of pride; in me, herself, or us, I couldn't be sure. As soon as I'd finished straightening my shirt, Estelle opened the inner blinds to bring the outer office into view. Brian and Natalie were in the same positions as before, working away and oblivious to anything that had just gone on between me and Estelle.

'Shall we head home then?' I suggested flatly as the aftershocks of adrenaline drained from my system.

Estelle sat behind her desk. 'I'm sorry Luke. I still have some work to finish. I won't be too long though. Why don't you head home and start dinner, and I will join you as soon as I can?'

'OK. Try not to be too late though. You've barely stopped the past couple of weeks.' I tried to conceal the fact my adrenaline was turning into disappointment.

'I won't, I promise,' she smiled. I picked up my jacket to leave. 'Oh, one more thing,' she called as I got to the door.

'Yes?'

'Keep the suit on. It's not just dinner that I'm looking forward to when I get home.' Her left eyebrow was raised as high as it could be, and the light was dancing in her eyes again.

I headed home, suppressing a smile as I passed Brian and Natalie on the way out.

Chapter 17

To prevent any of the overseas offices being tipped off in advance of her visit to them, and much to Salter's and Mitch's frustration, Estelle had been keeping the precise timetable for her visits under tight wraps to *'reduce the risk of anyone inadvertently letting on when to expect her'*. She wanted to see them in action without any pre-polished preparation or fuss. I had no doubt that Salter would have already given them all the heads-up that a visit could be expected at some point over the next couple of months, but at least a mild element of surprise remained.

Peter diligently followed all of Estelle's wishes to the letter and kept all information relating to the review saved securely on a central drive with restricted access to his team, me, and Estelle. Any hard copy documentation was always locked away, infuriating the other Directors who considered Peter's loyalty to Estelle to be foolish and too rigid. Salter had consistently been trying to undermine Peter by messaging Carl, Brian and Natalie, all separately, to tempt them to spill the beans. I felt proud of them when I saw them all respond separately with similar messages of rejection. Peter may be perceived by many as the least charismatic of Directors in the firm, but there was no questioning his team's loyalty.

It amused me that Salter hadn't even bothered trying to get any information out of me. He knew better than to try. But I enjoyed the fact that he was starting to view me as a barrier – competition even – to what he wanted. I, of course, was on the constant lookout for any goings-on in the firm that might derail the success of the visits or throw up any evidence of wrongdoing on Salter's part.

To date, Estelle had completed audits of the offices in New York, Denmark and German offices on her own, spending two days in each. Peter and I had been busy compiling the resulting reports, analysing the answers to the performance questionnaires, and preparing draft recommendations for improved profit. The Denmark office had already been left with revised end-year targets that aimed to increase their profits to HQ by 300%. Failure to achieve the target would leave them with the very real threat of the termination clause in their contract being invoked. Although that conversation was confidential, news of the threat had spread to the other international offices who were now dreading Estelle's visit.

However, much to my frustration, nothing had yet been uncovered to suggest any financial wrongdoing between their arrangements with HQ. Nor had the extra hours I was spending monitoring Salter's online conversations managed to throw up anything incriminating. But it seemed clear, even at this early stage of the review, that we'd be able to report back to the Board with a strong and positive plan to increase future profits.

To add to my frustration, Estelle had eventually been forced into involving the other Directors in the overseas office audits. Salter had gone running to Gordon to complain about his lack of direct involvement *"and that Madame Butterfly was fluttering about without a clue what she was doing"*. For all his posturing as the office alpha male, he really was nothing more than a slimy insecure shit.

Gordon had caved and '*strongly encouraged*' that Estelle reconsider her veto on the other Directors accompanying her on future trips *"to make sure they can provide her with a proper understanding of how the offices function"* (words I recognised as coming straight from Salter) and to demonstrate a bit more HQ unity and collaboration. And so, to appease Gordon, their presence was being built into future visits. Mitch was due to accompany Estelle to Amsterdam and Salter to Rome. The thought of Estelle being subjected to their lecherous company for two days apiece sickened me. Not only did I not like the thought of them trying their creepy charm on her (although I knew she was more than capable of handling herself in that respect), but I had also been quietly hoping that I might be able to join Estelle on the Rome visit and that we could experience a Roman Holiday vibe together.

To stoke my unease further, only a day earlier, I'd been following a particularly coarse exchange between Salter and Mitch in which Salter, after describing in some detail *"what would really loosen Madame Butterfly up…"* went on to challenge Mitch to a £5 bet to see which one of them could sleep with her when their overseas visits came round. The £5 stake had offended me as much as their fantastical schoolboy descriptions of what they'd like to do to her. In fact, their exchange had rattled me so much I'd taken the rare action to bring their conversation to a premature close by taking control of both of their systems remotely and shutting them down.

I'd feigned total innocence when they turned up in front of my desk with their laptops minutes later asking me to fix the gremlins in their systems. Without looking up, I'd told them to leave their laptops with me and I'd see what I could do.

The only good to come out of Gordon's diktat to involve Directors in some visits was the fact that when Peter had declined joining Estelle on the combined Brussels and Paris trips due to *'some stuff going on at home'*. He had, however, suggested that perhaps I be given the opportunity.

Estelle, in responding to Peter's suggestion, had put on a great performance of looking disappointed and pressed him a bit too hard on whether he thought I was ready for it. Especially as I was sitting on the bank of the desks along from Peter at the time she was talking to him about it. Eventually, and with a deliberate sigh in her voice, she turned to me and asked if I could accompany her on the trip. I tried my best to respond as indifferently as I could muster but I have no doubt that, to everyone else who could hear the exchange, I responded too quickly, sounded too goofy, and probably looked like one of those cartoon characters whose eyes pop out their heads when Jessica Rabbit walks into the room.

Sure, it was predominantly a work trip, but I'd be away with Estelle for almost a week! An opportunity to find some neutral territory to focus on each other and explore where we were heading together. I couldn't help myself, but I was already visualising drinks in Brussels' Grand Place, an evening river boat trip on the Seine, the Eiffel Tower lit up in the background, or. if we had time, an arm-in-arm stroll around the cobbled streets of Montmartre. Somewhere in the distance I could hear Estelle and Peter continuing to talk about the review's milestones, but I wasn't listening to a word they were saying.

My mind was already in Paris with Estelle on my arm.

Chapter 18

As Estelle's Amsterdam trip with Mitch approached, the knot in my stomach had been steadily tightening to the point it felt like a solid ball of corrosive acid sitting just below my ribcage. My appetite was non-existent, my sleep light, and I was weakening by the day. My determination to make sure that Project Butterfly – and Estelle – was a success, were the only things keeping me going. Logically, I knew there was no real reason to worry. The project was completely on track (RAG-rated 'green' in terms of delivery, thanks to our combined efforts), and its developing draft report was safely under wraps with a sufficient number of recommendations already to be able to demonstrate to the Board that improved performance, and thereby profits, were just around the corner. It was success waiting to happen.

Estelle and I had settled into a comfortable routine of absolute professionalism by day, and unbridled passion by night. The awkward moments between us had lessened and, dare I say it, we had found a routine.

She was no more looking forward to being away from home (we both called it home now) and in close company with Mitch over the next couple of days away than I was. I'd noted that she'd picked up my habit of wincing with a look of distaste whenever Mitch or Salter's names were mentioned in conversation. She knew they were taking every opportunity to undermine her and she no longer needed me to constantly remind her of that. In fact, it was she who was reminding me that, as a woman, she had spent a lifetime of having to navigate her way around predatory men who wanted to undermine and topple her. Or fuck her. In the same breath, she was also keen to remind me that she wasn't going to start relying on another man to 'protect' her from that reality. I took her point, but that wasn't going to stop me supporting her behind the scenes.

Estelle was more than capable of taking care of herself, I knew that. But emotionally, my feelings of distrust towards both Mitch and Salter ran deep and meant I couldn't help but feel threatened by the situation. My fears were completely unfounded, of course, but there was still a part of me that felt they might somehow use their tried and tested combination of charm and manipulation to fuck everything up for me again. Especially Salter. His swagger in the office had morphed into a prowl of late that was completely nauseating.

Insecurity, paranoia and jealousy are ugly traits in a partner, so I'd been trying hard to keep a lid on my neurosis in front of Estelle. It'd been nearly two months since Estelle walked into my life, moved into my apartment, and turned my world upside down. In the best way, I mean. We'd reached that cosy stage of a relationship where it was perfectly acceptable to spend the evening at home, windows open to let the warm summer air breeze through the rooms, slouching about in underwear and oversize t-shirts, unable to keep our hands off each other until we fell asleep spooning. It was the perfect relationship routine: wake, sex, breakfast, shower, sex, work, dinner, music, sex, chat, fall asleep and repeat. Despite the ease and comfort with which our relationship was developing, the doomsayer voice within me kept reminding me that each time we spent the night together could be the last. On the plus side, this negativity did at least come with the benefit of treating every night together as if it could be our last.

It was no surprise that Estelle had last night picked up on my general unease at her impending departure and suggested we get up at 5am to share a morning coffee and cigarette before her taxi to Stansted airport arrived. We'd sat on the garden bench together blowing streams of smoke into the fresh morning air, me smiling sheepishly at her, while she did her best to remind me that she'd be back the following night and that I probably wouldn't have time to think of her anyway. I hadn't even woken up properly by the time she stubbed her cigarette out, kissed me on my cheek and headed back through the flat towards the taxi waiting out at the front.

Our last exchange of words rolled round and round my mind, as if stuck in a time loop.

'I know it's only one night, but I'm going to miss you.'

'Don't be silly, Luke. It's only one night and I will be back as usual tomorrow night.'

'Promise?'

'I promise.'

'I love you.'

'I'll see you tomorrow. Bye.'

I stayed on the garden bench for another cigarette and, for the first time in a long time, felt awfully lonely.

Chapter 19

I was enjoying being the first to set off the automatic lighting control system as I walked along the Effective Solutions' eighth floor corridor, overlooking the atrium below at the ridiculous hour of 07:08. Returning to an empty bed without Estelle had seemed too sad, so I'd determined to make the best of the day by taking a long hot shower, having a clean wet shave, waxing my hair back and putting on my navy three-piece suit. I was still physically weak and tired but also wired from the morning's nicotine and caffeine intake on an empty stomach.

I made the most of being in the office alone by walking up and down the vacant workstations where the CHImps and Sales teams usually sat. Territories I usually avoided in preference to hiding behind my screens in the corner. Weirdly, it felt good and, in a mischievous way, I found myself looking forward to the day ahead.

Lesley, true to character, was the first to arrive, waving as soon as she saw me in the distance from the lifts, smiling broadly as she threw her coat off at her reception area, flattening non-existent creases down the sides of her skirt as she slinked towards my desk. I made a conscious effort not to smile too broadly or make direct eye contact as she approached.

'Well, good morning, handsome,' she said, tilting her head to the side. 'Someone's been making a bit of an effort lately!'

'Just trying to keep my job and blend into the corporate background a bit better,' I replied coolly. I'd known Lesley long enough not to have to pretend any different.

'Well, I always knew you had it in you, so I for one am pleased to see you're starting to show it. You deserve it.' Lesley had a habit of saying things that made me feel good about myself. 'Have to say, as well, I've noticed you seem happier too.' She smiled and squished her nose up, the same way a rabbit does. 'It's nice to see after so long.'

'Thank you,' I replied, returning her smile. 'I appreciate you noticing. It feels good to be back.'

'Good!' she declared definitively. 'Coffee?' she offered.

'Ooh, I'd love one please.'

Lesley squeezed my arm with a wink before wiggling off to the kitchenette area, glancing back a couple of times in the short distance it took to get there. 'Gotta look after the firm's rising talent!' she called back playfully.

Peter and the rest of the accounting team started trickling in from 08:30. Customary team salutations and banter followed - *'What's up Luke? Couldn't sleep?'*, *'Looking sharp today; hot date, or court appearance?'*, *'the boss is out today; no need to dress to impress!'* Cheap laughs at my expense out the way, they were quick to revert to their robot-like lives and lose themselves in accounts, invoices, and spreadsheets.

Mitch and Salter's team, by contrast, dribbled in much later than usual with an air of *'while the cat's away'* about them. I made a point of greeting everyone as they filed past my desk on their way to their work area - Sophie, Judith and Jaqueline from Mitch's team. Elaine, Sandra and Vicky from Salter's. Salter swaggered past a couple of times, annoyingly invading my space by trailing his hand along the edge of my desk. I made a deliberate point of ignoring him, although I could feel his eyes were on me. I kept him in the corner of my eye as he sat on the edge of Peter's desk and attempted to strike up a conversation. Peter was having none of it and replied to every exchange with monotone, one-word closed answers.

'Annoying, isn't he?' I commented, once Salter had given up and moved on.

'He's alright. Just a bit much for me today. I've got a lot on.' Peter's voice was flat and he kept his eyes on his screen.

'Anything I can help with?' I offered.

'Nope. Need to keep my head down and power through, that's all.' A clear unspoken instruction for me to leave him alone. Peter was the best manager I'd ever had. In fact, he was the only person who'd ever really managed me in the sense of being supportive and helping me develop some useful skills. But I knew when to steer clear if he was having one of his withdrawn days. Which today clearly was.

11:21. I checked my phone. Nothing from Estelle, although I knew she should have arrived at the Amsterdam office by now. She wasn't big on texting, although I did think it would be nice if she sent me the occasional nugget of reassurance.

Concentrating on completing any actual work was impossible. Whether or not it was down to the lack of food or sleep over the past few days I couldn't tell. My mind was buzzing, and yet I couldn't hold a single thought for longer than a couple of minutes. Meanwhile, Peter and the rest of the team drones were glued to their screens with only the sound of clicking keyboards for company.

My attention wandered around the office. Peter's team aside, there was a holiday feel in the air. It was a measure of Estelle's newly established authority within the firm that you could feel the change in atmosphere when she wasn't around for even a day or two. It made me feel proud of her - if that's not too patronising a way of describing the emotion.

Salter's team was making no pretence to work. Chairs spun round away from their screens to face each other, they were openly dissecting the events of the previous night's Love Island and the upcoming challenges set for the Great British Bake Off. Sophie was noting frappuccino and muffin orders on a post-it note for the next Starbucks run. Salter was reclining at his workstation, chipping into others' conversations with what he thought was witty innuendo, his whole demeanour worthy of admiration from David Brent himself. As I glanced round, I caught Lesley's eye in the distance from reception, giving me a not-so-subtle smile of encouragement.

Only a couple of months ago, I viewed these very same people as being the engine of the firm, the ones who were getting things done while I hid in my corner, observing the world from a distance behind my computer screens. Today, up against the passion, fire and dedication that Estelle brought to the firm, aside from Lesley, and Peter's team, who were consistent workers, all I saw were lazy, overpaid, narcissistic leeches. Harsh and hypocritical? Most definitely, especially given I was doing absolutely fuck all other than people watch and read their conversations, but at least my integrity was intact, and my loyalty to help Estelle deliver Project Butterfly was pure.

The more I watched and listened to them, the more predictable they became. They morphed into larger-than-life caricatures of themselves before my eyes as they continued to exchange anecdotes, opinions, news, gossip, each of them taking turns to glance round at each other for signs of approval, satisfaction, fear, flirting, confusion. All screaming 'like me' at one another through their body language and eyes. I had to blink and shake my head from side to side to remind myself that these human-sized puppets were living beings, rather than NPCs in some virtual reality world.

Tiredness was kicking in. I stood up and stretched my arms above my head to snap myself out of my daydreamlike state and get another coffee. I caught my reflection in the empty glass cage that was Estelle's office and had to take a double take. Wavy hair waxed back, sharp suit, stubble-free jawline, and the knowledge that Estelle was coming back to me tomorrow evening. I was looking good! Life was good! I wasn't being narcissistic; I'd earned this.

I thought back to my years of hibernation as an unshaven IT Contract Manager, living life through the window of my screen, often wearing the same t-shirt all week. I despised my old self. I could see why the rest of the firm had left me to my own devices and why I'd been put on the redundancy list. But, with thanks to Estelle, I'd found my way out of the fog and back into the real world. Not only had she saved me at work, but she'd also given my life purpose again. I was strong again. And yet, still vulnerable to know that I was missing her presence in the office already.

I stretched again and, in my peripheral vision, could see Salter sat upright at his desk, disengaged from his team, staring straight at me. No attempt to disguise it. He had the look of a concerned bystander on the brink of intervening in a situation. Salter was not an NPC, of course. He was most definitely a player to keep an eye on for unpredictable combat.

It was not just Salter who had eyes on me though. I'd noticed that while the conversations amongst his team were continuing, they had slowed down in pace and quietened to inaudible levels, while they took turns to steal glances in my direction. Could it be that I was becoming the subject of some office gossip? That would be a first in a long time.

*Click. The present slipped away to twelve years previous. I was standing in almost the same spot in the office watching past scenes play out before me. A similar group of attractive young female consultants had wheeled their chairs to form a small circle, heads huddled together, whispering and giggling. Taking turns to glance and point in my direction. Occasionally dropping their jaws in animated displays of shock, shrieks of laughter ringing out, as - no doubt - further details of tittle-tattle were released. A younger Lesley at reception looking on with concern. I was frozen to the spot as it dawned on me that **she** was at the centre of the huddle. That **she** was the one leading the cabaret of gossip entertaining everyone. That **she** was talking about **me**. That **she** was no doubt betraying any last shreds of confidentiality that remained of what was left of* *our relationship. The high spirits and laughter I could hear were **her** doing at **my** expense.*

*And then those words rang out that would haunt me forever: "I mean, seriously…look at **him** and look at **me**. If that geek had any common sense, **he'd** have known it was never going to last. **He** was lucky I stuck around for as long as I did! What is it they say about not settling for a hamburger when you can have steak?". The cruel cackles that followed rattled round my head like gravel in a tin bucket.*

*The reality of the situation translated itself into a lump in my throat, a dry mouth and burning eyes. I looked beyond the huddle and who could I see? Smirking, smug Salter, clearly relishing the drama **he'd** caused and the victory **he'd** achieved at **my** expense. Frustration and anger were boiling inside me, but the pain in my heart had rendered me powerless.*

Click. But that was then.

The memories swirled into the background recess from which they'd emerged. I took a deep breath, composed myself and checked my older and wiser reflection; a visual reminder that today's reality was very different. The only similarity was the fact that Salter, now bald, and wider around the waist, was still staring at me from across the office in that self-satisfied way of his. But I had no lump in my throat or wobbling lip. I matched his gaze and stood firm until he turned away. This was now.

I knew my presence rattled him. And I knew how much he hated anyone interfering with his team which he very much viewed as an extension of his own importance. So I decided to swagger towards them, relishing the uptight look on Salter's face as I approached.

'Morning, all,' I said cheerily as the group shushed themselves into silence. 'How's everyone doing today?' They instinctively rolled backwards on their chairs towards their respective desks, like a group of schoolchildren who'd been caught doing something they shouldn't.

'All good here, Luke. How about you?' replied Vicky quickly, shamelessly looking me up and down. Vicky was one of the newest arrivals in the firm and had only been here for just under a year. She was probably one of the brightest amongst the team, and also one of the most confident. 'You're looking very sharp today,' she added with a playful giggle, while working chewing gum round her mouth. I could see Salter in my peripheral vision, frowning.

'Thank you,' I replied stiffly. 'You're looking very professional yourself today too,' I lied, noting her blank screen behind her. 'Busy day?' I asked, ignoring the fact that an irked Salter was now grimacing in my direction, itching to intervene.

'Yeah, always plenty to do. You know how it is. We was just chatting, that's all.' Elaine and Sophie suppressed giggles while Vicky just about managed to keep a straight face. Salter's face was turning pink. 'Anyway, better get on, I suppose,' she said with a sigh as she spun her chair round to enter her login details.

'Good, good,' I said. 'Me too, I guess,' and headed towards the kitchenette, not bothering to turn around to see what the sound of giggling and gossip that had started up again behind me was about.

As I reached up to the cupboard above the sink to pull a mug out, I was aware of someone approaching me quickly from behind. The speed and weight of the footsteps meant it was no surprise when Salter appeared by my side, positioning himself against the kitchenette worksurface to face the office. His lips were tight, his brow furrowed and his jawline pulsating.

'What the fuck do you think you're doing?' he spat through gritted teeth. I opened the cupboard again to search for a teaspoon. Found one.

'I'm serious. Who the fuck do you think you are, coming over and meddling with my team?' His head was jutting towards my direction, but he was careful to keep his volume low enough for only me to hear.

I reached down to the cupboard to the right of the sink and pulled out a small tin of Millicano coffee.

'I don't know what game you think you're playing,' he continued, 'but keep your distance from my team and stay out my way.'

I filled the teaspoon with coffee granules and tapped the spoon against the side of the tin three times to level the measure. I didn't want it too strong. In my sideview of Salter, I could see that he was twitching with rage. Ignoring him was having the desired effect.

'Don't fucking ignore me, Luke, do you hear?'

I held my cup under the hot water dispenser and moved my cup around in small circles as the water poured to better dissolve the coffee granules.

'Oi,' he continued through his twisted face. 'You're wasting your time if you think this new you is going to get you somewhere with Madame fucking Butterfly. She's a fucking Ice Maiden and way out of your league, so I don't know why you're wasting your time trying to suck up to her in your fancy suits.'

Oh, how wrong Salter was and how I was enjoying seeing him getting so wound up. I felt the sides of my mouth curl into a smile.

'Mind you,' he continued, 'you could always join our £5 sweepstake if you fancy your chances with her, although you've never had much luck in that field.' Typical Salter – crude, competitive and quick to take a cheap shot at me to assert his dominance.

My smile turned into a frown at the thought of Salter running a bet on who could sleep with Estelle first. He was such a creep.

'Excuse me,' I said, gesturing for him to move away from the fridge. He made a point of pausing for a second before stepping out of my way.

'I don't even know why you're still here anyway,' he continued. I poured a dash of milk into my coffee and returned the carton to the fridge. 'You should have left years ago.' I stirred my coffee three times anticlockwise and then three times clockwise to make sure the milk was evenly distributed. 'It's fucking creepy how you're still hanging about here like some kind of fucking Jeffrey Dahmer weirdo.' I rinsed the teaspoon and placed it to the side of the sink. 'You should have left when **Sarah** left.' Another cheap shot.

Mention of *her* name brought us both to a standstill. I don't think anyone in the office had spoken her name out loud since she'd left. I turned slowly to face Salter, squeezing the tip of my shortened ring finger between my thumb and middle finger to keep myself calm. If eyes really are the window to our soul, Salter would have seen an inferno blazing through mine.

'You should have left when **Sarah** did,' he repeated cautiously, his eyes darting around the office, looking for somewhere to avoid my gaze.

'Why?' I asked coldly, stepping towards him. I imagined the satisfaction of smashing my fist upwards and diagonally into the side of his skull, straight into the corner where his nose meets his left eye.

'You know why, Luke. There's nothing left for you here,' he stood to face me squarely, brogue to brogue. 'After everything that's happened, it's just weird for you to even want to stay around. You need to move on.'

'And yet, here I am,' I replied coolly, imagining I was some character out of Goodfellas or something.

Salter tipped his head from side to side while he studied my face for cracks of willpower.

I lifted my cup to my lips slowly and took a steady sip of hot coffee, my little finger and shortened ring finger outstretched on display. 'Does it look as if you bother me?' I asked without a quiver. 'You're just an attention-seeking bully who's not used to being stood up to.'

My words were left hanging until Salter mumbled *'Fucking weirdo'* before turning away. 'Just don't mess with me or my team, Luke,' he added once he was a couple of steps away, returning to his seat. 'That's all I'm saying.'

I stayed at the kitchen point for a couple more minutes, sipping my coffee and surveying the office, enjoying having won the 'battle'. I was unashamedly basking in the sense of achievement from not reacted to hearing **her** name after so long, but also for having finally adjusted the balance of power between me and Salter.

How I had managed to resist confronting him for so many years, I could barely remember.

Chapter 20

When I arrived home from work, the click of my key in the front door was louder than usual and the atmosphere inside colder than the walk home through the park. The only downside to having Estelle in my life was the reminder of just how cold and empty it was when she wasn't around. I checked my phone. Still no message. I imagined she would have finished her meetings by now and be out dining or having drinks with the Amsterdam team. Schmoozing, I think they call it. Salter's £5 sweepstake came to mind, and I cursed him for being so…him.

While changing into some comfy jogging bottoms, I looked at my suit hanging up and reflected on what a good day's performance I'd put in. The sight of my new suit hanging up made me feel as if I was an actor who had just finished another show. It was all roleplay, but being able to confront Salter face-to-face and show him that I wasn't prepared to take his shit any more had been the highlight of the day. Making my way to the kitchen, I decided that I deserved to crack open one of the bottles of Sancerre Estelle and I had bought in as a reward to myself.

'Santé, ma chérie,' I said, raising my glass to the bowl of leftover pasta rotating in the microwave. I imagined that, somewhere far away in a bar in Amsterdam, Estelle could hear me and was breaking away from her conversation to look away and raise her glass back in my direction. The Amsterdam office visit was not expected to throw up any surprises, so I imagined she could have finished the day early and would be relaxing now. I sent her a quick WhatsApp to say I hoped she was enjoying the evening, and that I looked forward to seeing her tomorrow. I thought about adding an emoji heart to the end of the message but opted for a more mature 'x' instead. I continued to stare at my phone after hitting send, hoping for an immediate response that never arrived, until the microwave pinged, prompting me to take my glass, dinner, and the bottle through to the living room and settle down.

I had the TV on for company in the background while I ate, but all I saw was moving shapes and sounds, without really taking in what was happening. I was sitting at the table for two by the window, which had become our regular home dining spot (Estelle was adamant she wasn't going to get into the habit of eating off her lap in front of the TV and I felt as if it would be betraying her if I reverted to that habit while she was away). However, although the TV was on, I didn't have the attention span to follow what was happening and found myself staring out of the window while my mind raced.

My mind replayed the day's events, starting with me sitting with Estelle in the garden in the morning, then chatting with giggly Vicky and the other CHImps and then seeing red-faced Salter getting all worked up in the kitchenette. It had been a long day. For me, at least, although I did note that most of the rest of the team had followed Salter to the pub shortly before 5pm. I'd stayed on for another hour, filing emails away and making a jobs list for the following day. By the time I left, only Peter was still beavering away silently at his desk.

I stabbed away at the steaming bowl of parmesan-topped pesto pasta in front of me, only just realising how hungry I was. I hadn't eaten all day. The fresh citrussy tones of my cold glass of Sancerre were disappearing a bit too quickly. The first large glass was to wash dinner down. The second to celebrate standing my ground with Salter. A wave of calm washed over me.

The TV continued to drone on in the background as I stared out the window, watching passers-by returning home from their busy days. I reflected on how maturely I had responded to Salter's mention of *her* name – *Sarah* – earlier in the day and how well I had done not to give him the satisfaction of any show of emotion in response. I knew I was still experiencing the occasional flashback, but they were shorter, less frequent and less intrusive than they used to be. It was all a long time ago.

I bundled up the last four pieces of fusilli onto my fork and used them to wipe up the remaining smears of pesto from the side of my bowl before pushing them into my mouth. Aside from the TV, the flat was silent. Traffic was rare down my road, and I was blessed with neighbours who kept themselves to themselves. I continued to sip away at my Sancerre and let my mind drift.

It all felt very civilised until I realised how light-headed I felt. 'Deep breaths, Luke,' I told myself. 'It's been a long day. Hold it together.' The TV news was on and seemed to be repeating the same script over and over.

From somewhere in the distance, I heard someone calling 'Luke! Luke!'. It sounded like *her* although I knew that was impossible. I rushed to turn the TV off in case the sound was coming from there. The room fell absolutely silent while I froze, ears pricked for further sounds. I must have held my breath for almost a minute when I heard the same voice call out from what sounded like the back of the flat.

'Luuuukkke!', it called. The hairs on my arms stood upright while a chill ran down my spine. I put my glass down and moved cautiously towards the back of the flat, looking into the main bedroom as I passed. Nothing but a crumpled up duvet on the middle of the bed. Past the bathroom - dark cold and empty. Past the empty kitchen and into the small second bedroom at the back of the flat. Nothing.

'Luuuuke, where are you?' I heard from the front of the flat now. My hands ran cold and numb. I paced back to the front of the flat only to find myself back in the empty living room with nothing but an empty bowl staring back at me. Nothing, although the voice was unmistakably *hers*. Again,

I stood as still as a statue to allow my ears to focus on any further sound but all I could hear were waves of wine rushing through my veins. Or was it panic? I held my hands out in front of me to steady myself and immediately focussed on the half finger on my left hand. I imagined that this must be what it's like to be haunted.

The flat lay silent. Nothing to hear aside from my own breathing. I checked my phone for messages. Still nothing from Estelle. Not even a read receipt. I took my empty bowl back to the kitchen and decided to take the remainder of the wine out to the garden and have a cigarette. It hadn't even been 24 hours, but I was already feeling desperate for Estelle to come home.

I took up my usual position on my bench and went through the comforting ritual of tapping a cigarette against the side of the box three times before putting it in the corner of my mouth and lighting it. It was early dusk, and the sky was starting to turn pink. Strangely, it felt warmer in the garden than inside the flat. Each stream of smoke I blew upwards seemed to relax me more. Or was it the wine? I could no longer tell.

Somewhere, in the distance, I could hear my name repeatedly being called but, when I turned by head to concentrate on where it was coming from, it seemed to fade. Some kind of spooky auditory illusion I should ignore.

I switched my attention to the cherry tree which had a carpet of fallen blossom as its feet and small cherry buds on its fingers. It warmed me to watch yet another annual life cycle of the tree. I always found it reassuring that however bare it would become over winter, buds, florets, flowers, petals, and finally cherries would return year after year.

To distract my mind from the distant calling, I started pondering how the annual cycle of a cherry tree compares with that of a human. How the cherry tree has a cycle of beauty to admire, whereas we just slowly and steadily deteriorate over the course of a lifetime with no obvious shows of blossom or springtime signs of rebirth to appreciate along the way.

That said, I remembered reading somewhere that the billions of cells that make up the body completely replace themselves over the course of a seven-year period. Not just through vigorous exfoliation and cutting your toenails either, but organs, eyelashes, even brain matter. I finished my glass and topped it up with the bottle's remains and started questioning if, after seven years of every cell dying and being replaced, we're still the same person we were previously? And what about our memories? How are they carried forward, or do we only remember memories of memories if they're over seven years old? Do our mistakes expire within the same timespan?

I swilled more wine round my mouth and watched the sky blur into a palette of pink and turquoise brushstrokes. Small birds chirped away as they made their last calls before turning in for the night. And yet, busloads of questions continued chugging through my consciousness. If our bodies are constantly replacing cells, how do they take on the gradual appearance of becoming older? Or is it just that they can't replace themselves quickly enough to keep them looking young? Were we really no more than more complex versions of Trigger's infamous broom, with its numerous replacements of heads and handles that bear no actual link to the original? Do we retain no physical links to our younger selves? Keeping my mind occupied with these questions did at least have the benefit of keeping imaginary voices at bay.

'Fuck!' I spat, as the red-hot ball of embers fell out of my cigarette, burning my fingers and causing me to spill wine on myself. Bringing a natural end to the evening's calm, I put the cigarette stub in the empty bottle and made my way inside, intent on googling these life-critical questions.

Banging my shoulder on the back door as I entered the kitchen, I grabbed hold of the worksurface to steady myself and reacclimatise myself to my cold empty flat. My ears were still buzzing and desperate to play further tricks on me. If I concentrated hard enough, I could still hear the voices of the day chattering away somewhere in the background. Sadly, Estelle's soothing tones were absent from the hubbub taking place in the recesses of my mind. The only distinguishable tones I could make out were those of *her* cackling in my direction, and the gruff tones of Salter whispering various threats. I knew it wasn't healthy to give them the attention they craved so, to refocus my attention, I headed towards the living room, running my elbow along the hallway as I went, to find my work laptop.

I checked my phone while my laptop was booting up. Still no response from Estelle. I didn't want to make it seem as if I was hassling her for a response, so I sent a cool *'Heading to bed now. Night x'* message in the hope that she'd try and call back quickly before I fell asleep. Part of me wondered – or hoped – that she might have finished the Amsterdam audit early and be heading back tonight. Wishful thinking.

My laptop finally opened up where it had left off, on the C.R.A.P screen. I'd forgotten why I'd logged on so decided to browse through the messages which had been exchanged since I'd left work. I made sure that my online status was set to 'offline' so that my green light didn't appear visible to others. No one likes to be seen as one of those sad fuckers who are logged on every minute of every day checking their emails like an office brown-nose.

I chuckled to myself as I saw various exchanges between Salter's team, presumably sent from their phones to each other while they were in the pub, talking about which pub to move onto next and whether they should message me to see if I was still around to join them. These were sent about three hours ago and I hadn't received any direct messages from any of them. It seemed Vicky thought it would be brilliant fun if they could *'drag me out for the evening'* and see what I'm like with a few drinks inside me. Elaine, Judith and Theo had all responded immediately with an emphatic *'do it, do it'* messages, but Sophie had brought the suggestion to a close by saying she'd just spoken to Salter who was clear it was a *'team-only drinks evening'*.

I wouldn't have been keen to immerse myself in their group even if they had asked, pubs not really being my thing, but was flattered that so much chat had been about me. My new look and approach at work was obviously making a good impression in more ways than one. I even wondered if they might have their own version of a £5 bet between themselves...

I skimmed through other messages looking for gossip or useful bits of information I could bank for future use. Disappointingly, there was nothing of any significance and Salter's online communications were becoming more formal and less informative, presumably because he was increasingly switching to WhatsApp to communicate with his team over anything that might be useful. Which was annoying. The last messages sent from him to his team were to remind them of the various client progress reports that needed be finalised before Estelle's return to the office at 15:00 tomorrow. 15:00? How did he know that? I thought I was the only one who knew which flight and what time she was due to return tomorrow. Had Estelle messaged him separately, I wondered with a pang of jealousy.

My eyes were getting tired and blurry and my head spinning as it was losing the battle against the early morning start and the bottle of Sancerre. I was about to logoff and stagger to bed when I noticed that Peter's online presence was showing a green light. Had he really been working all this time? He'd been working flat out and withdrawn all day. Come to think of it, he'd been withdrawn for a few days now. If it wasn't for the fact that I was now too drunk to string a sentence together, I might have dropped him a message to offer a hand with whatever was keeping him up so late. His online messages (always very brief and factual) gave no clue as to what might be causing him so much stress lately.

I switched applications from the C.R.A.P. to Peter's private teamsite area to see if I could find out what was keeping him so preoccupied.

Two files were open; 'Journal.doc' and one which had been created this morning simply called 'Vicky.doc'. He'd taken the trouble to save them in a restricted format so that only he could view it. Well, only him and the systems administrator, of course, which people often forget. However, I liked Peter and did pause for a moment to consider whether I should open them or not.

Unsurprisingly, curiosity (or plain nosiness) got the better of me and, as I read the outpouring of emotion unfolding on my screen, felt an incredible pang of deep sadness and concern for my newfound colleague and manager who had shown me nothing but kindness since I joined his team. I always got the impression from his level of personal detachment that he was dealing with stuff outside of work, but I had no idea just how bad it was affecting him.

It just goes to show, you never really know what anyone is going through behind their workplace masks. I had long since learnt from bitter experience that the expression of emotions through the keyboard could too easily betray the best of us. Peter's letter was just the latest reminder to myself as to just how much power I wield within the firm, being able to tap into everyone's psyche. Except, for a change, Peter was one of the good guys who I felt needed help.

I used CTRL C and P to copy and paste the Vicky file across to my own private teamsite area and vowed to speak to him first thing the next day and find a way of helping him. The difficulty would be raising the issue with him without letting him know why I might be concerned. But I could worry about that tomorrow.

His words were still circling round my head as I brushed my teeth. I looked up in the mirror to see that black circles were already forming under my bloodshot eyes as my wooziness had somehow managed to fast forward itself to a full-blown drunkenness. I bounced along the walls before falling into bed, determined to get as much sleep as possible and get myself back on track for Estelle's return.

Estelle. I checked my phone one last time before closing my eyes.

Still no response.

Chapter 21

Urgh! I swung my body from left to right, my eyes tightly shut, and buried my head in my sweat-soaked pillow in the hope that the pulsating throb in my head would ease. No such luck. All I achieved was shifting the poisonous lump of headache inside my brain to gloop its way from behind my right eyeball back through the core of my nervous system, like an ugly fluorescent blob of wax in a lava lamp.

I cursed myself for drinking too much and staying up too late. In addition to my headache, a dry hollow feeling in my stomach threatened to work its way up to the back of my throat if I moved too fast. And, to top it all, my heart was thumping, a sheen of sweat covered me, and the thought of going to work filled me with dread.

It wasn't just the hangover though. Something didn't feel right. Was it nightmares, the after-effects of night traumas, or something else? I tried to piece together the events of last night to bring logical order to my senses, but everything was a jumble. I could remember hearing voices. Various flashbacks to past scenes being played out. Me and Salter squaring up to each other. Salter and *her*, laughing at me. Estelle soothing me with her soft caresses and confidence-boosting whispers. *Her,* calling my name out, but without me able to see her face. Me, rushing through crowds, looking for Estelle and calling out her name, but being unable to find her. Ghosts of past and present, all mixed up together and taunting me.

No, there was something else that was niggling away at me that I couldn't quite recall. My bladder was under pressure but that wasn't it. I forced my crusty eyes open to squint at the clock. 08:12. Fuck! I was running late again and with Estelle returning this afternoon, I wanted to have everything fresh and tidy at work and home to ease our way into the weekend.

I checked my phone. One missed call and a voicemail. I pressed play while carrying it to the bathroom. *'Bonjour mon chéri. Sorry I missed your messages last night, but you know what I'm like with my phone.'* It was true. *'The Amsterdam office was very straightforward and I finished early and went back to the hotel to catch up on my sleep. I'm going to work from my room this morning and fly back after lunch. I'll see you in the office this afternoon. Oh, and one more thing mon chéri...'* her voice softened, and she paused for effect. *'I hope you're feeling well rested too because I'm coming back very hungry!'*

I again cursed myself for letting myself get into such a state, but her message gave me the reassurance and motivation I needed to get a wiggle on. Having relieved my bladder, I decided to pop to the kitchen to get some coffee started before returning to shave. Heading down the corridor, I was struck by how extra cold the flat felt despite the sunshine that had been streaming into the bedroom. The reason was apparent as soon as I entered the kitchen. The back door to the garden was wide open, keys left in the lock, the cold breeze making me shiver.

I must have forgotten to close it when I came in from the garden last night. It wouldn't have been the first time I'd been so absent minded and, contrary to popular belief, Bethnal Green doesn't have a steady stream of opportunistic burglars patrolling back gardens at night. Everything in the kitchen was untouched so I wasn't worried. I stood on the back step and looked out to the garden. Inhaling the fresh morning air seemed to reduce the lava lamp blob of pain in my head. The garden looked lifeless aside from the branches of the cherry tree, swaying in the morning breeze, scattering pink confetti-like petals everywhere. It seemed to be taunting me with its carefree sprinklings of joy.

I slammed the door shut, flicked the kettle on, and returned to the bathroom. Thankfully, the fresh air had gone some way towards clearing my head and washing my face twice had brought some colour back to my cheeks. However, something troubling continued to niggle away in the recesses of my mind that I still couldn't determine.

As I whipped up my shaving cream into a lather, I visualised the day ahead. I had no reason to stress. I was on top of my work and, other than wanting to maintain a visible office presence, there wasn't any real reason for me to rush. Estelle would be back this afternoon and I was looking forward to seeing her. I ran the razor over my cheek, first downwards, and then in the opposite direction to get the cleanest shave possible. Her voicemail had certainly sounded as if she was looking forward to seeing me too. With half a face still covered in shaving cream, I put my razor down for a moment to send her a quick text *'Good morning beautiful! All good here and looking forward to seeing you later! x'*

I returned to scraping the shaving cream off the left side of my face while trying to fathom out what was causing my sense of impending doom. There was no immediate threat from Salter or Mitch to worry about. No reason to be nervous about work. I rinsed my razer through and washed my face again, this time with cold water to close the pores.

As my fresh-faced self-stared back at me from the mirror, the shock of the cold water having re-wired my brain back to normal, it hit me like a thunderbolt. Peter. God, he needs help. How could I have forgotten in such a short space of time? I thought I was messed up until I'd stumbled across his online journal and that letter to Vicky last night. In contrast to the cool, calm, and professional front he presented at work, his written words revealed a troubled, tortured and intense soul, crying out for help.

Only slightly relieved that I'd worked out what was niggling me, I stiffened up with the intention of reaching out to him today to find a way - any way - in which I could offer him some help. Empathy in the workplace was not my forte, but I'd grown to like Peter and was troubled at the thought of him suffering in silence. If he didn't want to open up to me, I could perhaps direct him towards the firm's Employee Wellbeing contract for some free counselling. I must be able to do something to help.

I took my coffee through to the living room and opened my laptop to re-read Peter's letter. The sense of something not feeling right returned as I checked each one of my personal folders without being able to locate Vicky.doc. I ran a full system search and the only place the file was showing up was the original copy on Peter's drive. I was sure I'd saved a copy to my own drive. Had the hacker been hacked, I wondered? My copy couldn't simply have disappeared.

My heart thumped faster as I tried to figure out what was going on. I closed my eyes and tried to visualise myself saving the document last night, desperate to reassure my sanity. As hard as I tried, I couldn't recall actually saving the file. My stress turned to panic as I considered the likelihood of me clicking on *print* last night instead of *save as*. If that were the case the document would have been sent straight to the print queue in Columbus House.

'Shit,' I said out loud as I rushed to open *devices and printers*. 'This could blow everything.' I scolded myself at the scale of my stupidity as I waited for the *queued print jobs* option to open in the desperate hope that it was there and I could delete it. Why was it that computers always seemed to operate at their slowest the more urgent a task was?

The print queue finally opened, confirming my worst fear. *Columbus House>Eighth Floor>Shenstone, Luke>Vicky.doc>job completed.*

Fuck. I needed to get to the office as soon as possible.

Chapter 22

'Fuck. Fuck. Fuck.' I scolded myself repeatedly as I pushed my way along Bethnal Green platform and squeezed into a carriage just before the doors closed, attracting scowls from my fellow commuters as everyone was forced to shuffle down a few inches.

The adrenaline rushing through my veins was neutralising the hangover I should be feeling. All I could think about was getting to the office as quickly as possible to retrieve my printing before anyone else could get to it. The thought of anyone else picking it up before I could get to it made me feel sick. Not only would it cause Peter intense embarrassment, and God knows what else, it risked questions being asked about how it had landed up on the printer, which in turn could expose my digital snooping. And what would Estelle think if she found out? What an awkward position I'd be putting her in.

I was grateful Estelle wouldn't be around to see me fuck up so royally. A headmasterly voice in my head boomed *'you've let Peter down, you've let Estelle down, but most of all you've let yourself down'*. I was a complete fucking idiot.

I did consider phoning ahead to ask Lesley to remove it from the printer and put it to one side for me or, better still, feed it to the shredder. But I knew she wouldn't be able to resist reading the document so I was going to have to risk it and deal with it myself. This was my cock-up and, to paraphrase the words of the platform announcement, it was down to me to see it, say it, sort it.

I shot out of the carriage and through the crowds to change onto the Victoria line as soon as the doors opened at Oxford Circus. I calculated that if I jogged to the office from Victoria, which was only two stops away, I should be able to reach Effective Solutions before 09:45. Peter and the team would have been at work for around an hour, and it

137

was likely that Salter and his team would only be starting to arrive, and unlikely that any of them would have settled into their work so much as to need the printer yet. I was cutting it fine but it was still possible for this nightmare to end well.

Zig-zagging my way through the morning crowds and running up the street from Victoria station to Columbus House had left me panting with an all-over film of sweat coating my face. I checked my phone briefly for messages as I waited for the lift. One from Estelle, *'Me again, mon chéri…hope you slept well and I look forward to seeing you sooner than you think x'*. Estelle's texts were like London buses - none for ages and then they all come at once.

I put my phone back in my pocket and dabbed my forehead dry as the lift doors pinged open at the eighth floor. I walked down the glass panelled walkway that looked down onto Columbus House's grand atrium, steadying my pace as best I could to avoid attracting attention to myself. I needed to get to that document as quickly as I could.

'Morning handsome!' greeted Lesley as I approached reception.

'Morning, cheeky!' I fired back, convinced that I was coming across coolly. The reality was, I was resisting the urge to run across the office to the printer.

'Everything OK today, Luke?' she asked, frowning. 'You look a bit twitchy if you don't mind me saying.'

I took my hanky from inside my suit jacket and dabbed my face dry again. 'I'm good, thanks,' I replied, suddenly conscious that my voice had raised an octave. 'Just a bit overheated from a stuffy tube ride, that's all. Are you alright?' I was keen to get the morning niceties out of the way quickly.

'Oh, you know…' She was speaking too slowly for my liking. '…same old, same old. Looks like everyone else is keyed up about something today though.' She nodded in the direction of the general office behind her.

Peter was sitting in his usual position, crouched over his laptop, as was the rest of his team. As I looked deeper into the office, my heart sank. Salter and the majority of his team were already in. He was upright, looking full of swagger as he laughed and joked with the rest of his team who had their chairs pulled up around him.

'Oh really? What gives you that impression?' I asked Lesley while continuing to eye Salter over her shoulder. It was too far to hear what any of them were saying, but they all looked extra lively and jovial which unsettled me.

'Well, it's Friday for one, isn't it? And the boss being back early seems to have got everyone going.'

'What, Gordon?' I asked, confused.

'No, silly. He's not due in till the next Board meeting. Estelle, of course. She got an earlier flight back.' My jaw dropped. I was more confused than ever now. 'I'd have thought you'd have known, given you seem to be her golden boy around here at the moment.'

Estelle's unpredictability was one of her many charms, but how and why she'd chosen to return early and come straight to the office without letting me know was not the sort of unpredictability I found charming. I parked the thought, politely excused myself from Lesley, dumped my backpack at my desk and headed to the printer.

I had to pass Salter's team's area to get there. As I approached, it was obvious that they were lowering their voices and suppressing laughter on my account. My heart sank as I was left in no doubt that they were avoiding any eye contact with me and, as I got closer, it looked as if Salter might be hiding a piece of A4 paper behind his back. Could it be...? Shit! I quickened my step to the printer and, as my back was turned, could hear Salter calling.

'Lukey boooy,' he called, with all the charm of Chucky from Child's Play. He was waving a piece of paper in the air. My toes gripped the ground like a child playing silent statues. I was frozen with fear at the realisation that he was going to read it out. Bastard!

'*Dear Vicky,*' he started with a mock sympathetic tone. A couple of his team members creased up laughing, while others looked away. I couldn't tell if it was from amusement or embarrassment at what they knew was to follow. '*I'm not sure why I'm writing this, but it's 3am, my cheeks are wet with tears of emotion, and I feel as if I might die if I don't at least attempt to express the turmoil that lives within me.*' He paused to make an exaggerated sad face.

'*You will think me mad.*' he continued, hamming up the emotion in his voice. '*Logically, I know my feelings are totally irrational and that my mind is probably playing tricks with me. But emotionally, we're soul mates, destined to meet, and despite the circumstances being totally wrong, fate has thrown us together.*' I was unable to speak or move, as if Salter's cruelty had cast some sort of spell over me.

'*We've only exchanged small talk at the tea point a handful of times, but each time your presence has wobbled me, made me stutter and mix my words up. I know you probably don't even give me a second thought, but I've been watching you from afar and have grown to find you funny, caring, warm, deep, understanding, and a genuinely beautiful person inside and out.*' The smirk on his face as he drawled out those last words made no secret of the fact Salter was in his element and enjoying himself. Behind him, I could see that even Peter and the rest of his team had turned their chairs to listen in.

Vicky, realising that Salter's poorly judged humour was also making her the focus of attention, spoke up. 'Stop John,' she pleaded. 'It's not nice.'

He ignored her and continued, striding up and down, reading from the page as if he was reciting Shakespeare. '*I love it when I get the chance to talk to you in person. Or to look into your clear blue eyes. Or hear you laugh. Or watch your face break into that wonderful dimple-framed smile...*'

'Enough,' Vicky said more firmly. In the background, I could see that Peter had stood up from his desk and taken a couple of steps closer. Salter held the page back up in front of him to continue. Did his cruelty know no limits? No one was laughing any more.

'SHE SAID ENOUGH!' I spat, before he could continue.

True to character, he ignored me *'Or...if I'm feeling brave, imagine how soft your thighs might feel...'*

'Please stop,' I interrupted, hoping that a softer approach might have more impact. 'No one needs to hear any more.' Looking round the office, it was clear that the mood had shifted from any pretence at banter towards an awkward stiltedness. Peter had listened to the whole charade and, if his bowed head and sloped shoulders was anything to go by, was looking more broken than I knew he was already.

'What's the matter, Lukey boy?' Salter challenged, squaring up to me. 'Can't take a joke?'

It was all one big power game with Salter, and always at someone else's expense. I snatched the page from his hand and stepped right up to him, meeting his gaze head-on.

'It's not my letter, you fucking moron.'

Chapter 23

*Click. As I faced Salter and stared deep into his eyes, the page scrunched in my tightly clenched fist, I felt as though I were in the presence of the devil. Fire must be met with fire, I told myself, refusing to look away from his defiant smirk. Memories danced inside my head, taunting me, dragging me away from the present day to a time many years ago when he had similarly humiliated me in front of the office. When he had boasted openly of the seedy affair that he and **her** – **Sarah Reynolds** – the firm's top-performing Change Implementation Manager and **my** girlfriend of three years had been having behind my back. How **he** had laughed at having trashed what I thought was love between **me** and **her**. How **he** had taken joy in making sure everyone else knew about it. How **he** had managed to publicly shut down any sense of self-worth and confidence I had just to feed his own ego. Of course, I knew Salter was not solely to blame for my past pain. **She** was to blame too. **He** had simply given **her** the opportunity to show **her** true colours and **she** had fallen for it, hook line and sinker. The messages they'd sent to each other had proved how duplicitous they were – to me and each other. The pain, humiliation and upset they had caused had cut deep, but at least they'd opened my delusional eyes up to the truth.*

*The only difference between the two of them was that **she** was long gone, and **he** was still here in my face, smirking at me, continuing to cause pain. Click.*

But this situation was not about me. It was about Peter who, staring at his feet in the middle of the office like a lonely child in a raucous playground, looked physically deflated, his shoulders sloped with complete humiliation and defeat. The awkwardness that cloaked the office sent team members back to their screens to pretend to work.

Lesley was peering over from the reception desk to see what was going on, and, for the first time that day, I could see Estelle from within her glass walled enclosure, watching the scene unfold from within. A small smile crept across her face as she caught my eye. Pride? Love? I could still never be totally sure what she was thinking. She looked every ounce the Chief Operating Officer as she viewed her domain with authority, her neatly pressed two-piece suit giving her added presence to the smart casual look favoured by the general office.

'If you'd have turned the page over, you'd have seen that it was Peter who wrote this, you idiot,' I said through gritted teeth, holding the crumpled page up to his face before throwing it to the ground. 'This isn't anything about me, you complete dick.' Salter's dim smirk was replaced with a look of confusion.

I turned to Peter, who remained statuesque. 'Peter, I'm sorry.' He chose not to hear me. Instead, he turned his back to us and made his way robotically back to his desk. There was something about the way he moved that told me something wasn't right. There was something totally detached about him, as if everyone in the office was invisible to him.

'Peter?' I called again as I stepped past Salter. No response. Peter remained with his back to me, the rest of the office silent and being careful to look anywhere but at Peter for fear that their role in his humiliation might be acknowledged.

Behind me, I could hear Salter muttering sheepishly 'Shit, how was I supposed to know?' I glanced back to see him unfolding Peter's fateful letter to read the second side, the words of which had etched themselves into my permanent memory:

"The truth is, I'm struggling. I need help and don't know where to begin. My sanity is slipping away from me. The

pain I carry in my heart, leads me to imagine a better life, to fantasise, and these fantasies bring me crashing down to reality. My hope in writing this letter is that it will provide some form of release to help me find a way forward.

I won't spell it out here - it would be too painful to see the full reality written down before me , but my children need help – one needs round-the-clock emotional and medical care, and the other has gone off the rails and barely cares. My wife has long since given up on me and the lot of us - the Sunday Times Wine Club subscription and her not-so-secret long lunches with our neighbour are her only true passions these days...

I know that my feelings towards you are phantom. A way of reaching for light amidst the darkness that surrounds me. Irrational, foolish and desperate.

It is with a heavy heart and tear-stained cheeks, that I bid you farewell. For now, I must put a lid on this Pandora's box of fantasies, continue to wear my Director's mask, and find a way to mend my family. I wish you well and hope that life's gentle winds will guide us both towards brighter horizons.

Your fantasist admirer from afar,
Peter x"

'Shred it.' I spat in Salter's direction. 'Now.' I snapped.

Salter, in a moment of total submission, scuttled off towards the shredder. Estelle watched the scene unfold from her office, a subtle but definite smile on her face. I still had no idea how she'd made it back to the office so quickly and why she didn't let me know she was returning earlier than planned, but that could wait. For now, I needed to focus on Peter and try to repair the damage I'd caused. And, yes, I was acutely aware that this whole mess was of my making.

Peter had picked up, and was staring at, the framed photo of his two small sons from his desk. His munchkins, as he often referred to them. He wiped the photo clean with his fingers and placed it in his inside jacket pocket.

'Peter?' I called softly, stepping closer towards him. Was I the only one who cared, I wondered, noting that the rest of the office appeared oblivious to the fact that anything out of the ordinary was going on, ignorant to the damage that their teasing and laughter had caused.

Peter continued to ignore me. A chill crept from my scalp down my spine, telling me that something sinister was sweeping the air. Peter's movements were controlled and mechanical, as if his mind and body were somehow disconnected from each other. As if he was being controlled by an external force.

Continuing to ignore my presence, he placed one foot carefully in front of the other, lugging his shell of a body towards the walkway to the lifts. Perhaps to take some time out and get some air? His actions could barely be called walking; they were too robotic. His movements were heavy, his posture devoid of life. The situation was clearly too much for him to bear.

I followed him down the corridor. I needed to apologise and let him know I wanted to help him in whatever way I could. Glancing back at the office, I despised each and every member of staff for their lack of compassion and indifference towards Peter. But mostly, I despised myself for my carelessness at having created the situation.

A stream of light shone through the roof of the atrium at the top of the walkway where Peter was standing in front of the lift. His head remained bowed. He appeared oblivious to his surroundings. The lift doors opened and closed without Peter getting in. Peter remained frozen to the spot. Something felt very wrong.

I quickened my pace towards him and again called out his name, this time more loudly.

'Peter, no!' I was desperate to gain his attention now.

I was about five paces away from him when he looked up to acknowledge my presence. His face was wet with tears and his jaw was pulsating furiously.

'Peter, please?' I pleaded, this time more softly.

Without saying a word, he turned his head slowly from side to side while his eyes blazed from within their puffy red sockets. His jawline and lips working themselves into some kind of spasm. What followed happened so fast it was difficult to comprehend it really happened.

Quick as a flash, and with no time for me to stop him, he took two quick athletic steps towards the edge of the walkway, gripped the handrail with both hands, and vaulted over the edge.

The sound which followed could not be described as a scream. It was a deep-bellied, animal-like roar that will forever be imprinted in my own memories of pain. Equally distressing, was the abruptness with which the dull thud and crunch from below brought the sound to an abrupt end.

For a couple of eerie moments, absolute silence took hold of the building, as if time itself stood still, before it was broken by yet another chilling sound. This time, the more humanlike screams and shouts from those who had been unfortunate enough to witness Peter's arrival at the ground floor.

An overwhelming sense of responsibility told me that I needed to look over the edge and face up to the result of my actions. I felt woozy. To steady myself, I held onto the walkway barrier with my right hand while my left hand instinctively started rubbing the silky scar tissue of the stump of my ring finger, in the same way that some people like to twist their wedding ring round their finger like a security blanket for grownups.

I was only able to look for a second, but that was more than enough for my photographic memory to make an indelible print of the blood-bone porridge mix seeping out of a suit eight floors below.

Chapter 24

Suppressing the urge to vomit over the balcony railing, I pushed myself away from the edge and managed two steps backwards before my legs buckled and I found myself rolling backwards on the ground. Salter was pacing towards me, a look of disbelief on his face. I pushed myself onto my knees and held out my arms to prevent him from getting past me to look over the edge.

'Did I just see what I thought I saw?' he asked with disbelief pained all over his face.

'You did. Don't look over. It's horrible.' Despite my dislike of Salter, I wouldn't wish the sight of Peter's crumpled body on anyone. 'He was fragile and we're responsible for this. You really don't want to see the result.' I stood upright, held Salter firmly by the shoulders and looked him in the eye. 'He's gone.'

'Dead?' Salter asked, bottom lip quivering.

'Completely,' I replied softly. 'I tell you what we're going to do. We're going to turn around slowly and get back into the office before anyone else thinks about coming this way and having a look.' I gently steered a compliant Salter around by his shoulders in the direction of the office, gripped his elbow and led him back, step by step. At the end of the corridor, I could see Estelle standing beside Lesley at reception, waiting for our return. She had all the air of a headmistress waiting to scold two naughty pupils. In contrast to my and Salter's shaky demeanours, she looked very firm and upright.

'What do you mean "we're" responsible?' Salter muttered, regaining his confidence.

'Just that Peter wouldn't have jumped if it weren't for the humiliation and shame he was feeling on top of everything else. You caused that, John. No question.' I let my anger speak.

'I would never have read that letter out if I knew Peter had written it, and you know it.' His eyes glared back accusingly.

'And Peter would never have known about it if you hadn't chased the opportunity to get some cheap laughs at someone else's expense.' I tightened my grip around his elbow.

We were about five metres away from Estelle when a thought crossed my mind.

'Did you shred the letter?' I asked.

'It's in my pocket,' Salter replied, gesturing his eyes towards his left jacket pocket. I suspected he might have kept hold of it. Out of sight from Estelle, I slipped my hand into his pocket and stuffed it into my own back pocket.

'There,' I said firmly. 'What's done is done. I suggest for both our sakes you make no mention of this letter to anyone ever again.' Salter didn't reply, nor did he challenge. We continued walking towards Estelle.

'What I want to know,' Salter whispered through gritted teeth, 'is how you knew what was in that letter before I'd even finished reading it.' He shot me a sideways look that suggested he knew the answer. 'And how you got hold of it? It's not right to be snooping into people's personal lives like that.'

I avoided answering his questions directly and whispered back, 'Like I said, I suggest for both our sakes you make no mention of this letter ever again.

Estelle had her arms folded as we approached. She did not look happy. The stern look on her face told me she was in 100% work mode. There was no glimmer of personal reassurance to be seen.

'What on earth is going on?' she asked, seemingly unaware of what had just happened.

Salter and I exchanged a glance before Salter stared at his shoes which I took as a signal for me to reply.

'It's Peter, Estelle. There's been an accident.' In the distance behind us, the sound of distressed cries could still be heard rising from the ground floor of the building.

'What do you mean "an accident",' she asked, shaking her head from side to side quizzically.

Before I had a chance to answer, a scratchy sound broke through the building's Tannoy system before a wobbly voice announced that there had been an incident on the ground floor and that everyone should remain at their desks in their offices on the outer edge of the building and avoid entering the central atrium area until instructed otherwise. The message was read slowly and repeated twice.

Estelle seemed unfazed by the announcement as she calmly turned to Lesley and asked her to rearrange all meetings with external visitors for another day. She then turned to the rest of the office, clapped her hands to gain everyone's attention, and repeated the instruction for everyone to remain seated at their desks until further instructions were received, and she could ascertain what was going on. She then turned back to me and Salter and snapped, 'My office. Now.'

She marched into her office with me and Salter shuffling behind, feeling very much like we were about to face some sort of punishment.

'Sit there,' she demanded, pointing to the beige sofa area usually reserved for visitors.

We sat silently while she remained standing behind her desk and picked up her phone to speak to security. She introduced authoritatively herself as 'Estelle Merisier, Chief Operating Office of Effective Solutions' and demanding to know what was going on. Her face showed no sign that she might already know, despite the fact that I had thought she'd been able to witness the situation unfold from within the comfort of her office. If she did know, she was playing the role of ignorance very well.

She listened intently to the voice at the end of the line before putting the phone down with a click that filed the room. She turned her attention back to us.

'I'm guessing you know already, but security have just told me that they have a dead body in the atrium that has either fallen or jumped from a higher floor, and that the emergency services are on their way. I'm informed that formal identification will be needed, but the security pass attached to the body's waist suggests it's Peter.' Her tone was very matter of fact, and in total contrast to the white-faced composure of both Salter and me. My hands went cold.

'As Senior Responsible Officer for the firm I have asked them to contact me as soon as the police arrive. In the meantime,' she continued, 'what I want to know is what the hell you two are playing at, and, more seriously, do you have anything to do with this?'

I was shocked at the blatant accusation but knew a strong denial would only indicate guilt.

'I'm still in shock,' said Salter, breaking the silence. 'It all happened so quickly. I have no idea why Peter might have jumped.' Estelle turned to me.

'Luke?' she prompted.

'Nor me,' I mumbled. 'I knew Peter had some stuff going on at home but had no idea he was feeling so bad as to do something like this.' I avoided looking directly at Estelle as I spoke.

'Then what was going on between you all before…' she paused. '…this happened?'

'Nothing,' Salter and I said in unison.

'Just a disagreement about team boundaries,' said Salter cautiously.

'Nothing serious, and nothing involving Peter,' I added, perhaps a bit too defensively.

'Are you sure there is nothing more I need to know before I have to speak to the police about this?' Estelle demanded gravely.

'We're sure,' we replied, again in unison.

'OK then,' she said with an air of acceptance which was not matched by the look she fixed on us. 'This is a terrible shock for us all, so I suggest you make your way back to your teams and show some professional leadership for a change by reassuring them that the situation is in hand. Make sure they stay at their desks until further notice as instructed and I'll be out to address them shortly. As soon as we have the all-clear from security to move around, I suggest we give everyone the rest of the day off if they need it. I expect they will.'

Salter and I mumbled our compliance and got up obediently to leave, reaching the door at the same time. I think we were both relieved not to have to face any further questions about the sequence of events, and no doubt Salter was keen to get to his team and tell them not to make any mention of the letter he had been reading from so cockily just half an hour earlier.

As I held the door open for him, Estelle called out from behind me.

'One minute, Luke, please.' I closed the door after Salter and turned to face her.

'You look rough. What happened?' she looked more concerned than critical.

'I told you. I don't know.' I replied, still in defensive mode.

'I meant what happened to you, Luke,' she clarified. 'You really don't look good.'

'Well, this business with Peter is stressful, plus I didn't sleep well last night. I couldn't settle without you by my side,' I admitted. 'Anyway, how come you're back so early? I wasn't expecting you back until this evening.' A smile crept across her face.

'I thought I would surprise you, that's all. The meeting with the Amsterdam office was very straightforward and showed nothing of interest so I left Mitch there to finish up the audit and caught an early flight back to the office this morning. That way we can get to start our weekend together sooner once we're finished with work.' I was relieved to hear that, despite her tough demeanour in front of Salter, I was still in favour on a personal level. I stood smiling at her like a lovestruck teenager, until she snapped us both out of the moment.

'I also wanted to have a word with you without John present to discuss what this situation means for the firm.'

Her train of thought left me confused.

'I will have to clear the appointment with the Board, of course, but, thinking ahead, we will need to cover Peter's role...'

She surely couldn't be thinking about this already, could she?

'...and I was thinking that you would be the most suitable person, on a temporary basis at least. The rest of the team are all accounting specialists and have none of the project management or leadership potential you are showing.'

I was speechless. Ordinarily the thought of working even more closely with Estelle and being on a level playing field with Mitch and Salter would excite me but, truth be told, I was still feeling the stab of pain for bearing the responsibility for Peter's death. I forced a smile and said, 'we'll see.'

'I will, of course, need someone to help me manage the Paris trip, and I may think about extending that visit to incorporate a short break south if you're interested?' The sparkle in her dark eyes was dancing around mischievously.

'That would be amazing,' I replied, my smile returning to my face.

'Good. Leave that with me then. For now, you need to get back to your team.'

Making sure to wipe the smile off my face before returning to the general office, I turned and reached for the door.

'Oh, and one more thing,' Estelle called out as I turned the handle.

'Yes?'

'What's that piece of paper sticking out of your back pocket?' she asked through narrowed eyes and eyebrows raised.

'Nothing,' I replied, stuffing it deeper into my pocket and out of sight.

'Right answer,' she said as she picked up her ringing phone, which I guessed was security announcing the police's arrival.

Chapter 25

'C'est la vie,' I thought as I surveyed the office from behind my new desk. Well, not new exactly. It was Peter's, but I'd repositioned it to give this section of the office a new feel, as well as making sure that my back was positioned against the wall and my screens out of sight from prying eyes. Carl's, Brian's and Natalie's desks had been repositioned to form a bank of desks leading off from mine.

It had been only three weeks since Peter's untimely demise and already the office had reverted to its former self. The regular hum of activity, the symphony of ringing phones, sales patter and clicking of keyboards providing the perfect soundtrack to my professional ascent. Surprisingly, my temporary promotion had been approved unopposed in a private meeting between Gordon Freeman and the other Directors without any need for it to go to the Board. Estelle had told me that the fact that I was playing such an instrumental role in Project Butterfly, was focussing on my self-development, and the fact that I was the only talent within the organisation that could oversee the combination of IT, accounts and Project Management, meant I was the only realistic solution if the firm were to avoid an expensive and lengthy external recruitment. Even Salter seemed to have chosen compliance over confrontation on this point. Of course, I made it clear, I was not letting go of my IT Contract Management or Data Security responsibilities.

So here I am, surveying the office both visually and online from behind my new ultrawide monitor screen that now sits on my desk, a material representation of my elevated status within the firm. And, yes, it was bigger than anyone else's. I was perfectly positioned to see straight into Estelle's office, keep an eye on visitors at reception, and always have Mitch and Salter in my line of vision.

I let my fingertips glide across the polished wood of my desk, a tangible reminder of my new role and status, as was the comfort of my new made to measure suit - a little promotion gift to myself. The tailored fabric draped over my shoulders to match the newfound confidence within me, symbolising the transformation I'd undergone over the past few months. Estelle was right; I should be proud of myself. Given how worried I'd been about questions being asked about Peter's letter being bandied about the office, I felt like a cat who'd just landed on his feet after falling eight floors.

The days when I was happy to plod along as the firm's IT geek seemed like a distant memory. Fair enough, I'd worked hard to turn myself around, but I couldn't have done it without Estelle's support and encouragement. And the will to impress her, of course. She'd been my anchor, just as I had been hers. I still gave her daily insights into what the mood and gossip was amongst staff so she could always present herself as being in the know and having her ear to the ground. We were the perfect team.

It had also been a relief to me how the team I now led had so easily switched their dedication and loyalty for Peter into supporting me and helping me make a success of the role. It had only taken a one-hour team meeting to reallocate Peter's outstanding tasks and responsibilities amongst them, during which they had all made it clear that none had wanted the responsibility that came with being Director. Still, the adaptation can't have been easy for them.

If I'm honest, it wasn't always easy for me. I did have genuine respect and appreciation for him. So much so, that I had set up a brand new AI Agent with a persona modelled on Peter based on all his past teamsite emails and documents. It made it easier for me to accept if I felt he was somehow still around. If ever I was stuck wondering how to lead the team, how to phrase an email, or set out a financial recommendation for the Board, I had Peter's very own omnipresence to seek advice from and provide me with drafts.

Carl had commented only this morning that it was impressive how much of Peter had rubbed off on me during the short time we worked together, even down to the little words of team encouragement I used to bring my emails to a close. I took that as high praise. Respecting Peter's legacy in this way gave me a form of solace which helped ease my conscience. As did the status and financial package, of course.

I was getting fit as well. Since my cock-up with Peter's letter, I'd been using the times when Estelle was away at international offices, or started work early, to fit in early morning runs before my first coffee and cigarette (it's important not to change too much in one go). It was paying off and I couldn't help but notice that the women in the office (and Carl) would eye me up and down when they thought I wasn't looking.

I thought back to Peter's last day. The tragedy had cast a dark, but thankfully short, shadow over the workplace. There had been tears, silence, disbelief on the day itself as emergency services took over with the clean-up operation, initially securing the scene, before taking cursory statements from everyone in the office before being allowed to leave.

The young police officers attending the scene were more focussed on adhering to their standard operating procedures - no doubt only recently learned - than digging too deep into what might have caused Peter to jump. The atmosphere throughout the whole building had been solemn as people were released floor by floor to state whether they knew Peter and confirm their contact details in case any further questioning was needed.

It had been some time before we on the eighth floor were told we could leave, at which point everyone had withdrawn into silence, muttering only the bare minimum to get out of the building. That didn't stop me getting myself worked up about someone mentioning Peter's letter to Vicky though. Salter had signalled he wouldn't be letting on, although I didn't like the way he kept looking over at me and shaking his head judgementally.

I needn't have worried though. By the time it was my turn to speak to the police, I was trembling so much that their focus quickly shifted from asking me to relay the events leading up to the incident, to providing me with support and counselling. Hooray for today's wellbeing culture!

Those same police had returned to the office the following week to request access to Peter's laptop in the hope of uncovering anything that might shed some light on his state of mind. Naturally, I had been keen to help and gave them a rebuilt replica of Peter's laptop, minus the personal folder he'd set up for himself. I'd even offered to show the officers how to conduct searches of the hard drive for any words associated with self-harm or suicidal thoughts, but they seemed happy enough to take it as it was. I imagine they're still wading through the volumes of company files and accounts that Peter's work drive held.

Estelle had the unenviable task of contacting Peter's wife to make arrangements for payment of his final salary, death benefit and pension. She had returned home from work quiet that day and described it as 'not pleasant but necessary'. We never spoke about it in any more detail than that.

A card and flowers had been hastily arranged; the gestures of kindness written within it contrasting sharply with the lack of support shown during Peter's life. His wife had sent through a short thank you card with details of the funeral but had only sent it through the day before it took place, so I'm not sure she really wanted any of us there. I don't think I'd have gone anyway.

Instead, Gordon Freeman made a point of attending the office on the day and orchestrating a minute's silence at the time of the funeral as a mark of respect for our former colleague. Other than that, the topic of Peter's death remained taboo in the workplace. No doubt the guilt and shame felt by those who had laughed along as Salter read Peter's letter out had helped to bury the reality of the situation.

Peter's death wasn't even mentioned once in anyone's communicator chats.

My success and temporary promotion may well have had a bittersweet tinge to it, but the thought of my upcoming trip to Paris with Estelle, followed by a mysterious couple of weeks somewhere in the south of the country, gave me the motivation I needed to stay focussed and professional.

I watched Estelle through the glass walls of her office, pacing up and down while chatting away into her phone. She had a spring in her step and kept tipping her head back with laughter. She was well and truly settled into the firm now and any initial resistance she'd received from Salter and Mitch seemed to have evaporated for the time being. She stopped pacing when she caught my eye, causing me to sit bolt upright and start shuffling through the folder of papers in front of me. She maintained eye contact and laughed some more before continuing pacing up and down.

I looked down at the documents in front of me. A pile of dull audit-related documents for the upcoming Paris visit with a pair of Eurostar tickets and a hotel reservation for one night clipped to the front of the folder. Behind them was the car hire confirmation that Estelle had arranged for the following two weeks. My stomach churned with the anticipation of the unknown.

I had no idea where we were heading, or what she had planned, but I was sure it wouldn't be boring.

Chapter 26

'Come on, Estelle!' I encouraged, trying not to march too far ahead of her on King's Cross station's concourse. Despite the early hour, she looked immaculate in her new two-piece skirt suit as she click-clacked behind me, her wheeled travel case gliding beside her.

I'd accounted for us arriving at the Eurostar terminal an hour in advance of the train's departure time to allow for check-in and customs, but Estelle was adamant we didn't need that long and had taken longer than usual to get dressed that morning. When she was finally ready, she'd insisted on not leaving home until she'd had a coffee.

Fair enough, it was an early start, but I did wonder if she was deliberately testing my stress levels to prove a point.

'Slow down, Luke,' she called back, stopping to switch her case into her other hand. 'I can't walk as fast as you'. We might have been able to move faster if she'd have taken my suggestion to wear trainers while travelling and change into her smart shoes at the other end, but that was a ridiculous idea apparently.

'Can I take your case?' I offered, hoping that might speed her up a bit.

'I can manage, thank you,' she said, ignoring my outstretched hand. 'You just need to slow down and stop panicking, that's all.'

I wasn't panicking, but there was no point in saying so. There was also no way I could say so without sounding as if I was panicking. I just didn't want us to miss our train. Departure times made me anxious, and I wanted to get the Paris office visit out of the way so that we could shed our work personas and spend some time being Estelle and Luke.

To my relief (and slight annoyance) we breezed through check-in and customs quicker than I had expected and managed to board our train and settle into our seats with plenty of time to spare.

'There,' Estelle said with a self-satisfied smile as she set her laptop up on the table between us. 'Plenty of time to spare, no?'. I said nothing and stared out the window watching the guard walk down the platform, slamming doors as he went, suppressing the urge to smile.

'This is it then,' I said as the train pulled out the station, unable to keep my enthusiasm to myself any longer. 'Paris, here we come! The start of our holiday.' I hadn't told Estelle, but this was my first time abroad anywhere. She gave me a faint smile and turned her attention back towards her laptop.

'It feels like a fresh start, doesn't it? Away from the office, the meetings, the games, I mean?' I was trying to encourage Estelle to shed her COO cloak and share some of the excitement I was feeling. She glanced up from behind her laptop, the click of the keyboard continuing, to give me the briefest of polite smiles, before returning her attention to her screen.

'Sorry, Luke, but I want to go over the Paris office operations again before we arrive. I was attached to them for a while, remember, and I need to make sure I've got a complete grip on the detail.'

'Of course,' I replied, pulling out my own laptop to feign similar commitment. 'Focus.' Inside, I yearned for our simpler, unguarded moments together.

I spent the next couple of hours staring at my screen in silent meditation, breaking only to answer Estelle's occasional questions about forecasts and performance. My thoughts could not help fast-forwarding to when our meetings were over, when we could finally be left to our own devices.

Chapter 27

'Luke? Luke?' I smiled without opening my eyes as I felt Estelle's hand on my shoulder, her voice was soft and distant. 'Come on Luke, we're here.'

I opened my eyes. Estelle was standing in the carriage aisle, wheely case by her side and handbag over her shoulder, ready to disembark. The train was slowing into Gare du Nord. Passengers were already squashing their way towards the exits as if it would somehow give them an unbeatable head start off the train. Estelle tapped her watch, her eyebrows raised to indicate impatience.

'Good morning, sleepyhead,' she purred. 'If we can find a taxi quickly, it should only take us about 20 minutes to reach the office. I hope your little sleep has left you feeling refreshed and ready to make a good impression?'

'I will be,' I replied, wrestling to put my suit jacket on. 'Sorry about that. I must have been more tired than I realised.'

'Don't worry, chéri. I have been emailing ahead and Mathéo and Éliott have a full agenda planned. They seem keen to impress us, and I am keen that today is not all about them, but that we show them the professional side of HQ and that we mean business. It's going to be a long day.'

I nodded vigorously to demonstrate focus, but what had really caught my attention was that Estelle had called me chéri. The word tugged on my heart every time she used it. It was a small reminder that the real Estelle, my Estelle, was still by my side. As far as I was concerned, the sooner we could get work out the way and start our break together, the better.

I already knew what Mathéo had planned for us, of course. I'd been monitoring his online chat with Salter for the past couple of weeks. He'd been trying to find out what to expect from our visit and how to play it. He could have chosen to contact either Estelle or me directly but, no, he'd chosen the sneaky option of bypassing us in favour of gossiping with his mate Salter who had in turn advised him to pad the day out with stock marketing presentations, leaving us with less time for us to focus on what we needed.

Reading Mathéo's derogatory remarks about my rapid rise within the firm hadn't bothered me. I expected that. What had really pissed me off was Mathéo and Salter's so-called banter about Estelle, totally undermining her position and ability and reducing her to no more than a *'pretty little thing'*, describing her as *'a bit too uptight'*, arrogantly stating that *'needs to learn to leave us to get on with it'*, and taking their exchange right down to the sewer with *'she needs a good seeing to'*. Their language was so dated, it read like a script from a crappy old 70s cop drama. The ultimate insult was when Salter had coaxed Mathéo into joining his £5 sweepstake to see who could sleep with Estelle first, followed by 'lol'. They were both so base, I hated it. Salter may have backed off trying to intimidate me since the Peter incident, but he was still out to undermine Estelle, and I was not having it.

We didn't have to wait long for a taxi. In fact, I'd only puffed my way through half my cigarette –only my second of the day – before our Taxi Parisien, a navy Peugeot, came to a smooth halt in front of us. With the air of a film star, Estelle put on a large dark pair of sunglasses and climbed into the back, leaving me to heave her luggage into the boot.

We slid silently out of the station grounds and onto the city's streets. Paris was alive with an energy that felt different to London's organised chaos. I stared out the back window like a kid on a school trip, admiring the passing buildings' architecture with their ornate balconies and intricate ironwork.

'This is fantastic,' I said, beaming.

'It is too crowded for my liking,' Estelle replied from behind her sunglasses. 'And dirty,' she added as we passed a rubbish truck. 'But it is a beautiful city.'

The taxi turned up a narrow street which led us onto a wide avenue that took us past picturesque cafés where patrons lingered over coffee, before bringing us up towards the iconic ironwork lattice of the Eiffel Tower. Estelle stared out of her window blankly. It was just another work trip for her, but I was struggling to contain my excitement. London had its impressive landmarks, obviously, but there was a certain romanticism and intimacy about Paris. It was a lot smaller and more compact, but there was something about the twisting cobblestone streets, the way the Seine snaked its way through the metropolis, and the grandeur of structures like the Champs-Élysées and Arc de Triomphe that demanded attention. The fact we were here together also marked the start of a new and exciting chapter for us.

I reached across the backseat, found Estelle's hand, and gave it a squeeze; a silent signal that it was us against the world. She pulled her hand away, leant forward in her seat and said something to the driver in French which I couldn't understand. This prompted him to take a sharp right and grind to a halt outside a tall narrow building in a deserted side street. A small brass plaque outside the entrance stated simply 'Effective Solutions (France)'.

'Here we are,' announced Estelle, switching back to English. 'Time for business. Let's get this done, Luke. Trust my lead, and I think this should go very smoothly.' I didn't doubt it. I had absolute faith in her.

A frosty woman who introduced herself as Brigitte met us inside and took us up to the second floor in one of those old-fashioned lifts I had only seen in films before. The sort with creaky concertina doors that let you watch each floor pass by. Our luggage made it a tight squeeze and I held my breath with my arms folded in front of me until we were safely out of our cage.

Brigitte punched in a security code to the double doors opposite the lift and opened them for us to be met with an onslaught of bilingual bonjours, hellos and welcomes, accompanied with handshakes, kisses and pats on the shoulder. Thankfully no man hugs. The whole office, around 10-12 of them, had formed a welcoming horseshoe around us, all smiling and asking us about our journey and where we're staying. They spoke so fast I didn't catch all their names.

I hadn't met Mathéo or Éliott before, but it was obvious who they were from the way they dominated the group and fussed around Estelle. I vaguely recognised Mathéo from an old corporate photo I had seen in a publication, although he was clearly much older than the photo suggested. Close up, I could see a marked contrast between the wispy grey hairs at the nape of his neck and the shoe-polish shade of the hair on the rest of his head. I guessed he was somewhere in his fifties. He repeatedly congratulated Estelle on her appointment, referring to how well she'd done to reach such heights after working on such small projects, and, if I didn't know better, I would have thought that he genuinely meant it.

Estelle looked over his shoulder and gave me a subtle raised eyebrow which told me she was on guard. She said she hadn't met them face to face before but had had some dealings with them while working remotely from the south of the country on a couple of sub-contracts.

Our coats were taken from us, and we were led down a corridor adorned with motivational posters into a small conference room. Everyone looked so bright and shiny. Well-fitted clothes, smartly polished shoes, and clouds of competing cologne that made my throat tighten. I couldn't help but notice that Mathéo and Éliott were not so different from Salter and Mitch. Full of charm and sales swagger but with perhaps a dash more gesticulation and shrugging. It was all very clichéd. The same but different.

We were ushered into our seats around a large central table with an array of warm pastries in its centre and the inviting scent of fresh filter coffee filling the air. We'd only been here two minutes and I was already suffering from a sensory overload. We were heavily outnumbered by their team and had somehow been steered into a seating arrangement that meant that Estelle was sitting at the upper end of the table, close to a large digital screen, flanked by Mathéo and Éliott, while I was stuck at the opposite end. There was no chance of us being able to exchange any private words throughout the meeting although, luckily, we had become adept at being able to communicate the basics of agree, disagree, or signal that something's not right through a series of subtle facial gestures.

I sat upright and stiff, feeling conspicuously British, as the rest of the room continued to chat with ease amongst themselves, flitting in and out of French and English. I hated small talk and found it difficult to participate. I knew that it was an essential conversational lubricant in the business world, but I really didn't see the point in exchanging non-controversial opinions on random irrelevant rubbish such as the weather, travel timetables or TV shows.

'And what about you, Luke?' Mathéo called out from across the table, catching me by surprise. 'Do you have any holidays planned this year?' It's almost as if he'd been reading my mind, sensed my awkwardness, and decided to throw me off my ease further.

I froze for a second longer than I ought, looking to Estelle for a clue as to how to respond. I couldn't read her, so blurted out 'France, of course! This is it,' with a smile that I hoped made it clear I was not prepared to elaborate further. Mathéo thought this was hilarious and clapped his hands together in amusement, laughing and winking to his colleagues. Estelle smiled at me reassuringly, but the subtle and slow shake of her head told me I'd said something wrong.

Thankfully, the spotlight moved off me as quickly as it had arrived as Mathéo signalled the start of formalities by inviting everyone to introduce themselves and say a bit more about themselves and their roles. Creeping death for introverts like me. And for extroverts like Mathéo, an opportunity to brag in front of a captive audience. Estelle gave an impressive introduction on behalf of both of us, clearly setting out the purpose of the visit and defusing any suspicion that it might be an inspection by emphasising that she viewed the relationship as collaborative rather than authoritative and that we were all working towards a shared goal of increased business and profit. She even managed to namecheck each individual with a nugget of praise. Heads bobbed along rhythmically as she spoke; there was nothing anyone could disagree with. And, simple as that, she had won them over.

I did my best to cheerlead Estelle along through subtle eye twinkles, smiles and nods as she spoke and during the questions that followed. Not that she needed it. She really was magnificent. Confident, relaxed, authentic, self-aware, engaging and warm. I could go on. She was a great listener too, pausing to face and really engage with whoever was speaking, leaving them in no doubt that they had her undivided attention. My contribution to the discussion was nil and I felt totally undeserving when Estelle described me as bringing both an increased focus on delivery and essential strategic vision to the firm. Did I? Other than being able to give her the occasional piece of advice or tip off I'd picked up from other's gossip I felt superfluous. But it was good to be given such public high praise, even if it was met by Mathéo's screwed up face.

Niceties exchanged, and the positive tone effectively set for the day, the team launched into a series of dry PowerPoint presentations, detailing their office structure, projects and blah, blah blah.

I topped up my coffee, sat back and braced myself for a day of pretending to look interested. My only real interest was Estelle, who was in her element and in full control. I assumed the role of observer for the rest of the day and took pleasure in watching her immerse herself enthusiastically into each session, flitting effortlessly between English and French depending on who she was talking to.

The rest was just fluff. A five-hour corporate endurance dance to endure before we could start our adventure together.

Chapter 28

'Here you are, Luke,' Mathéo said, sliding a thick plastic folder with neatly flagged page tabs decorating one side down the table in my direction. I slapped my hand on it just in time to stop it knocking my coffee over. 'Printouts of everything you've seen today, just in case you missed it - presentations, project timelines, forecasts... It's all there.' All eyes turned towards me, while Mathéo stood tall, hands on hips, looking like some corporate Superman.

I fanned through it, begrudgingly admiring the effort that had gone into producing such a clear volume of graphs, chart and tables.

'Thank you,' I replied. 'I'll take these away to study.'

'Take them! They are for you!' he said with a dismissive flick of his wrist. 'We are an open book here. We are Effective Solutions' oldest overseas office. We pride ourselves on leading the way.' I felt like I was on the receiving end of a cheap double-glazing sales pitch.

'Take it away,' he repeated, running his fingers through his hair. 'Read it. Share it. Do what you want with it.' His face betrayed the true meaning behind his words - 'shove it where you want'.

'Thank you,' I said again. 'I'll let you know if I have any questions.'

Mathéo turned his back on me before switching to French and muttering something to Estelle. She was, if I read her correctly, signalling to me that she had no concerns to follow up with.

'OK everybody,' Mathéo announced in English, clapping his hands together and holding them in a prayer position. 'Ten minutes to freshen up and we meet downstairs.'

Everyone shuffled about to collect their belongings, leaving me and Estelle alone.

'What's happening?' I asked.

'Mathéo has booked a table for dinner. He insists we join him and his team so we can spend a little time to get to know each other better.' I sighed. 'It is to be expected, Luke. He is being polite and wants to act as our host while we are here.'

'But we've got everything we need from them now. Do we have to?' I realised I sounded like a petulant child but the whole experience had reminded me why I preferred to work behind the scenes. Too much people contact for my liking.

'Come on, Luke,' she said, lowering her voice. 'Hang on a bit longer and we will be on holiday together very soon. Patience, mon chéri.' She glanced round to make sure no one was watching and gave me a playful wink.

'You know what though?' I said, feeling more relaxed about the situation. 'We could have got all the information we got from today's meeting in a single email. We didn't even need to be here.'

'Aw, poor Luke,' Estelle mocked. 'And where would the fun be in that? We are here in Paris, this office is one of the most efficient and well run I have come across and - who knows – you might even enjoy yourself if you relax a little! Also, don't forget I have a surprise for you to look forward to after this.'

She was right. Things weren't so bad, and I'd let myself get worked up over nothing. It had felt like an extra-long day purely because everyone had been slipping in and out of French, meaning I only ever caught half of what was being said. Estelle was right that the team did come across as high-performing and there was certainly no evidence of any underperformance or wrongdoing. I wasn't sure if I was relieved or disappointed. Mathéo's material would certainly make it easy for me to summarise their performance and incorporate the recommendations into Project Butterfly's overall report.

I still had no idea what surprise she had planned for when we could start our leave though.

We freshened up and met the rest of the team downstairs. The August heat hit us as we stepped out onto the street. Ties were off and their chatter, predominantly in French now, had a much more relaxed tone than it did within the office. I was relieved to see a couple of them were smoking so I pulled out my own to take the edge of my social tension with cigarette number three of the day. Estelle declined when I offered her one, instead choosing to walk hands-free alongside Mathéo as they led our small group in a southerly direction. I was left to trail behind as I struggled to keep control of Estelle's wheely case bumping across the cobblestone street, while laden with my own backpack and trying to enjoy my smoke at the same time.

I didn't mind being relegated to bag-carrier. Estelle was right. I was enjoying myself now that I'd let myself relax. OK, so I hadn't discovered any incriminating information on Salter connecting him to any impropriety with the Paris office, but the day wasn't exactly taxing. And I was enjoying the evening stroll behind the group, hearing their laughter, animated chatter and footsteps echo out against the charm of the architectural backdrop. A small part of me wondered whether corporate life wasn't so bad after all.

As we turned a corner, one of the team hung back to help relieve me of Estelle's case, freeing me up to enjoy the fading light casting a golden glow on the facades of the quaint buildings we passed. Before long, just after we passed a row of old storefronts, the herby aroma of French cuisine filled the air, marking our arrival at the restaurant.

'This is it,' announced Mathéo proudly, stopping outside the entrance. 'Nothing fancy. Just good quality French food, just like we have at home.'

The announcement was for my benefit, I was sure, as everybody else looked as if they were familiar with the place. Estelle looked relaxed and perfectly at ease as she continued to chat and laugh away with her newfound colleagues, who had clearly taken to her with a healthy balance of respectful friendliness.

'This way please,' invited Mathéo, holding the door open for Estelle and putting his hand on her lower back as she entered the restaurant. There was something about him that made me uneasy. He had camp mannerisms but had been fawning all over Estelle all day. It was as if he was trying hard to present himself as a safe pair of hands, but there was an underlying simmer of threat that kept me on guard. Not that Estelle couldn't take care of herself, of course. I recalled our first meal together in the ill-fated *Il Fagioli* when she was on the receiving end of unwanted attention.

The restaurant was a throwback to another era, with high ceilings adorned with intricate mouldings, while antique mirrors and vintage paintings adorned the walls. There was no music playing. Instead, the sound of enthusiastic conversations between guests sitting in cosy proximity on long, wooden tables, filled the air, along with the clink of cutlery on porcelain. The scents of slow-cooked stews, grilled meats and delicate herbs hit the back of my nostrils, making me salivate with hunger.

Mathéo, accompanied by a couple of waiters dressed in crisp white shirts and black waistcoats, led our group to a long table with a gap in the middle separating seasoned locals chatting away in rapid-fire French at one end from a group of tourists admiring the authenticity of the restaurant at the other. We were seated in between them.

Estelle mouthed 'sorry' across the table as it became apparent that I had again ended up being put as far away from her as possible. I had the accounts team sitting around me which meant I had to lean forward and call up the table if I was to communicate with the top team.

'Is everything OK down there, Luke?' Mathéo called down the table to me, winking, before turning to laugh with

Éliott. I said nothing but smiled politely back before shooting Estelle a look, pleading for help. She gave me a small smile and shrug which I could only interpret as 'what can I do?' Mathéo and Éliott had switched to French again and were roaring with laughter which, although I couldn't be sure, I suspected was at my expense.

I wished Estelle would have stepped forward to insist I was brought to their end of the table, instead of leaving me to field questions about which London football I supported (I didn't) from the office B team at my end. They were doing their best but the conversation was strained by both my lack of French and inability to make small talk.

Baskets of warm bread, small bowls of olives with toothpicks in them, and three small carafes of red wine were dropped off on our table by waiters who appeared to glide from one end of the restaurant to the other. This prompted Mathéo to stand up and encourage everyone to raise their glasses up high while he boomed 'Santé! To future success and new relationships.' As he said 'relationships' he shifted his gaze directly towards me and held it for a second before sitting back down, leaning into Estelle and clinking his glass against hers.

I raised my glass politely and smiled in turn at the colleagues immediately beside me, all the while keeping Estelle in my sight. She caught me watching her and sent me a signal of reassurance in return, reminding me that it would very soon be the two of us, alone to start our holiday together.

As if reading my mind, the woman beside me asked me in English where exactly in France I would be heading for my holiday. I'd forgotten I'd mentioned I was tying this visit up with a holiday in France seeing as I was here.

'I'm not sure exactly. It's an adventure,' I replied. Which was, of course, true. She looked at me with interest, expecting me to elaborate. I was struggling to think of a suitable non-committal reply when menus were being handed round by the waiting staff, buying me some more time.

'Somewhere south to start with, I think,' I continued, opening the menu, and immediately realising that I could only pick out a couple of words. It was situations like this that I wished I had Estelle by my side to help. I looked up the table to try and catch her eye when I noticed her face suddenly change from being relaxed to one of surprise and shock, followed by pushing her chair along from Mathéo with her legs to increase the gap between them. Her back was stiff, and her lips pursed. I raised my bottom off my seat and craned my neck just enough to see Mathéo's hand withdraw sheepishly from behind Estelle's lower back.

Being tactile seemed to be part of Mathéo's nature (with everyone but me, that is). His team seemed to accept this as part and parcel of who he was - slightly camp, completely disrespectful of others' boundaries, but overall safe. But there was something about Estelle's look of absolute chastisement at Mathéo that told me that she, at least, was left with no doubt that he had crossed a line.

Mathéo looked surprised and confused by Estelle's reaction. He was talking quickly, smiling nervously and, by the look of it, desperately trying to bring Estelle back into the conversation and reset the situation. I tuned my ears towards his end of the table but couldn't understand a word - it was all French. Estelle was looking around the restaurant, anywhere to avoid his eye contact, until she caught my gaze and gave me a pleading look while tapping her watch.

Watching Mathéo continue to chat away at 100mph to backtrack from his mistake, and Estelle to his left sitting bolt upright in a state of discomfort, I thought what an idiot he was. Up until that error, he was on track to finishing the day on a high. The presentations they'd provided were better than expected and, here he was, instead of impressing

Estelle with his Billy Big Bollocks act, had instead managed to piss both her, and me, off in one fell swoop.

Estelle was more than capable of handling herself, but what worried me was her tendency to go over the top. Estelle had so far gained the respect of, and endeared herself to, the whole of the Paris office and I didn't want her doing anything that might harm her reputation or position, here or within HQ. Estelle continued to stare impatiently at me, clearly ready to leave. The sight of the carafe, lit candles and serrated meat knives on the table were making me worry about the possibilities the situation could go in.

I put my menu down, stood up and stared angrily at him until he noticed.

'Is there something I can help you with?' he called down the table at me, feigning surprise that anyone might be prepared to call his behaviour out.

'Is there a problem?' I asked, surprised with my own confidence, my gaze flicking between from him to Estelle and back again. Estelle signalled a small smile of encouragement.

'No problem, here, my friend,' he replied dismissively. An air of awkwardness wafted across the rest of the group. 'Sit down,' he said making a patting motion in my direction. 'Choose something from the menu, my boy.' He laughed and turned to no one in particular to make a side remark of some sort in French and looked around the table for support. Everyone on our table, aside from Estelle, busied themselves behind their menus.

'I'm sorry, but what did you say?' I challenged, in no mood to back down. 'Firstly, if we are going to make this new relationship work, then I suggest you adapt your behaviour to show some respect. And secondly, I suggest you speak in a language that everyone around the table can understand.'

A painful minute's silence followed as Mathéo considered how to respond and the rest of the table froze in anticipation.

'What can I say?' he eventually said, releasing the tension in the air. 'I am sorry, Luke,' his words were as thick as syrup. 'Sit down and let us continue our meal. Please?' I remained standing, in no mood to waste any more time in the company of this oily man whose body language made no secret of his dislike of me.

'No, we have all we need now, and I think we can consider the business element of our visit concluded. I see no reason for us to stay any longer.' For some reason, the stiff Britishness in me came out stronger than I'd intended. I turned to the Paris office colleagues sitting immediately beside me and apologised for our early departure and thanked them for their time and hospitality.

'Do you not think you should see what your boss thinks first?' Mathéo countered, his patronising nature rising to the surface once more. He had misjudged the situation yet again though, for Estelle had already folded her napkin and was on her feet putting her jacket on.

'Thank you Mathéo,' she said to him with an air of finality. 'We will no doubt speak again soon.' She turned her back to him to heap praise on his team for their warmth and welcome. Mathéo looked stunned.

I walked around the table to similarly thank him for his time and couldn't resist adding 'we'll no doubt be in touch in a couple of months when we consider your contract renewal'. Overseas office contracts were routinely extended after their standard two-year duration unless there were any reason for concern, but I couldn't resist throwing Mathéo off his ease. He smiled falsely and thanked us for our time but looked furious. As did Éliott with Mathéo.

'What can I say?' said Mathéo defiantly. 'This is disappointing, but you have what you need. Go!'

As Estelle and I walked slowly towards the exit, side by side, smiles on our faces, I couldn't help thinking of Bonnie and Clyde. I took one look inside the restaurant from the street and saw Mathéo and Éliott exchanging cross words with each other while Mathéo was simultaneously talking into his phone held against his ear. I wondered if he was trying to feedback and defend his failure to Salter before anyone else might.

As soon as we were out of sight of the restaurant, Estelle grabbed my hand and quickened our pace, causing the wheely case that I was dragging behind me to bump loudly against the paving stones. I was almost skipping to keep up with her. Before long, we found ourselves beside the Seine, its navy/black water sparkling with the glow of streetlights. We slowed our pace to match the evening mood.

'You're not cross with me then?'

'Luke, you were brilliant,' she replied, beaming. 'I was looking forward to throwing my wine in his face but watching you get so worked up was far more fun.

'Phew!' I said, pausing against a railing to admire a river boat cruise glide into view on the river. 'I was worried you might think I overstepped my mark there.'

'You were great and have absolutely nothing to worry about, chéri,' she said, causing me to break out a sheepish smile. 'Nor does his office. They were great too, but he was a creep and deserved to let it be known.' We continued pacing forward slowly, enjoying the waves of calm that the river seemed to emit.

Estelle squeezed my hand and gave me a playful look while biting the corner of her bottom lip.

'How about we go straight back to the hotel, and you can show me you being all boss-like again?'

'But we haven't had dinner yet,' I teased, suppressing the urge to grin like the cat who got the cream.

'Fuck dinner', she giggled, pushing me against towards the riverside wall and flinging her arms around my waist and kissing me hungrily.

The holiday had most definitely started.

Chapter 29

I closed my eyes and let the shower spray jets of hot water over my face to revive my senses. Estelle seemed to have boundless energy. She was already awake, dressed, and had gone on ahead to the hotel lobby for breakfast, clearly excited for the day ahead. I, on the other hand, was still tired from yesterday's travelling and the variety of creaking doors, floors and pipes that our antiquated hotel had emitted throughout the night.

As I filled my palms with hair and body wash, I noticed the red circles around both my wrists, reminding me that it was not just the hotel's age that had kept me from sleeping. So much for me getting the chance to act boss-like. I briefly wondered if I had enough stamina to last the week ahead but dismissed the thought as quickly as it arrived.

As hot water pounded my head and shoulders, bringing short-term relief to my aches and pains inflicted from Estelle's power games, and despite my lack of sleep, and raging appetite from not having eaten anything last night, it dawned on me that I felt a lot more calm and relaxed than I had in a long time. My flashbacks and haunting memories had all but stopped and I was spending more time thinking about the future than the past. Both good signs.

By the time I was washed, dressed, and downstairs for breakfast, my energy for the day ahead had returned. I spotted Estelle as soon as I entered the breakfast hall. As always, she looked absolutely stunning. She was sitting on her own on a table for two in the corner of the room with two large ornate mirrors behind her, treating me to a view of her from every angle.

In contrast to her usual smart business attire, she was wearing a white A-line dress with small black polka dots. Her sunglasses were resting on her head, her hair wavier than usual, and still slightly damp from her morning shower.

She was reading something on her phone, and I found the way in which she was looking at it with childlike intensity, her mouth tightly shut and her dimples prominent, incredibly attractive. I put three croissants, some butter, and a small pot of honey on a plate from the self-service area and made my way towards her.

'Bonjour chérie,' I said cheerily. 'Sorry to keep you waiting.'

Estelle grinned, popped her phone into her handbag and replied with an exaggerated English 'good morning' and, reading my mind, filled my cup with coffee. 'I hope you slept well,' she added with a raise of her eyebrow, knowing full well I hadn't.

'Eventually.'

Keen to take the edge off my grumbling stomach, I bit into my croissant and sent a cloud of crumbs everywhere but my plate. Estelle giggled.

'So, what's the plan?' I asked, licking away a never-ending trail of croissant crumbs from around my lips. I still had no idea what the plan was from this point forward. Estelle had only asked me to book one night in this hotel while she had explicitly told me to leave the arrangements for the following morning onwards to her.

'Ah, Luke. Do not worry. Everything is arranged. All you need to do is finish your breakfast and relax. Our car will be here soon and then we can leave.' She was enjoying keeping me in the dark. Me, less so.

'But when are you going to tell me exactly where we're going?' I was guessing that she was going to take me to the hometown or village she'd described to me as growing up in, but she'd so far refused to confirm one way or the other. I knew her parents were no longer alive, and she'd never spoken of any other family, and I had no idea whether she owned any property in the region, so couldn't imagine what she had in store. A quiet gîte, perhaps? Or a relaxing spa hotel somewhere near the sea?

'All you have to do is sit back and enjoy the view. I have a surprise for you that I think you're going to love. Everything is arranged and you have nothing to worry about.' I wasn't actually worried about anything until she said that.

'Well, you ought to at least let me know where we're heading if I'm driving.' We hadn't discussed who would drive, but I was keen to reassert some level of boss-likeness into our partnership.

'Oh, OK,' she replied, eyebrows raised. 'I did not even know you could drive. It seems we are both going to learn a lot more about each other on this trip then,' she said mockingly. 'Well, in that case, I suppose I ought to tell you. We will need to head to the Dordogne region, and I will reveal specifics when we get there.'

I wasn't familiar with the different regions of France, but had heard of the Dordogne and was aware that it was a magnet for Brits seeking cheap property abroad (pre-Brexit at least). In my mind's eye, I painted a canvas of rolling hills covered in wildflowers and vineyards, punctuated with quaint little villages and, I think, the Dordogne River winding its way through the countryside. That was enough for now. I'd have to indulge Estelle's wish to maintain some mystery to fill in the gaps when we got there.

My curiosity remained, however, and there was something about the breadth of her dimply smile, and the sparkle in her eyes, that told me I was in for more of a surprise than she was letting on.

Chapter 30

Estelle's phone rang at full volume across the breakfast hall, causing both of us to jump. I brought my other hand to my coffee cup to steady myself while she fumbled to retrieve it from her bag.

'It's our car,' she said after hanging up. 'It's outside already.' Her eyes sparkled with excitement. 'Hurry up, Luke. Let's go and see it.' She was up and had left the table before I had a chance to reply. A bit more breakfast would have been nice, but it was impossible not to find her enthusiasm infectious.

Estelle was in the hotel parking bay with a young man in a branded polo shirt from a car hire firm, signing papers on the bonnet of a small white Renault Twingo. 'Now our holiday can officially start,' she announced, waving the papers in the air before handing them back to the bored-looking man. 'Look Luke. Isn't it perfect? I wasn't sure they'd have this model, but they do - it's a Twingo!'

I wasn't familiar with the car, nor did I share her excitement about it. It was a small two-door jobbie that looked as if it was only made for trips to the supermarket and back. I smiled to mirror hers but inside my stomach was somersaulting at the realisation that I hadn't driven for a good number of years and this model looked as if it might have trouble keeping all four wheels on the ground on the motorway. Not to mention the fact that the steering wheel was on the wrong side.

'It's lovely,' I said unconvincingly. 'Do you think it might be a bit light and lacking in power for the motorway?' I did my best to hide my nerves.

'It will be fine, Luke,' she said dismissively. 'Besides, we won't take the autoroute. It is boring. We will take the country roads. It will make the drive more scenic and interesting.'

'As long as you'll help direct me. I have no idea where we're going, remember?' Estelle rushed towards me and gave me a big hug and a kiss on the cheek before sending me back inside the hotel to fetch our bags and check out.

When I returned, Estelle was already in the passenger side, with the engine running and the satnav set. I climbed into the driver's seat, faked a confident smile, and announced, 'let the holiday begin!' I then spent a couple of minutes figuring out how to adjust the seat and familiarising myself with the controls. I could see Estelle in my side vision, staring ahead, patiently waiting for me to pull out. It was getting hot in the car, so I fiddled with the aircon temperature to make it cooler while she loosened her silk neck scarf. I wasn't sure if it was the heat or nerves that was causing beads of sweat to drip down my back. The sickly scent of the lavender car freshener hanging from the rear-view mirror wasn't helping me feel any less queasy either.

'Are you sure you wouldn't prefer me to drive,' she offered after a further minute of us remaining stationary.

'I'm fine, thank you very much.' I replied. And with that we were off. Fairly smoothly as well, though I say so myself. I responded to Estelle's directions obediently and found the quiet streets OK but was quickly overwhelmed by cars approaching from all directions as we joined the busier avenues in the heart of the city. My forearms burned from gripping the steering wheel and I was conscious that my twitchy reactions and sharp intakes of breath to the numerous hazards being thrown in my direction were making Estelle flinch. The constant cacophony of horns, exhausts, revving and people shouting at me reminded me why I had given up driving in London all those years ago. If driving in London was tough, Paris was worse. And despite my window now being fully open, I couldn't keep pace with the need to keep dabbing my forehead dry.

It therefore came with a sense of relief, and not a loss of pride when, while sitting in traffic, Estelle broke her silence to say, 'Luke, my darling. I have seen this all before. If you want me to drive so you can enjoy the view, I don't mind, you know.' It was a kind way to keep my pride intact, so I pulled over and we switched seats.

However, my relief at not having to drive was replaced with a different kind of stress as Estelle sped off, leaving my stomach behind, and causing me to grip the side of my seat with one hand and the internal door handle with the other. We swayed from side to side as we wove in and out of traffic, more like a motorbike than a small car, nipping in and out of gaps too tight for other vehicles. Estelle's driving was a complete contrast to mine. It felt more like we were sitting on a fairground rollercoaster when she took ninety-degree corners at speed without applying the brakes at any stage. The sound of drivers shouting and horns blaring filled the air as the Twingo stole road space that other drivers were too slow to occupy.

As if oblivious to the road chaos around us, Estelle was chatting away to me with a sense of calm totally at odds with her rally-style driving. She reeled off the names of cathedrals, museums, and other points of interest as we passed. Occasionally, she'd break off from being a high-speed tour guide to spit a French swear word out the window at anyone whose driving she didn't approve of. She was full of little nuggets of information, and I was enjoying listening to her speak with such passion for a city she pretended not to love. She was particularly enthusiastic when she told me about Eiffela, an art installation and mini twin replica of the Eiffel Tower that had been placed beside it earlier in the year. It was no longer there but, according to Estelle, it was only about thirty metres tall, and she'd managed to take a photo of them both in the same shot during her last visit at such an angle that made them look as if they were the same size. I'd nodded along with genuine interest, wishing she'd keep her eyes on the road rather than keep turning her head to talk to me.

Thankfully, before long, the chaos of Paris's streets was replaced with more open and straight roads that looked more industrial than residential before we steadied out to a more constant speed. It was only when I relaxed my grip on the door handle, and let my shoulders and neck relax, that I realised how tightly coiled I was.

'Destination Dordogne!' I said, pointing ahead as Paris reduced to a distant speck in the side mirror.

'Don't get too excited too soon,' she replied, turning to face me. 'We have another six hours before we reach our destination. Even if we keep going at this speed, we won't get there until early evening. Especially as I expect we'll need to stop for some lunch and a break along the way'.

'Keep your eyes on the road please,' I cautioned. 'I'm still curious to know where we're heading. Are you at least going to give me any clues?'

'Oh, but Luke. I've already given you plenty of clues! You really must pay better attention.' I liked to think I was pretty good at picking up on subtle hints and was fairly sure I hadn't missed anything. I didn't like not knowing anything about where we were heading, but Estelle looked happier and more relaxed than I had seen for a long time. We were together, away from work and happy, so what was there to stress about? I settled down to enjoy the view and resigned myself to the fact that she was in charge and I would just have to wait to find out what was in store.

We chatted all the way. First, I was treated to a beginners lesson in French to make sure I could pronounce the basics; *bonjour, au revoir, la carte s'il vous plait, du vin, merci* and counting to ten. I don't think Estelle was impressed with my attempts at pronunciation as we moved onto trying to form full sentences and, after much laughter – mainly hers - we concluded that it would be much better if Estelle did all the talking at restaurants.

We then moved on to playing 'what if'.

'What if I wasn't your boss, would you still love me?'

'Of course!'

'And what if you found out something about my past that you did not like, would you still love me no matter what?'

'No matter what!' I replied, not sure what she might be alluding to.

'What if there was something about your past you did not want people to know about, would you tell me?'

I looked at her, wondering what she might be getting at, but her face gave nothing away. 'Of course I would,' I replied, slower than I should have. 'Why, is there something in particular on your mind?'

Estelle turned took her eyes off the road for a moment to face me and said, 'No why? Is there anything you think you should tell me?'

Even after all this time, I still found her difficult to read. I sometimes wondered if she could read my mind. Was she asking me random questions for fun, or was there something behind them? Was she giving me an accusatory look, or simply leaving the door open for us to tell each other everything about ourselves and our pasts. I couldn't be sure, and before I could give it any further thought, the questions continued but this time of a more playful nature.

'What if you had to spend the rest of your life with me?'

'I can think of nothing I'd want more,' I shot back without flinching. I meant it.

'Really?'

'Yep.'

'But really, really?'

'Yep'

'Hmmmm….' she said, scrutinising my face for cracks in my confidence. 'Let's see if you still feel the same after a couple of weeks with me.'

'I won't change my mind,' I said resolutely and fixed my gaze at Estelle's profile until I saw the corners of her mouth curl upwards. Neither of us spoke for a while. We'd created a moment between us that felt perfect and needed savouring.

Despite the air conditioning, it was hot in the car. I opened the window to let a breeze circulate and was hit by the sweet aroma of lavender, mingled with a fragrant blend of wildflowers and sun-ripened fruit. I was falling in love with the French countryside. In contrast to the grey networks of motorways, cities and towns of England, here the landscape was painted with bold splashes of green, violet and amber as we passed endless fields of vibrant sunflowers and vineyards, heavy with grapes, that stretched on for miles.

Occasionally, Estelle would take her foot off the gas and cruise at a more reasonable speed as we passed through picturesque hamlets, allowing me to admire the stone cottages with their faded pastel shutters and old stone churches which even seemed to ring out with a French accent. It was so different to the grey bustling streets of London that I was used to. It was dreamlike, idyllic, a place where time moved at its own rhythm. It was one of those moments that you wish you could freeze and make it last forever.

'You like it here then?' asked Estelle, as if reading my mind.

'It's beautiful,' I replied, looking up at the tall poplar trees that lined and shaded the road we were on. 'I had no idea it would be like this.'

'I thought you would like it,' she said with a sense of satisfaction. 'So, what if we ran away together and never went back to work?' She kept her eyes on the road ahead while waiting for me to reply. Again, I wasn't sure how seriously she was asking.

'Where would we run to?' I asked.

'Anywhere,' she replied. 'And what do you think they would say if they found out we had run away together?'

'I think they'd be very surprised and would have plenty to say about it,' I replied, grinning at the thought. It wasn't something I'd considered much before. Since we got together, we had always worked on the assumption that we'd keep our private lives private and had never given much thought to what anyone else might think or say about it. I was sure that we seemed like such an unlikely scenario that the possibility of us being together wouldn't even cross others' minds. Estelle laughed out loud at the thought before briefly switching back into work persona to remind me that the question was completely hypothetical as she was sure that such a revelation would not end up well for her.

'Don't worry, Luke. I don't mean to scare you,' she said, giving my knee a reassuring squeeze. 'I have only just managed to escape this country. I have no plans to return any time soon.' I smiled, secure in the knowledge that our relationship was on more solid ground than I'd ever hoped for.

'But maybe one day, huh?' she added with a mischievously raised eyebrow.

She did like to keep me on my toes.

Chapter 31

It was nearing 18:00 but felt much later. Our final destination was, apparently, not much further. Estelle had turned the satnav off half an hour ago, proudly stating that she no longer needed it. I'd tried to figure out where we were heading by looking at the map on my phone but Estelle had snatched it away, saying she was confiscating it for the rest of our holiday to 'make sure I was fully present, break my screentime addiction and not spend the holiday staring at my phone from a different location'. I didn't feel I could argue with that.

She'd calmed the pace of the drive down to a leisurely cruise, allowing the Twingo's engine to stop screaming in pain and catch its breath. She was taking advantage of our relaxed speed to look around in a way that suggested familiarity. Her eyes darted left, right, up and down as she peered out the windows to inspect her surroundings, creating the impression she was checking everything was as it should be. I knew that the village she originated from was somewhere in this region, so guessed that was where she was aiming for, and I was itching to get out and stretch my legs.

I was tired. Again. And sore from last night. As with her driving, Estelle did not always pick up on my signals to slow down when her passion overtook my pain threshold. I couldn't find a comfy position to settle in, so had taken to shuffling restlessly from side to side. We'd stopped off for lunch a few hours ago in the *centre ville* of a pretty village we'd passed through. Tables outside, parasols creating shade, the civilised sound of clicking cutlery on plates and light conversation for background. An elderly gentleman with a wide bushy moustache and a single coffee cup in front of him looked as if he had spent all day there. I had imagined he lived the perfect life. Estelle had, very sensibly, opted for a light salade niçoise and sparkling water, whereas I might have self-indulged a tad too enthusiastically in the plat du jour, opting for a filling steak frites for mains, followed by a cheese board, all washed down with a carafe of St-Émilion red wine.

I'd been fighting the urge to doze off during the afternoon's drive. Not only would it have been unfair on Estelle, who had gallantly insisted on continuing to do all the driving, but it would have meant missing out on the passing scenery. Everything felt so much fresher, softer, more relaxed and with more variety than the same old over-familiar grey views I was used to in London. I was absolutely in love with France. The air was honeysuckle sweet, the countryside more colourful, and the bite-sized villages tucked in between gentle sloping hills and rivers each seemed to carry their own unique brand of quaint. The people I observed along the way moved differently. They seemed to carry themselves in a state of relaxed comfort in their own skin. Gone were the etched lines of stress, strain and suppressed rage that defined London's mood. It may have been a case of me seeing the world through rose-tinted French spectacles, but I imagined that any lines or wrinkles here must be the result of either smiling too much or from the sun.

And there was Estelle, of course. The deeper we got into the countryside, the happier she seemed. The angles of her cheek and jaw lines seemed to have smoothed out, and with the sight of her in a light summer dress as opposed to one of her pressed business suits, it really looked as if she'd left her COO persona in Paris. Even her voice had taken on a new lightness and musicality I hadn't heard before. It warmed me to see her looking so happy and relaxed. Her shoulders and arms flowed fluently between changing gears, handling the steering wheel, and keeping the car controls in check. Occasionally we'd catch each other's eye, and our smiles would broaden without a spoken word. It was incredible to think that it was less than three months since we first met, and yet I struggled to remember life without her.

Maybe a future living in France wasn't such a far-fetched suggestion after all.

I braced myself with one hand on the dashboard as she took a sharp right onto an unmarked road that wound its way up towards a small village on the top of a hill that appeared to consist almost entirely of sandstone-coloured houses with pointy terracotta roofs.

'We are nearly here,' Estelle whispered, leaning in towards me as if fearful someone would hear us.

'Is this the village you're from? The one you once told me about?' I asked.

'Yes,' she replied, still whispering. 'This is it. Lusignac.' She spoke the word with an emphasis that suggested it should mean something more. I did not know what. 'I have not been back here for some time now.'

She put the car in second gear and slowed down to a crawl as we passed the first house of the village. Her eyes continued to dart from left and right as if she was looking for something specific.

'It's very pretty,' I observed, admiring the blue shutters and rows of colourful outdoor plants in pots outside the first house.

'It is also very quiet and sleepy,' she replied, as we passed what appeared to be some sort of outdoor café or restaurant with a deserted seating area. A middle-aged woman wearing an apron and headscarf was sitting in the doorway to the house immediately adjoining the area. Her head followed the movement of our car while her eyes widened with curiosity. She stood up from her chair, perhaps in hopeful expectation that we would be her first guests of the evening, but Estelle cruised past.

'Haha. Nosey as ever, I see,' Estelle muttered to herself as we paused at a stop sign before a T-junction.

'Are we nearly there yet?' I asked, mimicking a restless child.

'It is just round the corner,' she replied, eyes fixed on the road ahead 'You won't have to wait much longer for your surprise.' We took another right turn. 'In fact, you can almost see it from here.' I still had no idea what sort of place we might be staying at.

'It looks very residential round here. I'm guessing you've booked an Airbnb somewhere?'

'Oh, Luke,' she laughed, tipping her head back. 'Better than that. We still have our house here.' She bit the corner of her bottom lip playfully.

'We?' I asked, my face screwed up in confusion.

'Well, I did say I had a surprise for you.' Her eyes were twinkling with playfulness. That same mischievous twinkle I was never sure would lead to fun or danger.

'Don't worry, Luke,' she said, pulling over onto a grass verge at the edge of the village outside a farmhouse with large double-fronted wooden doors on the outside with two small hearts carved into the top. 'We've arrived.'

She switched the engine off, took a deep breath and stared at the house silently, expressionless, her hands resting loosely on the steering wheel. I couldn't put my finger on it, but there was something about the situation – or location – that gave me a chill. Estelle's stillness and silence reminded me just how unpredictable she could be at times. Love her as I did, I was not comfortable with this side of her. Surprises were not really my thing.

'Er...shall we get out?' I suggested.

'Just one minute,' she murmured, continuing to stare ahead.

The vista from the edge of this small village was idyllic. The road ahead was clear, the view to the left led the eye down a tree-lined slope and the houses on the other side of the road were covered in a mix of climbing ivy and bougainvillaea. It was so different to anything I knew; I felt

I was on the other side of the world rather than 600 miles away from my Bethnal Green flat.

Suddenly, making me jump, Estelle's hands shot back from the steering wheel as she bounced back and forth in her seat, beaming with delight at the sight of a young woman approaching us from around the side of the farmhouse.

It took me a few seconds to process and accept what was before my eyes as I saw a young woman, waving at us with both arms in the air while calling out Estelle's name.

'Estelle, jumelle,' the young woman called as she moved closer to our car.

'Giselle, jumelle,' Estelle called back through the open window, beaming.

I stared in disbelief, aware that my jaw was hanging open, as Estelle flung herself out of the car and ran towards Giselle with her arms outstretched. My reality switched to dreamlike slow motion as I watched them embrace each other affectionately, both rolling themselves up on their tiptoes and rocking from side to side in glee. It was like stepping through the looking glass into some sort of alternate universe that left me not only with questions but questioning everything.

How could she not have told me that she had a twin sister? And an identical one at that. I was sure I couldn't have missed her mention something as significant as this. Could I?

I was mesmerised, amused and unnerved by the sight of them. They were the same height, had the same kinks in same places in their sleek dark brown hair, and were even wearing almost identical dresses aside from the fact that Giselle's was black with white polka dots whereas Estelle's was white with black.

After some squeals of delight and an exchange of words I didn't understand, they eventually broke their embrace and squeezed each other's shoulders before turning to face me with identical dimpled smiles.

'Well don't just sit there,' Estelle called. 'Come and say hello!'

Chapter 32

Fumbling with the door handle, I managed to stumble out of the car. My legs wobbled as I made my way towards them, almost tripping myself up as I walked the short distance to where they were standing. I cursed myself for turning into such a clumsy, tongue-tied goof. Estelle and Giselle exchanged amused smiles as they stood patiently, appearing to enjoy my every movement.

'Bonjour Giselle,' I said, extending my hand.

They both laughed disproportionately hard, and Giselle turned and said something in fast-paced nasal French to Estelle which I couldn't catch. I wished I'd bothered to learn at least a few words before this trip.

Giselle brushed my awkwardness, and my outstretched hand, aside, flung both arms around me and gave me a tight hug which made me squeak. I could feel her hands on my back, locking me in position while her warm firm breasts spread themselves against my chest. I looked helplessly over her shoulder towards Estelle, who was clearly enjoying watching my state of discombobulation.

'Hello Luke. Welcome to Lusignac and our humble home. It's fantastic to finally meet you.' Giselle said in carefully pronounced English, much to my relief. Her accent and rhythm carried the exact same speech pattern as Estelle. 'I've heard a lot about you.' This immediately got me wondering how. None of Estelle's emails ever carried any information of a personal nature, let alone mention me. I sometimes forget that some people still talk by phone.

'Well, it's lovely to meet you too,' I managed once she relaxed her squeeze on me, releasing the scent of fresh lavender and baby powder as she stepped back. 'And what a lovely surprise this is too,' I added, mirroring their amused smiles as I looked from one to the other of them.

Estelle stepped forward to stroke my arm, possibly to reassure me that everything was OK, possibly to reassert her status with me, while Giselle stood back, inspecting me up and down. There were smiles all round. 'See. Surprises can be fun,' Estelle said triumphantly. 'Why don't you bring our luggage from the car, and we'll see you inside?'

That suited me. I needed a minute to get my head round what was before me and figure out what I was feeling. Shock? Surprise? Amusement? Something else? I wasn't sure, but a whirlpool of emotions flooded my thoughts that needed defragmentation and reordering to restore calm. I found it almost unfathomable that the one woman who I'd fallen so deeply for, who was so unique in character, beauty, and passion for life, could have a complete replica that I knew nothing of. They turned and walked slowly towards the house, their hips and bottoms moving at the same height and in time with each other. Estelle turned and blew me a kiss as they disappeared behind the front door.

The house was impressive. It had a tall stone façade with small, box-shaped windows, framed with duck egg-coloured shutters at the top. A row of window boxes sat in a line outside of the front of the house containing bright red begonias. Or were they geraniums? I could never remember. I carried our luggage to the door and paused before pushing the door open, feeling a need to remind myself that this situation was real, not a dream, and that I needed to make a good impression to them both. First impressions last forever.

The entrance to the house was cool and dark. I put our luggage down on the flagstones at the bottom of the winding wrought iron staircase on the assumption that I'd need to take them upstairs later. The only sound in the hallway came from a tall mahogany grandfather clock that tick-tocked soothingly and sent rippling echoes to the top of the high ceilings. From the back of the house came the sound of Estelle and Giselle chattering away at fast pace. It was impossible to tell their voices apart from sound alone and I only guessed that they were both speaking, rather than just one of them, from the pauses left between sentences which hinted at the fact it was an exchange rather than a monologue.

I followed the sound down the corridor towards an ornate, wood-panelled door and pushed it open. Estelle and Giselle were both standing in the middle of a large, high-ceilinged kitchen with a thick wooden table in its centre. A variety of different shaped copper-bottomed pots hung from suspended hooks above the table. They both stopped talking and turned their heads towards me as I entered. Estelle was holding a tall glass of what looked like sparkling water with a slice of lemon bobbing about on top, while Giselle was holding a large bowl-shaped wine glass with a modest amount of red wine swirling around its bottom.

'Come in. Sit down,' Giselle gestured to an empty wooden seat with arms at the end of the table. 'What can I get you to drink?' she offered holding her glass up. 'Some wine, perhaps?'

'Or if you need the bathroom to freshen up first, you can find it on the left at the top of the stairs,' Estelle interjected.

'I'm fine, thank you. And...' I sat down and turned to Giselle. 'a glass of wine would be lovely, thanks.'

I folded my hands in my lap, partly out of politeness and partly because it had become habit to hold on to and shield my stump of a third finger when feelings of social awkwardness returned. Questions were still racing around my head, but not settling fast enough for me to think of something sensible to initiate a conversation. The ridiculous 'So how long have you been twins then?' kept pushing its way to the forefront of my thoughts, so I maintained my silence and smiled sweetly while Giselle went to the corner of the kitchen to pour me some wine.

My eyes flicked between the two of them, taking in every detail. They must surely have coordinated their complementary contrasting dresses together. It was too much of a coincidence. The pair of them looked so polished, so full of effortless chic, in their polka dots. In the corner of my eye, I could see that Giselle was watching me as she removed the resting cork from the top of a bottle and poured me a measure of wine twice the size of hers. I glanced up in her direction and caught her big brown eyes twinkling at me in the same way as Estelle's did and, judging from the way she was keeping her lips pursed together, she seemed to be suppressing the size of her smile if the prominence of dimples were anything to go by. Estelle took a few steps around the table, reaching out to trail her hand across the front of a kitchen cabinet as she moved, looking around wistfully.

'The kitchen looks so different now,' Estelle said as she stared wide-eyed at the six-ring stainless steel range gas cooker against the far wall. It was certainly a big step up from the ceramic hob in my Hackney flat.

'Well, the whole kitchen needed a refit, didn't it?' Giselle replied, nonchalantly. 'It was completely unfit for purpose before.' She turned and made her way towards me, her eyes on the full glass of red wine she was carrying.

It was impossible not to make comparisons between them both. I played a quick mental game of spot the difference as Giselle approached. Her hips moved with the same twist as Estelle as she placed one flat pump shoe in front of the other. Her waist was similarly slender, although her hips carried more of a curve that created slightly more movement as each foot touched the floor. Her calves were more muscular and defined, hinting at the fact she spent more time on her feet than Estelle. Her breasts were slightly fuller and looked as if they were being restrained by her dress. Her face, although at first glance a precise replica of Estelle, was softer with fewer of the sharp angles around her cheekbones and jawline that Estelle carried, and her skin tone carried more colour, no doubt a result of the warmer outdoor environment. They were similar, not identical, twins.

That said, there were enough facial similarities between the two of them for me to convince myself that Giselle carried all the memories and knowledge that Estelle did. That she might know as much about me already as Estelle. Most unnerving of all, was the way in which Giselle looked at me. Her eyes contained the same enigmatic energy. They were warm, inviting, cheeky and gave off an air of us sharing a secret conversation together; almost as if she could read my mind.

However, although visually similar, there was no sign that Giselle could, or would want to, step into the sort of senior corporate role that Estelle had. I wondered what past events had led them to end up living such different lives. Whatever prompted Estelle to leave this house and its idyllic surroundings for a life in London? Giselle was standing squarely in front of me when I realised I was staring. I looked away, embarrassed, as she put my glass down on the table.

'Voilà,' she said before spinning around and pulling Estelle back towards her. 'To family!' She picked her glass up and raised it above her head. They hugged each other again, each being careful to hold their glass out carefully behind the other's back. 'It's good to see you again, jumelle,' Giselle declared. They squeezed and released each other a few times before gleefully taking seats side by side at the table.

I sat forward, resting my hands on the table, still careful to conceal my stumpy finger, and attempted to crack my shell of awkwardness with some conversation. 'So, apologies if I look a little in shock, but you do know I had absolutely no idea where we were heading for our holiday, let alone that Estelle was going to introduce me to a twin sister I knew nothing about?' I directed my question to Giselle, and held my glass towards my mouth, taking in its rich fruity scent. Estelle rocked back in her chair laughing, still delighted at having been able to surprise me on this scale. 'There aren't any more of you are there?' I added, pleased with myself at being able to inject more humour so coolly.

'Oh, she is very naughty,' Giselle replied, resting her hand on Estelle's knee. 'How could you not tell this fine catch of a man about your beautiful twin sister? Since when did I become a secret, hmm?' Giselle shot me a glance that looked like another shared secret.

Estelle leaned into Giselle affectionately, resting her head on her shoulder. 'Not a secret, jumelle, just a surprise.' Estelle looked up at her sister with doe eyes. 'You know how funny some people can be about twins. Some people might think we're weird.'

'I know how funny some twins can be about twins,' Giselle replied, and they both burst into another round of laughter. 'Anyway, I think a lot of people round here would say that one of us is enough, let alone two.' Hysterics followed as if they were the ones with a shared secret now.

'Well, I don't think it's at all weird,' I reassured once their laughter had died down. 'Perhaps a little strange not to have been told before, but it really is lovely to meet you.' I meant it and raised my glass again towards Giselle and was rewarded with the clink of both of their glasses in return. 'Besides, who thinks twins are weird anyway?'

'Only the rest of the village,' Estelle snapped back. 'That is why I moved away more than two years ago. This is my first time back since then. They are not very accepting of us.'

'Why's that?' I asked. I couldn't recall ever having met identical twins before. I'd perhaps passed a few on the street but that was it. They made me curious rather than think of them as weird.

'This is a very small village with very small minds in it,' Giselle sighed.

'It is very conservative and traditional. They don't like anything out of the ordinary here,' Estelle added.

'Or strong women who are prepared to be different and stand up for themselves,' Giselle said flexing her arm in a jokey display of strength.

Estelle tipped her head back and laughed again. 'It probably didn't help that we were made to dress the same,' she added, frowning.

'And have our hair arranged in the same loose braid ponytails,' Giselle added.

'Or the way we used to walk to school in step together.'

'Or pretend to be each other to confuse the teachers.'

'Or finish each other's sentences.'

I found myself giggling as my head turned alternately between the two of them as if I was watching a game of tennis. This break was going to be more fun than I thought!

'Yes. If anyone around here thinks twins are weird, I think we only have ourselves to blame,' Giselle concluded, laughing again. The laughter went from mono to stereo as Estelle started up again. It was going to be a long evening.

I sipped my wine, taking in the rich creamy cherry flavours, while Estelle and Giselle exchanged quick-fire questions and answers about Estelle's job, Giselle's new kitchen, what London was like, how the garden was coming on, which places Estelle had so far visited in London, and how the drive down from Paris had been. I was grateful that they were both polite enough to stick to English, which they were both extremely efficient in and which made the situation more comfortable for me. Aside from their subtle differences, it was like watching mirror images at play, and their voices were almost indistinguishable from each other. Occasionally, they'd slip into fast-paced French for a sentence or two which I guessed was when they were either talking about me, or something they didn't want me to understand, as it was invariably followed by them glancing in my direction and laughing.

Realising that my glass was nearly empty, and to bring myself back into the conversation, I complimented its flavour and asked which wine it was, as if I might be familiar with the answer. 'Saint Émilion,' Giselle replied, pronouncing the words as if they were one. 'It is less than an hour from here,' she said casually as if everyone sources the world's best wines from their doorstep. 'Let me get you some more,' she offered.

'Not at the moment, thanks,' I said, realising that my head was already buzzing. 'But would you mind if I smoke?'

'Not in the house,' Giselle replied. 'I like to keep the house fresh and free from fire risks.' More laughter between them which carried a certain menace as I recalled my first date with Estelle. We still hadn't spoken about what really happened that night. I wondered if she'd ever spoken to Giselle about it.

Giselle, possibly sensing my unease, stood up and smoothed her dress down with her hands from her waist to her thighs. 'Why don't I show you to your room and give you a chance to freshen up and then we can move into the garden together for the evening?'

Estelle, answering on my behalf, stood up beside Giselle and said, 'That sounds like an excellent idea. Thank you, Gigi.'

'Come on then, Stella,' Giselle said as they linked arms and marched out of the kitchen, in step, like a couple of giggly girls preparing for a sleepover. Giselle again looked me up and down suggestively as if I was either on inspection parade or for dinner. I followed them out the kitchen and upstairs, picking our luggage up on the way while they ran up ahead.

The house was simple but stunning, with beams of sunlight streaming across the stairway through a small window at the top that lit up floating dust motes, and small scenic paintings of what looked like local landmarks on the walls on the way up. As I lugged our luggage up the last few steps, Giselle was waiting for me on the landing with a look of formality, while Estelle wandered wistfully into the room to the left of her. She pointed out each room to me with the same indifference that an estate agent trying to sell a house might. Main bathroom and toilet at the end of the corridor. The spare room at the back of the house, next to the bathroom, had a spare bed and some armchairs in it which was mainly used as a quiet space for reading these days. And to the right of Giselle was her bedroom which, she was careful to emphasise, *'...is never locked, so don't make the mistake of entering the wrong bedroom at the end of the evening.* She raised her left eyebrow suggestively in exactly the same way that Estelle might.

Was she teasing or flirting with me? Or testing me to see my response? My face must have betrayed my thoughts because she saw fit to lean into me and add *'...and I know what you're thinking, you cheeky boy,'* before stepping into the room to the left to join Estelle. My face flushed as I did indeed wonder if she knew what I was thinking and, with that suggestion planted firmly in my mind, left me thinking of nothing else.

I followed Giselle into the bedroom to see Estelle with her back to us, staring out of the window at the back of the room onto the garden, which was lined with treetops surrounding an open, sloping meadow that was littered with an array of colourful wildflowers. The garden looked as if it took care of itself and was a complete contrast to mine. There was a large bed in the middle of the room with a small pile of clean towels at its foot, a chest of drawers with a candelabra and clock, and a wardrobe in the corner. I put the luggage down, out of the way, against the wall.

'Ok,' Giselle said, clapping her hands together. 'I'll leave you two lovebirds to settle in. The wardrobe is empty and has some hangers for your clothes and I'll see you in the garden when you're ready. I prepared a cold dinner as I wasn't sure what time you'd get here so we can eat whenever you are ready.' And with that, she left, tweaking my arm playfully on the way past and commenting to Estelle, *'you've found herself a good one here'*.

Estelle responded with a muted 'Yes, jumelle. You're right. I have.' But Giselle had already left and I'm not sure that she heard her. Estelle looked around the room subdued, as if the day's driving had suddenly caught up with her.

'This is lovely, chérie,' I said, giving her a gentle hug. 'Such a beautiful house. I still can't believe I've known you for three months and you didn't even tell me you had a twin.'

She smiled wearily at me, her energy clearly waning from the excitement of the day. 'There is a lot you don't know about me Luke, but this break will give us a chance to get to know each other properly on some neutral ground.' My heart was skipping with joy at her words. This break was not just a break but a chance for us to deepen our bond with each other. To take our relationship to the next level. I wasn't sure about this being the neutral ground Estelle suggested, but I took her to mean away from work, which it was. Thoughts of Effective Solutions and of the recent events with Peter were distant memories already.

'I'm glad you like it here though.' Estelle added. 'And don't take too much notice of Giselle's teasing. She has been curious to meet you ever since I first told her about you.'

'Really?' I replied as coolly as I could manage. 'Well, I can see that she's obviously a big part of your life, so I'm looking forward to getting to know her as well.' I blushed involuntarily. 'Anyway, shall we freshen up and go back downstairs and join her for a cigarette and something to eat?' I added, hoping that my flushed cheeks had gone unnoticed.

It was strange, but the fact that Giselle was so similar to Estelle meant that I had felt the same butterflies in the pit of my stomach as I did when I first met Estelle. And similarly, when Giselle had joked with me about her room not being locked, I had felt the breath leave my body while my knees went weak. I had also tried my best not to imagine it, but I hadn't been able to resist wondering whether they looked as similar together naked as they did clothed.

Which, when I think about it, and despite what I said about twins not being weird, is actually a bit weird.

Chapter 33

'Take your time, chéri,' Estelle called through the bathroom door while I was stripped to the waist giving myself a half-body wash over the sink. 'I will see you in the garden. Straight through the conservatory at the back of the kitchen, OK?'

'OK chérie!' I replied, giving some oomph to my French pronunciation. Keen not to be left out for long, I quickly brushed my teeth, smoothed some oil over the unruly waves in my hair and sprayed some Dior Sauvage on my neck. I took the stairs two at a time, swinging myself round the wrought iron banister rail as I reached the bottom. I paused to check my reflection in a decorative mirror in the hallway, almost not recognising the fresh-faced, clean-cut, success of a man looking back at me. Gone was the ponytailed, unwashed, geek of the past. I had finally come into my own.

I opened the kitchen door and was immediately attuned to the sound of Estelle and Giselle laughing from beyond the open window. As I crossed the kitchen to make my way outside, the movement of an unshaven man wearing a short silk female dressing gown that could have done with being a bit longer caught my eye. His feet dragged as he shuffled forwards with a full glass of red wine sloshing back and forth precariously in one hand and a folded newspaper in the other. His eyes were dulled and the chest hairs poking through the opening of his gown carried the same mix of salt and pepper as his unshaven face. His long skinny legs, covered with a layer of black wiry hair, brought to mind an image of an ostrich.

'Bonsoir,' I greeted confidently.

'Ello,' slurred the man with what sounded like a disinterested and gruff south London accent. I noticed the English tabloid in his hand and immediately felt foolish for my salutation. The feeling that I'd stepped into some weird kind of wonderland returned. Mr Ostrich Legs turned his back on me and took a couple of large glugs of wine, causing his gown to lift up as he raised his elbow. I decided to head to the garden.

'Good evening,' I announced, stepping towards a large wooden table that sat underneath a sprawling oak tree that provided a natural canopy and cast a dappled set of shadows across the table. The early evening sun filtered through the leaves creating a serene ambiance. The air carried the sweet fragrance of evening jasmine releasing its scent. At the centre of the table were Estelle and Giselle, now both wearing matching pale blue cardigans over their dresses, the day's remaining sunlight lighting up their faces as they finished their exchange in French.

'Wow,' said Giselle, standing up. 'Someone has made an effort.' She again looked me up and down without shame. 'Nice shirt,' she added, her eyes twinkling in the sun, successfully turning my already flushed cheeks bright scarlet. Estelle stifled a smile.

'And may I say how lovely you both look this evening,' I replied, attempting to deflect attention off myself. 'And this all looks fantastic,' I added, gesturing towards the food. A feast for both the eyes and palate was laid out before us. Giselle, unlike Estelle who was always happy to leave food preparation to me, clearly carried the culinary artistry gene out of the two of them. A platter of thinly sliced French baguette, accompanied by an array of inviting cheeses of differing shapes and colours, beckoned. Delicate bowls of olives marinated in fragrant herbs, and jewel-toned cherry tomatoes that glistened like edible gems. To the right of them was a large wooden serving board with prosciutto, salami, and chorizo, arranged with precision. If the Darling Buds of May was set in France, I imagined it would look something like this.

'This looks amazing,' I said, a lump of happiness forming in my throat. 'Thank you. I hope we haven't put you to any trouble.'

'Trouble? This is not trouble. This is normal. Anyway, it has been a long time since I saw my sister.' They squeezed each other's hands and exchanged dimpled smiles. Giselle passed me a fresh glass of Saint Emillion and we settled down to fill our plates over light conversation.

The situation was so dream-like, I had almost forgotten to mention it, but I asked if Giselle knew she had a strange man in her kitchen. She rolled her eyes and gave a shrug of despair before answering. I noticed that neither of them spoke without giving the other a quick glance for reassurance or warning.

'Oh, that is Steve, my completely fucking useless partner. For now.' I couldn't help snigger at Giselle's casual swearing. 'I am sorry, Luke, I should have introduced you, but you haven't missed much.'

I jumped as, without making any effort to move, Giselle called out his name, sending shockwaves through the peaceful evening air, before ordering him to tidy himself up and come and be social for half an hour. I think I heard a grunt of acknowledgement from somewhere within the house. I wondered if Estelle was as capable of reaching such volume as Giselle. I had never heard her shout. My ears were still ringing when Giselle and Estelle reverted to their more eardrum-friendly level of conversation.

A few minutes later, Steve shuffled his way into the garden, glass in one hand, bottle in the other, with all the manner of Jack Nicholson in the final scenes of One Flew Over the Cuckoo's Nest. I was pleased to see that Steve had found some jeans and a shirt to wear.

'Steve, this is Luke, Estelle's partner. And this is Estelle beside me, if you hadn't already figured that out for yourself.' Giselle's sass made me giggle. 'Luke, Estelle, this is Steve, my current partner.' She emphasised the word current.

'Pleased to meet you,' said Estelle with a polite smile and small wave from across the table.

'Hi Steve. Pleased to meet you.' I said, forgoing the handshake. 'Whereabouts in England are you from?' As a fellow Englishman I felt obliged to show some level of interest.

'Nicetomeetyou,' he replied. His eyes were empty, incapable of focusing. He was clearly a man of few words.

An awkward silence followed while we refilled our plates. In doing so, Steve managed to drop a hunk of cheese between his legs as it fell off the piece of bread he was shoving into his mouth. In his attempt to dust off crumbs, he inadvertently splashed wine down the right side of his shirt. Estelle smiled sympathetically, the way someone does when they're glad it's not them embarrassing themselves, while Giselle stared frostily at him, her nose and lip curled upwards in total disgust.

'Have you got no self-control?' Giselle snapped at Steve. 'You are disgusting!' Estelle and I looked down at our plates to avoid being drawn in. 'Take your plate and take your wine and get out of my sight until you are sober!'

Estelle shielded her face from Giselle's view and pulled a face in my direction to signal the cringe-worthiness of the situation. Steve fumbled some more food on his plate and shuffled off towards a reclining deckchair in a shadowed corner of the garden, leaving Giselle muttering out loud to herself.

*Click. 'You disgust me!' echoed the distant voice from my past, accompanied with the memory of a spray of **her** spittle in my face, causing those standing in our vicinity in the pub to either turn away with embarrassment or stare unashamedly at the free entertainment. 'Why are you so weak?' **she** snarled. My only crime had been to follow*

Salter's instruction to pay compliantly for the round of drinks that he had just ordered for everyone. I'd thought it might bring me – us – into the fold a bit easier, but all it seemed to achieve was more humiliation and isolation. 'You should't be spending money on drinks that he's ordered,' she spat. 'You should be keeping that money to spend on me!' The words reverberated around my head like a ghost floating round the rooms of a locked house, trying to escape. I took a deep breath, slammed the lid shut on my ghosts and opened my eyes to the present. Click.

I looked up to see Estelle's big brown eyes looking across the table at me, her eyebrows crinkled up with concern as if asking if I was OK. I nodded to signal that I was. I could no longer allow the past to taunt me.

'I am so sorry,' Giselle said while shaking her head in annoyance. 'Believe it or not, he was quite a catch when I first met him.' She uttered the words through pursed lips. 'Interesting, intelligent, humorous.' Giselle sipped on her wine as Estelle and I listened attentively. 'Apparently, he used to run a book shop in the south of England. Used to sell books in the local market here every Sunday. Used to do a lot of things.' She put her glass down so she could gesticulate more freely with her hands. 'Good for nothing now!' She turned her head to watch as Steve collapsed into the deckchair. 'Now he spends all day drunk and doing nothing!' She shook her head to herself, prompting Estelle to do the same.

'Anyway,' she continued. 'It was foolish of me to think that he would be capable of anything at this time of day. Please. I am sorry for any embarrassment.' She rested her hand on Estelle's arm, and I saw the twinkle return to her eyes as she turned her attention to me. 'Let me get to know your fine new man better.'

'These olives are delicious,' I said, still keen to deflect attention off myself.

'He is adorable!' Giselle declared to Estelle; their dimpled smiles returned. 'Tell me again how you met?' And with that, I was free to sit back, enjoy the food and watch as the two most beautiful women in the world caught up with each other.

I was careful not to be seen to drink my wine too quickly for fear of being seen as another one of those 'alcoholic Englishmen' that Giselle kept talking about, so left my glass a third full and politely excused myself to stretch my legs and go for that last cigarette of the day. Giselle suggested I offer Steve one so 'he can blow himself up with all that alcohol in his body'.

I walked tall and slow, aware that both Estelle and Giselle would be watching me from behind until I found myself standing beside an unresponsive Steve in his deckchair. I paused, momentarily captivated by the serenity of the view. The garden, being the last of a row of houses, rolled endlessly downhill. The fragrance of jasmine lingered in the air and the sound of crickets provided the perfect backing rhythm for the peaceful setting. The scene was a picture of beauty, unlike the slouched pile of human despair in the deckchair in front of me.

His face was bloated, he was breathing heavily, and his untucked shirt seemed to have collected a few more stains since he left the table. A near empty bottle of red wine was propped up alongside the side of the deckchair.

'Evening again,' I said to gain his attention.

Steve, barely able to lift his head, mumbled something that might have been a groan of acknowledgement. It might have just been a groan. His eyes showed no sign of recognition.

'How are you doing?' I asked.

He shuffled into a more upright position and shook his head and spluttered without saying anything. I took a cigarette out and lit it, the orange glow of its embers glowing against the background of the deepening hues in the sky.

'Looks like you've had a heavy day. Smoke?' I offered, pushing a cigarette out of the box and holding it towards him.

He raised his hand, grabbing at the air a couple of times before giving up. 'Nah, you're alright mate. I've had enough of everything for one night.'

'Fair enough,' I replied, turning my attention to watching the sun going down while exhaling swirls of smoke into the evening air. I looked back towards Estelle and Giselle sitting side by side in their polka dot dresses and matching cardigans, rocking back and forth in conversation as they lingered over the remnants of their evening.

'Luke, is it?' came a sound from the deckchair. I looked round to see Steve sitting upright, his eyes now sharply focussed on me, and an amused smile on his face.

'That's right,' I replied, turning my back on him to watch the sun setting.

'You didn't know Estelle had a twin, did you?' He let out an unhealthy wheezy chuckle as he spoke. I decided not to reply. He was drunk and, like most drunks, was becoming annoying quickly. I took another long drag on my cigarette and looked round in annoyance at him. To my surprise, his eyes were still fixed on me with a concerted look of concentration. He picked up his glass from the grass and knocked back its remains with a distasteful suck of his purple teeth and said, 'If you didn't even know she had a twin, you're in for a few more surprises yet, mate!'

Then, as if the effort of dropping that cliffhanger had drained all his remaining coherence, he closed his eyes and threw his head back into the deckchair, signalling the conversation was over.

Chapter 34

When I returned to the table, Estelle was leaning into Giselle, telling her all about Effective Solutions, her big eighth floor office with panoramic views of central London rooftops, her ambitions, the people. As she started describing the office politics and personalities, Giselle nodded along attentively, while keeping her twinkly eyes fixed on me as I took the seat opposite. Her eyes followed my every movement as I put some more grapes, cheese and crackers on my plate. Even as I popped an olive in my mouth, I could see her eyes following my hand to my mouth and back to the table as if we had started playing some sort of unspoken game. I would have felt uncomfortable if it wasn't for the fact that she looked so similar to Estelle, I could be fooled into thinking that I already knew her. I had to consciously remind myself that, despite the visual familiarity, I didn't know anything about her yet. Not. One. Bit. And that, up until a few hours ago, I didn't even know of her existence. The fact that Estelle had chosen not to mention her to me until now also reminded me that I still had a way to go before I could really say I knew Estelle. In one sense, my introduction to Giselle was like being welcomed into something special. In another, I was left feeling that a haunting loneliness loomed in the background.

A sheepish grin crept onto my face as I realised Estelle was talking about how much I'd helped her settle into her role, what a rock I was to her, and how much my feeding her inside information about the workings of the firm had helped her. She described me as *'invaluable as well as adorable'* and told Giselle about the daily notes and background briefing packs I used to put together for her before every meeting. I felt my cheeks heat up and flush, causing Giselle to giggle. Playing it cool, I busied myself with my food, squashing a sliver of soft blue sheep's cheese onto a cracker and popping it into my mouth along with a grape, creating a refreshing creamy aromatic crunch, all the time, while I avoided looking at her directly, I could see Giselle's eyes continue to follow my every movement.

After a while, the spotlight of the conversation moved towards Giselle who, very unenthusiastically, described recent life in the village. Now it was me who could not take my eyes of her. Watching this living, breathing, carbon copy of Estelle exist side by side with her was fascinating; almost unbelievable. Her lips moved with the exact same pout and curl for emphasis as Estelle's when she spoke; although perhaps slightly more relaxed and at ease with herself. Her dimples appeared and disappeared with each broadening of her smile, as she described each day in the village being very much the same as the last. She referenced the names of people who ran the restaurant and coffee shop and was apologetic about the fact that she didn't have any gossip to share other than what she'd managed to grow in the garden over the hotter-than-usual summer. She played down her news in comparison to Estelle's by reporting that her highlight was, apparently, the higher-than-average yield of plums and figs from the garden.

A calm washed over me as they chattered away, as much with their hands as with their voices. Their melodic voices soothed me, blowing away the oppressive dark cloud of tension that I had felt standing next to Steve a few minutes before. I sat back and soaked up the scene, feeling under no pressure to participate, other than to give the occasional smile or nod of appreciation. I was happy. Happier than I had been for as long as I could remember. Watching them interact with such grace was sheer poetry personified and I found myself slipping into a dreamlike state as I tried to take it all in.

Giselle, perhaps sensing my increasing detachment, gently raised her voice and shifted her position to sit back from leaning into Estelle so she could address both of us more equally.

'Anyway, you know what this village is like,' she continued. 'Nothing ever happens here, and nothing changes here. You have no idea how bored I am!' Her last statement was accompanied with a facial gesture in the direction of the garden that Steve was still slumped in.

'Oh, it is not that bad,' Estelle dismissed. 'I seem to remember there was always something going on when I was here. It just happens at a different pace, that's all. What did you always tell me, Gigi? Life is what you make it?'

'Hmph!' pouted Giselle, poking her bottom lip out towards Estelle. 'That is easy for you to say with your new London life.' She sounded more playful than bitter. 'Perhaps I should come to London and get myself a job and a good-looking Englishman to go with it?' More smiles and laughter. However, I couldn't help but notice that while Giselle was rocking fluidly from side to side, Estelle's back stiffened. The dynamic between them was difficult to read and I wondered if one of them was more dominant than the other growing up. Or now.

Giselle, perhaps picking up on my wandering mind, turned her attention to me. 'And what about you, Luke?' she asked. 'What are your first impressions of Lusignac?' They both looked at me expectantly.

'Well, from what little I have seen of it so far, it looks idyllic.' They stared back at me in silence, expecting more, forcing me to make a defensive-sounding squeak of a laugh. They remained motionless. 'Very quiet and peaceful. To be honest, I had no idea the French countryside was so beautiful, but I haven't seen enough of it to form an opinion yet. I'm still taking it all in, including the pair of you, but the house, garden and everything looks amazing.' I must have said the right thing because simultaneous smiles of approval beamed back at me.

'So you think you could get used to it here?' Giselle asked, while Estelle's back straightened further.

'Who knows?' I replied evasively, popping another grape into my mouth. 'Maybe we could have a proper look around while we're here? It seems like a lovely place. Anyway...' I continued, '...I'd be interested to hear more about you two. Did you always live here? What was it like? Who was the naughty one growing up?' I was being nosy, but I was still curious to know everything about them as well as move the conversation away from me.

They paused to exchange a knowing look before taking turns to fill me in on their life growing up in the house together. Giselle revealed that their mother was French and their father was German. Their mother, I was told, was known for her singing in the local 'église' but had died sadly just after they had started school. They mostly knew of her from old photographs, hazy memories and stories from others. She was, according to neighbours, extremely beautiful and was always immaculately presented. They told me, in a very matter-of-fact way - presumably because they had been so young when she passed - that their father never really recovered from the loss of his beautiful wife. He ended up shunning his previous church attendance in favour of seeking solace in the depths of endless wine bottles. They alternated sentences between them as they relayed the story to me.

As their father increasingly withdrew into himself, the twins were left to bring each other up, getting themselves ready for school, preparing food to eat and making sure they did their own homework while their father sat slumped in his armchair at all hours. Until one morning, during their mid-teens they had come downstairs to find he wouldn't wake up and had taken his last sleep. It could have sounded quite tragic if it weren't for the fact that both Giselle and Estelle didn't seem to show any emotion for the series of events, saying that they didn't really notice the difference after his death as he'd checked out from living years before, when their mother had died.

'Typical!' Giselle declared at volume. 'What is it with men in this house being useless?' she said, attracting a scornful look from Estelle.

I also learnt that Giselle was the slightly older one of the two (by half an hour) and that their mother had named them and chosen Estelle and Giselle, purely because she liked the sound of them, and they were compatible with both French and German. Giselle had subsequently discovered that the meaning behind the name Estelle was 'bright star', while Giselle meant 'hostage', which she jokingly felt had sealed her fate at birth to remain in this village forever.

'Just imagine,' Giselle joked with that twinkle in her eyes coming to life again. 'If our mother had decided to give us each other's name; I could be the bright star in London and you working for me.' She sat back and folded her arms with a sense of triumph. Estelle raised an eyebrow and took a theatrical sigh. Giselle then went on to explain how she has been trying ever since to encourage the use of Gigi and Stella as nicknames, which she felt would be adequate compensation for the meaning behind their full names.

Estelle scrunched her nose up and said 'Hmmm, it never really caught on though, did it?'

Giselle turned to me and said 'What do you think Luke? Gigi sounds much sexier than Stella, no?'

I took a sip of wine to avoid answering. Giselle's question appeared to trigger something between them as their gentle teasing of each other increased in pace to the point they appeared agitated with each other and switched into French, presumably to prevent me from understanding. I couldn't follow what was being said and was relieved when, eventually, a cold blanket of silence fell over us all, making the crunch of my cracker seem much louder than it had a few minutes before.

From behind me, I could hear the uneven shuffle of Steve making his way back to the table. He took up position at the far end, safe from the wrath of Giselle and poured himself some water.

'It's gone a bit quiet here, hasn't it?' he muttered.

I felt it only polite to respond. 'I'm afraid I lost track of the conversation when they switched to French,' I replied cheerily. 'I'm just taking a break to refuel and enjoy the evening air while they catch up.'

I heard a 'pffft' sound from Steve's direction, causing me to turn and face him. His eyes were still unfocussed and only half open. He drank thirstily from his glass, leaned forward, and, as if he was whispering a profound nugget of knowledge, said slowly, 'it might sound like French to you, but it's not. They've got their own coded language when they don't want anyone else to understand them.' He paused for effect, tapping the side of his nose knowingly. 'All I know is, they might look sweet and innocent but they're fucking dangerous when they get together. At least one of them is, and I wish I knew which.'

Like a pair of Siamese cats with pricked ears, both Giselle and Estelle sat bolt upright, the same piercing glare and wild look of unpredictability on their faces as they stared down the table at Steve. Without taking her eyes off him, Giselle put a comforting hand on Estelle's forearm and said very calmly, and with the controlled tone of someone refusing to be dragged down to another's level, 'You're drunk Steve. Go to bed. Now.' She said it in the same tone that a non-negotiable parent might tell a child that it was past their bedtime.

Steve used both arms of his chair to lift himself up and, slurring what sounded like a submissive apology. Giselle spat 'useless pig!' out as he headed back towards the house, swaying left and right as he went.

'Once again, Luke. I am so sorry you had to experience that,' Giselle said in the same controlled tone she had used with Steve. 'It is not the sort of welcome I had in mind for you.'.

And with that, the conversation resumed in English with Estelle asking Giselle if she was planning to make any jams or chutneys out of the garden's abundance of fruit. I marvelled at the way in which they shifted the gears of intensity of their relationship so effortlessly.

Chapter 35

The next morning, I awoke to the gentle sound of birds chirping outside the open window. Streams of morning sunlight crept their way across the crisp cotton cover that enveloped me and Estelle. The fresh fragrance of garden plants waking up to the day wafted across the room, up my nostrils into the core of my senses, rousing my consciousness with a sense of calm I hadn't felt for a very long time. Beside me, Estelle lay in serene bliss, her lashes casting delicate shadows on her flushed cheeks as she slept, slow steady breaths vibrating from her slightly open mouth.

'Bonjour, ma chérie,' I whispered, gently moving a lock of hair that had fallen across her cheek behind her ear. No response. She was either deep in sleep or didn't want to be wakened. Careful not to disturb the cocoon of bedding around her, I swung my legs off the edge of the bed and lifted my weight off the mattress without creating so much as a ripple. I grabbed my washbag and tiptoed barefoot towards the door.

The corridor was streaked with rays of light invading the house from the rooms that led off it. The pastel shades of the walls seemed more vivid than the previous day, as did the watercolour paintings that adorned it. If a house could be designed to emit a sense of serenity, this was it. I paused, still on tiptoe, as I picked up the scent of fresh coffee working its way through the house, drawing me towards the top of the stairs in the opposite direction to the bathroom.

I placed my hand on the wrought iron banister, peered over the edge and inhaled deeply. The rich bitter scent wafting up was strong and invigorating. The house was completely still aside from the rhythmic tick-tocking of the grandfather clock at the bottom of the stairs and, if I turned my head to the side slightly, the distant sound of some tuneful humming which I could only assume was coming

219

from Giselle in the kitchen. I kept my breathing short and shallow, my hand glued to the handrail, and my feet rooted to the wooden floorboards as I let the sound of her humming wash over me, tempting me to follow it like some mythological Siren.

Should I head downstairs on my own, or should I wait for Estelle to wake up so we could head downstairs together, I wondered?

I assumed that she was alone downstairs as I couldn't imagine that Steve would be able to wake for some time yet. I smiled to myself as I recalled how Giselle had snapped at him and sent him to bed like a child last night. It was clear who was boss in that relationship. Steve only had himself to blame for getting so drunk in the first place. I resolved never to let myself slip down that slope. It was not who I wanted to be nor how I would want to present myself within a relationship.

The friction displayed between Giselle and Steve last night made me think of past events with *her*. *She*, who used to seem to enjoy exerting her power over me and belittling me in front of others at every opportunity but, unlike Giselle, for no apparent reason. *She*, who would think nothing of weaponising the love I once felt for her into something that could enhance her own standing in front of others at my expense. *She*, who was entering my mind less frequently these days and becoming more of a fading ghost than a haunting presence.

Twelve years had passed since I'd allowed *her* to control my feelings and rob me of my self-confidence and self-respect. I reminded myself that since then, my whole body would have died and replaced itself. Every layer of skin would have totally shed itself; every hair would have grown and been cut so many times that none of the original remained; every cell of my liver and other organs would have died and been replaced by new cells. Even my brain tissue would have renewed itself, making me a completely new person to that of the past. Like a snake shedding its skin, I was a totally new and refreshed version of my old self with no reason to allow old memories to gatecrash their way into my present. I questioned whether they were real memories, or just memories of memories? Either way, the here, the now and the future was what really mattered; the past needed to stay behind closed doors.

I snapped out of my trance as if a door really had slammed shut, let go of the banister and made my way to the bathroom. It was unusual for Estelle to sleep in longer than me. It was usually her who was up first, ready to tick off the list of successes she had planned for any given day. The long drive and late night must have finally caught up with her. I peeped round our bedroom door on the way and was pleased to see Estelle fast asleep and looking so relaxed and blissful. It would be unfair of me to disturb her, and the smell of coffee downstairs was too tempting to ignore. I'd be decent enough to go downstairs in my loose pyjama shorts and t-shirt, but I did need to freshen my breath and sort my hair out to make myself at least half presentable first.

As I was brushing my teeth, I recalled Estelle's whispered words to me at the end of the night when we were alone in bed together. 'I'm really pleased you like her and get on. She is a big part of my life, but don't believe everything she tells you, OK? She has an overactive imagination and likes to tease.' I was too tired to ask what she meant at the time but remember thinking it sounded overly critical. Giselle seemed to me to be nothing other than entertaining and welcoming and, if there was any teasing, it was with a sense of fun more than anything else.

Fresh-faced, hair tamed and with minty breath, I tip-toed my way back past our bedroom and followed the scent of coffee. Giselle had her back towards me as I entered the kitchen, busily wiping surfaces down and moving dried plates from the draining board to the shelves above. Her hips moved in synchronicity with her humming as she stepped from side to side, making the activity look more fun than a chore.

'Good morning,' I said, causing her to spin round and face me with a hand on her chest.

'Oh, Luke!' she said, exhaling heavily. 'You made me jump. I didn't hear you come in.'

'I'm sorry,' I said. 'I was trying to be as quiet as possible. I wasn't sure if anyone else would be up at this time,' I lied.

'Oh, I am always up early. Once the sun is up and the birds start singing, I can't bear to waste a moment of the day. How about you? Did you sleep well?'

'I did, thanks. Yesterday was a long day and, what with the drive, I don't think I've slept so deeply for a long time.' She smiled one of those smiles that made her eyes twinkle. 'Actually, Estelle did most of the driving.' I felt compelled to give Estelle due credit for taking the pressure off me. 'I expect that's why she's still fast asleep. She's usually up before me.'

'Let her sleep. This is your holiday, no? There is nothing to rush for today.' Her dimples came out to accompany the warmth of her eyes. 'Coffee?'

'That would be lovely,' I replied, taking a seat at the table.

I watched as Giselle placed a cup in front of me and, spinning round to take the stovetop coffee maker off the hob behind her, leant forward and slowly filled the cup with steaming brown liquid. She was wearing a simple, pale pastel orange crepe mini dress; the sort that forced you to notice the woman before the clothes.

'Milk?' she offered, making it sound like more than it was.

'Yes please,' I replied, keeping my eyes on my cup.

Conflicting emotions stirred within me, a mix of familiarity and an unexpected attraction towards Giselle. I had to make a conscious effort to remind myself that i) I only met her less than 24 hours ago, and ii) that feeling this way was purely a side effect of loving my sleeping Estelle upstairs. Yes, their likeness was uncanny, but with the fresh morning light, and perhaps a little more familiarity than yesterday, the subtle differences between them were becoming more apparent to me. Giselle's greater flow of movement, the playful mischief in her eyes, the way she liked to twist locks of hair around her finger when talking to me, like a bashful teenager. The trouble with that was that her differences were as seductive as the similarities.

Judging from the way Giselle kept studying me when she thought I was looking elsewhere, she seemed to have equal curiosity about me.

'Did you sleep well?' I asked, keen to break the silence that had crept in between us.

'Hmph,' she said, resuming wiping clean surfaces down. 'I did once I got rid of that snoring pig from my bedroom.' The circling of her cleaning cloth sped up.

'I didn't want to ask, but how is Steve today? He seemed to be very tired last night,' I enquired, deliberately underplaying the obvious. She left the cloth on the surface, put her hands on her hips, and turned to face me with a look of resigned patience.

'One night! One night of being sober is all I asked for and look what I got! Drunken, snoring pig!' Her tone was neutral rather than emotional. 'Luke. I am sorry again for his behaviour last night and thank you for understanding. I do not think we will see Steve before lunchtime.'

'Don't worry,' I reassured. 'I thought nothing of it, and you have absolutely nothing to apologise for.'

She let out a deep sigh. 'To be honest with you, it suits me that he will be out of our way today. I am not in the mood for him, and it leaves me free to enjoy some time with my sister and you.' I gave her an understanding smile and we held each other's gaze for as long as it took for my cheeks to flush, causing me to look away and bring my coffee to my mouth as a diversion, hiding the fact it was still too hot to drink. In truth, I was relieved to hear that Steve wouldn't be joining us today. I'd never been keen on male company and the thought of having Estelle and Giselle to myself for the day was a fun proposition.

As I watched Giselle return to busying herself with chores, putting cups back in cupboards, sweeping imaginary crumbs out the back door with the grace of a choreographed dancer, all while humming peacefully to herself, I concluded, despite only having spent not much more than an hour in his company, that Steve was a fool for not appreciating her more. I found it impossible to take my eyes off her as she continued to move back and forth from one end of the kitchen to the other, finding things to move from one place to the other, pulling out different cloths and sprays for different surfaces, spinning round with such speed and ease that the bottom of her dress would flair out occasionally. Giselle looked completely content within herself, and within her environment. It struck me at the same time that I had never seen Estelle do much more than make a cup of coffee in the kitchen at home before, let alone display such total command. Perhaps I had not made Estelle feel welcome enough at the flat to use it as she saw fit? Perhaps Estelle and Giselle were more chalk and cheese than their appearance suggested? While Giselle was clearly comfortable being the boss at home, she had shown no sign of having the same sort of fire in her belly to tackle the corporate world that Estelle did.

'It is good to see that my sister's taste in men has improved better than mine,' she said with a chuckle, pausing her humming. 'I can see from the way that you cannot take your eyes off her that you like her a lot.' Her raised eyebrow made this sound more like a question than a statement.

My cheeks burned hot as my brain raced to find an appropriate response. Although I had not been asked, it felt as if I was being asked what my intentions with Estelle were. Instead, I was itching to ask about Estelle's previous choice of men or make a self-deprecating comment about myself to attract further compliments. Before I had a chance to say anything, Giselle looked me in the eye and added, 'Perhaps I will have to visit London one day and find a nice Englishman of my own to play with?' I raised my coffee cup to my face to hide my bashfulness while imagining Giselle having fun with me instead.

'Jumelle!' Giselle said excitedly, looking towards the door behind me.

'Good morning, darlings,' Estelle called out, causing me to dribble some coffee down my chin as I jerked my head round to see her.

'Good morning, chérie,' I blurted. 'I thought I'd leave you to sleep a little longer seeing as you looked so peaceful.' It took a couple of seconds, and for me to look from one to the other a couple of times, to realise that Estelle was wearing the exact same simple, pale pastel crepe mini dress as Giselle, but in a shade of lilac. 'Wait, when are you two co-ordinating your clothes with each other?' They both responded with the same laugh.

'You know I don't like to sleep in, Luke,' she said, running her hand across my shoulders and taking the seat next to me. 'And our dresses are pure coincidence.' I was sure I saw Estelle exchange a knowing wink with Giselle. Giselle, meanwhile, unveiled a platter of previously unnoticed pastries from the corner of the kitchen, placed them in the middle of the table, and handed me a piece of kitchen towel and tapped her chin, gesturing for me to wipe mine. Estelle tutted at the sight of me dabbing coffee off my chin and turned to Giselle to say something in what I assumed was French, sending them both into ripples of infectious laughter.

When I laughed along with them, and it was impossible not to, they only seemed to laugh harder. I wasn't sure what the joke was but felt sure I was at the butt of it somewhere. If that was the case, I didn't care. I was surrounded by beauty in the happiest place on Earth. I also knew that if I needed to work hard to keep up with Estelle's quick mind and energy, I was going to have to work three times as hard to keep up with the pair of them.

Chapter 36

Estelle and Giselle dominated breakfast conversation as they discussed options for how to spend the day. I'd teased them about the fact that all their proposed plans seemed to involve food; visiting farm shops where they could pick up local specialities (their voices reaching fever pitch at the prospect of finding some truffle-infused cheese) or speculating on what foods I 'absolutely must try' while here. And all this before I'd even taken a bite out of one of Giselle's breakfast pastries!

They'd decided on a visit to the nearby Friday market in Riberac which they thought would tick all boxes. I'd been sent upstairs to freshen up and make myself decent as quickly as possible. I ignored the shuffling and hangover groans coming from the study as I rushed about upstairs, slipping on a pair of chinos, polo shirt, spraying some aftershave on and grabbing my sunglasses before meeting the twins at the front of the house. They were ready to leave and patiently waiting when I got downstairs, looking even more indistinguishable from each other than normal with their two large floppy hats and matching oversize sunglasses to protect them from the sun.

'I cannot believe it is still running,' Estelle said as Giselle swung open the large wooden garage doors.

'Of course!' Giselle replied indignantly. 'Le Papillon Bleu is one of the family. She will never leave us. Luke...' she said, stepping to one side and motioning inside the garage. '...meet Blue Butterfly.' I squinted to adjust my vision to see into the dark corner of the garage to see a weathered sky-blue Volkswagen Beetle, asleep in the corner looking very much like a relic from a bygone age. Hearing the word butterfly automatically reminded me of our Effective Solutions project but I kept that thought to myself.

'Wow, that's a real classic,' I said admiring the dusty chrome bumper and whitewall tyres. 'Those tyres make it look like it's wearing tap shoes with spats.' Blank looks in response. My attempt to describe what spats were might as well have been explained in hieroglyphics judging from the way in which their attention shifted away from me.

'This car has been with us forever,' Giselle explained. 'It belonged to our father. He bought it new when we were very young. I think he loved it more than us, even though he spent more time cleaning it than driving it.'

Estelle's face did not appear to share Giselle's affection for the car. 'These days you must spend more time taking it for repair than driving it. We could always take our car. It'll just about fit us all in.'

Giselle frowned and tutted. 'No. Le Papillon Bleu is our car for today. He might have cost a little bit along the way, but it is not so bad for something with so much character. Anyway, it is only a short trip into town. So…are we going to go now or what?' She entered the driver's side, bum first, carefully navigating the rims of her hat inside. Estelle suggested I sit in the back so that she could get into the front seat without disturbing me once Giselle had driven out and she could lock the garage doors.

And so, within an hour of waking up, I found myself sitting in the middle of a musty backseat of a Beetle, tinged with the scent of petrol, catching glimpses of scenery through the narrow line of vision I had between Giselle and Estelle's oversized floppy hats, a cracked windscreen to the front and the rattle of the engine coming from behind me. The car undeniably had a lot of character – that of a wheezy old man, coughing and spluttering and unsure if he was going to make it. Still, I could see why Giselle felt a level of affection towards it.

Giselle drove slowly for the whole of the journey, allowing her and Estelle time to commentate on everything and everyone they passed. More than once, people would stop and stare in wonderment as we rolled by, disbelieving eyes wide open as their heads turned in perfect sync with the movement of the car. I chuckled to myself as I supposed how I might stare if I was watching from the side of the road and saw such glamorous twins driving around in a such a noisy and funny looking classic car for the first time.

Before long, we were bumping along the cobblestones on the outer edges of Riberac's *centre ville* square, where crowds were milling around dozens of market stalls, bursting with the colours of crimson tomatoes, emerald lettuces, and golden peaches, complemented by the more orderly stripey overhangs of the stalls, protecting customers from the increasing heat of the sun. The back of the car was hot and airless, and I was looking forward to getting some fresh air. Giselle took her foot off the gas and let the Blue Butterfly roll in frontways diagonally between two cars up against the kerb, pulled up the handbrake and proudly announced 'Voilà. That's good enough!'

As they waited for me to clamber out of the back, they looked like a pair of film stars waiting for their gofer to catch up as they stood side by side in the sun surveying their surroundings. Again, their presence was causing several heads to turn which only made me feel even more special for being their companion for the day.

The market itself was positively thriving. To escape the sun, they headed straight down the central aisle of stalls to the market's centre. I don't think Estelle or Giselle heard my suggestion to take a more orderly approach towards exploring by starting at the left of the market and working our way systematically up and down each aisle towards the right. My voice must have got lost amongst the banter echoing out from stall vendors or drowned out by the pair of students playing guitars and singing through an amplifier in the middle of the square.

Giselle and Estelle linked arms and led the way as we meandered slowly through the market, stopping every few steps to admire the array of fresh produce, handcrafted goods and local delicacies on offer. Heads continued to turn and people whispered as they passed, obviously fascinated at the sight of seeing such similar looking twins together. I'd never really thought about just how nosey and indiscreet some people could be about twins until now. Fair enough, my eyes were spending more time on them than the stalls, but strangers made no attempt to even disguise their staring. It didn't seem to bother the twins though. They were engrossed with each other, chattering away non-stop, pausing only to point out items of interest as we went from stall to stall, Giselle slowly filling up her supply of string bags with items of produce.

The scent of ripe fruits, vegetables and artisan meats and cheeses filled the air, as did the sound of stallholders, customers and background music. 'Try this,' Estelle would call frequently, encouraging me to try an olive, piece of cheese, or slice of fruit 'let's get one for home!' she'd suggest at numerous pieces of handmade pottery, intricately woven baskets and various antiques stalls, each carrying the promise of hidden treasure amongst the junk being offered. I'd smile and respond positively to each suggestion, only for her to say she didn't really want it but appreciated the thought. Giselle seemed to find our interactions amusing as she took on the role of being the sensible one in charge of an over-excited child.

I was busy admiring a set of figurines and an old farmhouse crockery set, when I heard Estelle squeal with excitement from behind me. I turned to catch Giselle giving me a look of resigned patience as Estelle was dragging her by the arm in the direction of a jewellery stall glistening in the sun. 'You are with them?' a man sitting on a fold-out chair behind the stall I was looking at asked. He seemed to blend into the background of his open van so well, I hadn't noticed him before.

'Yes,' I replied, wondering how he knew to speak to me in English. I had thought I was carrying off the French look rather well.

'Hmm,' he said, his dark brown eyes tightening.

'Luke! Chéri!' Estelle called from the jewellery stall on the other side of the aisle, holding a pair of sparkly earrings and necklace to either side of her face. 'What do you think of these?'

I couldn't make them out in detail but nodded enthusiastically and gave her a thumbs up gesture. I was about to head over to her when I heard the stallholder tut twice behind me.

'I'm sorry?' I asked, curious as to why he was still staring at me. He let out a deep sigh and turned his beady eyes away from me, indicating that our interaction was over although there was something about his manner that left me uneasy. I left him and made my way towards the twins who now had their backs to me as they were in negotiation with the jewellery seller.

All three of them were talking over each other at pace and in French so I couldn't understand what was going on. I had at first assumed they were haggling over the price of the earrings but their snappy tone and the angry look on the stallholder's face left no doubt that some sort of altercation was taking place.

'Can I help?' I offered over the twins' shoulders, letting them know that I was there. Estelle looked round to face me, her eyes wide and her mouth curled with anger. 'Luke. Thank you. I was admiring this necklace and earring set.' She held the set up for me to see. The chain was fine and delicate and held a small pear-shaped pendant containing a sparkling clear gemstone, possibly diamond, which was matched by the two stud earrings. It was perfect for Estelle. 'But this man is so rude,' she spat, 'I forget how small-minded this place can be.'

Giselle was continuing to rant in the direction of the stallholder, whose sun-weathered face was getting redder by the second. Before I could figure out what was going on, he snatched the earrings out of Estelle's hand and flicked his wrists towards them both as if shooing scavenging cats off a tabletop. Estelle let rip with what I guessed was a torrent of abuse, to which he promptly turned his back to her, refusing to engage further. Giselle was tugging at Estelle's arm, encouraging her away from the stall while an even bigger crowd of people stopped to stare.

I was left standing bewildered at what had just happened, when the stallholder turned to me and said, in near-perfect English, 'It is not right. Those Lusignac twins should not be allowed out. It is wrong.' I held his gaze for a few moments, searching for where such an angry sentiment was coming from but saw only shock and fear in his eyes.

'How much?' I asked.

'Huh?'

'For the set. How much?' He studied my face with confusion before responding.

'200 Euros.'

I paid, slipped the boxed set into my pocket, and rushed through the crowds to catch up with the twins, eventually latching onto Estelle's free arm.

'What was that all about?' I asked.

Estelle ignored me and continued to march forwards, this time with no interest in looking at the passing stalls. 'If it was about the earrings, I'm sure we'll be able to find another pair somewhere else.' I didn't think it was about the earrings but felt a slight squeeze of encouragement from Estelle and caught her lips curl into a faint smile. I squeezed her arm in return as I noticed tears rolling out from behind her sunglasses.

Giselle, still holding onto Estelle's other arm, leaned forward and said 'I think it is best to leave it, Luke. She is upset. Unfortunately for us, Estelle is right. This is a small town with some small-minded people. It is best to ignore them.'

We continued pacing forward until we reached the outskirts of the market, where it opened up onto a quieter area full of home-grown pot plants for sale and paste tables open with second-hand English books for sale, manned by red-faced, silver-haired ex-pats sitting in direct sunlight. Estelle stopped suddenly, causing me and Giselle to stop in unison with shared concern. Very carefully, she took off her sunglasses, dabbed her cheeks with the back of her hands, straightened the sides of her dress down and said, very calmly, 'I think now would be a good time to break for some lunch, no?' Relieved that Estelle's mood appeared to be returning to normal, Giselle and I nodded in agreement, and we headed towards a corner bistro with shaded outdoor tables facing onto the market.

We took the only table that didn't have anyone sitting on adjacent tables and settled down to peruse the menu. It was hot and my shirt was starting to stick. The shade was a relief, as was the occasional breeze sweeping past, cooling my exposed arms. The bistro had a relaxed atmosphere - very rustic and homely. The background sound of cutlery against porcelain and peaceful conversations was a welcome contrast to the boisterousness of the marketplace. My eyes flicked back and forth between Estelle and Giselle over my menu to gauge their mood. They looked calmer now, the anger that appeared to threaten the day in the market had simmered down to nothing and neither of them seemed to be coated in the same moist sheen of sweat that I was. Their sunglasses were off, faces relaxed and the chatter had once again turned to food.

'What would you recommend?' I asked, fanning myself with the menu, having felt slightly overwhelmed by the choice on it.

'Anything you like,' Giselle replied without taking her eyes off her menu. 'All of the food is good here.'

'What's everybody else having?' I asked, seeking inspiration.

'I wouldn't get anything too heavy considering that Giselle seems to have bought enough food to feed the whole village!' Estelle advised, gesturing towards the collection of string bags sitting beside Giselle's feet, stretched to capacity with fresh herbs and vegetables, wrapped cheeses and even a protruding French stick. The three of us exchanged looks before bursting into laughter.

'Stop!' Giselle pleaded through giggles. 'I cannot help wanting to make sure we have enough of everything. There is no need to tease!' Our laughter provided welcome release for whatever remaining tension had followed us from the market.

I flinched as I heard coughing from beside me. A waiter, an elderly gentleman wearing a white apron over a black vest was standing patiently with a welcoming smile.

"Bonjour! What can I get for you today?" he inquired, as I fumbled to decide.

Estelle took charge and, having heard the waiter describe the blend of eggs, cream and smoked bacon nestled in a buttery crust of pastry, opted for a Quiche Lorraine for herself and Giselle to share. For me, she ordered the Salade Niçoise, reading out the description of fresh greens, tuna, olives, and hard-boiled eggs from the menu, checking through eye contact that I was happy with her choice.

'Could we have some sparkling water for the table please,' Giselle chipped in, followed by Estelle in French. 'Perhaps a bottle of white Bordeaux, Luke?' For a few uncomfortable moments, it felt as if time had frozen as they looked at me expectantly, waiting for my answer. Mischief flickered in Giselle's eyes, Estelle stared solemnly, the waiter smiled patiently.

'No thank you,' I replied, feeling as if I was under exam conditions. 'Sparkling water will be fine.' Smiles all round, as the waiter collected our menus.

'Perhaps half a carafe of wine and three glasses, please,' Estelle called out just as he was leaving, and then, turning to us, 'Well, it's not often I get the chance to spend some time together with my two favourite people.'

A smile crept across my face as I realised I would rather be no place else than in the company of these two, slightly strange, food-obsessed, volatile but incredibly warm and entertaining sisters. They were looking around the bistro now, scowling at any heads that were turned in their direction. Their company was like nothing else I had experienced, and a million miles away from the tedium of life at Effective Solutions. I was a lucky man.

The waiter returned with our drinks balanced carefully on a tray held high and set them out before us. Giselle took the lead and poured out a full glass of sparkling water each before emptying the carafe of wine into the three dainty wine glasses. The glasses were small and polite and looked much more civilised than the goldfish bowl-sized measures served in London. Before raising our glasses, I placed the small box from my pocket on the table.

'A small present from me to you to cheer you up.'

Estelle opened the box and removed her sunglasses to admire the necklace and earrings once more. They were sparkling as much as her eyes.

'I do not know whatever I did to deserve you, Luke, but thank you.' I will save these for a special occasion. She popped the box into her handbag, gripped my arm and rolled her eyes towards a group of people on the far table staring at us and said, 'You see what we mean about people finding twins weird, eh? This is why we would often choose not to go out at the same time together. Are you sure you're not freaked out by us yet?'

'Quite the opposite,' I shot back, freeing my arm and raising my glass. 'Two is better than one, surely!'

As we clinked glasses, I felt Estelle squeeze my left thigh under the table while, to my right, Giselle gave my arm a playful squeeze. It happened in perfect unison, and I was sure I caught them exchange a raised eyebrow between themselves at that same, precise moment.

Yes, I thought, two is definitely better than one.

Chapter 37

Estelle's chin was resting on her chest while her head rocked from side to side as the Blue Butterfly chugged his way back up the hill towards Lusignac. The sign of a good day out. Giselle had taken us to another nearby village to explore after lunch - Aubeterre-sur-Dronne. We'd visited local art galleries, mooched around independent shops and ended the day in the shade beside a sandy river beach to cool down, watching tourists splash about in the water. It was easy to spot who the tourists were. They were the ones running around unprotected under the full glare of the afternoon sun talking loudly in English, whereas the more sedate locals congregated under the shade of nearby trees and, like Estelle and Giselle, were often well shaded by large hats, sunglasses or full-length sleeves. Thankfully, the rest of the afternoon had passed without incident.

'Come on Le Papillon Bleu,' Giselle said, stroking the dashboard and seemingly unaware that Estelle was asleep beside her. 'Nearly home. Hang in there.'

Within minutes, we were home. Giselle let the car roll onto the grass verge just past the house and brought the car to a stop by pulling the old-fashioned handbrake up, causing Estelle to sit bolt upright, her eyes wide open while she oriented herself.

'Et voilà,' Giselle announced, swinging her door open triumphantly. 'Home!' She climbed out of the car, pulled her seat forward and ushered me out towards the front door with her shopping bags. She suggested Papillon could be left where it was for the evening in favour of getting the food shopping into the fridge as soon as possible. She was stressing over the cheese spoiling in the heat. Not wanting to rush off without Estelle, I waited for her to finish stretching and yawning before we headed towards the house together.

Inside the shadowy hallway, the coolness of the flagstone tiles and the gentle tick tock of the grandfather clock brought immediate relief from the bright light and heat of outdoors. The length of the day had taken it out of us all. Estelle excused herself for 'not feeling quite right' and needing to go and have a lie down or shower or something, while Giselle seemed overly focussed on me getting the shopping into the kitchen so she could start thinking about preparing the next feast.

All I wanted to do was to find somewhere cool to sit. Estelle declined to join me but reassured me that she had probably got too much sun and needed some rest. I watched as she hauled herself up the stairs one step at a time using the balcony rail for momentum, while Giselle reminded me to hurry up with the shopping.

Once in the kitchen, Giselle refused all offers of help and told me to sit down and relax while she put the kettle on the stove, offered tea and started unpacking the day's haul. She relaxed only once she'd got the cheeses, pâtés and cold meats in the fridge when she took a seat across the table from me to catch her breath. Her shoulders were slouched forward with tiredness, but her rosy cheeks and mischievous smile suggested that she was not drained yet.

'How did you enjoy today, Luke?' She exhaled a sigh of relief and stretched her arms across the table in the same way a cat reaches to stretch their back out. Her face glowed from the day's sun. I thanked her for organising the day and explained how different life here was compared to back home. I admitted that, other than the necessity of going to work, I generally chose to spend my life so far behind a screen at work or at home, and my occasional visits to Hackney's bustling Broadway Market were only to kid myself I was getting out and seeing the world. It was all a far cry from the beauty of French rolling hillsides, rivers and general pace of life of the region.

'I am so pleased you like it here,' she replied, her smile broadening while she bit her lower lip gently with her top teeth. She reached across the table with both hands, took mine, and gave them a squeeze.

'Do you think you could ever swap London for somewhere like this?' She released my hands to stand up but remained leaning forward with her hands on the table. I did my best to pretend I hadn't noticed the clear view down the top of her dress and looked thoughtfully towards the top corner of the room.

'Hmmm…I've never really thought about it. I mean, I've never really had a choice. It's never been an option.' It didn't feel right to explore the answer to this question without Estelle being present. 'Maaaybe,' I concluded. 'It's an interesting thought. I guess it's something Estelle and I could think about one day. I think she seems pretty committed to her job and London for now.'

Giselle gave me an impenetrable look and moved to the back of the kitchen to place teacups on a tray. I tried to imagine what life here might have been like when Estelle lived here too. It was hard to see. I found it difficult to imagine Estelle realistically swapping her corporate life for life in the countryside or this small village. Even at the market, Giselle had taken the lead in selecting what food to buy, led the conversations around future meal options, and the kitchen was most definitely her domain. The Estelle that I had seen was always so work-focussed and had never shown any interest in the kitchen or the domestic side of living. I couldn't imagine her having the patience needed to slow down to the pace of village life. Even the scene at the jewellery stall had become overly heated and I wondered how that might have panned out if Giselle wasn't there to drag Estelle away.

'Well, if you did come back, you might have to rely on me to get you through market days safely.' She pursed her lips and squinted at me, immediately giving off an air of seriousness. Could she read my mind, I wondered? She turned again to fuss about with teaspoons on saucers. I felt the implication of her statement was deliberately provocative and perhaps even edging towards being critical of Estelle. I was also uncomfortable at the thought that Giselle might be luring me into a trap of talking about Estelle without her being present. I wished she hadn't disappeared upstairs and left us alone. So I said nothing in response and let the silence hang in the air like a thick fog, muffling any further conversation.

The whistle of the kettle broke the silence as it came to the boil, sending a cloud of steam to the kitchen roof, prompting Giselle to spring into action again. My eyes followed her as she rinsed out the teapot with boiling water before placing three teabags in it and filling it to the brim. With her back towards me, she asked 'How has Estelle's mood been since she's been in London? Surely you must have noticed by now that she has a bit of a temper.'

The statement was delivered coldly. Matter of fact. In the same way that one might comment on someone's hairstyle or sense of dress. It was asked to provoke a response and to test my loyalty. My mind raced back to all the times I had witnessed Estelle's temper race from 0-60mph at the slightest provocation. The restaurant, driving, and on numerous occasions at work where I had stepped in to diffuse a meeting flaring up when someone – invariably a man - had attempted to patronise or deride her. The frequency of such occurrences often made me question whether I was being the patronising one by attempting to protect her from herself. If I was at fault, it was with the best intentions. While contemplating whether or how to answer Giselle, I leaned back in the hope of hearing Estelle emerging from upstairs. Or her shower running. But nothing. However, I was saved from answering by the appearance of Steve who had wandered in from the back door.

'Afternoon all,' he announced with the familiar cheeriness of a man who was seeking to come in from the doghouse. 'I thought I heard you were back. Did you have a nice day? Is there anything I can do to help?' He was red-faced, either from the sun or from last night's alcohol, I couldn't tell, and treading gingerly towards Giselle. His eyes were pleading, like a puppy begging for a treat. I almost felt sorry for him.

Giselle continued to prepare the tray of tea. 'No thank you. We are having some tea and have everything under control. I suggest you leave us in peace and disappear to your corner of the garden with this.' She had her back to him while she spoke, shielding Steve's vision from the large glass of red wine she poured out for him together with, if my eyes weren't playing tricks with me, a very large measure of brandy mixed in. She turned to face him, holding the glass out towards him.

Steve searched her eyes for forgiveness, found none, looked longingly at the tray of tea and then me, before accepting his offering and shuffling back out into the garden. Giselle returned to her tea tray, picked it up and placed it between us on the table with a warm smile, as if the appearance of Steve hadn't happened. She tucked loose strands of hair behind her ear and started pouring tea for us both. There were three cups on the tray.

'It is OK, you know,' she said while focusing on the tea. 'I know you don't want to say anything, but let's not pretend we don't know what she's like, hmm?' Her ability to speak what I was thinking was both uncanny and unnerving. 'She has always been like that. Fine one minute and then...' She put the teapot down and snapped her fingers. '...she becomes a different person. You must have noticed. I have always looked out for her, but she decided she wanted to chase her dreams in London, so what can I do, hmm?' She pushed a full cup and saucer towards me. There was a hint of sadness in her eyes.

'Thank you,' I said with a nod to the tea. 'I must admit, I know very little about Estelle's life before I met her.' Giselle leant forward, her eyes now sparkling with intent. 'As you know, I didn't even know she had a twin.' I was still wary about saying anything that might be deemed critical of Estelle and was keen to shift the conversation onto safer territory. 'Should we ask Steve if he wants a cup ot tea,' I suggested, pointing towards the empty cup on the tray.

'Leave him,' she said softly. 'He has his wine now and will probably be asleep before long. Anyway, I was hoping to have you to myself for a while longer.'

'Oh really?' I asked. 'Why?'

'So we can get to know each other better of course!'

'Sorry, I meant why give him so much to drink when he's only just recovering from last night? I saw you add brandy to his glass.' I was careful to make the statement about the brandy as playful as possible, rather than accusatory. She bit her bottom lip and gave a playful half-giggle in response.

'It makes life easier, you know? It gives me the space I need. And us a chance to talk.' She took a sip of tea. 'Anyway, his palette is so fucked I doubt he has even noticed he has been drinking brandy all this time.' She giggled again although I was not sure if it was from amusement or despair.

'Forgive me, but why are you even together if you don't enjoy each other's company?' I realised I was straying outside the boundaries of polite conversation, but Giselle's eyes looked so inviting I could not imagine that she'd be offended. She put her cup back into its saucer without taking her eyes off mine.

'You are right.' She sighed and looked away. 'He was fun once. But I doubt his wife would have him back now, so I am stuck with him. Like my name, I am "hostage", destined to be trapped here forever. Unlike Estelle, our lucky "bright star" with her sexy new Englishman.' She paused and let out a deep sigh. 'She has done well though,' she reached across the table and patted my hand. 'I was not sure if poor Estelle would want to put herself through another relationship after what she has been through.'

This seemed overly dramatic and self-pitying for afternoon tea conversation. I did wonder how much of it was being put on for my benefit. There was something about Giselle's account and perceptions about Estelle that didn't quite add up. I don't think anyone could realistically describe Estelle as poor. I put it down to the fact that Giselle hadn't seen her strong, independent, and dominant sister in the workplace. Sure, Estelle could be volatile at times, but implying that she was in some way a victim didn't sit right with me.

Giselle continued, unfazed by the fact our conversation had turned into a monologue. 'Who knows? Maybe she has something to prove to herself. I don't know.' She stared into her teacup as she spoke, but I got the feeling she was observing me closely with her peripheral vision. 'If she is happy then so am I. You are a good man, Luke. Please look after her. Her husband was such a bastard I did not think that she would ever trust another man.' She wasn't looking at me directly, but I knew she was watching for my reaction.

I brought my tea to my mouth as steadily as I could manage. My arms felt heavy, my stomach churned with acidity, and the kitchen walls appeared to jump forward by a metre from every direction. I was stunned. Lost for words. As tempting as it was to pump Giselle for more detail before Estelle returned, I was determined not to reveal I didn't know Estelle had a husband. She said he was such a bastard. Was. Past tense. Presumably divorced and long gone. How could I be sure? How was I only finding out about this now? Why had Estelle never mentioned this to me? Who even was she? Hot tea sank to the pit of my stomach. I closed my eyes to collect my thoughts.

Click. The discovery of hidden truths. The feeling of humiliation. They're laughing at me. Life will never be the same. The heartache, pulsing its way through my body and ending in physical pain. The rage. The anger. The need for calm. I needed to get a grip. Click.

'Is everything OK, Luke? I hope I didn't say anything wrong?'

Giselle's words echoed round my head while her eyes searched my face for chinks in my armour. They say our eyes are the window to our soul. If that's true, although there was reassurance in the depth of Giselle's big brown eyes, I was sure I could see mischief dancing in the background. Not for the first time, my sense of reality warped as everything I thought to be true fell into question.

Chapter 38

'Bonsoir mes chéries!' Estelle's voice sang out from behind as she entered the kitchen. 'I am so sorry. I don't know what came over me.' She stroked the back of my shoulders as she moved around the table to sit next to Giselle. She had changed into a light pair of pedal pushers, a baggy t-shirt and was wearing a headband to keep her hair off her freshly washed face.

'What did I miss?' she inquired, noticing that Giselle was still staring at me.

'Nothing,' Giselle replied, placing an empty cup and saucer in front of Estelle. 'We were just talking. Tea?'

'Yes please.' Estelle spoke slowly and warily. 'Are you sure everything is OK here?' She gave me a quizzical look.

'All good,' I replied, more clipped than I would have liked. 'I think we're all a bit tired after today actually.'

'O…kay!' Estelle said slowly. She was not stupid, and I knew that she knew that something was up. Thankfully, Giselle stepped in to remove some of the awkwardness by announcing enthusiastically that we were thinking about what food to start preparing for dinner. Estelle laughed and reached forward to squeeze my hand in exactly the same way Giselle had done only minutes before. I gave her hand a reassuring squeeze back and stroked the back of her hand with my thumb.

'Thinking about the next meal already?' she asked with a light laugh. 'You will get used to this, Luke. Life revolves around food here.'

I tried desperately not to give off any sign that something was bothering me. Part of me wished I had gone upstairs with Estelle and stayed in blissful ignorance of her past husband. Giselle's casual mention of him felt like a low stomach blow. I hadn't worked out yet if I felt jealous, threatened, or simply hurt that such a significant piece of information had never come up before. Questions reeled round my mind. How long were they married? Did she live here with him? When did it end? Is he still on the scene? I had foolishly - perhaps arrogantly - assumed that it – us - was always just about the two of us and that we were each other's big loves of our lives. My throat tightened as Estelle gave my hand another affectionate squeeze and Giselle looked on with a mischievous smile. She knew she'd dropped a bombshell and appeared to be relishing it.

'I know!' Giselle announced with glee, placing her palms on the table. 'Isn't it great? Let's take the tea outside where it will be cooler, and we can talk some more about food!' Estelle was directed to top the teapot up and take the tray into the garden, I was handed another large drink to take out to Steve, who I suspected would not have finished his first yet, and Giselle said she would make some finger sandwiches and join us shortly.

As we stepped into the garden, a light breeze carried the warm scent of jasmine towards us, bringing some calm to my racing thoughts. Estelle paused, tray still in hands, and whispered to again inquire if I was OK. I did my best to reassure her that it was only tiredness catching up with me and immediately felt guilty for the look of genuine concern on her face. I was also hit with a huge wave of affection towards her as I realised that the thing that was bothering me most was the thought that our relationship could be wounded by a single revelation. I loved her. Was besotted in fact. In fact, I could no longer imagine life without her. I needed to pull myself together and not fuck up.

We settled into the evening, enjoying the endless trays of snacks, drinks and nibbles that Giselle set out on the garden table. Tea turned to wine, conversation changed to laughter and finger sandwiches were followed by a clay pot of wild mushrooms with garlic and a cheese board. Steve remained in his deckchair at the other end of the garden with Giselle making sure full glasses of wine were regularly sent in his direction. Whether he was at the other end of the garden out of choice or command, I couldn't be sure. One thing for sure was that he was going to have another hell of a hangover in the morning.

I was doing well to mask my inner turmoil over the discovery that Estelle had a husband but was aware that I had become more of an observer than a participant in the evening. Of course, I laughed along and offered words of encouragement and amusement where needed but I otherwise remained quiet and reflective. Estelle and Giselle, by contrast, were as animated and full of stories as ever. Despite me being perfectly content and self-sufficient, both seemed extra-attentive, constantly checking if there was anything more I needed. It was nice to be fussed over. Estelle was more tactile than usual, taking every opportunity to reach over to prod or squeeze me whenever I was mentioned in one of her stories. These simple gestures provided the reassurance I needed to stay calm. And Giselle had dialled down the level of intensity displayed earlier in the kitchen, which also helped me appear relaxed. She did, however, keep giving me a look that suggested our conversation was not yet finished. I was careful not to emit any signs of encouragement in return.

Observing Estelle and Giselle in conversation with each other reminded me of the way you can look at a painting and see something different upon each viewing. Yesterday, and even this morning, I had observed two sisters who had desperately missed each other and were delighted to be reunited. As if each one of them was half and only together were they whole. This evening, and I couldn't put my finger on it exactly, there were subtleties in their interactions that suggested they were more in competition than partnership with each other. Almost as if there was a polite strategic battle for control being played out to see who could be the most amusing, more intelligent, or more confident of the two. Occasionally, their conversation would speed up, become cryptic, complex, and show signs of passive aggression, which would quickly be pulled back towards safe ground before slowly ramping up again.

I enjoyed watching Estelle. She always looked good and seeing her so relaxed in the sloping garden of her childhood home with the backdrop of picturesque hills rolling as far as the eye could see reminded me how far we had come together as a couple. I reminded myself that it was me who was here with her now, not her husband. Me who had been let into her life behind the scenes of her corporate persona. And me who would be sleeping by her side tonight. I really had no reason to feel insecure.

However, the combination of the day's heat, food and wine had left me incredibly tired and, as the sun disappeared behind the furthest hilltop, I made my excuses, thanked Giselle for again going to so much effort to make a wonderful evening, kissed Estelle on the cheek and headed indoors. Steve was still slumped motionless in his deckchair at the far end of the garden, empty bottle of wine lying beside him, so I let him be.

I paused in the kitchen to drop off my empty plate and glass by the sink. Giselle's kitchen window looked out into the garden and beyond. The distant hills were draped in deepening shades of violet and indigo. The trees in the garden had become silhouettes and, below them, was the outdoor dining table bathed in the dim glow of solar lights and Estelle sitting in solitary contemplation, blowing streams of smoke into the air. I felt at peace.

'You look lost!'

I spun round, almost knocking over the glass I had just put down.

'Oh my god, you made me jump,' I said, putting my hand to my chest as Giselle crept in.

'You look thoughtful,' she said, sauntering towards me with a handful of empty serving bowls she'd carried in from outside. 'I just wanted to check you were OK? You seemed very quiet this evening.' The light in her eyes danced with mischief and showed no real sign of concern.

'I'm fine, thanks. I was just wondering where you keep the washing up liquid to wash my glass.'

'Leave it,' she said, reaching behind me to place her bowls in the sink. As she did, she rested her free hand on my hip and pressed her body against mine momentarily, triggering an electrifying sensation that left me tingling when she stood back from me, a look of triumph on her face. I looked out of the window and saw Estelle still looking out to the distance in quiet contemplation.

'Are you sure you are OK, Luke? You look...distracted?' I was not OK. My heart was thumping against my ribcage and my hands were trembling. I now had no doubt that Giselle was deliberately playing with me. Or testing me. It was too much. I needed to escape the situation.

'I'm tired,' I said unconvincingly. 'I need to go to bed.'

'But it is early, Luke. Why don't you come back outside and join us?' She shifted her weight from foot to foot as she spoke, her tongue rolling across the inside of her bottom lip.

'I'm sorry. It's been a long day, and I think I'll have to leave you two to it if I'm going to stand any chance of feeling fresh tomorrow.'

'That's a shame,' she pouted. 'If you go now, Estelle will surely follow, and then I'll be left sitting on my own again.' She stepped forward, placed her hands on my arms, and looked up with her big brown hypnotic eyes. 'Can I not tempt you at all?'

I turned to look out of the window to see Estelle, now standing with her back to the house, looking into the distance. I turned back to face Giselle, who was waiting expectantly for my answer.

'No. Sorry. I really need to go to bed.' Firm but polite was the best approach to not cause offence. But then, for some foolish reason, I saw fit to add 'you could always ask Steve to the table to keep the evening going.' Even before

I'd finished the sentence my words had slowed down to speaking them one by one. It was a stupid and provocative thing to say.

The warmth in Giselle's eyes disappeared instantly and was replaced by a precision coldness that sent a shiver down my spine. She held her gaze and was statuesque for long enough to make me look away, probably for only three seconds but it felt much longer, before switching seamlessly back into life, spinning animatedly round, and finding something from the table to put back in a cupboard.

'Oh Luke,' she sighed. 'Don't be so naïve. Surely you can see that there is nothing left between us. Look at me and look at him,' she sneered. 'You think a man like that can keep me happy?' She held her head high and smoothed her dress down along her hips and down her thighs, leading my sight down her shapely figure.

'I'm sorry Giselle, but I really don't think it's for me to say. If it's not working, that's probably a conversation for you and Steve to have.' I looked away and then added 'I never understand why people stay together if they're not happy.' What was wrong with me? Why did I have to share another provocative opinion?

'You think I don't know that?' Giselle snapped back. 'Maybe you are right, but it is not easy being stuck here alone you know. Do you think it's easy?' She looked hurt and vulnerable, and I wished I could repair the situation.

'I'm really sorry, Giselle. I didn't mean to speak out of turn. I'm overtired. Sorry.'

Her eyes softened. 'That's OK. Forget it. You are right anyway.' She bunched up the material from the sides of her dress in her hands.

'Anyway, er, I ought to head up. Enjoy the rest of the evening and I'll see you tomorrow.'

I stepped slowly around the kitchen, leaving Giselle rooted to the spot, rocking gently from side to side.

'Maybe I have been neglecting my own needs for too long,' she continued, ignoring the fact I was trying to leave. 'Maybe I have been waiting for an incentive to change and wake up to the life I deserve.' I turned again to face her. Her words struck a relatable chord with me. Gone was any look of vulnerability. She looked supremely confident and determined.

I repeated my goodnight but again she appeared not to hear me.

'Luke.' Her saying my name made me stop in my tracks. 'It seems to me that all the decent men around here are either past their best or already taken. What do you think my chances are of finding a handsome man like you?'

I sighed; the flattery resulted in me being unable to resist giving her the reassurance she sought. 'Giselle. Like Estelle, you are gorgeous. I can't imagine you'd have any trouble finding a decent man if that's what you want.' The look on her face told me I'd obviously said the words she was hoping for. I was again about to leave when she very slowly, and with a half-smile while biting the bottom of her lip, started to inch her dress up her thighs.

'So you think my legs are still attractive then? I haven't put on too much weight with all this food?' I froze as her dress continued to rise to reveal more of her shapely legs. It was impossible to look away. And impossible to conceal my blushing face which was on fire. Her dress continued rising until it revealed a small pair of white lace see-through underwear, not doing a very good job of concealing the silky black hair beneath it. Not for the first time in Giselle's presence, my heart felt like it was going to crash its way out of my ribcage.

'They look great,' I stammered.

Suddenly, the back door swung open violently, jolting me out of my trance and making Giselle jump, quickly pushing her dress back down her legs. I looked away as soon as I could, but there was no hiding the fact I had been staring, with what I had just seen firmly imprinted in my mind, keeping my face flushed. I faced Estelle and told her that I was just heading upstairs. It was not good though; I sounded hopelessly pathetic and self-justifying. She said nothing in response but looked from me to Giselle and back again, a look of scorn on her face, whether at her sister's behaviour or at my reaction I couldn't be sure. Giselle looked down at her feet. Eventually, Estelle broke the silence.

'Go to bed Luke. I want to speak to my sister alone.'

Chapter 39

I slipped in and out of sleep for what felt like hours when I heard footsteps on the landing, different doors opening and closing, and indistinguishable whispers between Estelle and Giselle. It had been eerily silent in the house since I'd left them downstairs. I'd left the bedroom window ajar so I could hear them if they moved back into the garden. But nothing.

I was curled up on the far side of the bed with my back facing the door when Estelle entered the room and tiptoed towards the chair in the corner to change into her pyjama set. I lay motionless and kept my breathing shallow. I had not been on the receiving end of Estelle's temper yet, but that didn't mean I wasn't fearful of it. As much as I tried, I couldn't interpret her mood from the sound of her movements.

She climbed into bed, seemingly careful not to disturb me, her back facing towards mine, and quickly assumed a position to sleep. There was no touch, no 'good night mon chéri', no gentle peck on my cheek. Nothing. She was absolutely motionless.

There was no chance I was going to be able to sleep like this. I opened my eyes and, without moving my resting head, looked around the room. The walls were tinged with a muted indigo glow from the small window where the curtains swayed in the evening breeze. Aside from the unfamiliar creaks of the house, it was completely silent. Unbearably so.

I rolled over to face Estelle's back, hoping that she'd turn to face me. But she remained frozen. I rested my arm lightly on her upper arm and shoulder, careful not to let its full weight cause discomfort, and shuffled closer to let the heat from my body warm her back. Our bodies really were a perfect fit, like two pieces of a jigsaw slotting together to make a whole picture visible. I took in her scent; a cloud of citrussy soap, fresh minty toothpaste and lavender from her hair. And a unique calm and reassuring scent of her own.

I gently stroked her shoulder to elicit some sort of response. Nothing. I leant in and pecked the back of her neck. Still nothing. I raised myself up onto my elbow to lean round and kiss her cheek. Her eyes remained closed, although I saw her lips part as she let out a soft murmur. I pulled her closer and again kissed her cheek. Again, she moaned quietly, while her eyes and lips tightened. I moved my hand downwards to rest on her hip and pull her towards me while trailing kisses from her cheek down to her neck. She screwed her face up and shuffled forwards, reintroducing some distance between us.

'I love you,' I whispered, stroking her outer thigh. She shuffled back and forth, as if to shake me off her. 'Is everything OK?' I asked, moving my hand back to the safer territory of her shoulder.

'Go to sleep,' she replied, staying tight-eyed, and bunching a handful of the covers under her chin.

I laid my head back on my pillow, feeling deflated. I let a couple of minutes pass in silence before leaning back towards her and kissing the back of her shoulder softly. 'Are you sure nothing's wrong?' I ventured.

She shook her shoulders, readjusted her position, and replied with a firm 'nothing'. I should have maybe left her to sleep, but I couldn't bear the prospect of spending the night staring at the ceiling wondering what repercussions I had to face. I wrapped my arm around her, placed my hand on her chest and held her close to me.

'Can you not, please?' She moved my hand away. 'I want to sleep.' Her tone was curt but was not so harsh as to discourage me. I gently repositioned myself to bring our bodies back into contact.

'Are you sure everything's OK?'

She turned onto her back, sighed, and opened her eyes.

'Luke. It has been a long day. I am very tired. Go to sleep.' She was looking directly at me, but her facial expression was hidden by shadows.

'I'm not sleepy yet,' I said with a cheeky smile, moving my hand back down her body towards her thigh.

'Pour l'amour de Dieu! It's not all about you Luke.' Her eyes widened, and we stared at each other for long enough to feel uncomfortable. 'You can always go downstairs if you are not sleepy. Giselle is still up.'

And there we have it. I never guessed that she might ever display jealousy, but her words were loaded with rage. I sat up and whispered words of reassurance to her, fearful that she might think I had in some way encouraged Giselle or deliberately engineered her exposing more than intended. Estelle, barely visible in the indigo dark of the room, remained motionless and said nothing while I went on to repeatedly remind her that I loved her and that she was the only one for me. Even as I said the words, I knew I sounded weak.

Foolishly, to shift the focus off me and trigger a response from her I asked 'And what about me? Am I your only one?' I regretted saying it as soon as the words left my lips.

Estelle flipped onto her back again. 'What do you mean? Have I ever given you reason to doubt me?' she said in a hissed whisper. This was not going well. I needed to reset the situation.

'I'm sorry. It's just that Giselle mentioned something about you having a husband earlier today. I should have said something earlier. I should have just talked to you, but it's been playing on my mind ever since. It reminds me how little I really know you. It just threw me, that's all.' I spoke in hushed tones, fearful that our voices would carry through the house. A dark spiky wall of silence hung in the air as she lay staring up at me. Eventually she spoke very softly and carefully.

'You are so stupid sometimes, Luke.' Her face was shadowed, and her voice was full of disappointment and sadness. 'You are also a fool for listening to Giselle. Can't you see she's been playing for your attention ever since we got here?' She sounded as calm and measured as she did at work now. 'It's always been like this. Even with my husband. If you must know, although it is none of your business, he is no more. He treated me badly and now he is gone and that is all. It was a very difficult time of my life and not something I like talking about. I was going to tell you in my own time.' A lump formed in my throat as I realised how hurt she sounded and what a fool I really was. I muttered an apology and tried to comfort her, but she shuffled away before I could reach her.

'I am also not feeling 100% in case you hadn't noticed. I need the bathroom.' She left the room and closed the door behind her without looking around.

I turned my pillow, reclined against the headboard, and gazed at the ceiling, where a sliver of lonely moonlight had snuck in above the curtain. My holiday excitement was suddenly replaced with a howling emptiness. Guilt crept in for letting my insecurities get the better of me and hurt Estelle. I strained my ears for sounds of movement in the house but, aside from an occasional breeze against the garden trees, the eerie silence remained. My mind replayed the events of the past couple of days. I had been wholly unprepared for meeting Giselle and was still figuring out the confusing dynamic between them. The situation had even left me confused as to what the dynamic between me and Estelle now was. I started to wish we had stayed within the safe confines of our life in London and our safe routine of home, work, eat and sleep; simple, but familiar and safe.

I must have dozed off on my side because the next thing I became aware of was Estelle's bottom reversing into my stomach for warmth.

'Mmmm…you're back,' I whispered, wrapping my free arm around her, and kissing her shoulder.

She wiggled tighter into me and let out a sleepy reciprocal moan that I took to mean all was well again. A tightness in my shoulders and chest that I had previously not been aware of relaxed, and a wave of warmth washed over me. I moved my hand onto her chest, which was noticeably colder than my hands, and breathed '*I love you*' into her ear. She let out a pleasurable sigh with no sound of resistance. I slipped my hand inside her pyjama top and stroked her breasts gently and continued kissing her neck. She let out a sleepy purr of encouragement but kept her eyes tightly shut. I braved moving my hand out from her pyjama top, along the side of her back and towards the front of her pyjama bottoms to undo the bow at the front.

She stopped me by gripping my wrist sharply and using it to push me away while she turned onto her back, her eyes now wide open.

'Don't, Luke. My body is not well enough tonight.' I knew what she meant and tried to free my wrist to give her a hug, but she kept a firm hold on it, twisted it round and sat up to face me.

'Stay where you are and do not make a sound,' her black silhouette whispered, while holding a finger to hush my lips. 'That doesn't mean I can't treat you,' she continued. 'Especially as you're obviously feeling so insecure tonight.' She trailed her hand down my chest, pulled the sheets back, and, with her left hand still holding my wrist tightly, gripped me firmly between my legs. 'Someone's not ready for sleep yet,' she whispered. I couldn't see her face clearly in the dark, but I could hear that she was smiling.

I reached up to stroke her, but she released her grip on me to swipe my free hand away.

'Hold on to the headboard,' she whispered, lifting my trapped hand over my head. Obediently, I moved my free hand to join it. With one hand holding both of mine in place, she moved her pillow over my face and told me not to peep. As if reading from a rule book, she reminded me that I belonged to her, to her alone, and that she was in charge for tonight. I nodded from under the pillow and tried to release a hand to stroke her, but she smacked it back into place and tutted, instructing me that I would not receive any treats if I let go. Again, I nodded obediently from under the pillow.

She returned one hand below towards my shorts, edging them downwards while I lifted my waist to make the job easier. The expectation of what was to follow lit a fire in the pit of my stomach. I gripped the headboard in anticipation of her touch and let out a moan when she finally took hold of me once again and started stroking me gently up and down.

A cocktail of relief and pleasure, coupled with my hands being pinned down and my sight effectively blinded by the pillow, sent my head into a spin that reminded me of our first night together. Visions and flashbacks to our previous encounters flashed through my mind as her hand explored between my legs with alternative speed and touch until I could no longer accurately interpret what she was doing, other than it felt good. I tried hard not to let the sight of Giselle in the kitchen with her dress hitched up, baring all, from entering the forefront of my thoughts.

If I rocked my hips in reaction to Estelle's touch, she would let go and stop, ordering me to remain perfectly still if she was to continue. I complied. She let go of my hands and moved down the bed to free up both hands on me.

'Don't let go, Luke, OK?' I regripped the headboard firmly in a show of compliance.

'It's a question of trust, right?' she whispered. I nodded, unsure whether she could see my head move from under the pillow.

'Close your eyes and relax,' she cooed, her free hand pushing my legs wider apart while she straddled one leg to pin me down and used her free hand to start tracing small circles between my buttocks. My heart started thumping with anticipation and nerves. I felt vulnerable and exposed, but remained compliant. I squeezed my eyes shut and bit my lip as she continued to stroke me with one hand and circle with the other. I had totally submitted myself to her.

'You are mine, remember?'

'Yours,' I replied, my voice tight. She removed her hand from massaging my anus and replaced it with something that felt cold and hard. Inanimate.

'No,' I said without letting go of the headboard.

'It's a question of trust, remember. If you don't like it, I'll stop. Promise.'

I let out a muted gasp as I felt something cold and thin, perhaps metal, slip inside me. I could not tell how far in or what it was. I had no sense of perspective down there. It was not comfortable but nor was it unpleasant. It was confusing; on one hand I felt like a king being taken to ecstasy and on the other I felt shameful and slightly dirty. I felt powerless to ask her to stop. I was hers.

'Are you OK?' she asked softly.

'Mm-hm,' I replied, embarrassed to admit how good it felt, my body rigid with anticipation.

The heat from the pillow was stifling me so, keeping hold of the headboard, I wiggled my head from underneath it to catch only a glimpse of Estelle, a beautiful silhouette in the moonlit room, crouched over me, her arms moving back and forth, before she pulled the pillow back over my face.

'No peeping,' she tutted and returned her hand to working the implement between my legs. I was overheating and finding it difficult to breathe. My skin felt as if it was being roasted. Despite the pleasure, I was not sure I could take much more.

'I'm too hot,' I whimpered.

'Shhhh,' was all the sympathy I got. 'You're mine, remember?'

'Yours,' I replied with a wobble. The room was getting hotter. 'Please Estelle...' I needed her to stop.

'Pardon?' she asked, feigning hearing loss.

My heart was racing with panic now as I felt a burning sensation inside me, intense pain overtaking any pleasure I had felt before.

'Stop!'

She ignored me.

The heat inside me was becoming unbearable. 'Take it out,' I pleaded, still fearful of raising my voice and drawing attention to ourselves. She remained frozen. My insides were sending hot shots of pain throughout my whole body. Still scared to move my body for fear of causing further damage, I threw the pillow off my face, placed my hands on the sides of my jaw and, through gritted teeth demanded 'Take. It. Out. Now.'

She jerked her hands back, giving my insides one last wrenching shot of pain, and threw down what looked like her cordless hair curler on the bed beside me. I watched stunned as she walked across the room to close a gap in the door, switched on a soft lamp, and went to the far side of the room to sit in front of the mirrored dressing table with her back to me.

I reached to my side and picked up the curling wand. Heat was still radiating from it. A sickness rose inside me as a raw tingling sensation, not dissimilar to pins and needles, pulsated through my lower torso. I was scared to explore, but it felt as if there was a gaping, weeping wound behind me. Perversely, I was as much worried about the shame of messing the sheets as I was about what lasting damage she may have done. I pulled my shorts on, swung my legs round, and sat upright on the side of the bed, my hands by my side to reduce the pressure on my behind. I was too fragile to express any anger.

'Estelle, really? That thing has burnt me.'

She sat motionless but I could see she was watching me through the mirror's reflection.

'It was an accident. You should have said.' Her tone that sounded cold and distant, as if it was somehow my fault.

'I did say.'

She remained seated without response.

'Would you like me to check?' she eventually asked.

'No. I'll take care of it.'

I lifted myself off the bed and, using my hands to feel my way, edged my way around the foot of the bed to head to the bathroom. As I opened the door, the hallway light streamed into the bedroom somehow making the situation more real. I paused to look at Estelle's frame sitting with her back to me at the dressing table in front of her reflection. She turned her head, her face expressionless, but her big brown eyes full of soulful innocence.

'I'm sorry,' she mouthed as I left the room.

Chapter 40

I lay alone in bed, eyes shut, the morning sun warming my face and a light breeze from the garden cooling my skin while the sound of morning songbirds without a care in the world started the day. Estelle must have pulled back the curtains and opened the window before going downstairs. I guessed she stayed awake all night because, whenever I woke, she was there to stroke my face and soothe me back to sleep. In a strange way, if it wasn't for the stinging shots of internal pain every time I moved, I could kid myself that last night was just a bad dream. That it didn't happen to me. It felt easier to accept that way. Except it did happen.

As much as I wanted to stay in bed all day, the pressure on my bladder demanded I get up. I was relieved it was only a wee I needed. I eased myself upright, involuntarily clenching my sphincter as I straightened up. My insides stiffened with caution as I pigeon-stepped my way towards the door. However, provided I kept my footsteps short and my anus and stomach muscles tight, I found my steps increased in length by the time I made it to the bathroom.

Lifting my legs into my trousers caused the most discomfort. Raising my knees made my backside feel as if it had a strip of sandpaper stuck up it. I made my way to the top of the stairs, gripped the handrail and edged myself down, step by step, to join the others for breakfast before my absence became conspicuous.

I paused behind the kitchen door before entering to psych myself up for masking my discomfort with some false swagger before swinging the door open.

'Good morning, mon chéri/Luke,' the twins said in unison, followed by an indistinguishable grunt from Steve from behind a newspaper in the corner of the room. They had chosen to both dress in matching light flowing floral cotton skirts and small plain white embroidered tops that accentuated their curves. Giselle was busy in front of the sink and Estelle was sitting at the head of the table holding a cup of coffee to her face with both hands. Steve was being Steve and might as well be invisible.

'Help yourself to coffee and pastry,' Giselle said with a nod towards the table. 'Don't wait to be offered. This is your home too now.' She smiled broadly before turning her attention back towards drying items of crockery from the draining board. I held the wooden arms of the chair to ease myself into a comfortable seated position and poured myself some coffee.

'How are you feeling today?' Estelle asked from behind her cup, her big soft eyes studying me from over its rim. Her eyes flicked towards Giselle's back before she mouthed 'I'm sorry'.

'I seem to ache all over,' I said truthfully, more for Giselle and Steve's ears than Estelle's. 'It must be all that walking we did yesterday.' I thought I saw Steve exchange a look over the top of his newspaper with Giselle who had momentarily paused her drying of a cup, as if listening for something.

'I hope you're not coming down with anything,' Estelle replied. 'Maybe we should take it easy and head back to the river and spend the day relaxing together?' She put her cup down, pushed it towards me and moved around the table to sit beside me, giving my shoulder a stroke of reassurance. She pressed her knee against mine under the table. I leant in towards her, taking the pressure off my behind, and rubbed the tip of my missing ring finger for comfort. Estelle's eyes were deep, dark, calming and honest. Pleading, almost. A pang of guilt hit me for even thinking that last night's accident could have been deliberate.

'That sounds nice,' I said. A day out of sight from the others and a chance to spend some time alone together would be good for us. 'As long as it doesn't involve too much walking.' I stroked her hand with my thumb and gave her a weak smile.

'Are you alright?' she mouthed silently. I nodded slowly in return.

'We can have a slow day. Just the two of us. We can find somewhere to sit together.' She spoke softly and with a kindness that eased my internal twinges. She put a small apricot pastry on a plate in front of me and encouraged me to eat it.

Giselle came to the table and placed a flat basket of fresh tomatoes, garlic, mushrooms and some sprigs of thyme in front of her. 'Estelle, jumelle. You must always be doing something. If he is tired, why not let him rest in the garden? We have everything here.' Giselle's nostrils flared as she spoke. Subtle but noticeable.

'I know, jumelle, but I just thought it would be nice to take Luke out for the day and see some more of the area while we are here. We can leave you in peace for the day.' Estelle rubbed her knee up and down against mine under the table.

'Peace? It is always peaceful here. We have sun loungers and even a hammock we can put up somewhere. You can go out tomorrow. Rest today.' Giselle avoided eye contact and spoke with a non-negotiable tone. Estelle opened her mouth to respond but was cut off before she had a chance. 'Is everyone happy with mushrooms and cream with some lamb tonight?' Giselle asked to no-one in particular, resting a hand on my shoulder as she popped a cherry tomato into her mouth.

'Oh Giselle,' Estelle sighed. 'I cannot think about dinner at this time. I haven't even finished my morning coffee yet.' With Estelle pressing her knee against mine under the table and Giselle resting her hand on my right shoulder, I felt as if I was trapped between a silent battle of wills. In the corner, I caught sight of Steve's red face peering over his newspaper at us, presumably wondering when he could start drinking again.

'Lamb with mushrooms and cream it is then!' Giselle announced, releasing her hold on me. 'Luke. Estelle can show you, but you will find a hammock and sun loungers in the shed. Estelle, would you be my favourite twin and go and pick up a kilo of diced lamb from the village please?'

Estelle sighed. 'Why would you suggest lamb for dinner if it's the one thing we don't have? We bought enough other food from the market to provide lots of other options?'

Giselle turned her back on Estelle and started rummaging around a lower cupboard and pulling out various sized chopping boards. 'Yes, jumelle, but that is before you all decided you wanted lamb!'

Estelle gave me a resigned look and mouthed 'I'm sorry' while holding her palms upwards as if to say, 'what can I do?' I took Estelle's hand under the table and gave it a squeeze to signal I was OK with everything. Giselle continued busying herself with moving various items around the kitchen, while chattering away to herself about all the things she needed to do to prepare for the day ahead. Steve remained hidden behind his newspaper. The fact that he hadn't turned a page since I'd entered the room told me he was either a very slow reader or he was using it as a prop. Either way, I didn't care. I was just relieved that neither of them showed any sign of knowing what went on in our bedroom last night.

I ignored the clatter of plates and cutlery that Giselle was making behind us and looked into Estelle's eyes. They seemed deeper and browner than usual and radiated calm. The innocent warmth I saw in them left me in no doubt that last night was nothing more than an unfortunate accident. Nothing more.

Chapter 41

The rest of the morning slipped away with little event and another pot of coffee while the twins chatted about shared memories, the garden, and people in the village. It was nice. A weak descriptor perhaps, but true - cosy and comfortable. Estelle had subtly given me a couple of painkillers and, through flexing and shifting my position, I was feeling more confident that no permanent damage had been done. I remained, however, apprehensive about my next substantive visit to the bathroom and turned down lunch for the very reason of wanting to keep my stomach contents light. Keen as always to be the ultimate host, Giselle had laid out an array of bread, cheese and salad on the table to pick from. For politeness's sake, I'd opted to fill my plate with salad.

Giselle reminded Estelle of the need for her to pick up some lamb for dinner before it got too late so that she could have a few hours to marinade the meat before cooking it. Estelle had again asked if I wanted to go with her but, before I had a chance to reply, Giselle interrupted to insist I remain and rest in the garden if I was not feeling completely well. She'd also teased that we could surely manage being apart for a couple of hours, which made it sound like a challenge. It was said in jest but, as often with her comments, there seemed to be an ongoing battle of wills or control being played out behind their façade of frivolity. A steady layer of simmering tension. Estelle grabbed my hand and insisted I at least follow her to the front door as she got ready to leave.

'Are you sure you are OK?' she whispered once we were in the hallway.

'I'm fine,' I reassured. 'A bit sore when I walk, but as long as I avoid sudden movements, I don't think any permanent damage has been done.'

266

'Good, but I meant about me leaving you here while I go to the butcher.'

'I'll be fine. I'll only be resting in the garden. No big deal. You'll be quicker without me anyway.'

Estelle lowered her voice to a barely audible level. 'I meant are you sure you are OK staying alone here with Giselle?'

'Of course. Why wouldn't I be?' Her question genuinely confused me.

'No reason. I am starting to wonder if bringing you here was a good idea, that's all. Perhaps we should have gone somewhere neutral where it was just the two of us.'

'It's fine,' I reassured again and pecked her on the cheek. 'I'm grateful to you for bringing me here and sharing your life with me. I honestly don't know why you're worrying.' I took both her hands in mine and held them tight. She smiled weakly.

'I'll be as quick as I can. Promise. Just rest in the garden until I'm back.'

'I will and please stop worrying. There's no need. Really.' Her eyes still showed disproportionate fear. I pulled her close and whispered in her ear. 'If you're worried about Giselle, you really have no reason to. I'll be in the garden waiting for you.'

She held my face and placed a kiss on my lips. 'Just take care of yourself. I'll be back soon.' And with that she turned and left. I remained in the hallway until I'd heard the Twingo disappear.

'I think I'll head into the garden and lie down for a bit unless you need a hand with anything?' I said as I re-entered the kitchen towards the back door. 'Did you say there was a hammock and some loungers in the shed?'

'Yes, but wait,' Giselle called, causing Steve's red eyes to peer over the top of his newspaper. 'You'll need this.' She produced a set of keys from her skirt pocket. 'The big key is for main lock and the small key is for the padlock.' A playful smile accompanied her patronising tone. 'Although I am sure you could work that out for yourself.'

As I reached to take the keys, she pulled them back out of reach. 'You will find loungers and the hammock in the far corner of the shed. Call me if you need anything, won't you?' I took the keys and meandered towards the bottom of the garden.

The garden sloped downwards which meant clear, uninterrupted views of the surrounding countryside. The thought of having a few hours to myself to relax and collect my thoughts was welcome. Behind me, I could hear Giselle's raised voice from the kitchen, no doubt in frustration with something Steve had or hadn't done. I blotted it out and focussed instead on the surrounding chorus of the crickets and serenading songbirds. I liked Giselle's garden. It was more meadow-like than orderly. The grass wasn't cut, and small colourful flowers seemed to sprout up from wherever they wanted. Clusters of wild thyme released their scent from beneath my feet and short fruit trees – apples, pears, figs - were dotted about providing pockets of shade and an abundance of refreshment within arms' reach. Above, the sky was clear blue, without a cloud in sight. I could imagine never wanting to leave the house if I lived somewhere like this.

I paused in front of the shed and inhaled the garden fragrances to untangle my jumbled recollection of last night's events. The pain had downgraded itself to mere discomfort now and I was looking forward to lying on a sun lounger for the rest of the day. I fleetingly revisited the thought that last night might not have been an accident, but the thought of Estelle's caring soulful eyes reassured me that I needed to stop overthinking to the point it destroys everything.

I took the keys from my pocket. There were five of them in total, but it was obvious which one was for the deadlock and, through process of elimination, which of the smaller keys was for the padlock. Two locks did seem a little over-precautious for a shed at the bottom of a garden in the middle of nowhere, but what did I know?

The door creaked as I opened it, releasing a stale musty odour of baked dust and cobwebs. There were garden tools, spades, forks, even a pickaxe, leaning against one side of the shed and dust-covered pieces of equipment, including a lawnmower, that looked as if they hadn't seen the light of day for some time. The door swung shut behind me, leaving the only source of light to be a bright, stage light-like stream through the rear window. An unfolded garden chair was placed in the middle of the rear of the shed, alongside which appeared to be the sun loungers that Giselle had mentioned. I was in no rush. I made my way to the chair, took hold of its arms, and eased myself into it so that I was facing the door.

Despite the smell, there was something about sheds that were peaceful and comforting. They provided an escape from the outside world. A safe bubble. Some privacy and time to reflect. To my left were the sun loungers and behind them a pile of seat cushions and blankets. I lifted them up to put them to one side, careful not to throw up too much dust into the air as I did. Underneath a checked blanket was what looked like a rolled up sleeping bag, but which I guessed was the hammock. And beneath that an attractive old antique trunk made of wood and steel with a padlock fastening its opening. I took a moment to appreciate the shed's silence and focus on the stream of light coming in through the window, but I knew immediately that I would not be able to resist opening it.

I took the keys from my pocket and shuffled my seat round to face it. The padlock popped open with a satisfying click, and, with surgical care, I slipped it off its resting place and lifted its lid, curious as to what could warrant such security. Inside, there was a shoe box, a black bin bag, some jars, and a bundle of cards and letters tied together with a ribbon. I picked the bundle up first and placed them to one side once I realised they were all in French and I couldn't understand a word. Next, I lifted the lid of the shoebox to reveal a stack of old photos. The sort of collection that no one bothers with anymore now that everyone keeps their memories on their phones.

I picked up a handful of them and looked through them one by one, smiling to myself. They were mostly of the twins at various stages of growing up. Some of them contained a tall strong man with wavy hair and features which suggested he was probably their father. I recognised the photos' backdrop as mostly having been taken in the garden, which looked much more organised and primmer than today's meadowlike layout. I held one of the photos of the twins under the light and studied their faces more closely. They looked as if they were around seven or eight years old and were, unsurprisingly, dressed identically with the same black pinafore dresses and white shirts covering their straight frames. My eyes flicked from one to the other of their faces and it really was impossible for me to tell which was which. In fact, it was impossible for me to find any feature that could have distinguished one from the other. The thought of having an identical self wandering the earth still amused me.

I put the photos back in their box and picked up the black bin bag and placed it on my lap. The bag was folded around a pile of *Sud Ouest* newspapers and a lever arch file containing official-looking documents in protective plastic sleeves. The front pages of the papers gave no clue as to why they had been kept and stored away so securely, until I came across one that had a photo of Estelle and Giselle staring defiantly into the lens of whoever was taking the photograph outside an official looking building. Above them sat the headline *"LEQUEL?" "CRIME PASSIONNEL OU MEUTRE?"*. The newspaper was dated just over three years ago.

A chill ran down my arms and my breathing wobbled as I flicked through more of the papers in the hope of finding something I could understand. A couple at the back of the pile were in English and contained the same photo of the twins on the cover directing the reader to page five for further details. Shaking now, I balanced the remaining papers on my lap and leant into the light to read.

"The mystery surrounding the death of Philippe Matthou, who was found wounded and who later died at the scene of normally sleepy village of Lusignac continues." A photo accompanying the piece showed the lower half of a man laid out on a tiled kitchen floor. Giselle's kitchen floor! His top half was covered with a blood-stained blanket, surrounded by charred and blood-smeared pine-varnished kitchen cabinets and worksurfaces. The surrounding walls were also charred black. The scene looked unreal, like hell on earth with black and red providing the only colour in the photograph. There was no doubt in my mind that it was Giselle's kitchen in the photos although it was barely recognisable from the pristine, calm and pastel coloured kitchen of the present day.

I read on, skimming for key details as quickly as I could while adrenaline surged through my veins. *Philippe was discovered in the early stages of a fire by neighbours, who reported hearing banging and shouting coming from the house earlier in the day...it was reported to have "sounded like a fight which was not unusual from that house", said one anonymous neighbour...it was only sometime after the shouting had stopped that the smell of smoke had drifted through the village, prompting a group of men to enter the property from over a side wall where they had found an unconscious and badly wounded Philippe lying in a pool of blood in a smoke-filled kitchen with multiple stab wounds. Neighbours had been able to extinguish the fire, which was thought to have stemmed from a burning pan on the stove, but exacerbated by the presence of spilled brandy, before the emergency services arrived.*

I paused to check my surroundings and steady my breathing. Despite the sun spilling into the shed through its rear window I felt cold. The sound of birds chirping and trees swaying created a peaceful backdrop to the increasing panic welling up inside me. I read on. *Philippe was dead by the time the ambulance arrived, according to the statement from an officer from La Gendarmerie, who described the scene as the most disturbing and unusual he had come across in his whole 23 years of service. There were no signs of forced entry (not unusual in a village where most doors were left unlocked). The extremely high levels of alcohol in Monsieur Matthou's bloodstream (again, not unusual in itself) would normally render someone unconscious and incapable of attempting to cook a meal which appeared to be the cause of the fire. That, alongside the sheer number and positioning of the multiple knife wounds to his body suggested that they were caused by a highly dangerous individual.*

I inhaled deeply in an attempt to steady my breathing. *Without releasing specific details, the officer was also quoted as saying that the nature of some of the wounds suggested that the perpetrator was not only highly dangerous, but probably unstable and not in their right mind. The piece finished with him appealing for anyone who might have seen or heard anything unusual in the area on that day, or the preceding days, to contact him in confidence to provide further details.*

I folded the paper carefully and replaced it in the pile and continued flicking through the collection to see if there were any other English language editions. I was in luck. This one was printed a week after the last and carried the sensationalist headline '*Innocent ou coupable?*' above another photo of Estelle and Giselle, hunched together side by side in matching floral dresses and button fronted

272

cardigans with their long hair tied back into ponytails, looking gaunt and tired. I skimmed the article, which spilled over to fill pages two and three of the paper and had moved on from the story of Philippe's death to focussing on the effect it had on the twins. Of course, the fact that they were identical twins, and attractive ones at that, no doubt gave the paper additional motivation to dedicate so many column inches to them.

I suddenly became very aware of the fact that Giselle would be able to see the shed from the kitchen window and might start to wonder why I was taking so long so I continued skim-reading as quickly as I could. The piece was written from the angle of them being strange, focussing on the fact they were rarely seen apart, moved in synchronisation with each other, and never spoke to anyone other than each other when they were growing up. The next few paragraphs contained numerous quotes from neighbours who described them with suspicion, as withdrawn and isolated. I skipped forward to see if the piece contained any further news about the incident itself.

Here we are…the circumstances of Philippe's murder repeated again but in more detail…and then a focus on the twins. *There were no eyewitnesses to the starting of the fire, nor any sightings of any strangers in the village that day. The only other occupants of the house that day were Giselle Merisier and Estelle Matthou (née Merisier), who were eventually found covered in Philippe's blood huddled together in tears under a bush at the bottom of the garden. They were described as being visibly traumatised, wide-eyed and muttering incomprehensibly to each other with tears streaming down their faces.*

However, the piece then shifted towards highlighting inconsistencies between the twins' versions of events once they were taken away to be cleaned up and comforted. I read on. *Suspicion amongst enforcement officers was first aroused as the sisters continued to gibber away and shout*

273

at each other in a language that no one else could understand as they were led away to separate areas to explain their version of events... subsequent interviews with each of them gleaned contradictory evidence that raised more questions than the answers provided. Estelle was quoted as saying that she had been upstairs taking an afternoon siesta when she'd awoken to the smell of smoke and the sound of her husband shouting. When she rushed downstairs, she claimed to see a man she didn't recognise standing over her husband before he fled the scene. She had been unable, however, to provide any form of description claiming that she was in too much of a state of shock and the smoke had made her eyes sting. When asked where her sister was she was only able to assume she was somewhere downstairs as she didn't see or hear her upstairs.

Giselle on the other hand was claiming not to have seen or heard anything until she found Estelle sobbing over his body in the kitchen, and she was quoted as speculating provocatively that 'Philippe was a pig of a man who was always mad and drunk who had probably decided he could not live with himself anymore'. Whatever the intention behind her statement, it had backfired massively as all it seemed to achieve was casting a cloud of suspicion over them both.

The only detail their initial statements agreed on was their attempts to revive him which was not helped by Giselle adding that *'they wasted their time and should have focussed on putting the fire out and saving the kitchen before that pig'.* Having sown the seeds of doubt in the reader's mind, the article concluded with a blunt statement confirming that the sisters had accepted legal advice not to make any further statements while charges against them were being considered. I folded the paper shut and again looked at the photo of them on the front cover, both looking totally devoid of emotion, tired and withdrawn, with none of their usual sparkle.

I put the papers back in their bag and returned it carefully back in the trunk, removing the lever arch file again to see if it contained any sort of conclusion. It would be so much easier if I had my phone with me to be able to take a quick photo and scan any French text into google translate. Estelle had kept hold of my phone since the drive down though, and I didn't pack any back up devices. Nor was there any time for me to get back inside the house, search for it, and back again without arousing suspicion. Plus, for all I knew, she may have kept it with her. So I thumbed through the pockets of documents, skimming their content for any English language, an increasing sense of urgency rising inside me. I was desperate to find the conclusion to the story. At this stage, given the fact that they were free, I could only presume that either a) no charges were brought against them, b) charges were brought against them, but they were cleared, or c) Philippe's killer was caught. I needed to know.

In a weird way, discovering this dark past in a dark shed allowed me to compartmentalise and create some mental separation between what I was reading and the reality of spending a morning sitting peacefully with the twins in their pastel-coloured kitchen. There was such a contrast between what I was reading and reality that I had to find out more.

Caught up in a bundle of what looked like legal invoices was a small collection of newspaper cuttings which stood out due to their difference in colour. They were all in French except one which contained the headline "*MYSTÈRE DU MEURTRE*". The text beneath was written in English and dated six months after the other papers I'd read. My heart continued to thump steadily in anticipation of finding the conclusion to the story.

The tone was neutral and factual, containing none of the sensationalism of the previous articles, and the content was focussed on the outcome of court consideration of charges being brought against Giselle and Estelle. I skimmed the cutting for keywords and, towards the bottom, caught the sentence '...*dismissed as having no case no answer...*'. I felt an immediate release of tension in my neck and shoulders. I took a breath and returned to the top of the page to take in the detail.

Philippe's cause of death was recorded as murder on the basis that it was irrefutably impossible for him to have been able to inflict the injuries he was left with on himself. Reference was made to the fact that La Gendarmerie had withheld the precise detail of the autopsy report on the basis that it contained details that only the murderer (or murderers) could know and that the mystery surrounding the case remained open. Other than referring to a redaction of detail, the reporting pointed towards them of "a gruesome nature, intended to inflict maximum pain and damage".

It was also noted that Philippe's blood alcohol level was so high it was extremely unlikely that he would have been fully conscious when his injuries were sustained. Analysis of the contents of the remains of the single glass of red wine in the kitchen showed it contained a high percentage of cheap brandy having been mixed into it, and that traces of brandy were also found in his clothing.

DNA collected from the scene failed to find any other than from Estelle, Giselle and Philippe. There were no witnesses to the events that took place in the house to provide evidence and the suspicions previously aired by neighbours were dismissed as speculation due to the lack of any corroboratory evidence.

Estelle's and Giselle's initial contradictory versions of events were deemed unreliable due to the shock and trauma they had suffered, and they had both subsequently stated that they could remember nothing from that day before the emergency services found them at the bottom of the garden. Numerous interviews with psychologists and La Gendarmerie had failed to tease any further information out of either of them. In conclusion, and despite media and public opinion, by the time the case was handed over to the Officiers de la Police Judiciaire (OPJ) and subsequently a Juge d'instruction, it was clear there was simply not enough evidence to put a case to trial, let alone be strong enough to secure a conviction of any sort. And so the case was dismissed.

I leaned back and stared at the page. My hands were still numb and shaking while the hairs on my arms prickled. In my peripheral vision, a stream of sunlight crept along inside of the shed and onto me, bringing with it a burst of warmth.

I looked up to see Giselle's frame standing in the doorway, hands on hips, and a half-smile on her face that I couldn't read. I lowered the cutting to my lap, unable to breathe.

'Did you find what you were looking for?' she asked, stepping inside the shed.

Chapter 42

Silently, I stared up at her and tried to read her face from her facial expression. The sunlight shone through her cotton skirt, revealing the curves of her thighs. Her eyes darted around my face as if she too was analysing my expression. Trying my best to release the tension in my face, I closed the lever arch file and returned it to the trunk.

'I thought you had been a long time, so I came to see if you needed help.' I noticed she had this habit of pausing without breaking eye contact both before and after she spoke which made every sentence more intense than it needed to be. A cold sensation ran down my spine.

I stretched, feigning a casualness at odds with the adrenaline rushing through my veins. 'I'm fine,' I replied with. 'I was just taking the chance to appreciate the shade for a bit.'

'Let me help you, silly,' she said, bending forward to pick up one of the sun loungers. 'It would be a lot cooler in the shade underneath the walnut tree than sitting in this stuffy shed.' I almost gasped when I saw her line of vision turn towards the open trunk. 'Oh dear,' she said, looming over me now. 'I didn't leave that open, did I?' The satisfied smile on her face suggested she already knew the answer. 'Some things are best left locked away, don't you think?' I nodded passively, suddenly wishing I could be transported back to the safety of my own garden, my own bench, and my own cherry blossom tree. 'Come on. Let's get these sun loungers set up so you can get settled.' She turned, lounger in hand, and headed back out into the garden.

I knelt before the trunk and straightened the bag and folder into the position I'd found them. I was about to close it when a cloudy jar with a rusty lid wedged in its corner caught my eye. I checked over my shoulder for Giselle before pulling it out. She was out of sight already. The jar had remnants of a label that looked like it was an old pickle jar and was full of cloudy yellowy-brown liquid. Curious, I held it to the light and swirled the vinegary contents around until I could feel the weight of something solid moving within it. I held the jar still as the sediment of the liquid started to settle and its contents became visible.

Vomit rose to the back of my throat as it became clear there was a lump of flesh bobbing within the liquid. It was brown and decayed and had torn, ragged edges, the sort of thing you'd imagine fishermen would throw overboard as bait, but the shape and remnants of hair attached to the meat remnants left no doubt that it was actually pickled male genitalia.

'You might as well bring all of the loungers out with you,' Giselle called from outside. 'And the hammock if you want.'

I swallowed down the lump of concrete that had formed in my throat down and carefully replaced the jar in the trunk, closed the lid and clicked the padlock shut over its catch. 'Coming,' I called back. I made my way towards Giselle, loungers in hand and squinting in the bright outdoor light. Giselle was leaning against the walnut tree watching me. I staggered towards her, feeling as if I was going to pass out while she looked perfectly at ease as she tucked a loose strand of hair behind her ear and relieved me of my load.

'You really don't look well,' she said, placing the back of her hand against the cold sweat on my forehead. She steered me beside the unfolded sun lounger. 'I know what you were looking at must come as a bit of a shock, but it is better now that you know I think.' She applied light pressure on my shoulder, encouraging me to lie down. I complied. 'Just rest and I will take care of these.' I lay still and watched as she set up the other loungers, chatting away as she did so.

'So now you can see what people really think of us,' she said, opening the legs of the second lounger. 'Newspapers, neighbours, so-called friends…everyone assumed we had something to do with it.' She stood up and folded back the lounger's headrest. 'Let me tell you…anyone could have killed that man, and he would have deserved it. He was a nasty drunk and Estelle would have plenty of reasons to have killed him, but she is too soft and would not want to.' Giselle spoke as coolly as if she were describing a leisurely stroll through the countryside.

'She is far too soft,' she repeated. 'If it was left to her, she would have remained his slave for the rest of her life. Whatever happened to him was a blessing for everyone.' She paused from what she was doing and stared at me, gauging my reaction. 'However, if she did do it then good for her.'

Her voice trailed off as she turned her attention to unfolding the remaining lounger. 'That woman has always been the lucky one though.' Now, it sounded as if she was talking to herself rather than to me. 'She escapes this village, she finds a job, she is invited to move to London, she gets to show off her new man.' She paused again to study my face. I avoided her gaze and folded my hands across my waist, holding the tip of my finger stub for comfort.

'Sometimes I wonder if I am cursed from birth,' she continued, sitting herself on the lounger beside me. 'She was our father's favourite too, you know? Always the first to be picked up, held, sat on his lap, everything. Always the one on his shoulders while I walked behind. Always the first. Always Estelle and Giselle, never Giselle and Estelle.'

I gave a smile I hoped was reassuring. 'I'm sure he loved you both equally,' I said, hoping to calm the intensity of her emotions.

'Oh, don't worry about me, Luke. I am fine. It is just how it is. I am just saying, that is all. It is always me who is left behind while Estelle moves on in life.' She stood up and ran her hands down her legs to flatten the creases of her skirt.

'Did you know that Giselle means hostage?' she asked.

'I did,' I replied.

'And that Estelle means bright star?'

'Yes, you told me the other night.'

'See?' she said, throwing her hands in the air with a Gallic shrug. 'It is written.' And with that, she clapped her hands and spun round to face the house. 'You rest. I will be back later. Would you like a drink or anything? Some wine perhaps?'

'No, thank you,' I called after her as she headed to the house. 'Just some water please.'

She didn't reply and had disappeared by the time I next looked around.

I was left with the serenity of the garden, with its sweet jasmine scents and backdrop of songbirds and crickets. The environment was a complete contrast to the storm of thoughts swirling around my head. I noticed, for the first time, that behind the various shrubs, jasmine and bougainvillea that lined the edges of the garden was a brick wall that did not appear to contain an exit. I folded my hands across my chest for comfort and closed my eyes to calm my mind and think.

It was now me who felt hostage.

Chapter 43

The sun warmed my face through the tree's canopy as I lay back and watched a red kite circling the cloudless sky, its wings scarcely moving as it rode the currents effortlessly. Songbirds fluttered from tree to tree in the garden, oblivious to the danger up above. My internal voice was in overdrive. What if Estelle did kill her husband? She does have a temper but is she capable of murder? What if it was Giselle? How well do I really know either of them? Could it have been an intruder? What was Philippe like? Did he deserve it? How much more to the story was there that wasn't in what I had read? Why had Estelle never spoken to me about any of this and left me to find out this way? The questions kept coming with no answers.

I sat up and noticed a jug of water with ice and slices of lemon in it had appeared on the small table next to me, a cloth over its mouth and a glass beside it. Giselle must have brought it while I was dozing. I felt a pang of discomfort shoot through my lower torso as I twisted to pour myself a glass. I drank greedily, the water was cool, soothing my dry mouth and throat as it worked its way towards my stomach.

A breeze swept over me, cooling my exposed arms and neck. The hills beyond the garden were lit up in full technicolour as the sun was reaching its peak. Looking around, I could see I was alone in the central point of the garden with only Steve in sight in the distance, laid out in his deckchair beside the house, his spot no doubt chosen for easy access to his next drink. The shed stood solemnly to my left, its open door swaying in the breeze, reminding me of the secrets that lay behind it.

Images of the trunk and the newspaper cuttings within it flooded the forefront of my mind, their words permanently etched in mind for future perusal, all tinged with that musty smell. And that jar of course. Did I really see what I thought

I saw? Or was my mind playing tricks with me? It seemed inconceivable that the French police could be so inefficient as to miss a mutilated cock and balls in their investigations but perhaps it was not there at that time?

I was tempted to return to the shed for a second look at everything now I'd had a bit of time to absorb its contents but felt sure that Giselle would be watching from somewhere within the house. And I didn't really want to have to face her again just yet. I needed more time to think.

I considered waiting until Estelle was back from the shops and casually bringing the subject of Philippe's murder up with them to see how they react in each other's company. Why was I only finding out about this now? Then I scolded myself for being so arrogant as to expect that I had any right to have been told before now. I mean, what right did I have over Estelle's past? None. She had shown me nothing but trust, love and affection since we met and if she felt her past was no concern of mine, then that should be good enough for me. Whatever happened with Philippe, some things are best left in the past. I, of all people, should know that.

I turned to look uphill, back towards the house. Giselle was standing outside the kitchen door in a square, confident stance, her hands resting on her hips. Her skirt rippled in the wind and loose strands of her hair danced. She raised a hand and waved, as if I was much further away than I was and called out to ask if I was OK. I shaded my eyes from the sun, nodded, and gave her a thumbs-up. Even from this distance I could make out her dimples punctuating the broad smile on her face. How could someone so warm present any threat?

Despite my initial shock at reading about Philippe's murder, and the horror I had felt at seeing that grisly photo of his bloody body lying motionless on the kitchen floor, I did not feel any sense of danger from either Estelle or Giselle. The case against them had been dismissed. In fact, it had been dismissed before it even became a case. I fleetingly considered whether I ought to report the presence of the pickle jar to the authorities in case it did actually contain that vital piece of missing evidence they were looking for. But I didn't trust my own eyes enough to be sure about what I'd seen and, in any case, what good would getting authorities involved now bring?

No. Who was I, after all, to make a judgement on the rights or wrongs of what went on before? Perhaps Philippe deserved his fate? Perhaps it was nothing to do with the twins?

I searched my mind for every interaction I had had with them both since I'd known them. From my first date with Estelle, the fire in the restaurant, her sometimes irrational temper towards men, the passionate dominance shown towards me behind closed doors, the accident with the curling wand. I clenched at the recollection. But then there was the lifeline she had thrown me at work, the quiet evenings over dinner at home, the handholding Sunday walks, the browsing through local markets and feeding the goats at Hackney city farm together. I really had no reason to consider her a threat to me, despite her occasional outburst of unpredictable volatility. None of us is perfect, after all.

And Giselle? I still barely knew her of course, and our interactions had been limited to relatively formal situations, but did she present a danger in any way? I simply didn't know her well enough to form a view. She didn't seem the sort of person to take shit from anyone, but was she capable of murder? Even accounting for the fact that her flirtatious nature might be skewing my judgement in her favour, I didn't think so. Even if she did have a hand in Philippe's murder, which I couldn't fully rule out, there was something about the way she treated me that left me feeling unwaveringly safe.

Yes, I had managed to talk myself into a much calmer place since finding out what happened to Estelle's husband. It's amazing how quickly the mind can accept different situations, however much of a initial shock they present. And yet, an uneasy niggle remained. Like I was missing something. I looked round the garden and felt its boundaries shrinking towards me, its tranquillity starting to suffocate me. I couldn't put my finger on it but had a strong urge to return to my Bethnal Green flat as soon as possible.

I lay back, closed my eyes and practised some controlled deep breathing while focussing on the continuing sound of songbirds exchanging whistles with each other.

*Click. My younger self was back in London, back in the office, in my corner, staring at my screen in amazement at my realisation that my access rights gave me the ability to read everyone's online messages at work. Without thinking about why, I had logged straight onto **her** account ~ "Reynolds, Sarah (CHImp)" ~ my girlfriend of nearly three years. Why I chose to snoop on **her** first, I can't remember but what I'll never forget is the exchange that was taking place on my screen between **her** and Salter. 'Book a meeting room...make sure it's one with an internal lock on the door...put a meeting in our calendars in case anyone asks...no one will...he'll never know...so what if he does...do you really care anyway...?' Within a minute a message arrived on my own account from **her**, 'I've got my performance review this afternoon so will probably be late home. Go ahead without me and I'll see you later. Oh, and feel free to cook one of your special dinners if you like – I've got an appetite on me today'. Before I had a chance to respond, more messages were appearing in Sarah's chat with Salter. 'Done...no need to rush...I even told him how hungry I'm feeling today...I hope you can handle me...'*

That was the precise moment that brutal reality smashed my cosy perception of the world into a thousand pieces.

Whoever said 'sticks and stones may break my bones, but words will never harm me' was wrong. The stabbing pain in my chest proved the opposite.

Like a serum injection working its way round my body, I was defenceless against a wave of feelings which morphed from hurt to sad to humiliation, before eventually settling on anger, rage and a deep wish for revenge. But I was powerless to act. Powerless aside from the fact that I knew what was going on and they didn't know I knew. Powerless aside from the fact that I could continue to read every word they exchanged between each other – and others – without them knowing. My only advantage in the sorry situation was to keep this knowledge to myself and to wait until Sarah returned home later that evening before confronting her.

Click.

I woke with a jolt. A midday nightmare in the middle of the garden. I rubbed my eyes and looked around. My head throbbed as I looked up to note the sun had shifted further round the cloudless sky. I topped up the glass of water beside me and drank thirstily. I swung my legs to the side of the lounger and rested my elbows on my knees. The shed door was closed and the padlock back on its latch, locked. My memory of the trunk and its contents felt dream-like and unreal.

From the direction of the house, I could hear the chatter of Estelle and Giselle. I surveyed the garden. Steve was still in his deckchair to the side of the house, either fast asleep or passed out. Like a lounging cat, he managed to pass hours without the slightest movement.

The twins' voices continued to carry down the garden from inside. Jovial, teasing, light-hearted. Groceries, shopping, food preparation, Estelle taunting Giselle about her obsession with food, Giselle mocking Estelle for not being able to cook and look after me properly. Estelle retorting by telling Giselle not to spoil me or I'll get used to it and she'll never be able to keep me happy when we get back to London. I chuckled to myself and reminded myself how lucky I was to be at the receiving end of both of their affections. If, one year ago, I could have envisaged myself sitting in the luxury of such picturesque surroundings, with two such beautiful charismatic women fussing over me, I would not have believed it possible. I turned my sight to the locked shed again. Whatever secrets lay within it could stay there for all I cared.

Their voices continued to carry and their energetic chitter chatter sounded as easy-going and fun as any siblings spending time together. That was, at least, until I started to question why they were talking in English unless it was deliberately for the benefit of me overhearing.

Chapter 44

'Good morning, sleepyhead,' teased Estelle, standing in the back doorway, shielding her eyes from the sun as I took small steps back towards the house. My shadow stretched out before me, telling me I'd been asleep for much longer than intended. 'Are you feeling better at least?' she asked, planting a kiss on my cheek, letting her lips linger for just long enough for me to feel their warmth. 'You looked so comfortable down there, I thought I would leave you to rest.' She searched my eyes, as if seeking to communicate an additional message without words.

The details I had gleaned from the newspaper cuttings earlier seemed like a world apart, and as if they were written about someone other than the person standing before me now. There was no way I could imagine Estelle playing any role in the tragic events. With her big brown eyes, her gentle smile, the kinks of hair she kept tucking behind her ears, she looked nothing but peaceful innocence.

'I'm sorry,' I replied. 'What time is it? I must have been more drained than I realised.' I rubbed my eyes. 'Can I help with anything?'

'Giselle is bringing the last pieces out of the kitchen now if you want to help. But don't worry. Sit down if you want. We can manage.'

The wooden garden table was already set with platters of salads, crisp green beans, and slender spears of asparagus. Fragrant herbs, presumably freshly snipped from the garden, speckled their surface and small bowls of olives were laid out across the table, within reach of every seat. It was another picturesque display.

I entered the kitchen, keen to show willing. 'You are awake! What perfect timing!' Giselle beamed, her face rosy from the heat of the roasting tray of lamb she was holding. Steam rose from the tray which was glistening with a mouth-watering creamy mushroom glaze. 'We are ready to eat, no?' Her head wobbled from side to side with a sense of pride at the pièce de resistance in her oven-gloved hands. She nodded towards the kitchen table and asked me to follow her out into the garden with the bottle of wine - a St-Émilion Grand Cru – and the three cut glasses placed on the table. 'Dinner is ready!' she sang.

As Giselle led the lamb to the table, Estelle stood to applaud her efforts while we all stared hungrily as the dish was slowly lowered onto a metal stand in the middle of the table. Steve had plonked himself at the far end of the table, ignoring the empty seats closer to where the food was laid out, his own bottle in one hand, empty glass in the other. His half-dead eyes told me he'd already checked out for the evening.

'Please! Sit down. Asseyez-vous.' Giselle ordered as she carved thin slices of lamb onto our plates.

'This looks amazing,' I complimented, causing Giselle to beam with pride. Estelle reached across the table and squeezed my hand affectionately, her eyes radiating warmth in the evening light. A collective feel-good moment. 'Shall I pour?' I offered.

'Please,' Giselle replied, continuing to fill our plates. I half-filled each of our glasses with ruby red wine and was about to lean towards Steve's end of the table to fill his glass when Giselle tutted and shook her head.

'Not for him,' she winked. 'He can drink the cheap stuff.' She spoke as if he wasn't present, which, in a way, he wasn't. I sat down obediently and wondered what Steve had ever done to deserve such ostracization. Or why their relationship continued to limp along. 'Pass this to him please.' She handed me a plate with some bread, cheese and olives on it. I stretched down the table to place it in front of him. He barely acknowledged my presence and remained slouched over his wine.

'Please start,' Giselle prompted.

They stared at me as I cut into the lamb, added a slice of asparagus to my fork and took my first mouthful. In my side vision I could see Steve using both hands to shakily lift his glass to his lips. The lamb melted in my mouth, disintegrating into a perfect buttery herby blend. Two pairs of unblinking eyes watched as I chewed.

'Mmmm. This is amazing!' I said, releasing both twins from their frozen postures as they moved in slow unison to pick up their own cutlery and start eating. As idyllic a scene as it was, I couldn't help thinking of Tweedledum and Tweedledee at the Mad Hatter's tea party with Steve playing the role of the sleeping dormouse.

Everything was cooked to perfection, full in flavour, rich in taste but light on the stomach. I complimented Giselle again on her culinary skills and commented to Estelle that I must get in the habit of using more herbs in our own cooking when we're back in London.

Estelle and Giselle exchanged a knowing look between them. Estelle placed her cutlery on the side of her plate.

'That reminds me, chéri,' Estelle said with a business-like air. 'We need to cut our holiday short and head back to London, I'm afraid.' Giselle continued eating. Clearly, this was not news to her.

'Oh?' I questioned. 'I thought we were planning to stay another week?'

Estelle pulled her phone out of her pocket and placed it on the table beside her, as if it in itself provided explanation. She sighed. Her face tightened up into the uncompromising Chief Operating Officer I was familiar with. 'Apparently, something urgent has come up and Gordon wants me in to talk about it first thing on Monday morning.'

This was disappointing news. I was still acclimatising to our holiday and felt it would be left incomplete if we left so soon. 'What does he want?' I asked. 'It's a bit over the top for him to expect you to cut your holiday short just so he can talk to you about something. We have our laptops with us if he could figure out how to use Microsoft Teams like the rest of us.'

'I know, but what can I do?' Estelle replied. Giselle kept her head down. 'I offered that of course but he wouldn't say what it was about and wants to see me in person.' Despite everything I had learnt this afternoon, I was genuinely sad at the thought of having to leave so soon after arriving. I wanted to spend longer getting to know Estelle away from work, see more of the region, and get to know Giselle better of course. I wasn't due back in the office until the following Monday but thought I may as well cancel my own leave rather than sit at home for a week while Estelle went in.

'I'm sorry, chéri, but the fact he's messaging me on Saturday means he must have something important on his mind. Anyway, I have arranged for us to fly back from Bordeaux tomorrow.' She sipped her wine. 'We can always come back or have other holidays,' she added. 'After all, this is still the beginning, not the end.' She smiled and gave me a wink. I believed her. We'd be back.

'No sad faces!' demanded Giselle raising her glass. 'If tonight is our last meal together for a while, then we should make the most of it! Santé!' She knocked back half of her glass in one go and replaced it on the table triumphantly. Her enthusiasm was as infectious as her smile and red cheeks.

'Santé!' Estelle and I replied in unison, knocking back our wine as if it were tequila.

Giselle encouraged us to eat, enjoy the food while it was hot and then steered the conversation back towards ingredient preparation, which foods pair with which best, and what dishes they could look forward to making during our return visit. Compared to the nagging thought as to what Gordon might have recalled Estelle to London for, life in Lusignac seemed a much happier and simpler place than the rat race of London. I wondered again what motivated Estelle to seek such a drastic change in lifestyle.

'Maybe, and if Luke agrees of course,' Estelle started, as if reading my mind, 'you could visit us in London someday? It's very different but I think you might like it?' They both looked at me expectantly.

'Of course!' I replied without a doubt. 'Bethnal Green is not as pretty as round here, but you'd be very welcome and I'm sure you'd like it.' I meant it and, as an afterthought, added, 'And Steve of course is welcome too if you wanted him to come.' I struggled to think how I might accommodate them both in my small flat, but felt it was the right thing to say. Steve's head was resting silently on his chest. He hadn't heard a word.

'Pfft!' said Giselle, knocking back the remainder of her glass. 'Who knows? Maybe I will come one day but I don't want to intrude on young love.' She looked towards Steve and added 'if I do come, I'll come alone though. I cannot see this one lasting much longer.'

Estelle rested her hand on Giselle's shoulder and reminded her that she'd be very welcome. Giselle then made a point to remind Estelle 'to leave a contact number this time' and asked me to leave my contact details as well 'in case she decides to disappear again'. Estelle apologised to Giselle for being out of contact for so long, excusing herself by saying she needed to focus on settling into London and launching her career first. Giselle looked the other way in mock scorn, playing on Estelle's guilty feelings.

'Luke, I'm serious. Give me your address and number, just in case,' she joked, biting her bottom lip playfully.

Estelle still had my phone so, playing along, I offered to enter our contact details into Giselle's phone. She then surprised me by explaining that she 'doesn't do the internet or mobile phones'. She used to have one but 'gave it up in favour of life instead'. She passed her paper napkin across the table and told me to write my details down, insisting I include my fixed home line because 'people are always changing their mobile numbers', with a sideways glance to Estelle. Estelle passed me a pen from her bag.

Once I'd written my details down, Giselle made a point of snatching the napkin, folding it into a small square and slipping it down her top and into her bra.

'It is a long time since such a handsome man gave me his contact details on a napkin!' she said, licking her lips. She then turned towards Steve and banged her hand on the table, causing him to jerk upright with a jolt. 'Do you see what is happening here, Steve? I will run away while you sleep one day!' He gave each one of us a confused look before letting his chin drop back down to his chest.

The rest of the meal and the evening passed peacefully, with Steve having shuffled off to bed early, leaving me, Estelle and Giselle to clear up and finish the night with a cup of tea and cigarette while admiring the stars in the night sky. It was a perfect moment to end the night on. Their presence made me feel calm and safe. Whatever the truth behind what had gone on in the past with Estelle's husband, being in their company felt cosy and secure. Despite their funny ways, their coordinated movements, their identical inflections when they spoke and their matching outfits, it was all comforting. They way they both fussed over me in a way I hadn't ever been fussed over before. I liked it. They felt as close to family as I could imagine.

At the end of the night, I crept into our moonlit bedroom and carefully lowered myself into the bed alongside Estelle so as not to disturb her. It was a hot night, and she was only wearing her short summer nightie with a single sheet for cover. Unsure if she was asleep already or not, I placed my arm carefully over her waist and leant forward to kiss her cheek goodnight.

Her eyes were wide open, staring ahead.

'She told you, didn't she?'

Her poker face gave me no clues as to whether she was asking out of curiosity or anger. I gave her hip an affectionate squeeze and kissed her cheek again.

'Answer me, Luke,' she insisted. 'She told you what happened to Philippe, didn't she?' She turned on her back to face me.

I said nothing but nodded slowly while she stared up at me, hollow-eyed. It wasn't anger I saw in her but something akin to upset and disappointment.

'We don't have to talk about it if you don't want.' I placed light kisses on her cheek down her neck. 'It doesn't have to change anything between us,' I reassured. 'Does it?' A surge of panic welled up inside me, worried at how Estelle might react to me finding out and whether or how it might affect us.

'I didn't kill him, Luke. Promise.'

Her eyes glistened from what little light was left in the room as they brimmed with tears. I wasn't expecting her to come straight out with that, or for her to say anything about the incident at all. It made me wonder what she was thinking I might be thinking. Of all the things I might have been thinking, it wasn't that she killed Philippe.

'I know,' I replied, lowering my head onto her pillow and wrapping my leg over hers. The trouble was, at that moment, I couldn't distinguish between what I wanted to believe and what I actually believed.

Chapter 45

The following morning was a blur. Estelle had been up since an unnecessarily early hour, packing and preparing to leave. The first thing I could remember was being encouraged to wake up and put on my loosest-fitting clothes that she'd laid on the chair beside me, especially chosen for a comfortable flight. After a muted farewell coffee with Giselle, hugs and kisses all round, and over-stated promises to see each other again soon, we were back in the Twingo and on our way to Bordeaux airport. And now, having drunk more in-flight coffee and munched a bag of salted snacks, we were only fifteen minutes from reaching London City Airport and back in familiar grey British skies, with its network of grey motorways and grey buildings below. It hardly felt welcoming.

I rubbed my eyes and stretched my neck and shoulders which were sore from being slouched forward. Estelle was sitting upright in the window seat beside me, looking as fresh-faced and alert as always, reading a magazine. She acknowledged my presence with a smile and said she was looking forward to being 'home home'.

Home. It felt good to hear her call it that. I was, of course, looking forward to returning to our own private bubble together, but it was also tinged with sadness that our holiday had been cut short so abruptly. Maybe it was the fact that I hadn't really wanted to leave. Maybe it was the fact that, rather than getting to know Estelle better, we were returning with more unresolved issues and mystery than we left with. Another Pandora's box of questions we'd never get round to opening. Maybe I was just tired.

Estelle did not seem to have anything other than getting back to work on her mind and started talking about it as soon as we'd got into our Uber and were heading towards Bethnal Green. Sunday lunchtime, and her mind was already back at work. She couldn't stop speculating on the reasons why she might have been asked to return from leave early. Her hands were telling the story as much as her words as she ran through her achievements since joining the firm, as if preparing her defence against any accusation of wrongdoing. She spoke of all the streamlined processes she'd implemented, the recommendations for increased productivity she'd applied across all international offices, and the successful direction of travel that her brainchild, Project Butterfly, was heading in. By the time she'd finished, she'd convinced herself she was being called back to receive praise, or to sort out an issue that no one else could solve.

I was less sure but didn't want to bring her down with negative speculation, so I nodded along encouragingly. I desperately wanted my laptop and phone back from Estelle to see what had been going on back in the office, but she had refused, insisting she wasn't ready to lose me to cyberspace quite yet and that she wanted me to stay in holiday mode for as long as possible. She failed to see the irony of her putting all her energy into talking about work. However, she was happy, and we were good, and that was the main thing.

The following morning, we were both up and out early. Estelle first, and already dressed in her familiar tweed two-piece set with a blouse that buttoned all the way up to her neck, looking every inch the professional while I was only just getting out of the shower. I had hoped we'd travel in together and grab some coffee along the way, but she was keen to head off immediately without me and get a head start on the day. She did, however, return my work phone and laptop – finally! – officially marking the end of our holiday.

We still followed the routine of entering the office at least ten minutes apart from each other to avoid giving rise to any suspicion from colleagues and, given it was still only 07:03, I decided to make the most of having some time to myself by taking myself off for some good old-fashioned bacon and eggs.

The Regency Café in Pimlico was a long-time favourite of mine, a ten-minute walk from the office, serving good old-fashioned English classics in an original art deco tiled interior, complete with half-length checked curtains at the window. There was no hierarchy in the Regency Café. Whether you were a smart-suited office worker like me, a plaster-splattered labourer, or a cabbie, standing in a queue to order a great English breakfast was a great equaliser.

I placed my order, collected my mug of tea, and took a corner seat by the window and waited for my order to be bellowed back to me for collection. I took out my phone to make a start on checking messages and emails.

One from Estelle. *'First in at office. No one else here yet. Take your time x'*

She wasn't in the habit of sending me messages ever, let alone of the type to check in on arrival. I'd like to think it was because our relationship had progressed closer towards consolidated coupledom, but I knew it was more likely that she was more worried about what was in store for her at work than she had let on. Truth be told, so was I. I didn't like not knowing what was going on.

I was itching to get back online and read through last week's conversations to get a feel for what was going on, but the café was too busy and with too little free table space to be setting up my laptop. This was a place where people sat elbow to elbow, the clatter of cutlery on plates was constant, and table turnover was high. A long customer queue for service was already forming to place orders, discouraging any of us seated to linger over laptops. I pulled my work phone out instead and waited for emails and messages to sync.

The woman behind the counter bellowed out 'Set breakfast with two eggs for the young gentleman in the corner,' prompting me to rush up and collect my plate as quickly as possible; I knew I'd be publicly scolded by the server if I was a moment late. I used a napkin to carry my plate back to my table to prevent my hand from scalding and admired the feast before me - eggs, bacon, black pudding, beans and toast. And a grilled tomato I was keen to get rid of by eating first.

I placed my phone beside my plate; the messages were still downloading. I placed a perfect forkful of bacon and toast, dipped in egg, into my mouth and started scrolling through messages while I chewed. Pure comfort food in a moment that felt like the quiet before the storm. My sixth sense could feel it.

The empty seats on my table were filled with a group of American tourists marvelling loudly at the ordinariness of the place. I shuffled deeper into my corner to make room for them while continuing to scroll through messages with a do not disturb expression on my face.

Most were emails from my team ('my team' – it still felt strange!), and for information only. Various purchase orders, client account reports and team forecasts. Boring stuff that could be marked read without reading and dumped into a folder in case needed in future. There was one email that caught my eye and sent a chill through me, however. It was from Mathéo in the French office. It was unusual in its tone. It was professional, apologetic and respectful. The last qualities I would expect from Mathéo, especially considering how we parted company in Paris.

He had emailed to send through the files he had passed copies of to me when we met, with an explanation of how he had revised some of the figures to bring them up to date, and confirmation of the actions he was putting in place for improved performance. There was a subservience to his message and an offer to supply me with anything else I needed to provide the Board with reassurance. The bit that made me feel uneasy was the way in which he had started his message with an apology for underestimating me and expressing a wish to make sure we could work well together in future. It was the statement 'I trust you both enjoyed your holiday' that really troubled me.

He had used the word 'holiday' instead of 'visit' or 'trip'. This was surely not a linguistic slip-up. He wasn't referring to the visit to his office but the holiday I had mentioned going on after the visit was over. And he had used the word 'both'. Could I – or we – have inadvertently let slip that we were going on holiday together? I doubted it. I would need to correct any assumptions on his part once I was online and before there was ay risk of gossip spreading around the firm. I started to eat faster, chewing minimally and gulping lumps of black pudding down, keen to get to the office and log onto the servers so I could check last week's communicator messages for any chat between Mathéo and anyone at London HQ.

At that precise moment, my phone buzzed with the arrival of a text message.

My first ever text message from Salter.

'*Good holiday? Lol*'

Chapter 46

I held my breath as the crowded lift made its way up to the eighth floor of Columbus House, stopping along the way to relieve its load of NPCs. It was just after nine. I swallowed repeatedly, trying to keep my breakfast down. Rushing down Victoria Street after wolfing it down had done my digestion no favours. So much for a relaxed start to the day.

I kicked myself for being so naïve as to think that we didn't need to concoct a story sooner to cover the fact that we were both taking leave at the same time immediately after our visit to the Paris office. It hadn't entered my mind or seemed necessary at the time. Panic was bubbling inside my brain as I replayed every interaction and exchange I'd had with Salter, trying to recall what clues I might have left him. Questions flooded my brain. How much could he really know? Was it a lucky guess? Was I worrying about nothing? I needed to know. Now. I'd always imagined we were above suspicion. I was the invisible, socially awkward, nerdy IT guy –deliberately so. Any suggestion that something was going on between me and Estelle would surely be laughed out the room. Wouldn't it? To the rest of this firm, we were an unlikely couple. Weren't we? What did Salter know?

'Good morning, Luke,' sang Lesley from behind the reception desk, grinning. 'I didn't think you were back for another week? Couldn't stay away, huh?'

'Haha. I'd only be sitting around at home if I wasn't here. Plus, I've got loads to do on this Project Butterfly.' I tried to sound blasé. 'Why? Did you miss me?'

Lesley's face lit up. 'What do you think? Of course! Now stop standing here chatting and get on with whatever you need to.' She turned her back towards me to type something into her laptop. I'd only taken a few steps away when I heard her call, 'Nice tan, by the way. Been anywhere nice?'

I stopped in my tracks and turned to look at her. She avoided looking at me directly, but I could see she had her tongue pushed against the inside her cheek as if she was deliberately winding me up. Could she know more than she was letting on or was paranoia getting the better of me? I needed to get onto the C.R.A.P. system fast. But first, Estelle.

The open plan area was eerily quiet considering most people were already in. Heads were down, studiously so. A few inaudible whispers were being exchanged but nothing like the usual boisterous morning banter.

'Morning,' I announced, making my presence felt. A few faces looked up in reply, but no one spoke. I scanned the office and wondered what crisis we had rushed back for. Why Estelle had even chosen to swap her laissez-faire life in Lusignac for the volatile and vexatious life in one of Victoria's two-bit consultancy firms remained a mystery to me. I wished we were still there. I imagined we'd still be having morning coffee in the garden at this time of day, planning the day ahead, what we might eat for dinner. And, instead, here I was, standing in the middle of a soulless office in a suit surrounded by people who didn't care for anything but themselves.

Estelle's office was empty. I scanned the outer offices for signs of life. In the enclosed meeting room at the far end, behind a closed glass door, I spotted Gordon Freeman, as red-faced and sweaty looking as always, standing in front of a table, his hands propping himself up as he leaned forward. Estelle was sitting opposite him, upright and stiff, her hands folded on her lap with her back towards me. Sitting at the side of the room were Salter and Mitch, looking very much like spectators to the main show. Even from behind, I could tell that Estelle looked uncomfortable. I couldn't help thinking of her as prey, trapped in a room full of predators and, as tough and ruthless as I knew she was, I was overcome with a wave of protectiveness for her.

Without a care for consequences, I strode across the office, swung the door open and demanded to know what the meeting was about. I was, after all, Acting Finance Director and there was no reason why they should be meeting without me being present. I realised how pathetic the word 'acting' in my job title made me sound as I said it out loud.

Four heads turned to face me. The room fell silent. Gordon straightened up in surprise, lost for words. Salter and Mitch were hunched forward with their hands over their mouths, giggling like a pair of pathetic schoolboys. Estelle turned round in her chair to face me. She looked like the only real professional presence in the room with her smart pressed suit and focussed expression. Her face and neck were sending out flushed distress signals, although I did notice the corners of her mouth curl upwards in response to my presence. Her eyes, although warm, looked as if they were pleading for help. She looked hurt.

'What's going on?' I demanded, surprised at the deepness of my voice. I shot a sideways stare in Salter and Mitch's direction and they both immediately froze behind stifled laughter. I imagined how satisfying battering them senseless would be. 'Did I miss a Senior Leaders Team meeting invite?' I asked Gordon in a deliberately sarcastic tone.

'You might as well take a seat,' Gordon replied, with unexpected tolerance. He gestured towards the empty seat beside Estelle. 'We have an issue.'

Apprehensively, I sat down. Estelle, still upright and stiff, blinked slowly and reassuringly at me as if signalling for me to tone down my aggression. It wasn't that easy. Our holiday had been interrupted. And for what? What games were these idiots playing?

Gordon grimaced and fiddled with his collar before speaking again. I couldn't recall a single time we'd interacted directly before now and, up close, he did not look as daunting as I had built him up to be in my mind. He looked old, uncomfortable, and as if he didn't want to be here any more than the rest of us. He stretched his jacket around his middle to button it up as if he was making a formal announcement rather than having a conversation. As if reading from a script, he then announced that he had received reports of unprofessional behaviour about Estelle that presented an issue for the firm.

'An issue?' I questioned.

Estelle snorted. 'This is ridiculous. Wait until you hear.'

Gordon cleared his throat, looked at the floor, and paced up and down as he spoke. He explained that, before explaining his position, he felt duty-bound to ask what the nature of my relationship with Estelle was. My back stiffened, mirroring Estelle's posture. I turned to her for a prompt. She simply bowed her head, giving me the green light to reveal all.

'It's none of your business,'

The clash of worlds between what went on behind closed doors and what took place in the office was uncomfortable and I was in no mood to let one seep into the other. 'We are getting the job done, and better than this place has been run for years, and that is all you should be bothered about.'

'Exactement,' Estelle chipped in before I'd finished my sentence. 'I have achieved everything that has been asked of me and more. You have no reason for concern or action.' Her face flushed redder and there was a distinct wobble in her voice.

Gordon continued pacing. Salter and Mitch remained silent statues.

'Action?' I asked, wanting to get to the nub of the point faster.

He ummed and ahed and stuttered his way through explaining that he had relieved reports of unprofessional and improper behaviour between members of his senior leadership team (he didn't have the balls to mention me or Estelle by name) that amounted to a breach of trust, a damage to the firm's reputation and, ultimately, had created a situation that undermined Estelle's authority as Chief Operating Officer that was simply not sustainable. Not here, and not with the international offices.

His heard his words for what they were - corporate bullshit. 'What exactly are you trying to say, Gordon?'

He took a deep sigh, 'We're going to have to let Estelle go.'

The buzzing in my ears intensified. From behind, I heard Salter let out a stifled snort of laughter.

'What?' I stood up and slapped my hands on the table, prompting Gordon to take two steps back. Estelle reached out to grab me by the hand and steer me back in the direction of my seat but I shook myself free. 'You can't do that. On what grounds? On what evidence?' I turned to face Salter who looked away – guilty as fuck. 'What have either of us ever done to threaten the firm's reputation? This is totally unnecessary and unreasonable. This is bullshit. You can't just sack us like that!'

My heart knocked against my ribcage, while my hands tightened into fists. Gordon grimaced and sat down before asking me, very politely, to remain seated. I complied. Estelle reached over and squeezed my hand. I could see that she was already three steps ahead of anger on the change curve and had reached quiet acceptance.

Gordon went on to explain that *we* weren't being sacked. It was only Estelle, as the senior officer, who was affected. He tried to soften the blow by explaining that her contract contained a no-quibble termination clause by either party within the first six months of appointment which meant she could simply be 'let go', rather than dismissed, thus leaving her free to pursue other opportunities. I, on the other hand, was not in such a senior position to give rise to any reputational damage and, additionally, I was on a permanent contract which would make 'letting me go' (or dismissal in layman's terms) more difficult. Gordon did, however, take the opportunity to emphasise words like 'currently' and 'at this moment in time'. Clear warning shots for me to toe the line.

No sources were referenced as to how our relationship had come to his attention, but I had no doubt that it had something to do with Salter and Mathéo from the Paris office. There was something about the way in which Mathéo had asked about where we were staying, where we were heading and how long we'd worked together that, with the benefit of hindsight, seemed more than polite small talk. Also, I now recalled him asking whether either of us had a family or partner waiting for us at home which seemed completely inappropriate. We'd both ignored him at the time.

My temper rose as the injustice of the situation sunk in. How Estelle managed to keep her controlled poise, I had no idea.

'Since when has it been reputational damage to the firm for a senior team member to be in a relationship...' I paused to look at Estelle. '....a *meaningful* relationship, with another member of staff? If those rules apply, then aren't there a few other people you should be getting rid of? Or "letting go"?' I shot a warning look at Salter. He looked as if he was going to say something, but Gordon silenced him with a hand gesture.

'It's completely different, Luke.'

'Different, how?' It wasn't. It was bloody hypocritical and stank of double standards. If anyone deserved to be kicked out the firm for causing reputational damage it was Salter. My cheeks flushed with rage. 'What about him?' I pointed at a smirking Salter. 'What about you?' My eyes burnt with rage.

'Luke, calm down,' Gordon started, his words winding me up further. 'You're not doing anyone – especially yourself - any favours. Listen to me.' He stood again. 'Your position is not in question here at...the... moment.' He mouthed the last three words slowly and with particular emphasis. 'I am *advising* you, Luke, not to rock the boat here. People shouldn't throw stones in glass houses.' Even his mixed metaphors were winding me up now. He droned on about the issue not being about Estelle's ability to deliver, but about professional conduct and needing to instil confidence in the Board and stakeholders.

'Let me reassure you,' he continued, 'that I have guaranteed Estelle an exemplary reference for what she has achieved in her time here. But that time is up. It is decided. It is what it is.'

His final words hung in the air like an annoying fly that needed swatting. The most pointless phrase ever to be introduced into the English language. The ultimate cop-out from having to explain or justify.

Estelle, silent until now, stood up, smoothed her suit down and, with a professionalism that far exceeded anyone else's in the room, said, 'Gentlemen. This is ridiculous. There is clearly nothing more to be gained from prolonging this discussion. Gordon, I will be consulting lawyers and appealing this decision. You will be hearing from me.' Gordon shrugged. 'Luke, I will see you later.' She stepped forward, gave me a peck on the cheek which would have been inappropriate and unprofessional under any other circumstances and gave me a subtle wink, reassuring me that she was OK, and that this was not over.

'I'll come with you,' I said, following her as she headed for the door. Salter and Mitch stood up in an unexpected sign of respect.

'No,' she said firmly, making a stop sign with her palm. 'You need to stay and finish what we started. I'll be back, you'll see.'

And with that, she left, closing the door gently behind her. I watched as she walked through the open-plan office, past heads that followed her movement, and then past reception and out of sight. A lump formed in my throat.

'Let her go Luke,' said Gordon from behind me. 'And remember, this isn't worth kicking a fuss up over. Keep your head down and I was thinking of removing the "Acting" from your job title.'

Did I hear right? Did he just offer me a substantive promotion out of this sorry mess? I turned to face him, then looked in turn at Salter and Mitch. Each of them had the same look on their face as that of a child wanting to be picked for the football team. There was nothing more to be said. Channelling some of Estelle's professionalism, I simply nodded and said, 'thank you' and left the room.

I walked tall, maintaining my pride and confidence, as the whole office's eyes followed me back towards my desk. As I approached, I could see something in the centre of it coming into focus, making the lump in my throat harden, my chest hollow out, and my eyes well up. For a split second, I could understand how the balcony edge appealed to Peter.

A deep feeling of shame enveloped me as two five-pound notes sellotaped to the centre of my desk came into clear focus. I ripped them off, scrunched them up and threw them to one side. I sat down, exhausted. The words of past teachers echoed in my head '...but most of all, you've let yourself down...'

I hated Salter and Mitch for being such childish, misogynistic shits. But part of me couldn't blame them for being themselves.

Who I really hated most was myself.

Chapter 47

Carl, Brian and Natalie did well not to ask me about the Paris trip, or the now notorious holiday that followed as I sat in silence behind my screen, scrolling through the C.R.A.P. to bring myself up to date with office gossip. Unsurprisingly, and contrary to the physical illusion that the rest of the office were actually working, Estelle and I were the hot topic of the morning. It wasn't possible to keep up with the exchanges taking place but clichéd phrases such as *'dark horse'*, *'it's always the quiet ones'*, and *'you never know what's going on behind closed doors'* would have dominated the word cloud if I chose to create one.

Gordon had chosen, probably wisely, not to make any official announcement about Estelle's departure, either verbally or in writing, but had instead encouraged us - the Directors - to cascade the news informally, emphasising that she had left *by mutual agreement* without giving further details.

Messages continued to buzz back and forth through the office, a relentless, electronic whisper campaign that reduced us to caricatures of our real selves. We'd been dehumanised from the people they knew on a day-to-day basis, to anonymous, fictitious characters on the latest series of Love Island. All online, of course. No-one dared say anything out loud. *'I wonder when it started?'*, *'I wonder how long it'll last now she's not working here?'*, *'Who do you reckon made the first move?'*, *'They should make this into a Netflix drama'*, *'Just think, they might have done it on your desk!'* The exchange of messages was endless and shameless.

And my shame at not having been able to protect Estelle from her fate cut deep.

I took some solace from the fact that a number of people – both male and female – were of the opinion that the decision to let Estelle go was unfair and unjust, the consensus being that what went on behind closed doors was of no one else's concern. Could this be an early tremor of rebellion against this stuck-in-the-past leadership team, I wondered? I hoped so. I wanted to bring the whole fucking place down.

What deepened my sense of shame and disgust was how, whenever Salter walked past my desk, he would nod respectfully and say 'alright?', as if I had completed some rite of passage that qualified me to join his club. I didn't want to be part of his club. I didn't want any of this. I just wanted Estelle. And for her to be happy. And yet, here I was. I fucked up again.

I could still recall that time twelve years ago when Salter was openly taunting me in the office after he'd messed things up between me and Sarah. Twelve whole years, yet it felt like yesterday. He had completely humiliated me then, and here he was, as if the past counted for nothing, trying to treat me like a mate and rewrite our history to suit his narrative. I was not going to let that happen, despite the fact they were all emotionless memories now, rather than traumatic flashbacks. Estelle was what was important now.

It wasn't just Salter either. Elaine, Sandra and Vicky, coincidentally all from Salter's team, had each found excuses to attempt to befriend me by bringing up some random invoicing issue before enquiring if I had a nice holiday. I kept them all at arm's length with a polite *'yes, thanks'* but that didn't stop them from trying to interrogate further details out of me, *'where did you go?'*, *'did you get up to anything nice?'*, *'I wish someone would take me away...'*. None of it was welcome. I just wanted to be left alone, have minimal interaction and get back home to Estelle.

The icing on the cake was when Gordon left the office at lunchtime and stopped by my desk to congratulate me in front of my team and personally deliver a letter confirming my position as the substantive Finance Director. He was his usual emotionally oblivious self when he patted me on the back and said, 'All signed and sealed, old boy. Looks like I'd underestimated your efforts in the past. I always thought you were a bit of a twat to be honest. But you've surprised everyone by your good work on Project Butterfly. Well done!'

We both knew he wasn't talking about Project Butterfly, but I took the letter, put it in my jacket pocket and thanked him. I decided then and there not to share this news with Estelle. It would only look like I was rubbing salt in her wound.

It was early evening by the time I got home, tired and mentally drained. I'd passed on Salter's offer to join him and his team for after-work drinks – my first invitation from him ever. Estelle hadn't heard me enter the flat, nor seen me from the dining room table in the window alcove as I made my way up the steps towards the front door. She was still in her work clothes, including her shoes, absorbed in her laptop when I entered the living room.

'Good evening,' I said as I knocked on the door frame. She continued typing without acknowledging my presence.

'Hi honey, I'm home!' I crooned to attract her attention. Still no response. I walked across the room, placed a hand on her shoulder and pecked her cheek.

'Hello honey,' she said robotically, without looking up. She was scrolling through a legal website. I caught the words *unfair dismissal* and *compensation*. Her focus was absolute.

I placed both hands on her shoulders and started giving her a light massage, but she shook herself free. 'Not now, honey. I'm busy.' The rejection stung and I hoped it wasn't an early indication of a chasm that work might drive between us.

'How was the rest of your day?' I asked.

'Bastards, Luke. They are all bastards, but I will sort this out, you will see.' Her eyes remained fixed on the screen.

'Can I help?'

She switched tabs and continued typing.

'I'll go and make us some dinner then, shall I?'

'Mm-hmm.'

I leant in to give her another peck of encouragement on her cheek, but she pulled away, making it clear she didn't want to be disturbed. Message received loud and clear.

I paused in the doorway to watch her before leaving the room. Her focus was intense - her notepad and pen lined up at ninety degrees to her right, a half-filled glass of water to her left. She sat looking the perfect picture of professionalism that she always did. Except she was a professional without status now. I was already worrying how that might upset our relationship while I was still at work. Although we'd managed to keep work and home separate up until now, the fact that she was – yes, was – my senior in the workplace had always seeped through into our personal lives. She'd always been the boss. I was thankful that she wasn't displaying any signs of resentment towards me for not losing my job too - yet. As much for my sake as hers, I hoped she managed to find another job soon. However, I didn't share her hope of achieving reinstatement at Effective Solutions. I was familiar with her contract.

In the kitchen, other than a just-in-date carton of milk and half a block of cheese, the fridge was devoid of any fresh ingredients. I scooped out the fur-lined cucumbers, tomatoes and shrivelled mushrooms from the bottom tray, threw them in the bin and pulled a pizza out of the freezer. I wasn't in the mood for eating out and didn't trust takeaways. I bit my lip and felt a moment of shame for thinking that Estelle could have used some of her day to pick up a bit of shopping for tonight. It was a petty but natural thought.

The clickety-clack of Estelle's keyboard from the front room sounded frantic as it made its way down the corridor. She had every right to be pissed off, and I was on her behalf too – really. But I did wonder if trying to fight Gordon and Effective Solutions was a waste of her time. They hired and fired as they saw fit and would never lose face by reversing a decision, especially one as visible as this. As I leant against the kitchen counter, waiting for the oven to heat up, I couldn't help wondering how Giselle might react in such a situation. Her simple, straightforward and practical approach to life seemed a world away from the tension I felt right now. It was impossible for me to visualise Giselle in such a situation because there's no way she would ever choose corporate city life over the idyll of the countryside. I looked out of the back window onto the garden with its solitary bench, cherry tree and overgrown lawn, boxed in by brick walls separating the patch from adjoining gardens.

It looked sad and was as far removed from the splendour and tranquillity of Giselle's garden as you could imagine. The flat suddenly felt very small and insignificant as I realised I was missing everything about our past week in Lusignac more than I realised - the relaxed conversation, the comfort of countryside, the constant flirting.

Estelle's keyboard continued to ring out from the front room. I thought of Giselle and wished she were here to inject some light-hearted calm and flirtatious banter to the situation. To bring that feeling of completeness back. I felt guilty and a sense of shame for even thinking it, but you can't help what you think, right?

Chapter 48

The next couple of weeks at work proved definitively that no one is indispensable. After an initial burst of gossip, the office had reverted to the lifeless shell it was before Estelle's arrival. Gordon was popping in more frequently and with more optimism than usual, casually sitting amongst the CHImps and Sales teams, enjoying the attention that his position attracted. Salter continued to assert his dominance within his teams, flitting between playing the macho manager one minute and spoiling everyone with coffee runs, doughnuts and after-work drinks the next.

For me, the void left by Estelle was vast and left the office hollow, empty, and dull. Everywhere I turned, I felt Estelle's absence. The management meetings, the exchanged looks across the office, the occasional raised eyebrow in my direction to let me know what she was thinking. Her office remained empty like a shrine, a constant reminder that the heart of the company had been ripped out. Although I seemed to be the only one who thought so.

I'd set up an alert for any mention of Estelle on the C.R.A.P. system. After day three of her departure the gossiping stopped, and she appeared to have been completely forgotten. However, it hadn't escaped my attention that both Sophie and Elaine had undergone mini-makeovers and had started wearing fitted two-piece suits, a small sign of Estelle's legacy within the firm. Sophie pulled the look off better than Elaine, due to her having a similar frame to Estelle. I also noticed they'd created some distance between themselves and Salter, perhaps hinting at a change in dynamic.

Sophie had even gone so far as to come over to my desk one evening and, in a low voice and quite sincerely, told me that, 'I always liked her. I hope she's OK. What they did to her was unfair.' I promised to pass her wishes on to Estelle.

There was still plenty of work to do to fill my days, but there seemed little point without Estelle. My presentation of Project Butterfly's conclusions was due to be delivered to the Board within days. However, Gordon, Salter and Mitch had watered it down to ensure that there were sufficient recommendations for savings and increased profit drive amongst overseas offices to allow the travel budgets and bonus schemes for HQ staff to remain the same. I didn't have enough enthusiasm to challenge them and so it seemed as if we had reached some sort of unspoken understanding amongst ourselves that we would leave each other alone while continuing to serve ourselves. Which suited me.

I was contributing very little. ChatGPT had written my narrative for the Board presentation, and my team had pulled the visuals together. I'd even created a separate ChatGPT persona by uploading all of Estelle's wise words and communications so that I could call on her virtual personality throughout the day to give me advice on how to handle different situations. Each time I consulted my virtual Estelle, I felt a mix of relief and guilt. It was a poor substitute for the real Estelle, but it was better than nothing, and better than troubling her for advice when I got home, which only seemed to cause irritation.

Of course, I felt awful and a total fraud for taking credit for the Project that Estelle had conceived and driven, but what was the alternative? As much as I hated the saying, *it was what it was*. I couldn't afford not to work. There was no point both of us losing our incomes.

I was, however, getting increasingly worried about Estelle. It became apparent within days of her dismissal – no, departure – that she was not coping well. Gone were her early starts, business suits and working her way through a list of daily achievements. In were the leggings, baggy t-shirts and lack of structure to her days that were throwing her off-course. Up until now, I didn't even know she owned leggings. She was solely focussed on overturning the decision to dismiss her and seek reinstatement. But deep down we knew that wasn't going to happen. Nor was any compensation a realistic option. I had no idea what her financial situation was and was too afraid to ask for fear of making it sound like I might be asking her to contribute in some way, but there was a desperate air in her demeanour that suggested that time was running out. Watching her glued to her laptop night after night, refusing to come to bed felt like the tide was coming in and gently washing away the sandcastle we had built together.

Estelle appeared to be OK with me keeping my job but, every now and then, there were signs of a simmering resentment that would bleed through into our conversations and make me think twice before opening my mouth to say anything. I'd been home for a good hour now and our initial exchange when I walked through the door had not gone well.

'Chéri, sit down, I have had a fantastic idea.' Her eyes were alight, and it was the first time she'd called me chéri in a long time. I hadn't even taken my jacket off when she sat me down on the sofa and pulled her chair away from the table to sit facing me.

'You are Finance Director, and you are in charge of your own budget, right?'

'That's right.'

'And you will need some additional resource to implement Project Butterfly, no?'

'Maybe,' I replied hesitantly.

'Then why don't you just take me on as a consultant Implementation Manager? No one knows the detail of what needs doing as well as me and no one can question how or who you choose to implement it.'

I envisioned the inevitable backlash that her return to the office would bring. My jaw must have visibly dropped because before I had a chance to say anything, her face looked crestfallen as she absorbed my non-verbal response. Her eyes filled with tears. I took her hands in mine.

'Chérie,' I started, hating how patronising I sounded. 'Honestly, how do you think that might work out?'

Her eyes searched my face silently while I did my best to look as sympathetic and understanding as I could. The whites of her eyes were mottled with red vessels and the surrounds of her eyes were shadowed. It had become usual for me to wake in the middle of the night to find an empty space beside me and the sound of her shuffling around elsewhere in the flat. Gone was the crazy passion that used to keep us up into the early hours and I was often too tired from spending full days in the office and then coming home to preparing dinner to nuance my words perfectly for every scenario. Estelle was always too busy to think about the basics of life, like food.

I maintained eye contact with her as her facial expression morphed from hope to questioning to disappointment and, finally, disgust. At which point she pulled her hands free of mine, took her chair back to her laptop and sat with her back towards me.

'Don't forget that you are only in that position now because of me, Luke. We were a team, remember?' Her words would have had less impact if she'd have spat them out, but it was their calm, controlled delivery that sent a chill through me.

'We *are* still a team,' I emphasised, sounding as if I was pleading. 'I just think it would be better all round for you to move on from Effective Solutions. You have more to offer the world.' She ignored me, leaving me feeling as if the tide coming in between us was stretching into an ocean.

'It should be me there, Luke, not you.'

She was right, of course but *it was what it was*. I internalised that thought while she took her frustration out on her keyboard. Clouds of bitterness and anger filled the air as she flitted between scribbling manically in her notebook and bashing her keyboard. A lump rose in my throat as I realised *this was it* and I didn't know how to navigate our relationship back to safer land. I desperately wanted to revive the connection we had just a few short weeks ago, to feel the warmth of her affectionate touch, to feel her leg resting on mine at night as we slept together. Everything was moving too fast and here I was, again wondering what she might be capable of if her anger took over.

'There!' she announced, spinning her chair around, her eyes boring into mine as she turned her laptop screen to face me. The text was still a blur from where I sat. 'Plenty of jobs on offer. Chief Technology Officer, Chief Operating Officer, Programme Manager…London and Paris, although the Paris jobs are showing much better potential and have better packages than London. You can blame Brexit for that.' She gave me a look that challenged me to doubt her. 'Don't worry, Luke, I will be out of your way soon enough. You will soon be free to enjoy yourself.'

I bowed my head and looked down at my folded hands. I could feel the waves of anger coming off her hitting me. A familiar sinking feeling filled my chest like a heavy weight, dragging me downwards.

'That's not what I want, Estelle. Not at all. I'm sorry.' She stared back at me defiantly. Something about her reminded me of the first time we met. 'Look. The past couple of weeks have been a lot for us both to take in and I'm sorry you lost…, no, were let go from, your job and I'm sorry if I haven't been able to help much but I don't want you to leave.' Her expression remained one of complete indifference. 'Please.'

'Options, Luke, I need options. I can't stay here like this. I won't be your kept woman. I need more. I'm sorry.'

Our eyes filled with tears as we held each other's gaze. I could not believe that all was lost. I had faith in us. These were angry words in the heat of the moment. Our story had still only started and was not ready to be cut short. This was not our destiny. I steadied the wobble in my voice, knelt before her and took hold of her hand.

'Estelle. I love you. I know you're not happy and I've been preoccupied with everything that's happened at work, but we'll get through this. Together. I value you over everything else in life.' Her eyes softened and her mouth curled upwards slightly.

'Tell you what,' I continued. We've not been out for weeks now. How about we make tomorrow night a date night? I'll get home from work at a decent time. We can dress up and get an Uber out. Somewhere special? Maybe The Ivy Asia? With views of St Pauls?' She pulled her hand free and held the side of my face and smiled as if I had finally managed to say the right thing.

'That would be nice. Thank you and I'm sorry too. But I can't continue with this misery. Something needs to change.'

Chapter 49

Friday morning. For the first time in a fortnight, Estelle was up before me with a cup of coffee waiting on the bedside before I was awake. As usual, I took it straight out into the garden to have my first cigarette of the day while she pottered about inside, humming to herself.

By the time I'd brushed my teeth, shaved and got dressed (in my new bottle green slim fit three-piece suit from Paul Smith – a promotion present to myself) she was waiting to usher me out of the front door with a small packed lunch.

'Mm, you smell good,' she'd said as she pecked my cheek goodbye, taking in the woody bergamot aroma of my aftershave. 'Make sure you come straight home today. I'm looking forward to tonight!'

I promised I would and gave her a big hug. I'm not sure if it was the promise of our date night, or whether Estelle had finally managed to rid herself of her dark clouds and radiate light of her own accord, but her whole temperament seemed different today. Brighter, more positive, and less intense. Her eyes had the same mischievous sparkle as when we'd first met. It was good to see, although I was still worried about her lack of appetite and her increasingly gaunt appearance. I hoped the menu at The Ivy Asia might tempt her to eat a decent meal later.

By lunchtime, I had already received a handful of playful texts from her, hinting that she was out shopping and choosing something special to wear for the evening. She'd attached a couple of cropped photos that appeared to be of a band of material against her thighs, asking if I thought it was too short. It was a tease as the message was set to disappear after only two seconds, and before I had a chance to zoom in and figure out exactly what I was looking at. It left me grinning at my desk though and it felt fun to sense her presence, albeit virtual, in the office again.

My newfound popularity in the office and unwanted attention I was attracting had meant I'd had to turn down invitations for after-work drinks throughout the afternoon as various colleagues added me to their group chats (a first!) and stopped by my desk to compliment me on my new suit and try and coax me out. The more resolute my refusals, the harder they pushed back. *Just for one? Aw, come on – it's my birthday* (it wasn't – I checked). My sights were firmly set on getting home early. I had no intention of falling into the trap of letting corporate culture take over my life.

It was overcast by the time I was quick-marching myself home through Victoria Park, but that didn't alter my sense of hope that today marked a fresh start for me and Estelle. I'd texted before leaving the office to let her know I was on my way, and she'd messaged straight back. *Great – ready and waiting x*. As I turned onto Gore Road to approach the flat, I could see two tall candles in holders, lighting up the dinner table in the upper ground bay window. I also saw Estelle's head disappear quickly behind the curtain from where she'd been looking out for me. I smiled and quickened my step.

I hadn't even reached the front door when Estelle swung it open, taking my breath away. She stood in the doorway, one hand on the doorframe at head height, the other on her hip. Her wavy hair sat naturally on her shoulders, perfectly framing her fine cheekbones and jawline. She looked me up and down as I stood rooted to the spot, admiring her slender neckline that led my sight down the spaghetti straps of a champagne-coloured satin slip dress, towards the embroidered pattern and subtle lace trim just above her knees. If she was wearing any makeup it was neither noticeable, nor needed. She was wearing the matching necklace and stud earrings I'd bought her from Riberac market. She was stunning.

'Bonsoir, chéri.'

'Bonsoir, indeed. New dress?'

'Thank you. Do you like it?' She spun into the hallway to give me a 360-degree view, confident of a positive answer.

'I love it. You look amazing.'

She led me by the hand to the living room where I could now see the table in the window was laid for two, complete with linen tablecloth, placemats, candles and proper cloth napkins in proper silver napkin rings. A step up from the sheets of kitchen towel I normally used. The candles made the cut wine glasses and cutlery sparkle beneath them.

'oo…ambience,' I commented approvingly. 'This all looks beautiful, but I thought we were going out this evening?' I made sure to show my appreciation. I didn't want to hurt her feelings.

'No,' she said wagging a finger. 'We do not need any fancy restaurants or tourist attractions to have a good time. Tonight is about us, like it used to be.'

She told me excitedly that she had been chatting with Giselle over the phone during the day and taken her advice over menu suggestions for the evening. 'If it goes well, you can thank me; if it turns out to be a disaster, you can blame Giselle.' Her dimples returned as she laughed. It was good to see.

Stroking my lapel, she told me I had ten minutes to myself to decompress while she finished our starters off. She was, however, very clear that she didn't want me changing out of my suit, which she complimented as being my best purchase yet. I took the opportunity to freshen up quickly in the bathroom before returning to the living room where a smiling Estelle greeted me with two glasses of wine.

'Santé, chéri!' she said, handing me a glass. A bottle of open Sancerre - the same wine as she had chosen for our first date - sat on the dining table. I looked around the room and realised that the whole place had been tidied. The books on the bookshelves had been straightened and reordered by size, sofa cushions had been plumped and laid out an equal distance apart, and I was sure I could detect a hint of fresh lavender in the air. Or was it the candles?

We sat at the table and chatted away with an ease that had eluded us for the past couple of weeks, light, effortless and without any of the edge that had tainted us recently. I expressed appreciation for the trouble she'd gone to make the evening special. She again reminded me that it was nothing and that she didn't need fancy restaurants to enjoy my company. She apologised for being so grumpy recently and put it down to her being so upset and angry about the way Gordon dismissed her so abruptly.

We laughed when I told her it was understandable and that she hadn't been *that* grumpy – we both knew it wasn't true.

I gave her a brief run-through of my day at work and apologised for having to spend so much time in the office while I was still establishing myself as a director, instead of with her at home.

She topped up my glass, frowned and, avoiding direct eye contact, adopted a more serious tone.

'Luke, achieving something for myself is important. I am never going to be happy without my own independence and some challenge. I have ambition.' My stomach tightened as I sensed the conversation was leading towards bad news. 'I loved my job at Effective Solutions, Luke. And to be honest, I didn't like how quickly you accepted your position while I was pushed out. It felt unfair.'

'But...' I started. She cut me off before I had a chance to rationalise my position.

'It's all right, Luke. I understand. What choice did you have, right? There's no point both of us losing our jobs, right?' There was no anger in her voice, only sadness.

'I'm still sorry,' I mumbled.

'Anyway,' she continued, recomposing herself. 'Let's look forwards, not backwards, right? I have decided to forget about fighting Effective Solutions and move on for the sake of my sanity and for our future.' She clinked her glass against mine, sending a chime echoing around the room. 'Effective Solutions is history to me now and, besides, I have a good track record and have plenty of other options to follow up that I won't bore you with.' Her raised eyebrow told me she had a plan up her sleeve. 'Tonight is about us. A celebration of what we have together.'

Her positivity and enthusiasm were good to see but only slightly reassuring. I was still worried about her lack of appetite and increasingly gaunt appearance, and I couldn't shake off the feeling of guilt that had been gnawing away at me about her losing her job.

We moved to the sofa while Estelle relayed news from her call with Giselle, who, aside from her usual routine of gardening, shopping and cooking, was finding life boring and asking when we would next visit. I suggested we aim to return before Christmas, as soon as work would allow.

'We'll see. The world is a big place,' was Estelle's lukewarm response. I hoped we would return soon and felt a pull back to Giselle's garden. There was something about that house and spending time with both twins together that felt like unfinished business.

Once Estelle had finished updating me on Giselle's news, she encouraged me to the table while she retreated to the kitchen to finish dinner preparations. The two glasses of wine I'd knocked back on an empty stomach had left me light-headed. Within minutes, Estelle was back with two starter plates of pâté de campagne with rocket on crispbread, and a fresh bottle of wine. She pulled the curtains shut 'to create the right ambience' and again topped my glass up, ignoring my request to slow down to prevent me falling asleep. 'Don't be silly,' she said, filling my glass to the brim. 'Enjoy tonight! You don't need to go anywhere tomorrow, do you?'

This was true and I was in no mood to disrupt Estelle's flow, so I relaxed into my third glass, alternating sips with crunches of crispbread starter, and enjoying seeing Estelle return to her old self. I was feeling very spoilt. The starter was superb, Estelle was on good form, and it felt as if our relationship was back on good tracks again. As Estelle cast dreamlike shadows around the room with her communicative hands, I wondered if perhaps our relationship might move towards the next stage, whatever that was. Something a bit more stable, I hoped.

It wasn't until we'd finished our starters that Estelle brought the topic of conversation back to work. 'Oh my, Luke! I have just realised I have been chatting away all this time and not given you a chance to tell me properly how your day went.'

'It's all fine,' I said, choosing not to tell her about the bonus I had been awarded for my presentation of Project Butterfly's recommendations to the Board. 'You know what it's like – the usual meetings, updates and reports. Nothing special.'

'Hmm. What about the Board? Did you present the project findings.'

'Yes. It went fine.'

'And did they accept all of it?'

'Yes, no problem. It all went through without fuss. Nothing more to say really.' I decided not to tell her about the watered-down recommendations for fear of spoiling the evening.

'Hmm. Ok. Well done you, I suppose. And did anyone notice your new suit today?' She reached across and stroked the breast pocket. 'You look very handsome in it.'

'Thank you,' I smiled, taking her hand into mine, recalling the compliments I'd also received from Lesley, Sophie and Elaine earlier in the day.

'I am sure some of the CHIMps noticed it?' she questioned, as if reading my mind. I chuckled to avoid answering. 'It is alright, Luke,' she laughed. 'You do not need to worry about me being jealous, you know. Who could blame them after all for finding you so attractive? And now you have the position and power to go with it, you must be irresistible to them, no?'

I wasn't sure if she was teasing or accusing me. 'I'm just trying to keep my head down and look the part, that's all.'

She reached over and squeezed my cheek with her thumb and forefinger. 'You are so cute sometimes,' she teased. 'It is OK you know, Luke. I know they like to flirt with you, and I think you quite like the attention too. It's not a problem. We are not teenagers and, besides, I trust you, you know.' I searched her face and could find no signs she didn't mean what she said.

'Sorry,' I said sheepishly, and we laughed together for a minute until it felt awkward, at which point she collected our plates and disappeared to the kitchen to bring the main course through. I peeped out through the curtains while she was gone. It was dark outside and the length of the street looked as if I was looking through a glass of water, all blurry, with no clear edges. The effects of the wine felt stronger than usual although the bottle said 13% abv only.

Estelle returned, carrying two steaming plates and proudly announced 'Voilà! Chicken in creamy mushroom sauce with sautéed potatoes and a side of tenderstem broccoli.'

'Oh, chérie. This looks and smells amazing. Thank you.' I meant it. It looked fantastic and I needed something substantial to help soak up the wine. Estelle beamed with pride, and we tucked in to eat. Estelle's cheeks were rosy from the heat of the kitchen, and I noticed that she'd undone the top couple of buttons of her dress to cool down. I also noticed that she had noticed I had noticed her undone buttons and seemed to be enjoying the fact that I was admiring her cleavage.

She continued to give off flirty vibes throughout our meal, occasionally stroking her breastbone to lead my eyes in that direction, tucking her hair behind her left ear to expose her slender neck – a known weakness of mine - and biting her bottom lip whenever I said anything remotely interesting.

By the time she disappeared to the kitchen again to fetch dessert, I was blissfully and totally intoxicated from her flirtatious presence and the wine. Dessert was a thin slice of New York cheesecake, a handful of raspberries, a drizzle of cream over the top and a side shot of amaretto. It was a solo portion. Estelle apologised for not joining me for dessert, saying she was too full and wanted to start clearing up. The fresh bottle of wine she'd brought with the main course was now empty. She must have been topping my glass up when I wasn't looking, which explained my wooziness. I ate my dessert to the sound of dishes clattering from the kitchen, followed by Estelle's footsteps rushing back and forth to the bedroom, and finally the door slamming shut. I could hear her rummaging around from behind the closed door. She was up to something mischievous, I could tell. I swirled amaretto around my mouth, imagining how the night might end.

'Chéri,' she called out from the bedroom. 'I have a surprise for you.'

Chapter 50

I tottered towards the bedroom, banging my shoulder on the living room doorframe on my way and pressed my ear against the bedroom door but heard nothing other than the blood rushing round my head. I opened the door slowly to let my eyes adjust to the darkness. The curtains were drawn, and the only light came from candles flickering in each corner.

From behind the door, Estelle grabbed my arm, pulled me towards her, slammed the door shut and pushed me against the wall, making me bang my head. These situations always look better choreographed in films. My head spun as I steadied myself, wishing I hadn't been so greedy with the wine. We kissed hungrily, biting each other's lips in turn. I felt self-conscious about Estelle's mint-fresh mouth encountering my mix of food remnants and alcohol fumes.

'I need to freshen up,' I said, pulling away.

'You are not going anywhere now,' she replied, keeping me pinned against the wall, the whites of her eyes shining.

I attempted to slide the straps of Estelle's dress off her shoulders, but she slapped my hand away and tutted.

'Don't be so greedy,' she scolded and led me towards the bed. Over her shoulder, I saw the bed had a towel laid out at its foot, and a variety of sex toys on it and, on the pillow, a blindfold and pair of handcuffs. In the corner of the room, the dresser held a tray with glasses, an ice bucket and various other implements reflecting the candlelight.

Estelle placed her hands on my shoulders and applied enough pressure to encourage me to sit on the side of the bed with my back to the implements laid out behind me.

'Shhh, no peeking,' she ordered, placing her hands on my cheeks to prevent me from looking behind. She pushed me on my back and instructed me to hold my wrists out towards the bedposts. I complied without question. We maintained silent eye contact while she clicked a set of cuffs onto each wrist and then stretched out each arm to each bedpost. Her playful glint turned to a frustrated frown as she realised the cuffs didn't open wide enough to fit round the bedpost.

'Too much girth?' I offered unhelpfully. She tutted and rushed across the room to fetch a couple of my work ties. 'They won't be strong enough to hold me,' I said dismissively.

'They will if you know the right knots.'

She clenched her jaw with determination as she looped and wrapped the tie around the bedpost and then through the cuff on my wrist, giving it a final loop and a tug that left little wriggle room. She moved to repeat the procedure on my other wrist, slowly as if completing a sacred ritual, while I remained compliant. I looked around the room, squinting to make out the glistening objects on the tray on the dressing table. I recognised the small chrome ice bucket with no bottle in it but could not make out what the other shiny objects were. Cutlery? Pens? Unfamiliar make-up applicators? There was also a glass jar. I scanned the rest of the room and noticed a small nurse's uniform hanging up and a suitcase brought out from under the bed. It was the suitcase that Estelle had first arrived with. What was she up to? Was she adding cosplay to her repertoire? I vaguely recalled mentioning the clichéd fantasy of her dressing up as a nurse, but I never expected it to become reality.

'I said no peeking, remember!' Estelle completed the knot on my other wrist and pulled it tight, causing me to squeak wimpishly. She straddled me, but only to put the blindfold over my eyes. I twisted from side to side to test my restraint. It was secure but allowed me to shift my weight a couple of inches in each direction. I still had a sliver of vision through the bottom of the blindfold.

Estelle climbed off the bed, presumably admiring her handiwork. I remained motionless. Slowly, she checked and re-checked her knots to the bedposts, giving each one a final tight tug. I remained passive and compliant. A silence followed, filled only by the buzzing in my ears and the occasional hiss and splutter of the candles, making me feel uncomfortable.

'What next?' I asked.

Estelle sat on the bed beside me and started undoing the buttons on my waistcoat.

'Chéri. I know things have not been easy for both of us for the past few weeks, so I thought I would arrange a little surprise. You just need to be patient, that's all.'

I tried to sit up, but my splayed arms kept me down. Estelle pulled my waistcoat open and started unbuttoning my shirt, pulling it out from my trousers, exposing my stomach. I tipped my head back to peep out the bottom of the blindfold and could make out her silhouette shadowing me as her hands worked up my chest.

'No peeking, Luke,' she said, pulling my blindfold down and returning me to blackness. 'This evening is about trust after all.' She pulled my shirt wide open, leaving my chest exposed while she undid my belt. 'You need to have complete trust in me tonight,' she continued. 'This evening is not about sex, although there may or may not be some involved. This evening is not about love either, although love is present. It is all about trust. I have put my trust in you completely and now you must put your trust in me.' Another silence followed as she went to the corner of the room and returned with the sound of ice against glass.

'Do you understand, Luke?' Her tone sounded official, as if she was channelling her workplace persona. I confirmed I did.

She undid my trousers and slowly trailed an ice cube down my chest and past my belly button. The cold sensation caused me to inhale sharply. She teased me by steering the ice cube away from below my waistline and dragging it along the bottom of my stomach, causing me to flinch forward as far as my bound wrists would allow.

'Stay still, Luke, or I will be tempted to punish you.' It was said playfully.

I nodded as she continued circling the cube up and down my stomach. I could feel trails of melted cold water running down my sides. I relaxed as best I could behind the blindfold and concentrated on suppressing the urge to giggle at the tickling feeling. I kicked myself for not having the foresight to use the bathroom before entering the bedroom. Again, I thought, the films never show the reality of these situations.

In addition to my bursting bladder, my head spun from alcohol and now my nose started to itch. I creased it up and wiggled it from side to side like a rabbit, bringing slight relief as it rubbed against the blindfold and increased the gap at the bottom. If I tipped my head back, I could see Estelle bent over me, her hair hanging forward over her face as she focussed on drawing patterns on me with ice cubes. I made encouraging noises in response but, if I were honest, I would have preferred some old-fashioned eye contact. Something a bit more vanilla, and perhaps a comfort break. However, given the tension and lack of any physical contact between us recently, I didn't want to discourage or disappoint her, so I stayed silent until the ice cube eventually melted to nothing. At which point, she got up, sighed, and moved to the back of the room.

'You will have to be patient while I get changed now. The blindfold stays on because I'm feeling shy tonight. For now, at least, you will have to use your imagination.' She continued talking to me while she got changed, reminding me that life's greatest pleasures are worth waiting for, and that I need to maintain my faith and trust in her.

Estelle had never described herself as shy before. I peered down my nose and out of the bottom of the blindfold to catch sight of her silhouette wriggling out of her dress and into the nurse's unform I had seen hanging up.

Ordinarily, I'm sure I would have found this arousing but, being strapped down with cold water running off my stomach while needing the toilet preoccupied my mind. Also, her emphasis on trust had made me start to question whether I should be trusting her or not. In the same way that when someone tells you not to think of an elephant; all you can think of is an elephant.

Perhaps egged on by the urgency of my bladder, I started wondering if tonight was about to deliver me a trick or a treat. My mind started spinning. *Is she really over losing her job? Is she OK with the fact that I'm sitting in a secure Director's role? Is her complete turnaround, from simmering resentment to wanting to spoil me tonight, realistic or wishful thinking on my part?* The faster the questions bombarded me, the more I started to doubt what was happening here.

I could just about make out her shimmying the nurse's uniform up her body through the bottom of the blindfold. I do love her, I do trust her, I do want a future with her. I voiced the words in my mind but would be lying if I didn't feel them battling against a sense of fear and panic. It was the trust part that was niggling away at my subconscious. Estelle had proved herself volatile and unpredictable in the past, yet it was her calmness that scared me most. We still hadn't spoken about what exactly happened the night her ex-husband was killed, and I wished I'd broached the subject with her more directly and sooner. I wiggled my hands in their bindings against the bedposts. Now was not the time to raise the issue.

Estelle sat on the bed beside me, coaxing my head forward while she put a small glass against my lips. 'A celebratory drink,' she said. I recognised the unmistakeable scent of almonds.

'More Amaretto?'

'It's medicine, chéri, and I am your nurse for the night. Drink it.'

Her voice wavered slightly as she held the glass to my lips. I swallowed it down in two gulps, sending a shot of warmth that spread through my chest and stomach. It was followed immediately with a cold kiss as Estelle transferred an ice cube from her mouth to mine, while running her free hand down my chest, over my stomach and into my briefs.

'Oh, chéri,' she said with genuine disappointment. 'Does your sleepy snail need waking up?'

I laughed at her turn of phrase as she lifted the blindfold off me to reveal herself kneeling on the side of the bed, facing me, her eyes dancing with flames as they reflected the candlelight. The uniform didn't fit properly. It was far too short and flimsy, but it had the desired effect. I was about to compliment it but she shushed me with a finger on my lips.

'Shhhh...don't speak, chéri. Tonight is about trust, remember. I might not be the boss at work anymore, but I am still the boss at home, right?' I nodded. 'Then you need to trust me completely.' I tugged my wrists against their fastenings. They gave way a centimetre but there was no doubt I remained chastened.

Estelle eased me out of my trousers and briefs, maintaining a look of seriousness as she threw them to one side.

'Now, point your ankles to the bedposts so I can tie them,' she demanded, turning to retrieve two more ties from the wardrobe. Her too-short uniform barely covered her bottom. I do trust her, I do love her, I told myself as I parted my legs proudly, adopting a starfish position.

She set about securing my ankles against the foot of the bed. Thankfully, my state of arousal had eased the urgency for me to need the bathroom. Estelle adopted an authoritative tone as she weaved and looped the ties round my ankles, clearly enjoying the role she was playing.

'You know, Luke, I don't think you realise just how attractive you can be. There is something very vulnerable about you, but also strong. That is what first attracted me to you.' Occasionally, she glanced up at me to check my reaction, but otherwise maintained an air of professional distance, focussed on the job in hand.

'You were pure and kind. Loyal and passionate. Attentive and respectful.' Her use of the word *were* jumped out at me. 'And completely unaware of your good looks,' she continued. 'No ego, just a man who was comfortable in his own skin. I could see that there was something different about you, and completely different to the other men in the office.'

I hid my unease at where this was heading and smiled as warmly as I could manage. Inwardly, panic was simmering, and I was regretting allowing myself to be tied up.

'You have come a long way since I first met you, Luke, and I am happy for you.' She paused, giving me a look that bore deep into my soul. 'But you have changed too and not all for the better.' I met her gaze squarely. This was starting to feel more like a performance appraisal than the promised night of passion. 'I have stayed true to myself and to you since we met, but I am worried that you have become infected with the toxicity of that firm. I need to know that you still believe in me if we are going to have a future.' Even in the dim light, I could see Estelle's eyes welling up.

Splayed out before her, I felt an urgent need to reassure Estelle of my faith in her as soon as possible before this one-way conversation took any wrong turnings. I was horribly exposed and vulnerable.

'Estelle, I know things have been…'

'No!' she cut me off mid-sentence. 'No talking, remember. This is an evening where I need you to show me you trust me with actions, not words.' My ankles sufficiently secured, she turned her back on me, blew out all but one of the candles in the room and retreated to the dressing table in the far corner with her back to me. Shadows filled the room.

'I need you to prove you are not like the rest of them, Luke.' She kept her back towards me while speaking. 'I have seen it before when a man becomes a legend in his own mind. It changes him. He can become a monster.' My heart now thumping, I wrestled my wrists and ankles round in their ties, trying to gain some more leverage and freedom.

'Like Philippe, my ex-husband,' she added.

Chapter 51

Mention of Philippe's name was a complete passion-killer. *Why mention him now? Why weren't we discussing this at the table? Why was I tied up and exposed on the bed? How had I let my guard down so spectacularly?*

Picking up on my unease, Estelle addressed the issue head on.

'I am sorry to mention his name, but this is about the trust between us. I need to tell you what happened to him. Just once, and then we never have to speak about him again. It is not easy for me to talk about.' My voice escaped me, so I nodded silently. 'I know Giselle told you about him, and I know that you read some newspaper cuttings about his death.' I noted that she chose not to describe his death as murder. My face stiffened up, betraying my fear, causing Estelle to laugh, 'She is my twin sister, Luke, and we might not always see eye to eye, but we do tell each other everything you know.' I couldn't help it, but I wondered what Giselle would make of this scenario.

'The thing is,' she continued, 'I do not find it easy to talk about the past, but that does not mean I don't trust you, OK?' I nodded. 'I trusted you from the first moment we met. I trusted you at work. I kept you on when everyone else wanted to get rid of you. I trusted you enough to take you to my home village and meet my only family. And I still trust you enough to let you know that I know exactly what happened to my husband the day he died.'

'Would you mind covering me up while we talk, please?' The urge to visit the bathroom had returned and I was not enjoying being so exposed and disadvantaged. Estelle tossed a sheet over my midriff, providing some semblance of modesty.

'I will tell you but only because I trust you, Luke.' Her shadowy figure paced up and down at the foot of the bed.

The whole scenario was starting to feel like a bad nightmare. I rocked my knees from side to side to ease my returning bladder pressure. 'Giselle was right about my husband. He died a horrible death and he deserved everything he got.'

My heart was now pounding, my ears filled with the whooshing sound of blood, while cold shots of adrenaline ran down my arms to my fingertips. This felt more like a lesson in fear than trust. It made me think of one of those scenes in a James Bond film when he's strapped down waiting for a circular saw to make its way up to his groin while the villain confesses all to our hero.

'I also know more about his death than I told the police.' She stopped pacing. 'I also know what missing piece of information they didn't release to the public, but I would not be here now if I let on any more than I knew.' An image of the cloudy pickle jar with all its gruesome contents flashed in my mind. 'So, you see Luke, I trust you completely. Enough to tell you everything.' Her voice trembled.

'I appreciate you, Estelle,' I croaked. My throat was dry. 'Why don't you come and sit beside me?'

She sat down and rested her hand on my chest. Her head was bowed so that her hair formed a curtain, preventing me from seeing her eyes. She opened up like never before, telling me about her unhappy marriage to Philippe. It was the furthest thing from pillow talk you could imagine, with me strapped naked beneath a sheet and Estelle offloading every detail of how her happiness and dignity had been stripped from her, layer by layer.

I listened with genuine sympathy as Estelle described how her dreams of a happy marriage had quickly devolved into a life of pain and abuse. Philippe, once charming and entertaining, had changed immediately after the wedding. Overnight he reverted to being a heavy drinking, womanising and violent man who would often be found asleep in the streets after his heavier sessions. He was a public embarrassment as well as a danger at home. She was abused, ashamed, and had taken to spending her days locked up at home.

I thought of Sarah and could empathise with the feelings of humiliation, disappointment and shame. I wiggled my hands in the hope of being able to free one to hold her hand. The ties loosened slightly but not quite enough to free myself. Echoes of Sarah's voice taunted me from within my mind's recesses.

Estelle shifted position and started a more detached monologue, wistfully describing her childhood and how she felt responsible for her father's happiness after their mother's death. How her feelings were controlled by his moods. How, despite the fact that Giselle always accused Estelle of being the *bright star* of the two, she was in fact *the prisoner*, always being controlled by someone else. How it was Giselle, apparently, who started the game of dressing the same and moving in tandem which, once they'd started, became difficult to break free from. Finally, she described with joy how she'd managed to escape the confines and controls of her past and escape to London for a fresh start.

She paused, tucked her hair behind her ear and looked into my eyes. Her eyes were wet and all I could focus on was the reflection of the one remaining candle dancing in her pupils and the smoky aroma of the extinguished candles overpowering the room.

'Do you not have anything to say?' she asked after a couple of uncomfortable minutes. 'I have told you everything now. What about you? Is there anything you want to share, Luke? I have heard you scream while you sleep, but I have never asked. Do you not have anything you want to tell me?'

My mind spiralled back to the past as every closed door to every painful memory swung open, flooding my thoughts with every humiliating, shameful and regretful moment I had ever lived. I could hear Sarah's voice in the back of my head, screaming *'go on, tell her what you did, you prick'*. However, words escaped me, and I felt too ashamed to face Estelle directly, so I looked round the room's shadows, taking in the upright suitcase by the door, the tray on the dresser with the ice bucket and other shiny objects on it.

'I'm sorry,' was all I could manage.

'You can tell me anything, however bad,' she coaxed. I shook my head. 'I need to know that you have as much faith and trust in me as I have in you.'

I thought about telling her, I really did. Perhaps I should, but could I really trust her, or was this a trap? What could possibly be gained by opening up and telling her all my secrets? Nothing. My stomach bubbled uncomfortably, and I needed the toilet. The evening was becoming memorable for all the wrong reasons.

'Can you untie me please?' My tone unintentionally cold and demanding.

Estelle tutted and shook her head. 'Not yet, chéri.'

She reached forward and pulled the blindfold back down over my eyes.

Chapter 52

Complete darkness followed. I wiggled my nose and peeped out the bottom of the blindfold. Estelle was at the dressing table with her back to me. I squeezed my eyes shut, hoping it would sharpen my other senses. The smell of burnt candles was still prominent, as was Estelle's sweet fragrance and the almondy aroma coming from an open bottle of Amaretto. I could hear a drawer opening and closing, a rustle of paper, the sound of something, possibly metal, being placed on the dresser and finally the sound of ice cubes against glass.

I pulled against the ties binding my wrists and ankles, feeling them give slightly. I was careful not to fully test whether a quick, sharp wrench might break me free completely. Not yet anyway. It would spoil whatever fun Estelle might have in store for me. Estelle was silent, her presence in the room a mere shadow. I couldn't even hear her breathing. My breath, by contrast, came in short, quick gasps, betraying the escalating panic that surged through me as worst-case-scenarios played out in my mind.

I tried calming myself with memories of our good times - the meals out, the walks through the park, late nights at the office – but my thoughts kept returning to Philippe's murder and Estelle's possible involvement in it. If tonight was a question of trust, then I was being tested to the full.

'What are you doing?' I asked, my voice trembling.

'Wait and see.'

'I'm not sure I like this.' I said fearfully as a metallic taste rose on the back of my tongue.

'Don't be too hasty to judge. You might discover you like something new.' Through the narrow sliver at the bottom of my blindfold, I watched her take slow, deliberate steps back towards the bed, carrying something with one hand.

She knelt on the bed and, with a swift flick of her wrist, whisked the modesty sheet away. I reflexively jerked my wrists and ankles against their ties in a failed attempt to shield my nakedness. Estelle giggled with amusement. 'Hold still,' she commanded.

The sound of ice against glass preceded cold drops of water being flicked up and down my body, making me jolt as if shocked by tiny electric sparks, while Estelle continued giggling. The sensation of cold water hitting my exposed body only increased my mounting discomfort and urgent need to pee. At that moment, given a choice, I might have preferred Estelle's hair straighteners to cold water on my bladder, although without 'the accident with the switch'.

'Oh, that's really cold,' I said, stating the obvious.

'You think this is cold? Just you wait,' she teased, straddling my left leg and resting her weight on me while she started running an ice cube up and down my chest and ribs, causing me to twitch at every nerve ending she brushed past. I screwed my face up tightly as she took the ice cube below my waist and slid it along my thighs, encouraging me to relax by whispering compliments about the firmness of my physique. I held my breath as she introduced the warmth of her free hand, alternating her strokes between the cold numbing effects of the ice cube and the reviving warmth of her hand. 'You're so strong, so firm,' she murmured, her voice melting away my anxiousness.

The sensation was disorienting and confusing, but it revived life in every inch of my body. Still blindfolded, warm tingles ran up and down my body with every stroke, easing me into a detached, dreamlike state. I focussed on Estelle's hypnotic whispers, my body relaxing and responding to her every touch.

But, as my mind drifted, another voice interrupted. It was not from the room but from a buried box of memories in the recesses of my own mind and it was clawing its way to the surface.

Click: It's Sarah. Drunk-screaming at me after she returned home at just after midnight after working late. We both know she hadn't really been in the office. She spent the evening out with Salter, leaving me to lose my mind – and dignity – with worry and humiliation. She has no shame and doesn't care and continues screaming at me without a thought for our curtain-twitching neighbours. I'm on my knees with tears running down my cheeks, begging her to reconsider what we have and our promised future together. She stamps on every last crumb of hope in my soul and ridicules my attempts to be a doting, attentive partner. She tells me I was only ever a cheap place to stay. A benefactor to tolerate. A stopgap before experiencing real excitement from 'real men like Salter'. My neck tightens. My heart spikes.

I beg her to stop and not leave me, losing every remaining shred of self-respect in the process. She scorns me for thinking that I was ever anything more than a passing convenience. Spittle flies out of her mouth as she screams resentment for the weekend walks I used to take her on which she found so boring they made her want to kill herself. She can't bear being near me, she wants excitement from men like Salter. My chest feels crushed. I feel hollow inside. Click.

I gasp as I realise I'm back in the bedroom, back in darkness, back incarcerated to the bed. I feel Estelle's warmth against my chest as she leans forward, kisses my neck and shoulders while pressing her warm thigh between my legs, the remainder of ice water now warming up to equal our body temperature. 'Shhh...' she whispers. 'Relax...trust me.'

Trust. That word again. The distant voice in my head has stopped screaming, but its aftermath is lingering, biding its time, on standby ready to taunt me. My heart thumps, I'm hyperventilating and, from behind the blindfold, I visualise my surroundings - Estelle dressed up as a nurse, the mysterious tray in the corner of the room, her suitcase upright by the door - while writhing my wrists and ankles against their ties.

I recall every moment spent with Estelle, the first night when I didn't know who she was, the incident in the restaurant, my surprise at finding out she had a twin sister, my shock at finding out she had been married. Giselle. Estelle. Philippe. The shed in the garden. The trunk. Its grisly contents.

My body turns rigid with panic. My internal monologue fires doom-filled scenarios at me. *This isn't about trust, this is about revenge. She's still bitter about her job. She's leaving you, that's why her suitcase is packed. She's got you where she wants and now she's going to kill you, just like Philippe. Worse, she's going to castrate or mutilate and leave you to bleed to death in agony.*

Estelle's soft whispers and caresses do nothing to soothe me. I reach full-blown freak-out mode and thrash against my restraints, desperate to free myself. Estelle, sensing my anxiety, sits upright, increasing her weight on my middle waist and paining my bladder.

A bolt of strength surges through me, allowing me to break free of my shackles and sit up straight with my arms finally free. At the same time, Estelle whips off my blindfold to reveal herself at her very best. She's straddling my waist, the nurse's uniform wide open displaying perfectly formed curves below an enigmatic smile and big brown eyes that give no clue as to what lies behind them.

'Shhh,' she soothed, as I reach my arms around her and pull her towards me. 'It's time to put you out of your misery. I want you to remember this.'

Click. I'm on my knees and Sarah is screaming abuse. 'You fool! We're over. Finished. This is it. Get over it.'

Emotions and logic twist themselves into a painful knot. Vomit rises to the back of my throat, pain throbs in my chest and numbness devours my limbs. Sarah's tantrum blurs into a continuous noise, a painful, stinging buzz that eventually hits a frequency within me that releases a wave of calm clarity that tells me how to stop the noise.

Pain turns to calm, confusion to purpose, and weakness to strength. I rise from my knees, step and pull Sarah towards me, wrapping my arms around her. I ignore her protests, her fading screams as I lock my arms around her neck and tell her she's never leaving me. Tears run down my cheeks. I continue to squeeze until I hear a final click and feel her body flop limply into my arms.

Silence and peace followed. It was that easy. The ease with which everything fell back to normal, the tying up of loose ends from her email account, the resignation, the deleted social media accounts, the fact that she hadn't told anyone where she was staying and that no one really cared enough to ask any questions about her disappearance. I feel a euphoric sense of relief, like being able to finally scratch an itch that's been trapped under a plaster cast for weeks. And I remember the fear I felt knowing how easy it had been to tap into this dark power that lay dormant within me. Click.

I open my eyes and find Estelle asleep in my arms, a picture of peaceful bliss with every perfect facial muscle relaxed. I place my finger on the bridge of her nose and trace my finger along her eyebrow, along her slender jawline, down her neck and across her collar bones. So fragile, so perfect and mine forever.

I hold her tight, close my eyes and feel the sting of tears running down my cheeks.

343

Chapter 53

I must have lain in bed for hours not daring to move, just holding her and trying to take in the full horror of the situation. The urgency to need the bathroom had long since been overtaken by inability to let go of Estelle. She looked so peaceful with her head resting on my shoulder, her hair fanned out against my chest, her eyes closed, and lips slightly parted.

My bladder had passed the point of discomfort and settled into a numbing throb that sent ripples of pain through my body. It was what I deserved. The pain peaked on the missing tip of my wedding ring finger, which pulsated and itched. I tried to imagine my finger as it used to be - part of a perfect hand, perhaps with a wedding ring that Estelle and I had chosen together, perhaps with my hand on the steering wheel of a car, perhaps driving up a hill in the French countryside. It was not to be, and will never be.

Aside from my own breathing and the occasional crackle of the lone candle in the corner, the room was silent - no creaks, no passing traffic, no sound from neighbours. That wasn't unusual for the early hours, but even my internal voices were silent, as if in shock, creating an uncomfortable eeriness. I slid my arm out from underneath Estelle and removed the ties that were still hanging from my wrists and ankles. Red rings remained where I had struggled my way free. These would need covering until they healed, but I was otherwise unharmed.

I stood up and crossed the room to the dresser, flicking the light switch on and blowing out the candle on the way. The overhead light was harsh, like a spotlight, and washed away any sinister air, or 'ambience', from the room. My steps were robotic, as if I was not in full control of myself. I felt heavy. Numb. On the dresser was a collection of shiny pens that Estelle used for writing. No implements. No danger. No other phantom tools. Just pens.

Propped up against the mirror was an ominous-looking envelope with 'Luke' written in Estelle's carefully drawn flowing letters. I opened it.

Mon chéri,
If you are reading this, then I have gone.
Do not be sad. I want only for you to be happy.
I am sorry but I cannot stay here anymore.
I think you need some time alone to work out what you want.
You are a wonderful person, but you have changed, and you scare me,
You have been consumed by the job and the power you never cared about.
You have withdrawn to a place that I cannot reach.
I have tried to talk to you about it, but you seem so distant. More so than usual.
I hope tonight has shown you that my heart is pure and I am ready to give you everything.
Please don't be angry with me or come to find me. I need some time too.
This is goodbye for now, not goodbye forever.
Yours, Estelle x

I stared at the letter, reading its contents over and over until my eyes stung and the words blurred. I turned towards Estelle. She lay unmoving on the bed, awkwardly positioned as I'd left her, her arms in an unnatural pose that no one simply sleeping would adopt. Her skin looked paler than usual. Her eyes and lips looked darker. She looked tired.

She was exposed from the waist down, as I still was, and still wearing her nurse's uniform. This upset me. It was unbecoming, demeaning and disrespectful to the woman I knew. The woman who had lived through so much, stood up to so much, and who had awakened a dormant passion within me. The woman I loved.

I wondered what had first drawn her to me and what had gone so desperately wrong to lead me to make such a sickening mistake. Was history stuck in a loop? No answers came. One thing I was sure of - she would remain mine forever. To love, to care for and treasure. I would make sure of it. The itch at the stump of my wedding ring finger flared up. I sucked on it to ease the sensation.

I put the letter back in its envelope and sat on the side of the bed and took Estelle's hand into mine. I would need to change her into something more fitting. Her polka dot silk pyjamas, maybe. Brush her hair. Remove the delicate matching necklace and pear-shaped earrings I'd bought her from Riberac market. I probably ought to change the sheets as well.

The whole scene was wrong, and shamefully vivid, like waking up from a hangover with memories of the night before threatening to crush me. Bile rose in my throat, burning me with its bitter acidity. I disgusted myself and felt the need for punishment.

I bowed my head, closed my eyes, and bit down hard into my wedding ring finger as tears spilled onto my lap.

Chapter 54

It's been a rough couple of weeks but, in a strange way, I'm looking forward to getting back to work. Ever since Estelle left, I've been all over the place and desperately need to return to some sort of routine. Luckily, I had an old photo on my phone of a positive COVID test that I'd taken during 2020 and no one had dared to question its validity when I sent it in to work and said I'd been hit hard and needed some time off.

I didn't sleep much last night, but it was at least nightmare-free; a small step forward. I took a long drag of my first cigarette of the day and blew the smoke upwards to avoid contaminating my suit.

It was grey and cloudy with a chill in the air - the sort of day that more hardy people would describe as fresh. To me, it was just a bit shit, considering it was still only the beginning of October. It felt like summer was definitely over. There was a back-to-school feeling in the air. I nestled my cigarette in the ashtray beside me on the garden bench, careful not to knock any ash on my clothes, and cupped my hands around my mug.

My finger throbbed but was healing well beneath its bandage. I'd given it a good wash and changed the dressing first thing this morning. As long as it didn't start weeping again, it was presentable for work. I hadn't done a bad job of the mess I'd made considering the only tools I had for the clean-up was a pair of toenail clippers, some Steri strips and a bottle of TCP. Thankfully there was enough skin left attached to make a decent v-flap and I was fairly confident it would heal neatly as long as I avoided infection. I was also confident it wouldn't attract any undue attention seeing as it was same finger as my original wound. If anyone asked, I was mentally prepared with a contingency story about carelessly chopping vegetables while dizzy with

COVID. No one would ask further questions. No one cares that much.

Today's appearance at work was more to show willing. I'd agreed to a phased return until I felt completely free of my COVID symptoms so wasn't expected to stay beyond lunchtime. I'd really exaggerated the after-effects so there was no pressure on me. Besides, I'd kept up to date with all the gossip in the office via the Communicator system, and my team were taking care of the business end of things. All that was needed today was to show my face, offer any steers, guidance or advice that they needed and get back home again. I wouldn't have to actually *do* anything.

Of course, I already had draft emails prepared and saved to send at regular intervals throughout the day. Most notably, those from Estelle's personal email account to her employment lawyer and various recruitment agencies, informing them that she no longer wanted to pursue her compensation claim or job applications due to her change of plan and wish to return to France urgently. No one would ask further questions. No one cares that much.

I took a final drag on my cigarette and stubbed it out. No more flicking butts all over the garden making it look like a rubbish tip. I stood and stretched to invigorate myself for the day ahead, smoothing the creases out of my waistcoat and trousers as I did so. I'd opted for the navy suit today. Paul Smith. Three-piece worsted wool, created in Italy. It looked good and although Estelle never got to see it, I knew she'd love it.

The thought of her brought an instant smile to my face. She'd made me feel alive again and saved me from letting my life stagnate behind a laptop. The love we had for each other would last beyond life itself. That and our memories gave me the security and confidence I needed to go on. I was ready for the day.

I paused to take in my surroundings. Although summer was ending, the garden was bursting with more life than it had in a long time. The pink cherry blossom in the far-right corner had completed its yearly cycle of buds, florets, blossom and fruit. Now, it stretched its naked branches to new heights in preparation for next year.

In the opposite corner, planted a month or two earlier than ideal according to the blurb on the packaging, was the most beautifully formed white blossom cherry tree I'd bought off the internet. The soil around its base was still a clean, fluffy brown, betraying its youth. It was compact and round and totally mismatched to the other tree, but it would grow strong. Described as hardy with green foliage that turns to fiery red in autumn, and with snowy white flowers expected next spring, it was perfect - prunus incisa 'The Bride' tree. Absolutely perfect.

I fought to swallow down an involuntary lump that had formed in my throat and stepped forward to stroke the trunk of my new tree. A spider's web had formed between a couple of the lower branches. And then some more. Why are there so many webs around? On closer inspection, I noticed a small pale blue butterfly, struggling with the stickiness of a web, trying to extend and flap its wing to free itself.

'Papillon,' I said out loud, remembering the French word for butterfly. I'd always been impressed by nature's design, allowing a creature to metamorphose from one state to another so impressively. And also that, in its incarnation as a butterfly, it has a clever set of detachable scales on its wings that enables it to pull itself free from any web it should find itself caught up in.

Yep. Here it goes. I watched as the little blue butterfly freed itself and flew away, over the fence into the next garden, leaving a frustrated looking spider peeping out from a nook between the branches. The thought of Papillon made me think of Giselle and wonder whether I ought to get in touch with her following Estelle's departure. There was no clue of an email address for her in Estelle's email account which didn't surprise me given Giselle's aversion to all things IT-related. But what could I tell her? Why would I call her anyway when the natural assumption would be that Estelle would get in touch if she had any news to share. No. As tempting as it might be to make contact, no good could come from it.

Before I could give the matter further consideration, my thoughts were interrupted by the sound of the home phone ringing from inside the flat. I froze, rooted to the spot, while it rang out. No one ever calls the home phone.

Within seconds, it started up again, its intermittent cry increasingly insistent with every ring.

Chapter 55

I didn't rush inside. The persistent ringing suggested the caller wasn't going to give up. It was demanding and needy. I stared at the phone, unused and dust-covered, and let it ring four more times while I mulled over whether to ignore it. No. I'd only be delaying the inevitable.

'Fuck.' I winced as I picked up the receiver with my left hand, forgetting about my finger and hoping I hadn't triggered it weeping again. I cleared my throat and answered, 'Luke Shenstone.' I don't know why I answered so formally. I could have just said hello. It's not like I didn't know who it was.

'Allô?'

'Hello. Estelle?'

'Ahh, allô Luke. No, it is Giselle.' I could hear the grandfather clock ticking away in the background and immediately pictured Giselle in her hallway, maybe leaning against the wrought iron staircase or standing barefoot on the flagstones. I'd forgotten how similar to Estelle she sounded. If I didn't know better, it could have been her. I slid my back down the wall and sat on the floor, my chest aching. I wasn't ready for this conversation.

'Is Estelle there?' she asked.

'No, I'm afraid not.' An awkward silence hung over us while the grandfather clock tick-tocked in the background.

'Where is she?' her voice wobbled.

'I'm afraid I don't know, Giselle.' It was impossible not to sound tearful. 'She left and didn't say where she was going.' My dry mouth clicked as I spoke. 'I was hoping you might have heard from her?'

'Hmmm.' Another long pause followed.

'Giselle?'

'I am still here. I am thinking.' I could almost hear her biting her bottom lip, just like Estelle used to when she was concentrating. 'Something is not right, Luke. We used to speak every week and then nothing.'

'She left me. I don't know where she is.'

'Really? She did not give me the impression she was going to leave you. Quite the opposite in fact.' I detected an accusatory tone to her voice.

'You know how quickly she makes her mind up about things and how strong-willed she can be. I begged her to stay.'

'I spoke to her just over two weeks ago and she said nothing of this. Did she say where she was going?'

'I'm afraid not.'

'Do you have her mobile number?'

'I do. Don't you?'

'No. She never gave it to me and she would always call me. Since she moved to London, she said she preferred to keep what she called a healthy distance from me.'

'Hmmm.' It was my turn to add a judgemental tone to the exchange. 'I can give it to you but can tell you it's been disconnected.' Which was true. 'That was the first thing I tried.'

'Yes please.' I gave her Estelle's defunct mobile number.

'I'm sorry I can't help more, Giselle. I wish I could.'

'Hmmm.' The grandfather clock ticked away in the background, as if prompting the conversation along. 'Luke?'

'Yes?'

'Something is not right. I want to find her. I do not want to lose her again.'

'If I hear from her, I'll let you know and tell her to call you.' As an afterthought I added, 'and I'd be grateful if you could do the same, please.'

'Luke?' Her voice sounded as if it was about to crack.

'Yes?'

'Can I come and stay with you? I really want to find her.'

I leant my head back against the wall, closed my eyes and let a strange feeling wash over me.

'Yes, of course. You'd be very welcome. Do you have my address?'

'You wrote it on a napkin for me, remember?' I did indeed remember her folding the napkin in four and tucking it into her bra on our last night in France. The corners of my mouth curled upwards at the memory.

'And what about Steve? Will he be coming too?'

'He's gone.' She said the words with such finality it was clear that no more details would be offered, nor was I inclined to ask. My heart pounded with adrenaline.

'Giselle?'

'Yes?'

'I'm really pleased you're coming.'

'Good! So am I.' Her voice carried an element of hope.

'I've found it quite difficult since Estelle left,' I added.

Giselle expressed sympathy and said she'd be back in touch as soon as she'd booked travel.

I took a cigarette out the pack and headed to the garden for another smoke.

Work can wait.

About The Author

Brendon is a London-based writer whose work explores the psychological territory where dreams collide with harsh realities.

His debut novel, *Hoodie*, is a work of contemporary literary fiction that follows a London teenager's devastating summer after stealing from his school's most notorious drug dealer: a powerful and heartbreaking story of friendship, misplaced loyalty, and wasted potential. Like 'Hoodie', Brendon grew up on a council estate, attended an inner city comprehensive and left school at 16. In his youth, he was a hoodie. Today, he writes.

Brendon's second novel, *A Tangled Web*, ventures into psychological thriller territory and explores the dangerous territory between obsession and love, passion and manipulation.

Printed in Dunstable, United Kingdom